# Ψ The Doctor, the Witch and the Rose Stone Ψ

by

Joanne Coyle

**W**itchy **W**ays

Copyright © 2025 Joanne Coyle

All Rights Reserved.

ISBN: 978-1-917601-98-6

# Characters

Scotland

**The Accused**

Agnes Sampson: Midwife and healer
Gelly Duncan: Servant and healer
John Fian: Schoolmaster

**The Accusers**

Mr Seton: Gelly's employer
Mr McPherson: Witchfinder
Reverend McLaren: Minister
Sheriff MacKay: Local lawman
Commissioner Baxter: Royal Court
King James VI of Scotland

France

*Paris*

Assen Verey: Physician
Gérard Xavier: Physician
Theo Verey: Assen's father
Uncle Manny: Assen's uncle.
Dr Broussard: Head physician St Marcel's Plague Hospital
Dr Brisbois: Head of the Faculty of Medicine in Paris

*Vézelay*

Madame Lambert: Midwife and healer

*Beaune*

Abbott Antoine: Abbot of Hôtel-Dieu (House of God)

North Berwick, Scotland

October 1590

A man creeps along the edge of the wood and into the garden. No one is about. The door of her cottage is still ajar from where they kicked it in.

Through the darkness, he makes out the denser black of her bed and the fireplace. Feeling along the range wall, his fingers find a loose stone and scrape it out.

Diving in again, they settle on the box draped in linen rags. He carefully removes it and stuffs it into his satchel. Outside, the torch is where he left it, propped against the wall under the window. It is as dry as a broom. He used to do this as a boy, hunkering down, rubbing the stick against the stone and blowing.

'Come on. Light!'

It catches. He walks to the corner of the house where the thatch is lowest and holds the flame to the straw. It crackles.

He does the same on the other side and throws the torch on the roof. After stepping back, he turns and disappears into the forest.

# Part I

# Chapter One

Storm at Sea, December 1589
Off the Coast of Denmark

It's witchcraft, King James is sure of it. When they left Copenhagen, the weather was serene and the red northern sky the night before promised a calm crossing. Now sheer, cliff-high waves loom over the ship, forming a wall of impregnable gunmetal grey.

'It's the Devil's work, sire!' his admiral bellows. The words whip from his mouth and sweep overboard in a torrent of wave, spit and foam. 'We have to turn back!'

'Never!' He will not be thwarted by the Devil. A battle with the Prince of Darkness is his destiny. Is he not God's representative on Earth, and is Scotland not God's country? On several occasions, walking down the long gallery in Holyrood Palace contemplating some point of philosophy or history, he has felt a demon's hot breath on the back of his neck. William Balfour said the Devil wanted to stop him from writing his treatise on demonology. That shows he's getting too close to the truth. Now this storm. It is no coincidence.

'I'll get my bride back to Scotland this night!' the king hollers over the deafening roar. He has just married Anne of Denmark and is desperate to get his new queen back to Scotland. It is not a country that tolerates absent monarchs; the fate of his mother testified to that, and he has no intention of joining her head in the basket.

The negotiations were long and tortuous, and his rebellious nobles forcibly expressed their impatience at the Privy Council in the preceding weeks and months. But this lucrative alliance for Scotland will swell her coffers with much-needed gold, enabling James to divvy out royal favours, pitting aristocrat against aristocrat instead of the Crown.

But the sea cares nothing of the dalliances of kings and commoners. It recedes, creating an abyss that might swallow an island. The ship pitches downwards as if aiming for the seabed, her bow deep into the crevasse of the wave. Walls of water as high as the cliffs of Edinburgh Castle rise on either side of the craft.

They have lost four men already. The admiral is not inclined to lose more. 'Witchcraft!' he shouts.

Confirmation, if the king needs any. He recently read in *The Hammer of Witches* how it is common for covens to whip up storms to defeat their enemies. The book told of fishing boats setting sail from a calm harbour only to return with shredded sails, rotting fish and their crew nowhere to be seen. It turned out their neighbours and rivals had conjured up a spell to bend the weather to their will and destroy their opponents. There were many such tales. But the tome is over one hundred years old, and things have moved on. It needs to be updated, for the Devil has become more wily, and the king has tasked himself as the man to do it. This is meant to be.

As the ship pitches skywards, the boom on the main sail breaks free and smacks the helmsman across the ship, knocking him out cold. The wheel spins chaotically as other crew members cling to ropes, rigging and poles, frantically trying in vain to keep control. The ship lurches and tumbles like a possessed roller coaster in the ever-deepening swells and troughs.

King James and the admiral stand apart from the mayhem, perched on the bridge.

'We have to go back, sire. We can't fight the Devil tonight. He's too strong; he'll send us to the bottom of the sea!'

The king's stomach tightens; defeated by the Devil on his triumphant voyage home with his Danish bride and a new profitable alliance. 'Damn it! Very well. Turn around.' Gripping the rail spanning the deck, he makes an oath. 'This is not over.'

The ship's wheel eerily stops spinning and rocks gently from side to side, as if brought under control by an invisible hand. The king and the admiral look at each other. Two sailors grab the wheel and the king notices there is no resistance from the elements. One steps back and the other warily takes the helm.

'So be it. Plot a course back to Denmark,' King James shouts to his admiral. 'The gauntlet is laid down. I take it up gladly for God and for Scotland!'

'But not tonight, sire.'

'No, not tonight.'

The admiral lets out a long sigh of relief and the king gives him a withering look. He needs men of steel with strong stomachs for what lies ahead.

# Chapter Two

### Storm Over Land
### The Village of North Berwick

Across the North Sea, almost in a direct line from where the king's ship flounders, a tiny, whitewashed cottage with a thatched roof sits on the edge of a forest. A footpath from the front door joins a track skirting the woods to the village of North Berwick on the wind-battered east coast of Scotland.

A woman is sleeping in the straw bed in the corner, close to the range. Her long, wavy, silver-grey hair reflects the moonlight seeping through a crack in the shutter. The fire's embers glow faintly, brightening for a fraction of a second as they are fanned by a draught from beneath the door and through the cracked window frames, fading as the breeze recedes out to sea. Blackness descends.

She turns over and sighs, facing the fire, oblivious to the gathering storm and darkness. Her high cheekbones and smooth brow illuminated in the firelight still retain the beauty of her younger years, even now in her mid-fifties. She is used to the pitch dark. But it doesn't matter anyway for she is somewhere else, in a dreamworld she's been visiting more often of late. She did half-heartedly wonder why, but why look a gift horse in the mouth?

*Soft, moist grass under her feet, she walks through a luscious garden and catches a glimpse of the reeds and pond beyond. Lily pads float on its mirrored surface. A gentle breeze caresses her face and lifts strands of hair at the nape of her neck. She shivers and instinctively rubs it, feeling the prickle of goosebumps.*

*A man is sitting by the water's edge. His fingers are entwined around a stick he is using to draw shapes in the sand. He stands as Agnes approaches. Her heart stops for a fraction of a second – she's sure it does – then bump-bump ... bump-bump ... before jumping into her throat. This is the bit she enjoys the most.*

She lets out a long breath, then breathes in the heat of the fire. In the other world, she closes her eyes and feels the warmth of the sun on her face.

BANG! BANG! BANG! Loud rapping at the door startles her awake. *God save us!* She sits bolt upright, her heart beating a demented, chaotic rhythm. *Where am I? What is this place?* She jumps to her feet, squinting to make out the shapes in the dark. There's her dresser, two chairs, the table and the fireplace. She glances at the stonework above the range's mantle.

The frantic knocking continues even louder. Someone is shouting her name. 'Goodwife Sampson! Goodwife Sampson! Agnes, Agnes, for God's sake, open up!'

Agnes grabs the shawl slung over a chair, wraps it around her shoulders and stumbles to the window. Her fingers fumble in the recess and find the cold, hard metal of the ancient iron candle holder and the candle's long waxy shaft. Setting the holder on the table, she puts the wick to the fire and blows. More knocking. *Come on. Come on.* The wick lights.

'I'm coming!' She screws the candle back into its setting.

'Agnes! Help us!'

She recognises the voice. As she opens the door, candle in hand, the gale almost blows out the flame. 'Come in, John. What's…? What is it? What's the matter?'

Her old friend and neighbour, John Lockhart, is ashen and barely able to talk.

'Please be seated.' She leads him to one of the chairs by the fireside. The fireplace, like so many in these cottages, is a roughly hewn squarish hole cut deep into the wall with enough space to cook a whole meal in several pots at once. The only nod to decoration is a darkened horizontal beam built into the stone above the hearth.

John slumps onto the seat and awkwardly places his palms on the kitchen table.

Agnes says gently, 'Let me put on something warmer.' She takes the long bodice waistcoat and skirts slung over the other chair closest to the bed.

John turns to the fading cinders and picks up a peat brick from the haphazard pile stacked by the hearth. As Agnes dresses, she watches him close his fingers over it and gaze into the dying fire.

What can have happened? Whatever it is, she must be calm, collected and in control. There is no place for panic and drama in the life of a midwife and healer.

He throws the lump into the fire. It bursts into life, lighting up the room. 'It's Maggie.'

'But she's not due 'til next month.' Agnes checked on her only three days before.

'I don't know what happened. She got up ... she seemed to... I dinna ken, it happened that fast. She went down. There's blood, a lot of blood. Help us – please help us. God help us, Agnes!'

'Aye, of course, John, of course. Let's go.' She stops. 'Wait! Just a second... Go outside ... close the door. I'll just be a moment, I promise.'

As soon as he closes the door, Agnes rushes to the wall on the left of the fireplace. She glances over her shoulder and her eyes home in on a brick-shaped stone, much like any other. She slips her fingers into the sides and jiggles it free. It crunches and grinds as she slides it all the way out. The hole is cold and damp, but right at the back is the familiar, comforting texture of an old wooden box with its iron braces and keyhole. The key is long lost.

Breathing deeply, she pulls the box all the way out, opens it and rummages inside. She cradles an item wrapped in an old piece of cloth and places it in a hidden pocket in her skirt. Holding her breath, she closes the box without a sound, returns it to its resting place and replaces the stone. She breathes out only when satisfied it is well hidden.

Drawing her shawl tightly around her shoulders, she opens the door and heads out into the night.

# Chapter Three

The Dissection
A Medical Theatre in Paris

Assen glances at his friend. Two little worry lines have appeared between Gérard's brows.

'Honestly! Do you think this is really necessary?' Gérard asks.

The pair are standing on one of the wooden tiers of the round theatre in the prestigious Faculty of Medicine in Paris. The crowded hall is buzzing with excitement. Medical students and their fellow newly qualified physicians chatter animatedly, craning to get a better view of the centre stage. Some have even brought boxes to stand on.

Assen is enthusiastic. 'The new medicine! Think how much we're going to learn, how much we've learned already! Dissection is going to change everything!'

A cadaver lies on a huge table in the centre of the theatre. To the side is a smaller trestle table with saws, blades, clamps and all manner of implements unfamiliar to the eagerly waiting medical novices.

'It won't be long now,' another student whispers behind Assen.

A hush sweeps through the audience like a wave rolling to the shore as two men enter and position themselves at either end of the great table.

'That's the surgeon. He'll be assisting the professor. The second man is *his* assistant,' another student says authoritatively.

'Uh-huh,' Gérard replies, looking over his shoulder. 'And is anyone assisting the assistant assisting the surgeon?'

Assen ignores him. 'We're lucky to have Professor Lavigne here in Paris.'

'He robbed graves, you know.'

'Professor Lavigne?' Assen exclaims, looking squarely at Gérard.

'No! Vesalius. The one who started all this.'
Assen tuts. 'Hmm.'
'And took them straight off the gallows, just hanging there, nice 'n' fresh.'
'Scare stories. Made up by those who don't want progress or understand how humans really work.'
'We know how humans work!' Gérard says. 'They eat well, sleep well, enjoy the company of friends and family, have nothing on their conscience, then they live long and healthy lives. If they don't, they don't.'
'Things aren't as simple as that,' Assen says curtly, although he knows his mother, Bahdeer, would have agreed with Gérard. He still misses her.

'Give people hope, reassurance and the right remedies, and they will heal themselves,' she had told him when he first went to medical school. 'Be cautious, reserve your judgement, Assen. The new medicine doesn't have all the answers,' she'd added one day when he came home excited, wanting distilling equipment. 'The chemicals the court physicians are experimenting with are strong – too strong for the human body. They can throw it out of balance ... and they can be deadly in the wrong hands, or in inexperienced hands. Be humble, my boy. Ask God to guide you.'

Assen feels a dead weight the size of a boulder lodge in his chest and a lump rise in his throat, making it hard to swallow or even breathe. Lights flash before his eyes. He feels dizzy; he might pass out. *God, no!* That would be so humiliating. He grabs the rail in front of him. *Calm down. Focus on the lecture.*

'I think you'll find they are.' Gérard's words seem far away.

Assen releases one hand from the bar and places it on his chest. The small oval on its chain is still there. His shoulders slacken.

'Look,' he says, releasing his hand and pointing to the dissection table. 'With this method, we'll be able to see inside, see what's causing the problems, discover which organ is diseased, and then we can...' That's better; he's on solid ground now, talking about medicine and the body. The flashing lights start to fade and he can hear the conversations around him.

'And do what?' Gérard shouts back over the din. 'Create a big list of diseased organs and symptoms with no idea of how to cure them?'

It is exactly what his mother would have said. 'We'll find a way. One day, medicine *will* find a cure for every disease.'

Gérard raises his eyebrows but says nothing.

'In hundreds of years,' Assen continues, 'the new medicine will make sure no one ever has to live in illness or pain ... if it be God's will.'

Silence once again rolls through the auditorium like a swell as a gentleman strides from the wings to take centre stage behind the table. Unlike his assistants, who are covered from head to foot in long hide aprons, he is dressed in the height of Parisian fashion. He struts over in a dark-blue velvet doublet with gold trim around the buttonholes, hem and cuffs, and his hose are of a paler shade of blue. The outfit is topped by a deep-plum velvet cape and a hat sitting jauntily awry. Looking like he's just stepped out from the royal court, he hands his cloak and hat with a flourish to a man Assen hadn't noticed before.

'Talking of God.' Gérard coughs.

Assen laughs.

With a crook of his finger, Professor Lavigne calls over the surgeon and his assistant. They huddle for several moments, adding to the suspense. Some of the students playfully elbow each other and widen their eyes. Then the huddle breaks and the surgeon nods. The theatre goes deathly quiet. The show is about to begin.

The professor turns to the audience; most are straining to see and keen to hang on to every word so they can tell their non-physician friends in the taverns later. However, some, like Gérard, look on circumspectly.

'Gentlemen. You are here to witness one of the wonders of our time – the human body. We are privileged to have dispensation from His Majesty to conduct this dissection. You are deeply honoured, gentlemen. There are thousands who would stand where you are now.'

'They are more than welcome,' Gérard says deadpan.

'Shhhh.'

Professor Lavigne continues to address the audience. 'This is Mr Artois, a most skilled surgeon, and his assistant, Mr Tremblay. They will be performing the surgery as per my instructions. I trust you all have a good view.'

Gérard blows out.

The professor makes eye contact with the surgeon. 'Commence, Mr Artois, if you please.'

The surgeon picks up a large, sharp-looking knife. The blade glints in his hand. Pointing the tip just below the throat of the cadaver, he draws it steadily down the torso to the pubic bone, making a faint ripping sound like cloth being pulled apart. There is an intake of breath. Out of bravado, many stretch their necks for a better view; others, looking queasy, step back to let their classmates take their place.

'Now, gentlemen, for the first time we can see where the organs are in the body,' Professor Lavigne says.

He nods to the surgeon to peel back the skin. Some of the previously enthused students look a little less enthusiastic, affording those with a penchant for the macabre an uninterrupted view.

Gérard sighs but steps into a place vacated by a retreating novice student. Assen looks at his friend. Although Gérard is sceptical about the need for – or, more precisely, the usefulness of – dissections, he is not squeamish. He lifts his chin and stares unwaveringly at the table. Assen smiles and does the same. They'll talk about it later.

'We will start with the heart. Mr Artois…'

The surgeon walks over to the cadaver carrying what looks like a huge pair of sharpened pliers.

'Mr Artois will use these instruments to crack open the ribcage to give access to the heart.'

Gérard shakes his head. 'You think this will get us far?'

'Shhhh.'

'It's theatre … just theatre. Entertainment.'

'It will be useful one day.'

'Are you sure?'

# Chapter Four

### The Birth
### North Berwick

Stumbling in the pitch dark down the well-worn path to the village, Agnes wonders why she chose to live out here in the forest. Not convenient, not convenient at all for a village midwife and healer. But it was a sanctuary, and God knows she had needed one back then.

At last she sees the outline of the village, the black shapes of the buildings set against a marginally lighter shade of grey-black sky.

*Where's the bloody moon when you need it?* It's always popping up in fairy tales. Mind you, those stories never end particularly well. Agnes smiles to herself.

John and Maggie Lockhart would have to live on the other side of town. Heading towards the harbour, they take the short cut through the west wynd, a narrow, twisting alleyway of overhanging houses with a sewer trench cut deep down the middle like a gash that won't heal. They tread gingerly, keeping close to the walls.

As they emerge onto the wider main street, Agnes notices the soft glow of a candle in the Johnstons' front parlour. But the wind cuts through her like a knife, whisking her breath away and, with it, her curiosity.

'Jesus!' She clutches her shawl tighter around her throat, then remembers herself. 'Sorry.'

Not far now, thank God: nearly at the harbour. Her fingers are like claws, clutching her wrap tight around her throat. She braces herself for the onslaught waiting round the corner but it's more than she bargained for. A gust nearly sweeps her off her feet, and John has to grasp her forearm and pull her down. Her fingertips glance off the earth.

They crouch low and edge along the wall. Although they can barely hear each other over the crashing sea and roaring gale, they still shout pleasantries, more for comfort than communication.

'I've never seen nothing like this!' John's voice is lost to Agnes but she understands the sentiment.

'Aye, I ken.'

'I wouldn't like to be out at sea on such a night!' His voice momentarily booms as the wind drops precariously.

'May God protect them.'

'Amen.'

There is almost a full complement of fishing boats in the harbour. Praise God: it is comforting to know she and John may be the only people out on such a night. Agnes imagines everyone in the village tucked up in bed, warm and cosy. After nursing them for twenty years – or is it more? – Agnes feels protective towards all the lives she's saved, brought into the world or given solace to in their passing.

Nearly there. A light glows in the last cottage along the shore at the end of a row of low-slung buildings. It is whitewashed, like its neighbours, with two windows on either side of a dark-stained oak door.

They crash through the opening with a gust of wind, rain and sea, and the door bangs against the wall. The room is oppressively warm, a rare discomfort on such a cold night. A fire blazes in the hearth, and Agnes notices the forge glowing in the room beyond. That's where John spends most of his time, along with Maggie here, keeping the fires burning. A haze of smoke hangs in the air at chest level like the vapor off a peaty bog when the haar rolls in.

The simple surroundings make Agnes feel at home, like she belongs and is the same as her friends and neighbours. But that is wishful thinking. Yet Agnes is good at pretending, imagining, dreaming. She's had to be.

She shakes off her shawl and hangs it on a peg by the fireplace; it'll dry there. The hook has become her hanger, always left clear for when she visits, which she's done regularly these last two months. Maggie's confinement has not been straightforward.

The room is dusky, though there are several candles lit. The big bed has been moved closer to the fire, but it still takes up a lot of the room. It fleetingly crosses Agnes's mind that it is far bigger than her own wedding bed.

Maggie lies in the centre, her fawn nightdress crimson with blood around her lower abdomen and between her legs. The sheets encasing her are also sodden, forming a reddish-brown halo around her hips. Sweat glistens on her forehead and drips down her neck where strands of hair stick like seaweed around a rock. She is a paler shade of the off-white bedding that surrounds her.

Stretching out a hand, she implores weakly, 'Help me, Agnes. Please, help me.'

Agnes rushes over, takes the limp hand and squeezes it tightly. She looks at John. 'When did it start?'

John shakes his head. 'I dinnae ken, maybe two, three hours ago, wasn't it, Maggie?'

But Maggie lets out a piercing scream.

Agnes grabs her shoulders. 'Look at me. Babies come early all the time. They decide when they come, and everything turns out fine. Right?'

Maggie nods feebly.

'John.' Agnes points to his forge next door. 'Boil as much water as you can. Do you have salt?'

'Aye.'

'Get any cloth and linen you can spare and boil it in salt water. Quickly. I need to clear all this—' she gestures to the sodden sheets '—and see what I'm doing.'

Maggie releases another deafening scream, groaning and rolling with the waves of pain. She grabs Agnes's arm. 'Am I going to die? Agnes, don't let me die.'

'Of course you're not going to die. I'm here, I'm here.' She takes Maggie's hand firmly. *Keep a level head.* She digs deep into the long pocket of her skirt and takes out a small phial of dark-green liquid. 'Drink this. It'll take away the pain.'

Staring at Agnes with wide eyes, Maggie puts the phial to her mouth and takes two gulps.

'That's enough.' Agnes slips the bottle back into her concealed pocket.

\*\*\*

John returns with a pile of cloths, his face wan. Right now, he would do anything to change all this. He would be happy not to have a family. The Sinclairs over at the grange have no offspring and they seem perfectly happy – well off, too.

If only he could go back eight months, to the month after they wed on that balmy night in May, and not do what he did. They had been to the fair earlier in the day. Everyone was happy; funny how everyone gets along when the sun is shining. Agnes was arm in arm with Gelly, watching the Punchinello show. And Maggie – God she was beautiful, *is* beautiful. He sees her making a garland, twisting spring flowers – daisies, bluebells, buttercups – around a length of twine; stems and petals strewn over the kitchen table like scattered memories. He'd had too much ale, or perhaps just the right amount, for making a baby.

He stands staring into the fire, cradling a basin of cloths. The container made from a wine casket cut in half looks like a baby's bath.

'John,' Agnes calls, then a little louder, 'John!'

'Sorry.' Shaking off the past like a dog shakes off fleas, he goes over to Agnes. 'Sorry. I'll set it down here.' He places the basin on the chair and draws it closer to the bed within Agnes's reach.

Agnes begins to clean Maggie, then the bed.

John turns away, feeling obsolete. 'Can I do anything?' he asks.

A window shutter bangs open and shut as a gust of wind whips around the room. Glad of a task, he bounds over, closes the shutter and retrieves the baton blown from the ledge. Placing it in the slots, he fastens the window securely as the howling continues outside.

'Looks a bad one,' Agnes says matter-of-factly, and John is grateful to her for lending an air of normality to the situation.

He goes along with it. 'Aye. Like a couple of years ago. Midsummer, mind?'

'Aye. We were lucky… Not a soul lost.'

'A miracle.'

Agnes looks at him. She stands and stretches, reaching her palms to the ceiling. She slides her hand into her pocket again, pulls out a small piece of linen and carefully unwraps it to reveal dried herbs and flowerheads. 'Make up a beaker of tea with this please, while I attend to your wife.'

'Aye … Right.'

Taking the little bundle, he makes his way to the forge next door. He knows to take his time.

\*\*\*

Agnes tenderly brushes Maggie's forehead. 'How often are the squeezes?'

'All the time,' Maggie moans.

'Right. Let's see… May I?'

Maggie nods and Agnes pushes up her gown. She gently examines her lower belly and her opening; it is moist and wide. 'It won't be long now. You can ride the squeezes out with me.'

'Is everything all right? Am I going to be all right and the baby?' Maggie whispers, then lets out a piercing cry.

'You're going to be just fine.' Agnes squeezes her hand then positions herself between Maggie's legs, her hands braced against the younger woman's knees.

Another contraction, a strong one by the looks of it. Maggie writhes, panting heavily. An image flashes into Agnes's mind. She's running up The Law, a hill behind North Berwick, with the other villagers; they are all dressed in bright colours and with painted faces for Lammas Day. They are pounding up the hillside one after the other towards the ancient cairn. Can she do this? Get there to the top and run down?

'Maggie! Maggie! Look at me. Keep looking at me.' Agnes holds Maggie's face between her hands, forcing her to look into her eyes. 'Everything's going as it should… We're doing this together. Do you know how many babies I've brought into the world?'

'Lots.' Maggie offers.

That's right. 'Lots.'

Another picture streaks across Agnes's brain. She did it! That's right. First to the top on that Lammas Day, and first back down. The men calling behind her, their voices growing fainter.

'Let's do this, Maggie. This is women's work.'

Maggie stares into Agnes's deep, dark, mesmerising eyes. 'Aye. Let's do it.'

The sun streams in through the small recessed window by the front door, forming a compact corridor of light that bounces off a table littered with empty pewter beakers, a basin, stained cloths and rags. The storm has passed. A fresh, bright winter's day has taken its place.

Agnes is drying her hands with a clean cloth and tidying up the debris.

'I'll do that,' John says, picking up a rag and depositing it in the bucket.

She stands back, her eyes heavy with tiredness, and says soothingly, 'It's fine, it's fine. It's all part of what I do. Go to Maggie.'

He opens his mouth to say something, then looks at Maggie cradling and cooing at her newborn baby and heads over. His arm around his wife's head and shoulders forms a V-shaped pillow. Maggie's face is pale but unblemished, the lines of pain smoothed as if the agony never happened, or at least will soon be forgotten.

John kisses the top of her head and gently brushes the child's cheek with the back of his fingers. A smile of relief and sheer happiness transforms his face.

Agnes looks on. This is why she became a healer; after all, her chart foretold it. She smiles as she clears the table, dumping the rags, bowls and tumblers into a bucket. But her smile slowly fades as she recalls the chart's other predictions.

'Agnes,' the astrologer said on the day she had sat down looking around the dimly lit room in the back alley of that great city, 'it's going to get... hmm. There is darkness here... See.' His long finger pointed to a cluster of stars and objects in the top left-hand quadrant of the chart.

The room was filled with curios, she remembers, shelf after shelf. There was a white porcelain palm with the fingers pointing up as if newly severed – perhaps a lady raising her hand in greeting, then ... thwack. A cloudy glass ball teetered on the edge of his desk, and a lectern with an ancient manuscript lay open in the corner.

The shop was illuminated with pools of flickering yellow light cast from thick candles in sturdy iron holders, some as high as

Agnes's head; the one poised by his shoulder delivered a surprising amount of light. Row after row of scrolls stacked the opposite wall. She wondered if they were other people's charts; she knew he was very popular at court. The rest of the wall space was adorned with drawings of the heavens. She could make out a goat and a centaur traced in lines with little stars twinkling through their forms.

He was still looking at her astrological chart, frowning. She hadn't wanted to get it done but Madame had insisted. She'd said Agnes was as good as everyone else, and all the young ladies were having theirs done. Since then, there had been a good deal of talk and excitement about weddings and children.

But it had unsettled Agnes. Granny McLeod was against it; she said putting your destiny on paper made it too definite and didn't give the person a chance to change their fortune. People had to be able to redeem themselves, alter their course, or what was the point of living? Granny McLeod had a different way of looking at the world, but there was always some truth in her words.

'Agnes,' the astrologer started again. She had pulled her eyes from the gargoyle-like creature on the shelf above the door. 'You're going to encounter… umm…' he grimaced '…difficulties at this point… See…' His finger was still fixed on the cluster of stars in the far left of the chart. 'And at this juncture…'

Agnes could only see stars and illegible scribbles.

'Well, the thing is,' for a second he accidentally looked into her eyes, then drew his away, 'the thing is, I have to tell you … that…'

She didn't much believe in astrological charts after that.

'Agnes, are you all right?' John asks, cradling his newborn.

'What? Aye, John, I'm fine, fine. Just a bit hot.'

Brushing his fingers over the child's bumpy little skull, he passes the baby to Maggie and rises. 'Aye, it's hot in here. I'll open the windows a wee bit, maybe the door.'

'No, no, I'll do it. Stay with Maggie and the bairn.'

He sits back down and his wife passes the infant to him. 'She's beautiful. Just like you, Maggie,' he says, kissing the baby's forehead.

Maggie gives a tired smile. 'I dinnae think I'm beautiful just now.'

'You are!' he replies adamantly. 'You're the most beautiful I've ever seen you.'

Agnes laughs. 'Best not to argue, Maggie. Now, I think I will leave and let you both...'

John gently places his daughter back into Maggie's arms. 'Goodwife Sampson, I can't thank you enough. I don't know what to say... I...'

'I know, John. I ken. I'm just glad ... I'm glad I could help... Now,' she adds brightly, 'what are you going to call her?'

'I'd like to call her Agnes,' he says. 'What do ye think, Maggie?'

'Umm...' Maggie looks uncertainly from Agnes to the baby. 'I ... I ... I'm not ... sure... I'd like to, it's a lovely name, but...'

'Nonsense!' Agnes laughs. 'We've enough Agneses round here! It's not even in your family. Goodness knows how you managed to avoid it. What names were you thinking of yourself, Maggie?'

John answers. 'Margaret. Maggie's a good name. Two beautiful Margarets. I'd be a very lucky man.'

'No, no,' Maggie says quietly. 'I thought maybe ... *Hope*. It's pretty, ken?'

'Ah, Hope,' Agnes repeats, opening the window and looking out. The sea is as calm as a duck pond and only a couple of fishing boats are now anchored in the shelter of the harbour. 'Hope. I like that.'

'Hope, it is. To Hope!' John grabs a tankard of ale from the table.

Agnes and Maggie join in with pretend cups. 'To Hope!'

Maggie strokes her daughter's temple. 'I wonder where life will take this little one.'

Agnes's stomach flutters like little moths around a candle. *Strange.*

# Chapter Five

The Conspiracy Begins
Edinburgh Castle

'These are indeed dark times, sire.' William Balfour shakes his head sadly.

King James rests his elbow on the arm of a huge, ornate oak chair painted in gold leaf.

The private royal apartment in Edinburgh Castle, one of its smaller rooms intended for confidential conversations, has a gloomy air. The small, square, lattice windows and slits cut deep into the stone walls only permit the most meagre daylight to enter.

Sir William walks over to one of the archers' slits and looks down. Below, through the haze, is the Nor Loch, from which a broken cartwheel protrudes through the mud. There are sacks of God knows what on the banks and bobbing up and down on the surface of the brown water. Shapes move in the smog, taking the form of people picking up items from the mud. They examine them and either toss them away or put them into the bags slung across their shoulders.

A chill wind stings Sir William's cheek and he instinctively raises a defensive hand. He must proceed cautiously.

The king is no longer a child. He became King of Scotland before he was scarcely able to walk following the execution of his mother, Mary Queen of Scots; since then, he has relied on the advice of high-status Protestant noblemen like Balfour for the day-to-day running of the kingdom and deferred to them on all matters, whether philosophical or theological. But he is now a young man of some twenty-four years, and Sir William and other members of the Privy Chamber fear this dependent era is coming to an end.

For the time being, as the monarch's chief confidant and advisor, William Balfour still has the ear of the king but that is looking more precarious as each day passes. The king recently asserted his independence on several occasions in the Privy Council, demanding it ratify things His Majesty had already decided. Unless something is done, the power and influence of the inner sanctum of the Council – and hence the top echelons of the Scottish nobility – will be completely eclipsed.

Sir William breathes in the cold air and the stench of rotten eggs assails his nostrils. Lifting a handkerchief to his nose, he quickly turns back into the room. Even though it is only a little after midday, torches blaze in almost every holder in an attempt to dispel the darkness. Some are in sconces protruding from the walls, others are in huge iron candlesticks the height of a man. Two enormous silver candlesticks sit on a sturdy square table against the far wall, but they make little impression on the gloom.

Stretching from floor to ceiling behind the table is a tapestry of an old medieval battle, and behind it a door. Sir William is one of the few to know of its existence – an escape route if the time ever came. It reminds him of that hellhole in Tranent, the gaol with its ancient spiral-stone staircase leading down to the cells. They were dark times during the queen's rule.

Indeed, timing is everything, and William has calculated the timing is perfect. The king has just arrived home from Denmark, shaken and troubled by the storm that delayed the wedding celebrations in Scotland. All manner of dignitaries from England, Spain, France and the Low Countries have been hanging around the capital for days waiting for the monarch, but in the king's absence William has been most interested in the Danish emissary who brokered the lucrative marriage with Anne of Denmark. They both had something which could be mutually beneficial if it were presented correctly to the king.

'Aye.' Sir William clasps his hands behind his back and paces. 'These are indeed dark times, sire.'

Lifting his head, the king responds, 'Aye, good William. My bride has been much afflicted since we arrived back.'

Bowing deeply and glancing out of the window again, Sir William replies, 'Indeed, sire.'

The sky is dark grey and the heavens have opened. Scotland's weather never disappoints when you need atmospheric foreboding. It is time. 'I fear it is witchcraft mischief, Your

Grace,' he says ruefully, shaking his head and casting his eyes downward. 'Evil targets the virtuous.'

'What is this?' The king looks steadily at Balfour, who is careful to keep his expression unreadable. Balfour's spies have told him the king is contemplating witchery. But this time, His Grace doesn't just want sycophantic acquiescence for what he has already decided, rather evidence they've arrived at the same conclusion. Refreshingly, he wants genuine agreement.

Sir William turns to the gentleman standing noiseless and unmoving in the corner, and ushers him forward with a flick of the hand. The man emerges from the shadows and bows reverentially. 'Your Grace, you are acquainted with the Danish emissary,' Balfour continues. 'Our good friends in Denmark had the same problem. They had to act quickly, cut it out. Take up the sword of righteousness, as it were.'

'Oh, yes?' The king makes a steeple of his forefingers and rests his lips on their tips.

The diplomat coughs. 'You were correct, Your Grace. The storm that prevented you and Her Illustrious Majesty Queen Anne from returning to this most glorious country was undeniably supernaturally conjured. When we—'

'Of course I was correct!' the king barks.

'I beg your pardon, Your Eminence. Entirely correct, of course, entirely accurate... And when we investigated, it *was* indeed a coven in our own Copenhagen that caused the whole thing – the tempest, everything! But we rooted them out! We discovered the witches met and did their diabolical conjuring in the house of Karen, the weaver.'

King James leans back. 'You did, huh?'

Sir William runs his fingers along the window ledge and turns them over. He smooths the dust off with his thumb, willing the ambassador on.

'Yes, sire. She confessed the whole thing. They were in league with the Devil. He helped them, and the coven summoned up demons – little crawling demons. Then the fiends climbed up the keels of your ships, Your Grace, crawled all over them. But *your* ship had the most – it was covered in them, sire.'

'Hmmm. And you got all of them?' The king stares intently at the emissary.

'The witches? Yes, sire.'

'You're sure?'

'We were very thorough,' the envoy continues. 'The divine lives of His Grace and our most precious princess,' he bows respectfully, 'now Queen Anne, were almost lost. Our grief and fear were unimaginable, Your Grace. We had to take all possible measures to ensure it could never, would never, happen again.'

King James straightens. An almost imperceptible – except to William – smile plays at the corner of his mouth. 'That is only fitting.'

Sir William seizes the moment. 'That night, sire, it was not just Denmark. As you are well aware, a storm raged off our own coast, the place where you would have made landfall. God preserve and keep you ... your ship would have been smashed to pieces.'

The king sits back and mumbles solemnly, 'My dreams foretold as much.'

'They did, sire?'

'The Devil fills my dreams with lurid abominations, grotesque doings. I knew he was close at hand. He wants to destroy...' He trails off, eyes glassy.

'It is natural he would seek out God's emissary on Earth,' Balfour adds quickly.

The king scrutinises Balfour, momentarily catching his eye. Sir William hurriedly looks down. Has he said the right thing?

The king nods. 'Aye, good William, you are right.'

William breathes out.

'Where?' the king enquires.

'North Berwick, the place you would have landed. I have a contact there, a God-fearing minister, a man you can trust. He's been worried for some time. The women there –midwives, healers – there are too many in a small village. It is strange. They are disrespectful, too. There's been talk of miraculous healing—'

'What?' The king jumps up, paces from the fireplace to the window and back. 'There is no doubt, then. It is the work of the Devil.'

'It seems so, sire.'

'But,' the king adds, returning to his chair, 'in this kingdom no one can be condemned without evidence, without going through due and proper procedures. I am well known to be a fair-minded and just monarch.'

He rises again and stands by the fire. Lifting his head so he is a few inches taller, he adds, 'As God's representative on Earth, I will arbitrate over the fate of all our citizens and will carefully sift information to reveal the truth.'

'And if it does turn out to be the machinations of the Devil in our land, sire?' Sir William prompts.

'Then justice will be swift and merciless. This man of the cloth, the minister you have in – where was it?'

'North Berwick, Your Grace.'

'He is trustworthy? Loyal?'

'Aye, Your Grace. By all accounts, this reverend is a good, God-fearing man. But he isn't sure what to do. He knows something isn't right, hasn't been for some time, but he doesn't know how to proceed.'

'He must start now!' King James bangs his fist on the ledge of the fireplace. 'Who knows how long it has been going on, how long they've been plotting and scheming? The stars prophesised it long ago. My destiny,' he continues quietly, 'is to do bloody battle with the Devil, the greatest enemy on Earth, on this ground here in God's country.' He makes a fist and looks at his nails. 'Who is the commissioner?'

'Robert Baxter, sire, another good man. Keen, new, young ... ambitious.'

'Ambitious, young... I have seen him at the Privy Council?'

'You have, sire. He asked my wife, Lady Balfour, to dance the balletti during the wedding feast at the palace.'

'Ah, yes.'

Sir William recalls the king's eyes following Baxter as he sauntered confidently over to Lady Balfour, bowing and offering his hand. Baxter is a handsome man in his late twenties with dark-brown hair and an immaculately groomed beard. Standing a good head above Lady Balfour, his sturdy yet sculpted figure had guided her around the floor like an eagle circling its prey.

'Very well, send Baxter,' the king orders. 'He has my full authority. I want this evil rooted out. The time has come for me to confront the Devil, to lay down the gauntlet. If it comes to it – and I fear it will – I will defend my realm and God! I will gladly take up the sword of righteousness for my kingdom, my Lord and Saint Andrew. Now go! See to it!'

Sir William bows. 'Aye, sire. At once, sire.'

# Chapter Six

Festivities Before Contagion
The Marais, Paris

Assen takes a deep breath to steel himself. Every room in the house is lit up and the gates have been thrown open to welcome guests. He passes between the posts into the little garden where a path leads to the front door and another skirts around the side of the building. He hates being the centre of attention; he has had too much of it. Stopping, he looks from side to side. He'll go around the back.

A picture flashes in his mind of him aged seven throwing his satchel down on the table. 'I hate people looking at me!'

'They're just curious, darling,' his mother had said. 'It's because you look a little different. *We* look a little different.'

'I don't want to look different!' He dropped into a chair.

His mother had laid a consoling hand on his head. 'We're all the same underneath when it comes to it.'

He touches his temple; he's sure he can still feel her smoothing his curls.

He'll enter by the kitchen: it will buy him time. It has begun to snow, and a soft flurry settles on his hat and shoulders and tickles his nose. Through the drawing-room window he sees his father and a family friend, Dr Brisbois, standing by the great fire, glasses in hand. There is Uncle Manny, too, and Aunt Charlotte and his cousins, and many others he does not know or has not seen in years. How many did Father invite? Best get this over with.

He pulls his cloak tightly around his neck and shoulders and hurries to the gable end of the great house towards the kitchen and the servants' entrance. The door is ajar with a wedge of yellow light spilling onto the white ground. The noise within is almost deafening: pots clang on the range and the huge ancient kitchen table, and occasionally clatter on the floor. Crockery rattles on trays as the servers plonk them on every available surface. Cook curses, shouting something unrepeatable to the new serving girl they have poached from next door.

Assen quietly pushes the door open. In all the mayhem, he hopes no one will notice him.

'Why, Mr Verey!' an older man exclaims, tray in hand. He coughs. 'Ahem, I mean *Dr* Verey, sir! We did not expect you to come round here. Can we help you, sir? Marie!' he shouts to a serving girl with an armful of empty plates. 'Take Dr Verey's hat and cloak. Come sir, please. Your father wanted to make an announcement when you walked through the front door.'

Assen's heart sinks. 'Thank you, but it's all right, François. I prefer to enter this way. It has been a long day and a busy few weeks. I will explain to Father. He will understand.' He passes his cloak, hat and gloves to the waiting servant.

François doesn't look convinced. 'Yes, sir.'

Bracing himself, Assen marches through the kitchen and into the hall. The door to the great drawing room is half open and the murmur of voices and chinking glass leaks out. For a moment he stands behind the door, hand poised on the handle. He drops his shoulders and stretches his neck, puts one ear to his shoulder then the other, rotates his head from side to side.

*Right, come on, Assen, you can do this.* Flattening his palm on the panel of the door, he pushes it open. The room is full and his father hasn't seen him.

Someone slaps him on the back. 'Congratulations, my boy! I hear you distinguished yourself. Best the Faculty's produced! Where's your drink?' The older man is about to beckon François with a tray of drinks when Assen's father spots his son.

'Ah, here he is,' Mr Verey bellows. 'Come here, Assen, come here. Where have you been? It doesn't matter. Medical business, no doubt.' He laughs and looks at the gentleman beside him. 'Anyway, you're here now.'

Assen joins them before the roaring fire, the heat flushing his cheeks and forehead. He rubs the back of his neck. Looking around the panelled room, he notices the massive dining table pressed against the wall groaning under the weight of food. There are red and green grapes piled high on four corners, roasted chickens with some carved slices and carving knives angled neatly on plates to the side, and other cuts of beef poised on pewter platters. All manner of vegetables fill the spaces between: haricot beans, tomatoes of all colours, sliced artichoke, carrot, cabbage and ... hmm ... what looks like aubergine. He hates aubergine.

Drawing his eyes from the opulence, he notices tall chairs positioned at various points along the other two walls where some of the older guests are ensconced.

Someone places a glass of red wine in his hand. 'Congratulations, Mr— Dr Verey.'

Assen takes the glass and shifts awkwardly. 'Thank you, François. How is Monique?' he enquires, regretting he had forgotten to ask when they were in the kitchen.

'She is better, Dr Verey. Thank you for asking.'

Assen smiles. 'Good.'

His discomfort at the lavishness fails to evaporate. This celebration is not something he wanted, but his father and Uncle Manny had been very persuasive; they'd said it was what his mother would have wanted. He doubts it. She would have preferred a smaller affair, just family, a quiet celebration to talk about his plans, his hopes, and how he could best use his education. But his father and uncle had assured him she would have loved a big celebration. Funny how they remember different things about her, so much so they could be talking about a different person. Perhaps it is not so much the person they remember when reminiscing but themselves.

A servant carrying a pail of logs places more wood on the lively fire and the flames shoot up the flue. The elegant greystone fireplace is big enough for a man to stand in and nicely frames the yellow, blue, green and white dancing flames. Although the room is warm, it is surprisingly well ventilated. The haze from the fire hovers high above their heads, skirting the vaulted ceiling and escaping through the openings at the top of the long lattice windows spanning the length of the room. Some of the windows are also open at the bottom to admit the cool breeze, especially welcome to those a little red-faced from the punch.

Assen knows his father likes the house to be well aired, especially since the last outbreak. It didn't come anywhere near

The Marais, but Mr Verey is convinced the pestilence seeps in with the miasma and will suffocate everyone in the house. Assen doesn't know how many times he's heard his father counsel the servants to throw open the windows and let the odours disperse, even before mother died.

'Come, Assen, come. Here is Dr Brisbois.' Mr Verey pats Assen between the shoulders, bringing him closer.

'Good evening, Dr Brisbois. Thank you for joining us.'

Dr Brisbois is a dapper older gentleman in his mid to late fifties wearing, a little uncharacteristically for his generation, the latest Parisian fashion. His russet-silk doublet suits him and contrasts well with the cerulean and cornflower-blue of his pantaloons. They are a little longer than the younger gentlemen would wear, encroaching upon his knee. Below them his hose are an understated flesh colour, displaying a finely toned calf. The ensemble is topped off with a flawless, brown-fur, sleeveless over-jacket and a small ivory ruff around his neck, although the latest fashion is for wider ones. The impression is one of effortless elegance and class: a man at the top of his profession.

'And thank *you* for joining us!' Dr Brisbois clasps Assen's upper arm. 'You'll find many doors open to you as a physician at court. You'll attend the very highest in our society – noblemen and royalty. I predict a queue for your services, Dr Verey.' He winks at Assen's father, who raises his glass.

\*\*\*

In truth, Mr Verey would have preferred his son to go into the law but the boy showed no aptitude. He was always poring over those star charts and following his mother around the grounds, asking about the plants and herbs she was picking to use in her remedies. She wanted him to be a healer of some sort. But a court physician like Dr Brisbois? Now that would be something. Of course, it will take time to cultivate their aristocratic friends as clients, but there are many in The Marais who will be more than happy to acquire the services of young Dr Verey. This is indeed a good day.

Mr Verey watches his son chat with the doctor. It is easy to picture him as a court physician: poised, handsome and unselfconsciously elegant. He has the look and manner of someone for whom things have come easily, including his studies. Yet his boy is not conceited or entitled, merely at ease with his privilege. But he is not happy to be the centre of attention, not happy at all, never has been. Perhaps it is because he looks a little foreign.

Mr Verey glances at his dark-haired, olive-skinned son. He can see his wife's family, the Aldabehs, in him. His heart softens; that will appeal to the nobility at court due to the latest fashion for all things exotic.

Some think that was why Mr Verey chose his wife, Bahdeer, but it wasn't. Nor was it for the money, since both families were among the wealthiest in Paris. It was for the usual reasons: they liked the same things, had similar interests, the same sense of humour, had similar souls. But who is he kidding? He almost melted when he first saw her, not because of her exoticism, he barely noticed that; it was because of her easy grace and finesse.

Assen has absorbed that – he was always her boy. Yet, at this moment, Assen looks anything but comfortable, with his cheeks glowing crimson. Oh well, needs must.

\*\*\*

Dr Brisbois continues, 'We need good young doctors with vision, eh? The duke has promised patronage for our work.'

Assen blurts out without thinking, 'They say plague is abroad on the outskirts, maybe as close as…'

Mr Verey looks at Assen and his face drops.

Dr Brisbois responds tactfully. 'There are brothers who look after the poor, the needy. What we need—'

'With respect, Dr Brisbois,' Assen interrupts, 'I would help them. I would go where I'm needed, where I could do most good. I want to use what I've been given. What God has given me.'

His father's face is set hard.

'People need you at court,' Dr Brisbois continues breezily. 'You'll learn from the greatest physicians of our age. And you can carry out experiments – we have the stills, the salts, sulphurs. We can combine chemicals, compounds. Who knows what cures we will find? It is exciting, don't you think?'

'Y-yes,' Assen stammers, imagining a room full of distilling apparatus with phials and flasks of different coloured liquids gurgling over the flames. It's what he's been dreaming of – his own still. Just think of the fusions, elixirs and chemical cures they could create; they could change everything.

Little butterflies of excitement take flight in his stomach. To be involved in ... no, to be at the *forefront* of the new state-of-the-art medicine. Yet he has a duty, and he promised his mother to go where he was most needed. But perhaps he could save more lives this way. He furrows his brow and looks in the direction of the door.

A smiling, middle-aged gentleman, glass of wine in hand, is making his way over to the trio. 'Uncle Manny!' Assen exclaims, a smile lighting up his face.

'Assen, my good fellow! I am so proud of you. Your mother, God rest her, would have been delighted. A physician, a healer! You're so like her.' He turns to the group. 'Isn't he?'

'Thank you, Uncle. It was Mother who taught me about physicks, mixing herbs, roots, leaves, flowers and heavenly charts. How nature could heal and be made more potent... I aim to live up to her name, her memory.'

'You will, son, you will.' His father places a hand on his forearm. 'I wish she was here to see this.'

'Me too, Father.'

Seated at the far end of the room, a middle-aged woman is looking at the group. Uncle Manny calls affectionately, 'Charlotte, dearest, come over.' He holds out his hand.

Maintaining eye contact with her husband, she makes her way over. 'Congratulations, Assen.' She kisses him on both cheeks.

'Aunt Lottie.' Assen is delighted; he likes female company. He had precious little of it when he was young, after mother...

His aunt is a handsome woman, petite, almost Spanish in her looks and definitely in her dress. She prefers the Iberian fashion to the showy, jewel-encrusted gowns and headpieces in Parisian society. Uncle Manny once told him, she would much rather people noticed a comment she made, the sparkle in her eyes or the smoothness of her skin than a jewelled frock. Her velvet gown is a dark shade of wine, almost black; unlike across the sea in England, the skirt is slim at the hip, as is her shape. The dress begins at the neck with a high collar topped with a tiny ruff, and an embroidered delicate pattern of intricate bows flow in a horizontal pattern one after the other down its centre. The sleeves are long, almost cascading to the floor, slashed open from the shoulder to the wrist to reveal undersleeves of deep blue finished at the wrists with ruffs.

'You've inspired Émile, you know.' She smiles and sips her cordial.

'We blame you.' Uncle Manny gives Assen an affectionate nudge.

Aunt Charlotte continues, 'He talks about nothing but becoming a physician. He wants distilling apparatus!'

Everyone laughs.

'You will come and see your little cousins – Émile, René, Joséphine? They ... we miss you.'

Assen's gut tightens. He has neglected them; he should have visited his little cousins. They look up to him, and now young Émile wants to be just like him. But he's been so busy with all the lectures, visits to patients and the amount he has had to learn. No: he is not being truthful. He's also been enjoying the company of his fellow physicians, the heated exchanges late into the night about politics, the new medicine, the old medicine and astrology – and enjoying the claret. He *has* had time ... or he could have made time. He has been remiss.

'I'm sorry, Aunt Charlotte, Uncle Manny. I have been neglectful. I'll come soon, I promise.'

Uncle Manny slaps Assen on the back. 'Good boy. I'm very proud to say I have a nephew serving at the royal court. I know your mother was a regular and favourite. You will be too!'

'We don't have a royal court,' Aunt Charlotte corrects her husband.

'Well, yes, well... No, for the moment we don't, but it'll soon be sorted, I'm sure.' Uncle Manny smiles at his wife. 'But for now, we have a noble court! A very noble court and, of course, the duke and the League.'

'But it's not the king, is it?' Aunt Charlotte squeezes the fingers of one hand with the other.

'Charlotte is worried Paris will descend into chaos if we do not proclaim Prince Henry king,' Uncle Manny explains.

'Ah, but we cannot, I'm afraid, Madame Verey. He is Protestant.' Dr Brisbois sighs. 'It would not be acceptable.'

'But he *is* the king, and if he's the king he should have a royal court. He should be here. Surely the League can work with him?'

Uncle Manny takes two glasses of punch from a salver as a servant passes and hands one to his wife. 'Charlotte, dear wife, the duke has said—'

'Now, now.' Mr Verey waves a hand. 'This is a celebration of good fortune and hard work. There'll be no talk of politics or religion.'

'Quite right.' Uncle Manny nods.

Two of Assen's fellow young physicians enter the room and hover uncertainly by the door. 'If you'll excuse me,' he says quickly, 'Gérard and Lucas have just arrived. I must welcome them.'

'Yes, yes, attend to your guests, Assen. This is your evening,' Mr Verey says pleasantly before turning to warm himself by the fire.

As Assen stops to place his empty goblet on a platter on the edge of the table, he hears his Uncle Manny whisper, 'Is he really considering serving in a plague hospital? I'm sorry, I couldn't help overhearing.'

'A plague hospital!' Aunt Charlotte exclaims.

'Hush, my darling.' Uncle Manny brings his finger to his lips. 'Not so loud.'

Assen reaches for a plum in a bowl of fruit and studies it, holds it up to the light.

'Of course. I'm sorry, Theo,' Aunt Charlotte says.

'He *says* he wants to use his training to help the poor, to combat this dreadful pestilence when – *if* it should return to our gates,' his father explains.

'Doesn't that frighten you?' Aunt Charlotte whispers.

Assen can hardly hear; he tilts his head to the side, looks down and runs his fingers along the tablecloth.

'There has been talk of it in the villages to the south.' There is an urgency in Uncle Manny's voice. The top of Assen's stomach tightens as if he's just pulled a belt securely across his waist.

'Oh, it won't come to anything.' His father's voice is light.

'What? The plague or Assen going anywhere near it?' Uncle Manny presses.

33

'Husband, you think it will come here? You think it'll reach the gates of our city?' Aunt Charlotte's voice quivers.

'No, no, my dearest. You're right, of course, Theo. It won't come to anything.'

# Chapter Seven

Hanging in the Balance
North Berwick

Gelly raises her fist to bang on the door. Agnes said there'd been trouble here at the Johnstons'; she didn't know what, though, only there was a light on in the early hours during the storm. News came later. It was the poor bairn, Jennie. The minister's been and the doctor could do nothing, so they say.

A shadow flits across the upstairs window. Mr Johnston peers down at her, he disappears, then there's creaking on the treads of the stairs. He must be coming down. She rubs her palms and puts her eye to a crack in the door. A warm mustard ball of light is descending, glowing brighter as Mr Johnston pulls the door open and peers from behind his candle. 'Miss Duncan.'

'Gelly, sir. Please.'

'I don't know there's much you can do. But my wife asked for you.'

A gull screeches high above. A solitary call into the blackness of the North Sea. Somewhere over the ancient church of St Andrews at the harbour the call is answered.

'You'd better come in. Up here.' He nods to the stairs.

Putting her hand on the post at the foot of the stairs, Gelly slips past him. It is cold and hard. A lump forms in her throat. What will she find? Can she really help? Or is she just a stupid servant with a few herbs and teas?

She squeezes the linen bag in the pocket of her skirt. The leaves, buds, pods and twigs crunch. Her throat loosens. They've helped before. Besides, the Johnsons have tried everything else, so Agnes overheard the minister say.

'She's in here.' A sliver of light from a door fractionally ajar illuminates the floorboards furthest from the head of the stairs. He pushes open the door and announces, 'She's here.'

Gelly steps in behind him, hovering in the doorway with her hands cupped in front of her. She is in her late teens, wearing a

35

plain brown dress that's a little frayed around the cuffs and hem. Her light-brown wavy hair is mostly tucked beneath a white cap except for a single ringlet framing her smooth temple and delicate eyebrows. An off-white linen waistcoat tapered at the waist sits over her dress, as does a matching apron. The ends of the pinny are tucked into a belt at her waist.

Bobbing a curtsey, she says, 'Hello, Mrs Johnston. I'm sorry for your troubles.'

'Come in, Gelly, come in. Bring her in, for goodness' sake, Husband. We were just about to pray. Will you pray with us, Gelly?'

Mr Johnston steps aside and looks down at the child on the bed. Gelly follows his gaze. It's wee Jennie; Gelly has seen her playing on the shore down by the harbour many times. Out of sight of their parents, a ramble of shod and unshod bairns splash in the shallows and rock pools and chase each other up Parson's Lane towards the ancient ruins in the middle of Three Witches Wood, daring each other to go in.

Now wee Jennie is deathly white with a greenish tinge, and beads of sweat glisten on her forehead. Her sister Cathy, a girl of about twelve – four years older than Jennie – hovers at the end of the bed close to the open door. By her side is the youngest child, Simon, just seven, his eyes wide.

'Aye, of course I'll pray with you.' Gelly looks directly at the older woman.

A tear forms at the corner of Mrs Johnston's eye and trickles down her cheek, and she quickly brushes it away.

Gelly joins the children at the bottom of the bed. The children look at each other. Simon opens his mouth to say something, but his sister nudges him.

'She'll be all right, Ma... She's... She'll be all right, won't she?' Cathy asks.

'Aye, Cathy, if it be God's will.'

'Is it God's will?' Simon looks up at his mother.

'Shhhh.' His sister elbows him again.

'We hope so, Simon. We'll pray...'

Mrs Johnston gets onto her knees and places her elbows on the bed beside the comatose child. She presses her interlaced fingers to her forehead. The other two children jostle for position

next to their mother, pushing and tugging each other's clothes.
'Cathy!' Mrs Johnston cries. 'Go round the other side.' Cathy's shoulders drop as she gets up and trudges around the bed.

Gelly settles on her knees and clasps her hands to her chest. With their eyes closed and heads bowed, Mrs Johnston begins.

'Our Father which art in heaven,
hallowed be thy name,
let thy kingdom come,
thy will be fulfilled
on earth as it is in heaven... Amen.'

'Amen,' they chorus softly.

Getting up and returning to her seat, Mrs Johnston turns to Gelly who is still kneeling on the floor. 'We've heard you might— We've heard... That is to say...' She lowers her voice. 'We've heard you've helped other folk, right?'

'I've tried, Mrs Johnston.'

'Can you help our Jennie?' Mrs Johnston asks, her voice cracking.

'I'll try. Have the doctors been?'

Mr Johnston glances at his wife. 'Aye.'

'What did they tell ye?'

'Tae prepare. Send for the minister.'

'No! No! I will not have it!' Mrs Johnston howls.

Gelly has seen this before, a mother not letting herself think of what lurks at the back of her mind. To think of it would be to invite it in. For all Mrs Johnston's mild manner, kind presence and gentle protection of her children, she is a force of nature when it comes to things that threaten them.

Gelly looks at the children. Likely they've never seen their parents distraught. Their father is normally calm, strong and jovial, and their mother a quiet, reassuring and comforting presence. But in a way she is glad the physicians have left them no hope. *No toes to tread on.*

'Did they say what it is?' she asks.

'Umm...' Mr Johnston hesitates. 'Rising ... rising o' ... err ... rising o' the lights, they said.'

Gelly nods. 'Aye. Her chest's congested, then. She's had difficulty breathing?'

'Aye, that's right.' Mrs Johnston says. 'She coughed and coughed and coughed; coughed up some terrible stuff. Isn't that right, Husband? Then she just flopped down. I could hear it in her chest. She's been like this ever since.'

'I see. I have something… I cannae guarantee, mind.'

'Please. Anything.' Mrs Johnston looks at her husband. 'Robert, please.'

Mr Johnston draws his lips together. Gelly knows that if he doesn't agree there's nothing she can do. She holds her breath. 'Aye, alright, give her whatever you've got,' he says at last.

She reaches into the hidden pocket of her gown and draws out a pouch with herbs, seeds and berries, and a phial with dark-brown gooey liquid in it. 'Can you fetch a bowl of hot water, please? I need somewhere to prepare these.'

Mrs Johnston turns to her daughter, who has retreated to a corner of the room to watch quietly. 'Cathy, quickly. Take Gelly to the kitchen and get her whatever she needs.'

'Aye, Ma.' Cathy picks up a candle in a plain pewter holder from the dresser under the tiny window and heads to the door.

'Go with Cathy,' Mrs Johnston says to Gelly. 'She'll get you what you need.'

'Thank you, ma'am.' Gelly follows Cathy into the lobby at the top of the stairs, now lit by the soft warm glow from the candle.

When Mr Johnston is sure they are out of earshot, he quickly turns to his wife. 'I don't like it.'

'Shhh.' Mrs Johnston nods to the door. 'Ye heard what the doctors said.'

'Aye, but maybe we should just have done, ken, what the minister said…'

'What?' she hisses. 'Leave it? Wait and see if she dies afore the morning? No, Mr Johnston, I won't! I won't sit here and watch ma bairn…' She lowers her voice. 'You know what happened wi' Mary's father?'

'Aye, I know, I know.'

'Well, if ye ken, what's the matter with ye?' Again, she lowers her voice to a whisper. 'That wee lassie doonstairs brought him back. He would have been stretched out in the churchyard wi' all the other Hunters. A fine, fit man, and all.'

'Aye, I know, I know. It's just ... they don't seem to like it.'
'Pa! Doctors, ministers! Feeding off folks' suffering. Frightened they'll not get this.' She rubs her thumb and fingers together.

Gelly hears snippets of their conversation as she climbs upstairs. She lets her feet flop heavily on the steps to warn the couple she's close by. As she approaches the door, they immediately fall silent. She knocks and enters, carrying a bowl with steam rising off it. Mr Johnston steps away from his wife.

Pretending she hasn't noticed, and looking deferentially at Mr Johnston then Mrs Johnston, Gelly says, 'We need to get her to swallow some o' this.'

'Help me, Father.' Mrs Johnston props up the child. 'Jennie, ma dear, you have to try and take some of this. It'll make you feel better.'

The little girl's head lolls from side to side, and Mrs Johnston looks pleadingly at her husband, then Gelly. Mr Johnston sits and smooths the strands of hair stuck to the child's face behind her ear. Gelly walks over, carrying the bowl as if it were an offering to the gods.

Mrs Johnston tries again. 'You have to drink some of this, pet, then you can go back to sleep.'

Jennie's eyelids flutter and blink open, her stare resting and locking onto her mother's gaze.

'Mrs Johnston, ma'am, here, quick!' Gelly presses the dish into her hands. 'Now!'

Together they place the rim of the bowl on the child's lips. 'Take a wee drink, and ye'll feel better,' Mrs Johnston soothes.

The girl's eyes grow large as if she is trying to form a question, but she swallows. At first the brew dribbles out of her mouth, a tiny stream down her chin and onto her chest. Gelly pulls a cloth from her belt and wipes the trickle. 'If you're a good girl, Jennie, and you drink a wee bit more, you can have a nice long nap. You'd like that, wouldn't you?'

Jennie nods. They tilt the mixture into her mouth once more, and this time her throat rises and falls as she gulps the liquid.

Gelly stands and looks into the bowl; it still has half its contents. 'We have to give it tae her again when the sun is over the church clock, and then when it goes doon past the byre, and we'll see.'

There is nothing to do but wait. 'May I stretch out in front of the fire?' Gelly asks Mrs Johnston, her hands clasped in front of her.

'Oh course, my dear, of course. Cathy. Cathy! Where is that child?' Cathy pops her head around the door, her little brother peering from behind her skirts. 'Cathy, love, get a blanket for our guest.'

'Aye, Ma … ehmm… Yes, Mother.'

'And, Cathy…'

'Aye?'

'Go to bed. Jennie's sleeping now; nothing is going to happen 'til the morning.'

'Right Ma … ehmm… Mother.'

Mr and Mrs Johnston settle into the chairs on either side of the bed while Gelly pulls the coarse blanket over her shoulders and rests her head on her palm. The warmth from the fire caresses her forehead and cheeks and she closes her eyes. Has she done enough? She's never lost a patient. What would happen if she does? She opens her eyes and stares into the orange, yellow- and blue-peaked flames.

# Chapter Eight

Plague Arrives
Paris

Assen pulls the plush collar of his overcoat tighter around his neck and buries his chin deeper into the fur. Will he be able to persuade him? He seemed immovable, but if he offered him money or food, then, perhaps...?

*Jesus.* A bitter wind blasts him in the face as he rounds the corner of the square. The sleet is blowing diagonally, peppering his coat so it looks like he's been sprinkled with sugar by an irreverent baker. Bloody Paris in January.

He turns into a narrow back street where the overhanging upper storeys reach out to each other like branches, forming a dense canopy to keep out the light. Even so, the alley is crowded. Several women carry large round baskets covered with cloths.

'Can I tempt you with steaming hot pescods, risshes, sheep's feet, sir?' one asks, peeling back the cover and allowing the aroma of rotting meat and mouldy mushrooms to escape.

Assen suppresses the urge to cover his mouth and nose, and his fingers curl round the handkerchief in his pocket.

Another woman appears to his right. 'Can I tempt you with anything else, sir?' she says, half-mocking and half-hoping.

'No, thank you, ladies. I have business to attend to.'

Both laugh. 'Business, is it?'

He looks furtively around. Are these women here to distract him? Is he being set up? Is he going to be robbed at any moment? Everyone seems to be hurrying because of the cold, hats pulled down, heads buried in coats and shawls, scurrying down the multitude of lanes leading off the street. Several windows high above are open; a woman shouts from one to a boy below to hurry to the butcher's before every cut disappears. 'Yes, Ma,' the boy shouts as he takes off like a tornado, weaving in and out of the adults at hip height.

Assen realises there are lots of children, most reaching no higher than his elbows. They move nimbly and quietly through the crowds. With the falling snow deadening footsteps and voices and the cold stripping his senses, he'd hardly noticed they were there. He wishes he had worn more modest clothes; he should know the other side of Paris by now.

The narrow street is bustling with everyone jostling for position, trying to overtake. Someone knocks Assen in the shoulder as they pass; it is a large man wearing a long hide apron tied in the middle. Assen instinctively puts his hand inside his doublet to check for his purse. Still there. He chides himself. The man was probably a farrier, an honest, hard-working fellow. But times are hard with the pestilence; some people have lost their living. He needs to think more, be less rash, more careful. He sounds like his father.

The thoroughfare widens into a broader street where carts can pass on either side. This is the right area. *You shouldn't be here.* Assen ignores his father's voice. This is exactly where he should be; this is what he trained for. His mother's voice replaces his father's: *You have a vocation. It is sacred. Be guided by your heart.*

He squeezes two fingers into his collar, pulling it to loosen it as he passes several doors with white crucifixes haphazardly painted on them. Further down the road a cart is parked outside a house marked with the same insignia. Two men stand talking, apparently waiting. One is leaning his elbow on the side of the cart and the other has his arms folded. Carters, no doubt, given their dress and the long leather aprons.

He strides over. 'Excuse me, gentlemen.'

They eye him curiously and he is even more aware of how out of place he must look. One of them laughs under his breath. Assen feels the back of his neck prickle and heat rise under his collar. The fur is stifling. He must act as if everything is normal and he has a right to be here.

He coughs. 'Can you tell me where Dr Xavier is? The physician, Dr Gérard Xavier, if you please?'

'Never heard of him,' one of the men answers then spits on the ground.

'I beg your pardon.' Assen says, deflated. 'Sorry to have troubled you.'

The carter shakes his head with a grin and starts to stack the sheets in the back of the cart. Assen scans the street and beyond to the square, looking for similar carts. The doctor is in this district somewhere. He turns and steps away.

The other carter calls after him. 'Hey! Dr Gérard, you say? From Bordeaux, right? Young chap, fair?'

'That's right.'

'He's at the far end of the street. Past the two waggons.' He points. 'The door just before the church. On the other side.'

'Thank you.' Assen's shoulders unwind for the first time this morning. He ambles back to the man and drops some coins into his hand.

'Thank you, sir.'

A cart is parked outside the large house, whose door is open. No one is around; Gérard must be inside. As Assen reaches the house, a figure steps out covered from head to foot in a leather robe and wearing a large-brimmed hat, their face hidden behind a mask with a long beak. The figure is carrying extended poles and tongs.

'Excuse me, I'm looking for Dr Xavier,' Assen says hesitantly.

'You've found him,' Gérard replies, taking off his hat and mask and running his fingers through his hair. There are dark circles under his eyes and little parallel lines drawn deep between his eyebrows. 'You shouldn't be here,' he sighs. 'Go! I'll see you in The Marais, if I can get out. The whole place is quarantined, right down to the Seine. What are you doing here, anyway? No! I don't want to know! You shouldn't be here. Just go!'

Having predicted he might get this response, Assen says quickly, 'The same could be said of you.'

'I volunteered.'

'I'll volunteer.'

'You bloody well won't!'

Gérard beckons two men on the other side of the road. As they approach, Assen steps back. Standing a little way off, Gérard says something to them, which Assen can't make out.

'Wait,' Gérard commands the men. Pointing with his pole to a well at least twenty yards away, he orders Assen, 'Stand aside.'

Assen paces over to the well.

Gérard puts the mask back on, then the beak, hat and gloves, and enters the house. After several minutes he re-emerges and signals to his helpers.

'All of them?' the carter asks, stretching his back.

Gérard sighs. 'All of them.'

The men gather up sheets and sacks from the cart and head into the building. Gérard joins Assen at the well. 'I want to help,' Assen says earnestly.

'You can't. Come back when you've had the plague and survived, and I'll fit you out in this fetching attire myself.'

'That's what makes you invincible, is it?'

'No, but I've seen out three plagues since I had it.'

'I'm a doctor. This is what I trained for.' Assen takes off his hat and lets his hand drop by his side.

'Look,' Gérard says, 'maybe there is something you *can* do. Get food, good food, fresh, hot, as much as possible. Send it here. Get volunteers, but only those who've had the plague … yes? Pay them well… Go to the Sanitaire, the City Council – you'll get all the funds you need there.'

'I have the money. I can pay for it.'

'Fine. Get water and rosehip juice. We need more waggons to take away the bodies and more shrouds. We have to get them out of here as soon as possible. Do you understand?'

'Yes, right away,' Assen says excitedly.

Gérard sighs. 'Thank you. You'll be doing us a great service.'

Keen to make a start, Assen turns to head off. Gérard grabs his upper arm. 'If you see any of our colleagues treating these poor unfortunates, tell them—' he takes a deep breath '—tell them not to bleed them. It makes matters worse, a lot worse. Try to make them understand.'

Assen nods. 'Right. Anything else?'

'Pray for a miracle.'

# Chapter Nine

A Miracle
North Berwick

Is Jennie still alive? How long has it been? A sliver of light begins to form in the corner of the room on the far side of the fireplace. Eyes wide open, Gelly is still curled up in a blanket on the floor in front of the gently glowing fire.
*Dear God, dear Jesus, our gentle heavenly lord, the lamb of God, please help this little lamb. Spare her, please God, spare her.*
She gets up, sways and has to hold on to the back of a chair. Mr and Mrs Johnston are still fast asleep, sitting upright in two straight-backed wooden chairs. Mr Johnston's chin rests on his chest; Mrs Johnston's head is tipped to the side on a rolled blanket serving as a makeshift pillow. But there is movement in the bed, a ripple like a gentle wave slowly coming to shore.
The child begins to stir, sweeping her legs from side to side as if making a snow angel. Then she opens her eyes and stares at the ceiling. Gelly bites her bottom lip. *Thank you, Lord, sweet gentle Jesus.*
Pressing the heels of her hands down into the bed, the little girl pushes herself to almost sitting. Gelly follows her gaze as she looks to the left where her mother sits fast asleep, and then right at her father. 'Ma? Da?' she whispers. Her mother stirs then settles back down, breathing out heavily. Jennie persists, raising her voice. 'Ma! Ma!'
Gelly can't help but smile; her heart might just explode out of her bodice. *Wake up, Mrs Johnston, wake up!*
'Ugh? What?' Mrs Johnston says.
Jennie is sitting up in bed, cheeks flushed pink, staring intently at her mother. 'Are you all right, Ma? Did you read me a story? Did I fall asleep? Will you read it to me again? I don't remember it.'

'Aye … aye…' her mother stutters. 'I'm all right, I'm all right. I'll read you a story, any story you like, pet. Are you … are you … all right, too?'

'Aye,' answers Jennie with raised eyebrows. 'But…'

'What is it, love?'

Jennie sits up further in the bed. 'I had a funny dream.'

Mrs Johnston moves across to the bed, sits on the edge and gently strokes her daughter's cheek. 'Did you, pet? Everything's all right now. Praise God, praise God, oh God, thank you, thank you, thank you.'

Gelly retreats into the shadows, carefully folds the blanket and places it on the chair by the fireplace. Little does she or anyone know, but in the not-too-distant future wee Jennie will leave these shores never to return. She will grow up and raise her own family in a foreign land and become fluent in three languages.

'Gelly, my dear, dear girl. God bless you.' Mrs Johnston reaches for her hands and squeezes them. 'Thank you. We'll never be able to repay what you've done. Never. Robert, the money's on top of the press.'

Gelly looks down and shifts. 'It's just the herbs, ma'am, what Granny McLeod taught me.'

'No, no. it's more than that.' Mrs Johnston is still gripping her hands tightly. 'You have a gift, just like they said.'

'Who?' Gelly asks.

'Mama!' Jennie cries.

Mrs Johnston immediately releases the young woman's hands and turns back to her daughter who is staring at Gelly looking puzzled. 'Mama, is that Gelly? Gelly, Mr Seton's servant? Why is she here?'

'This is Miss Gellis Duncan. You weren't well, darling, and Miss Duncan helped you get better.'

'Did she?' asks Jennie, wide-eyed. 'Will you tell me all about it?'

'Aye, she did. And I *will* tell you all about it. It'll be your story. And when you meet her, darling, you must always say "Hello, Miss Duncan." '

'Yes, Ma.' Jennie sits up fully and places her hands across her stomach. 'Hello, Miss Duncan.'

'Please, just call me Gelly.' She glances quickly at Mrs Johnston, 'If that's all right?'

Mrs Johnston smiles. 'Gelly it is.'

'Hello, Jennie.' Gelly bends forward and smiles.

'Hello Miss ... Gelly.'

Gelly carefully places the blanket on the bed and backs away. 'If you'll excuse me, I have duties. I have to be at Mr Seton's.'

'Of course, my dear, of course ... and thank you.' The lines around Mrs Johnston's eyes and forehead have smoothed, restoring her full round face.

Jennie tugs on her sleeve. 'What? What is it, pet?' Jennie looks imploringly at her mother. 'Yes, pet, a story. I'll tell you a story right now.' Mrs Johnston slips into a world where only she and her daughter exist.

Gelly smiles, bone-tired but happy. She hasn't noticed Mr Johnston at her side. 'Thank you,' he says simply. This is perhaps the first time he has looked at her properly. 'Please, take this. It isn't enough, it'll never be... I'm so...' He drops the coins into her hand.

'Thank you, Mr Johnston, it is. It's fine. Thank you. I'm happy I could help.'

As Gelly moves to close the door, she hears Mr Johnston say under his breath, 'May God keep us all safe from evil.' She stops, her fingers stiff around the doorknob.

'What was that, Husband?'

'Nothing.'

Gelly clicks the door shut. An icy draft lifts the base of her cap and the back of her neck prickles She shudders and heads down the staircase.

# Chapter Ten

Holding Back the Tide
St Marcel's Plague Hospital, Paris

'How many?' Assen exhales heavily.
　'Seven. We lost seven last night.' Gérard folds his arms and looks down. 'Four in here and three in the Duplessis chapel.'
　'Really?'
　They are standing in the middle of St Marcel's large airy hall, the main body of the church, well out of earshot of the patients who are ensconced in beds lined along both sides. Assen has been working at St Marcel's hospital for a month now, much to the chagrin of his father. Above them are tall windows high up in the thick medieval walls, many of which open at their apex so a light breeze can meander through the space. There are also great fires at each end, giving the air a light, smoky quality. Most of the beds are occupied, some with two patients.
　'How are things at home?' Gérard enquires.
　'Don't ask.'
　'He just wants the best for you.'
　'I know, but … I'm not my father. I'm not a copy of him. I want to try to do things myself, my own way. Sometimes I think…'
　Gérard regards his friend thoughtfully. 'What?'
　'Am I being selfish?'
　'No, you're not selfish. Just your own person. We all need to be our own person.' Gérard smiles.
　'That's very revolutionary of you.' Assen rubs the back of his neck. 'But I'm not sure people want me to be my own person.'
　'Give him time.' Gérard turns back to the patients. 'Odds are half will recover.'
　'And the other half?'
　Gérard purses his lips.
　'Not good enough, is it?' Assen says.

'No, but we can only do what we can do. Come on, we'd better start. I'll take the far end.' Gérard turns and calls over his shoulder, 'If you need me, shout.'

'Right.' As Assen turns to walk away he glimpses the senior physician, Dr Broussard, entering the hall through the door in the far corner from the chapel.

Holding a sheet of parchment, the doctor is talking with one of the nurse brothers and pointing to it. Seeming to sense he is being watched, he looks up and locks eyes with Assen, who feels like a hare caught in a gamekeeper's sights. Slapping the page onto the monk's chest, the senior physician strides down the aisle towards Assen.

'Shit,' he whispers.

'Dr Verey. Not busy? Following the tradition of Nero, eh?' Dr Broussard places his hands on his ample middle, looking pleased with his joke.

Gérard hurries back. 'Sir, we were just about to start the round,' he says neutrally.

'Fiddling while Rome burned, wasn't it?'

'Yes, sir, we're familiar...' Assen's cheeks grow warm, well aware Dr Broussard is studying him with thinly disguised distaste. He imagines the older doctor sees an immaculately dressed young man confident in his opinion, privileged, wealthy, with a disregard for authority. *He probably thinks I'm one of those young fellows who thinks the rules don't apply to them, that I'm far above them.* Although that couldn't be further from the truth.

'Hmm. Are you indeed?' Dr Broussard hisses. 'So, to business. Brother Benedict tells me three more arrived in the night.'

'Yes, sir,' Gérard replies.

Dr Broussard looks around. 'We have been able to accommodate them?'

'Yes, sir. Six ... um ... left,' Assen explains.

His eyes like slits, Dr Broussard scrutinises Assen. 'Left?'

'Two recovered and were discharged at first light, and four ... didn't,' Gérard responds quickly.

'Hmm. And where are our new guests?'

'This way, Dr Broussard.' Gérard walks over to a bed in the middle of the row under one of the tall windows. A middle-aged man is quivering under the sheet. Stopping at the bottom of the bed, Gérard explains, 'The patient—'

'Mr Durand,' Assen interjects.

'—took ill at his place of work,' Gérard continues.

'Place of work?'

'He's a cobbler, sir,' Assen replies.

Without looking at Assen, Dr Broussard turns to the patient. 'Mr Durand! Do you know where you are?' he shouts.

Mr Durand lifts his head looking glazed. He nods and whispers, 'St Marcel's.'

'What? What did he say?' bellows Dr Broussard.

'St Marcel's, sir!' Assen bellows back. Gérard gives him a warning look.

'I'm cold,' rasps Mr Durand.

'Get him another blanket.' Broussard orders.

'Yes, sir.' Gérard calls over one of the brothers who has just removed a chamber pot from underneath a bed nearby.

'Has he eaten?' Dr Broussard says to the space in front of him, even though Assen is standing by his side.

'No, sir. He purged all night. He's had severe stomach pains.'

'You have the discharge here?'

'We do, sir.'

'Well? Get it!'

With a sharp intake of breath, Assen goes to the centre of the bed, reaches below and retrieves the pot. Dr Broussard peers into the bowl. 'Uh, ah… Right… I see. You can get rid of it now.'

Chamber pot in hand, Assen looks around for a nurse brother. Gérard grins. Dr Broussard is oblivious to Assen's discomfort. 'Any blackening of the extremities?'

Gérard takes the pot from Assen and gives it to a passing monk. 'Not that we could see, sir.'

'Hmm. Mr Durand, hold up your hands. Let me see them.'

The patient slips his hands from under the blanket and holds them up.

'Let me see the backs, too, Mr Durand.' Dr Broussard turns to the young doctors. 'And what do you observe?'

'Nothing,' Gérard answers confidently.

'And what does that tell you?'

'No blackening,' Assen quietly interposes. 'That would indicate plague.'

'Or progression of plague.' Gérard looks at the floor as he thinks.

'Quite.'

Dr Broussard returns to the patient. 'Mr Durand, please show me your neck.'

Mr Durand does his best to reveal his neck, awkwardly pulling down his nightshirt, his hands making fists at his collarbone.

'Observations?'

Assen is careful. 'No swellings ... at the moment, sir.'

'Right. I need to see more. Pull back the covers.'

Gérard reaches under the bed, pulls out two long tongs and gives one to Assen. Keeping their distance, they position themselves on either side of the patient's head, about three feet away. Opening the pincers, they grab the ends of the sheet. Gérard manages to catch hold the first time but Assen's instrument slips. He reddens.

'For goodness' sake!' Dr Broussard exclaims.

Assen tries again. This time it takes hold and he squeezes the pole tight, wincing as his fingernails dig into his palm. He looks across at Gérard, who nods. They peel back the blanket to reveal Mr Durand's entire body, his nightshirt falling just below his knees.

Gérard says gently, 'Mr Durand, Dr Broussard wants to see your feet.'

Dr Broussard comes closer and peers down. 'Hmm. Right... Enough.' He nods to Assen and Gérard to pull the blanket back up. Meanwhile a monk has returned with more blankets.

'He hasn't purged this morning?' Dr Broussard barks.

'No, sir.' Gérard takes the tongs from Assen and carefully places them under the bed.

'Right. A little light broth and warm milk. Something more substantial if he can manage it after vespers. Keep an eye out for swellings. No sweats?'

'No, sir.'

'Right.' Dr Broussard sweeps his hands behind his back as if to leave. 'Instruct Dr Rivett, the phlebotomist, to bleed this forenoon, and then—'

'I'm sorry, Dr Broussard,' Assen stumbles. 'I ... I have a friend who has much experience in treating these poor unfortunates. He has even had this pestilence himself.'

Gérard glares at him.

'Indeed?' Dr Broussard slowly turns to face Assen.

'Yes, sir. With respect, sir,' Assen continues quickly, 'he says that bleeding weakens the patients and might even hasten their death.'

'Did he? Did he really? And is he a senior member of the Faculty? Hmm? Has he learned his art in the finest medical schools in Europe? Sat at the feet of masters?'

'No, sir. But...'

'No, sir! No buts. Make sure this man is bled according to my instructions, once this forenoon and in the morning at first light.'

Assen's throat tightens. 'Yes, sir.'

Dr Broussard marches off leaving Assen and Gérard stranded in the centre of the hall. Once he is out of earshot, Gérard rounds on Assen. 'What was that?' he fizzes. '"I have a friend who says..." You think I can't speak for myself? You think I wouldn't have ... I wouldn't have spoken up? You think so little of me?'

'I'm sorry. I was just...'

'Honestly.' Gérard shakes his head and walks off.

'May I have a drink, please?' Mr Durand asks quietly.

Shaking himself, Assen replies with kindness. 'Of course. I will fetch it myself.'

'You're going to make a fine doctor.'

Assen looks at Mr Durand's open face. 'Am I? I don't know.'

'That is, if you don't kill us all first.' Mr Durand laughs heartily.

Assen chews in side of his cheek.

# Chapter Eleven

The Sermon
North Berwick

A ray of sun hits Agnes square in the eyes as she rounds the corner of the old church wall. *Hope I'm not late. That'll give him another excuse, daft git... Shhh, Agnes.* She rebukes herself, reining in the rest of her thoughts. *It's the Sabbath and you're nearly there.*

The sun is astonishingly bright for the time of year, with hardly a cloud in the sky. Some would say it's a good sign foretelling a warm spring and a bountiful early crop; others might warn it is a bad omen – the sun has appeared too early and is still setting too low in the sky, warning of a bad harvest being drowned in floods off the hills and overflowing rivers.

Agnes checks her white cap to make sure it's straight. 'Ach, we'll see.'

She sees Gelly with her stool under her arm. Most of the women and some of the men bring their own seats to sit on; it's either that or standing, and if you've been on your feet all day and all week…

'How's it going?' she asks Gelly.

The girl shrugs. 'Ach, ye ken.'

'Aye, I ken.' Agnes laughs.

The villagers mill about the church entrance waiting until the last minute to go inside. Reverend McLaren's sermons are notoriously long and tedious.

\*\*\*

The church is relatively new and austere, built only in the last ten years, unadorned by the statues of saints and other embellishments favoured by the old faith. Erected to the Reverend McLaren's specification, it looms over the centre of the town.

As he'd pored over the plans with the architect, the reverend reasoned it was the best place to administer to the flock since he could keep an eye on the comings and goings in the village and no one would have an excuse for their absence. He'd run a tight ship from now on.

'After all,' he had said to the draftsman, 'the good townspeople are paying for all this, so they must use it! I am here as a servant of God to save their souls.'

Before he arrived, it had got a bit lax with some folks harking back to the ways of the auld faith. As a young cleric, one morning he'd been walking by the whitewashed cottages on the seafront when he'd heard two older women deep in conversation over their spinning wheels. Between the click-clack-clicking, he heard them reminisce about the auld kirk by the sea, how it used to be the chapel for the Brothers' Hospital, giving alms to the poor, taking in the sick, sheltering pilgrims and other such nonsense. The Devil's breeding ground. Now all of that was gone and North Berwick was better for it – a God-fearing town.

'If you please, show respect for the Sabbath,' he says as he ushers the remaining stragglers into the church.

***

Agnes and Gelly are among the last to go inside. The hall is packed, with men standing along the sides and at the back. The two women turn immediately to the left where there is space in the row in front of the standing male parishioners to place their stools.

The interior is cold and bare and the windows tall and opaque, casting a muted blue-grey version of the sunlight outside. At the front is a raised stand with a lectern serving as a pulpit; sitting in several rows of plain wooden pews facing it are the wealthier members of the congregation.

Everyone who has seats takes them. As the church grows quiet, Gelly and Agnes look at each other. Agnes raises her eyebrows; Gelly looks down, suppressing a smile.

Uncharacteristically, Reverend McLaren walks down the central aisle, his black robes flapping behind him like a crow chasing a lump of bread. With a huge, brown, leather-bound Bible under his arm, he slowly mounts the steps of the pulpit.

A woman in front of Agnes and Gelly turns around, her questioning eyes wide. Agnes shrugs, sensing something is different. A thud reverberates through the church as the minister slams the tome onto the stand. Opening it at the place marker, he looks up and slowly scans the congregation.

'Ah, everyone in their place? Isn't it good, isn't it right, when everyone is in their place?'

Gelly blows out and says under her breath, 'Jings, what now?'

Agnes giggles. 'Shhhh.'

'Man and woman, husband and wife, a holy union.' He holds on to the edges of the book rest, letting his eyes settle on the married couples in the hall.

'Here we go.' Gelly rolls her eyes.

'Shhhh. I want to hear what shite he's gonnae come out with today,' Agnes whispers.

Gelly snorts.

Unabashed, the reverend continues, 'Timothy, Verse 2: 12 says, "I do not permit women to teach or have authority over a man."'

He pauses for effect and looks around the hall. Several men silently nod, others stare blankly; some women cock their heads to the side and narrow their eyes. '"She must be silent",' he goes on. 'In Verse 14, he tells us it was not Adam who was deceived, it was Eve. It was the woman who became deceived and was the sinner. She is weak, easy led…'

Gelly has had enough. 'Easy led into his bed … or so I've heard.'

Agnes raises her eyebrows. 'Aye?'

Gelly shrugs.

'I'd rather kiss Cochrane's prize boar…'

Gelly wrinkles her nose and makes a face.

'…'s arse,' Agnes finishes.

Gelly guffaws and has to turn away from her friend. Agnes's shoulders shake as she looks at the floor and grips the edge of the stool.

The reverend raises his voice. 'Women!' he shouts. '"Women," says Corinthians 34, "should remain silent in the churches. They are not permitted to speak, but should be in submission, as the Law also says."'

Maggie, sitting in front of Gelly and Agnes, turns her head, her chin level with her shoulder, and hisses out the corner of her mouth, 'You're right. He is an arse.'

The three titter. It's no use: Agnes knew she'd have the giggles with Gelly today, and the Reverend McLaren never fails to rise to the occasion. She'll have to look fervently at the floor if she's going to get through this one.

After an hour or so, the clergyman comes to the crescendo of his proclamations. 'For the head of Christ is God, the head of every man is Christ, and the head of a wife is her husband. Order, knowing we all have our place... Wife, mother, the most honourable place of a woman...'

*He must be going to finish now. What's it been? Two hours?* Agnes looks around. She'd heard him complaining to his usher last Sunday that people's attention span was not what it used to be. At one of his parishes, they had wanted four – even five – hours of scripture. She doubted that.

In the front row, Mr Maxwell's chin is on his chest, hands cupped in his lap; his quiet snores and the gentle prods from his wife show he isn't in a state of pious listening. Agnes smiles. With a quick glance behind, she takes in a row of men leaning against the wall, their heads resting back on the hats they've made into pillows.

*I wonder where they are, this flock. They're certainly not here in this draughty, plain building. Hope they're somewhere nice.*

Gelly's slow breathing next to her tells Agnes she's in a peaceful place, perhaps the bottom of Weir's meadow, dipping her toes in the cool, crisp waters of the burn. Agnes lets her shoulder's drop and closes her eyes. She is in an orange grove, the sweet citrus scent filling her nostrils. The setting sun is reflected in the water, a palette of gold, pink, orange, white and silver streaks. A warm breeze brushes her face bringing a hint of sandalwood...

'Ah-hem,' a gentleman coughs, breaking into Agnes's reverie. He coughs again, louder. 'Ladies, the sermon is finished.'

She blearily opens her eyes to see a tall man standing over her. Like her, Gelly is still slumped on her stool. Agnes pulls herself up and sits straight. 'Yes, thank you ... thank you, Mr Morrison. We were, um, enthralled.' She nudges Gelly.

'Aye ... enthralled...' the girl mumbles.

'Captivated,' Agnes continues. The man looks at her sceptically.

They get up, grab their chairs and head out into the bright sunlight. Agnes shields her eyes and Gelly rocks her stool from side to side like a small child. People are milling about, chatting in small groups. Gelly sees the woman from the row in front of them and heads over.

Agnes scans the parishioners. Where is he? She needs to talk with him. She locks eyes with Reverend McLaren instead. *Shit.* But he turns back to his group, nods and shakes their hands. *Good.*

She looks around again: there he is, but he's with his wife. Maybe she should leave it, wait 'til... Reverend McLaren is staring at her. *Shit! Shit!* 'Thank you, thank you, you are most welcome,' she hears him say before he heads over. But Agnes is too quick and makes a dash to join Gelly and Maggie.

'Good day, Maggie. Enjoy the sermon?' she asks a little breathlessly.

'Aye, Agnes. As much as getting slapped in the face wi' a wet kipper.'

'That much?' Agnes laughs, clandestinely glancing from side to side.

Maggie becomes serious. 'Actually, Agnes...' She lowers her voice, looking around. 'I've just been saying to Gelly, I'm not sure I want wee Hope christened here – you know, with the minister. He keeps asking, saying I better hurry up or she'll go to hell.'

'Dinnae listen to him. Wee Hope'll be just fine. She's an angel. But what's wrong? Why don't you want the minister? I know he can be a bit – I dinna ken – pompous, but you'll have to go a long way to the next parish. They'll ask why.'

'I know, Agnes. John thinks I'm mad, but I have this funny feeling about him ... that he's—'

Gelly nudges Maggie. 'Shhhhh. He's here.'

Reverend McLaren is closer to the group, talking with Gelly's employer, Mr Seton, one of the wealthier, higher status parishioners. 'I understand your frustration. I will pray for resolution. It has gone on long enough.'

Mr Seton shakes his hand. 'I am obliged to you.'

The minister quickly turns to the three women. 'I trust you will be reflecting on today's readings. The Devil's bile always seeps through weaker vessels.'

Agnes faces him. 'Aye, and they say he talks mostly through his arse.'

Bristling, the reverend glares at Agnes. Maggie and Gelly stare at the ground, lips drawn tight.

# Chapter Twelve

A Warning
North Berwick

Agnes knows what Maggie means about the minister: he has a deadness behind the eyes, an unending, unfathomable darkness. She shakes her head. *Come on, Agnes, stop scaring yourself. This is your morning off.* Such a rarity. No patients, no tinctures to mix, no herbs to brew, but still plenty to do. A tangle of weeds, vines and brambles lies at the far corner of the garden on the edge of the woods. Best get the ground ready for planting. Turnips and carrots as usual.

Agnes stretches her back in preparation and lifts the scythe leaning against the wall. It's heavier than she remembers, but she's done it every year, for ... what? Fifteen, twenty years? And every year she amazes herself at what she did the year before.

'Same again this year,' she says, taking her first swipe. 'And next year, God willing.'

She soon gets into a rhythm of slash, pull, slash, pull. A rivulet of water trickles down her spine, making her hot and cold at the same time. She pulls off her cap and wipes her forehead with a rag stuffed into her shoulder strap. With the rag wrapped around her hand, she tugs at the thicket of twigs and thorns.

Something catches her eye, a movement that shouldn't be there. Not at this time of year. Carefully, separating the branches, she peers into the undergrowth. There it is. The colour of fir bark, almost invisible among the stems, twigs and stalks: a hedgehog.

'What are you doing out, wee thing? It's too early. You should be tucked up sleeping.'

She looks around for its home. A fallen branch is perched against the trunk of a tree, its dead leaves thinning. 'Hmm. So, this is it, is it?'

Forest debris has attached itself to the screen, giving some protection, but the structure is too flimsy to see the little beastie through the bitterest months of winter.

'Right, first things first.'

Agnes heads back to the dark kitchen, squints and opens the shutters and front door. She retrieves her ladle from above the hearth and digs into the pot dangling in the fireplace. Inspecting the scoop, she shakes her head then plops the contents back into the pot and stirs. She tries again, carefully picking out bits of meat from the rabbit stew intended for supper. Oh well, she can easily pad it out with turnips and oats.

Once she has arranged the meat on a pewter dish, she heads back down the yard, collecting a small bowl of water from the stream on the way.

'Right, little fellow, this'll keep you going.' The hedgehog is where she left it snuffling in the undergrowth. Wafting the meat a few feet in front of it, she places the dishes down.

'Now. What are we going to do about this?' she says, looking at the rickety shelter. 'This won't do at all.' She looks around again. 'I know!' On the other side of the garden are two short planks of wood, no more than seven-hands long and four deep. Perfect. Now for some stones and a few short branches.

'There.' She stands back to admire her work. A much better place to spend what's left of the winter.

The hedgehog finishes its meal and resumes its search of the undergrowth, the tiny black nose twitching as it ventures towards the stream. Agnes digs into her skirt for a piece of meat she has held back and tosses it into the hibernaculum.

'Right.' She returns to her rhythmic scythe swinging.

As the sun reaches the top of the tallest Scots pine, little legs disappear into the sanctuary. Agnes smiles.

Darkness has transformed the sunlit day into a bitterly cold night so characteristic of the east coast. Agnes imagines the wee hedgehog curled in a ball surrounded by dried grass, leaves and twigs, and imagines she hears the raspy snores.

'Here. Sit down.' She scrapes a chair along the flagstones, a little closer to the fire. Gelly slumps down gratefully.

Agnes is bent over the fire, brewing barley tea. She notices Gelly staring at a contraption next to the fireplace. 'A cooking tree. A present from John,' she explains.

'The smith?'

'Aye.'

Gelly cocks her head. The contraption consists of a long thick pole at the side of the fireplace with arms attached at different levels.

Reaching across the table, Agnes picks up a small pail, loops the handle over the highest arm and pushes it into the fire with a cloth from her belt. 'I can boil the tatties with this one,' she says, pointing at the middle arm, 'and broth can go on the bottom.'

'That was good of him.' Gelly rubs her hands and stretches them out towards the fire.

'Aye, it was.'

'How is Hope, anyway?'

'She's grand now. Putting on weight like a suckling pig.'

Gelly sits back while Agnes stoops and stirs the tea with a wooden spoon. Satisfied, she swings the pot away from the fire and places it on the bench at the back wall under the tiny window, its imprint joining the other scorch marks. She pours the steaming mixture into two bowls, the aroma of sweet barley mingling with the smell of peat in the faintly smoky room like a fine island whisky. She hands a bowl to Gelly, who has turned her chair to face the kitchen table.

Unlike the rest of Agnes's humble furniture, the ancient oak table is not rough and fashioned with the materials, tools and skills available locally. Instead there is something fine about it. Agnes knows Gelly is used to seeing expensive furniture in the grand houses she's served in. She slides her palm along the surface. The grain is cold and comforting.

'Thanks. Brrrr.' Tossing back her head, Gelly releases her hair. The long, wavy, dark-blonde strands cascade down her shoulders and over her breasts under her drab brown-linen dress. She stretches out her slender legs, her knees little peaks beneath the earthy material.

Agnes watches her. There is something sensuous about Gellis Duncan, and more so for her being completely unaware of it. Agnes smiles, shakes her head and drops into the chair facing the girl. She lifts her own bowl to her lips, takes a sip. Placing it carefully down, she looks steadily at Gelly. 'Heard what ye did over at the Johnstons'. How is wee Jennie?'

'Great. She's back at the kirk school.' A smile engulfs Gelly's face as she recalls the wee lassie fervently waving to her outside the school with her friends gathered round. Then she sighs and picks up her tea.

'That's wonderful. I'm really pleased to hear that.' Agnes needs to tread carefully. 'And I hear you did wonders over at the Hunters'. Old Mr Hunter, wasn't it?'

'Och, it was nothing.'

'It *was*, Gelly, it was *something*. Ye've got a gift; it's a precious gift, but just—'

'Och. It was just things ma mother told me, and Granny McLeod. Dae ye remember her?'

'Aye, she taught me too… But, look, Gelly…' Agnes makes little invisible shapes with her forefinger on the table. 'There's folk around here that don't like what ye've been doing.'

Gelly sits up straight. 'What? Why?'

'You don't know?'

'No!'

'They don't like…' Agnes rubs the back of her neck. 'They don't like these … these… They're calling them … miracles.'

'They're no miracles!'

'Aye, I know that, but ye ken how folks are.'

'That's daft. It's just the herbs and that mould Granny showed us.'

'I know, I know. It's just they're calling it "miraculous healings". Just play it down. You have to play it down, Gelly. Tell folk not to talk about it.'

'Who's "they"?'

Agnes sees one old woman elbowing another as she passed, both falling silent until she was out of earshot. She recalls Mrs Robertson asking if the healings were proof they were going back to the old ways, the auld faith.

'Anyway, our Lord Jesus healed the sick,' Gelly says petulantly, leaning back and folding her arms.

Agnes sighs. 'Aye, that's just it. Minister McLaren's been going around saying *only* Christ can do miracle healings. If anybody else does it, it's the Devil pulling their strings. Just be careful. Watch what you're doing. Like I said, play it down.'

'I need the money. It's not much but, ye ken, with what folks give me and what I get at the Seton place, I can... I mean, I want... Ach, you'll think I'm daft...'

'I'll not. Tell me.'

'I want... I want a wee cottage like yours.' Gelly looks around Agnes's humble dwelling and sighs. 'With a wee stream at the bottom of the garden.'

'What, with a smoky fireplace and a roof that sags?' Agnes laughs.

'Especially the smoky fireplace.'

'It needs re-thatching. I'll have to work on it in the spring,' Agnes says, looking up.

Gelly stares over Agnes's shoulder at the inky blackness through the window. 'I want somewhere far away just for me – peaceful, quiet, you know?'

'Far away, eh?' Agnes joins Gelly in her daydreaming. 'Somewhere warm, where you could dip your toes in the pond, walk barefoot through an auld orchard, pick up a juicy apple and give it a big bite!'

In her mind, she sees her own hand lifting a plump red-and-green apple from the dewy grass, lifting it to her face and biting into its firm flesh. The smell of apple and hay fills her nostrils and the juice moistens the corner of her mouth. She can't help smiling at the sweet tangy taste. Another's hand gently wipes her lips and chin.

'You sound like Eve.' Intrigued, Gelly gazes at her friend.

Agnes laughs and rises from the table. 'There was no snake in the grass in my fantasy, not like here. You have to watch your every step. More tea?'

'Please. You went somewhere hot once, didn't you? Somewhere exotic?' Gelly looks into her dish then sideways at Agnes.

'It was a long time ago, but aye.' Agnes's tone is measured. 'Though I don't think you'd call France exotic. But it was...' She stares into the same blackness that Gelly drew her eyes from only a moment ago. 'Oh, Gelly...' The wistfulness in her voice is unmistakable.

Gelly looks up. 'Why didn't you stay?'

'I couldn't. Anyway, we're going off the subject.'

Gelly sips her tea. The door to Agnes's past closes once more. 'Which was?' she asks.

Agnes lifts a poker from the side of the fireplace and prods the fire, making it spark. She places another log and watches the flames lick around the bottom of it. 'Are you still seeing your man at the school?'

Gelly bites her bottom lip.

'For goodness' sake, Gelly. He's married! You're playing with fire.'

Gelly grabs her bowl and stands. She walks slowly to the other side of the fireplace and bends to pick up the large jug of water sitting on the floor.

'Leave it. I'll do that,' Agnes says.

Gelly puts the dish back down. 'He's kind and gentle, but strong. He makes me feel, you know… Ach, he was that young when he got married. They had to. You know, like, they *had* to.'

Agnes stares into the fire. 'Aye, I know. But listen. If you get into something, it might… you might … you would be an outcast. You couldn't do your healing. No one would take you on.'

'Don't worry. It'll all work out.'

What Agnes loves about Gelly, but also finds most annoying, is her unbridled, stubborn optimism.

Gelly walks towards the door. 'I best get going. Got to get up early. His Royal Majesty's got people coming.'

'Oh, aye?'

'We've to make bread, stew, a big joint of beef, the works. The whole house has to be scrubbed down.'

'Who's he got coming?'

Gelly frowns. 'I don't know really. The minister and some other folk.'

'Hmm… He'll not be doing all that just for the minister.'

# Chapter Thirteen

A Nightmare
Holyrood Palace, Edinburgh

Midnight has long since passed and it will be many hours before the first cock crows. Shadows flit along the outer walls of Holyrood Palace and the decimated abbey next door that was crushed under the march of the Reformation. The jagged shapes of tall pines creep across the windows and walls like long spidery fingers.

Inside one of the state bedrooms to the east, farthest away from the grand entrance, the king and queen lie sleeping. This was an unusual scenario, for like other crowned heads they more commonly slept apart. But lately the king craved his wife's presence, at least at night. It is not the grandest or most opulent room but it is the warmest, and in its modesty least likely to give away the monarch's location to would-be assassins. King James knows a great deal about exterminations. Both his father and mother, Mary Queen of Scots, were dispatched before their time.

But at least the young king has not made any enemies of the nobles that surround him. He likes to think he has been clever about that. William Balfour, his trusted older counsellor, has guided him in such matters, advising him to pit the powerful barons and clan chiefs against each other rather than the Crown, and it has worked. Unlike other monarchs, King James has little to fear from a shadowy figure tiptoeing through the antechambers into his inner sanctum to plunge a knife into his heart while his nobles whisper and divvy up the royal lands.

However, there is something else to worry about, an even greater threat than a disgruntled aristocracy: Auld Nick himself. James can't escape the feeling he is being watched. Someone or some*thing*'s eyes were boring into the back of his neck when he was in the old library signing the papers to redistribute the McNab lands, and the hairs prickled on his scalp. He could also swear he saw a strange creature lurking in the ruins of the abbey, creeping about on long spindly legs and crooked, hooked arms. Whether he saw horns poking out of its head, he's not sure. He might have.

Now, in the dead of the night with Anne lightly snoring and branches tapping at the window, the king is tossing and turning like a rowing boat cast adrift in a stormy sea.

*It is almost pitch black in his dream as he wanders lost through a dense, fern-choked forest. He feels the spongy moss beneath his feet giving way every so often so his leg plunges down a hole and he stumbles forward.*

*Something screeches deep in the woods – but where is it coming from? In front? Behind? Is it in pain? Is it attacking? He must escape! He must find a way out. The low growling is close by. A wolf! More growling, circling, twigs snapping. He sees it! A huge four-legged creature the height of his shoulder, with bared teeth, its eyes as red as cinders, ears cocked. It holds him transfixed in its glare.*

*Other wolf-like creatures emerge from the wood, encircling him. He is trapped! His eyes are drawn back to the hideous apparition as it begins to transform itself, its shape ripping and tearing, until it metamorphizes into – a woman! A woman dressed from head to foot in black, with a pointed hood. She has ruby-red lips and long, wavy, silver hair escaping from her cowl.*

*She points a long thin figure to his heart. 'You will die in flames, and our Lord and Master will claim your soul. You will forever burn in hell!' she screeches.*

*Laughter surrounds him and, to his horror, the wolves circling him have transformed into hideous women – a monstrous regiment of women. Knox was right!*

The king shrieks and sits bolt upright, eyes on stalks. He places his palm on his cheek; it is burning. Queen Anne sits up too. 'Your Grace, what is it? What's happened?'

'What?' The king recognises his bedchamber. He grasps the sheets, rubs the material between his fingers. Yes, it is real. He feels Anne, sweet Anne, sitting by his side, shoulder to shoulder. He turns to her; she looks terrified.

She stammers. 'You had a dream, sire?'

'A dream?' His cold, clammy nightshirt sticks to his back. 'A dream, aye, a nightmare.' He breathes out hard. 'A grisly nightmare. There were old hags, shape-changers, witches, horrible women, she-wolves.'

'It was just a dream, Your Grace,' Anne says soothingly.

'It was not just a dream, woman!' he retorts, glaring at her. 'It was a warning!'

# Chapter Fourteen

A Ray of Hope
St Marcel's Plague Hospital

'We must move with the times. Bloodletting, leeches, posies – they don't work. We know they don't work! Gérard, you've said it yourself.'

They are in St Marcel's apothecary. Assen looks at the rows and rows of jars containing dried herbs, roots and leaves of plants, powders, seeds, liquids and ointments. They are neatly placed on shelves reaching from floor to ceiling which is some twenty feet above their heads. 'We have to get Pierre to help us.'

'You wanted me?' Pierre stands in the doorway.

'Can you look at this?' Assen gives him a scroll of parchment.

Pierre Coutelle takes it, sighs and unfurls the sheet. He is the hospital's apothecary and has been for more than twenty years. He's seen it all: fashions coming and going, claims about this miracle cure, that miraculous potion.

He walks slowly towards the stepladders leaning against the farthest edge of the shelves near the tall, lattice window. Sliding them along the rows, he ensures the steps are dead centre. 'Well, Doctors Verey, Xavier, yes, I have most of these ingredients. One or two are rather…' he lets his eyebrows slide up his forehead '…singular. I'd have to send out for them. But yes, these are possible.'

Assen starts, 'We want to try something. A few things.'

'Oh, yes?'

'You will have tried elixirs and combinations yourself?' Gérard says diplomatically.

'Of course.' The apothecary regards him.

Pierre has seen Dr Xavier many times in the main hall tending the poor, asking for the apothecary's advice about this tincture or that root, which is best and the correct measures. Unlike others of his generation the young doctor has respect, even deference, for the apothecary's knowledge and experience.

What's more, the apothecary has observed in Dr Xavier a warmth and care for his patients many young, brash physicians – even the older ones, for that matter – don't have. Pierre has seen Dr Xavier wipe his eyes in the store at the back of the vestry when he thought no one was watching. Unfortunately someone is always watching; churches can be quiet, observing kinds of places. But there is something else about Dr Xavier that makes him different, something Pierre can't quite put his finger on. No matter; he likes him.

Pierre studies the two physicians. They make quite a contrast; they are not the opposite of each other but rather the same in reverse. Both are fairly tall, with sturdy but not heavy frames. There is no doubt they would be described as handsome by many, and they sport those fashionable, manicured beards carefully sculpted around the chin and upper lip. But Dr Verey is dark, with sallow skin, black eyes and thick, dark, unruly hair, whereas his companion is fair-skinned with blond-streaked hair and pale-blue eyes.

Their dress is also similar but differs in the subtlest of ways: the trim, the quality of the material, the weave of the cloth, the warmth of the colour. Both wear light-fawn doublets cinched at the waist, though not as tight as is currently fashionable; the young doctors favour comfort over fashion when tending the sick. They both have russet-coloured puffed pantaloons, tapered with a band just above the knee, and pale-taupe hose. Yet, if you look closely, Dr Verey's doublet is decorated with the tiniest of gold diamond shapes in vertical lines from shoulder to hem; there is also a fine gold trim at the collar where it meets his ruff. The colour of his pantaloons is a rich auburn, hinting they are made of velvet in contrast to the wool of Dr Xavier's.

Dr Xavier is certainly a gentleman physician, but he is cut from a very different cloth to Dr Verey. Dr Verey has an air that only privilege, social standing and wealth over God-knows-how-many generations can breed. His stature is effortlessly elegant, and the apothecary suspects the effect would be the same if the young man was in pauper's garb.

Assen looks along the shelves. 'Can we make theriac here?'

Pierre looks from the sheet to Assen, then Gérard. 'Yes, but it needs time to brew, ferment. Months.'

'We haven't got months. There's something I think we could add that would hurry the process. Then we can test it once and for all, see if it really works.' Assen stabs the parchment with his finger. 'See, if we use—'

'Brine from rotting fish. Well, it's not something I'm usually asked for, Dr Verey.'

'What if we could give it to the patients on the right-hand side of the great hall and compare with those on the left?'

Gérard laughs, shakes his head. 'You can't do that, it's immoral. You can't choose who to treat. Everyone who comes here gets treated with the best we've got. It's our moral duty – it's the principle on which St Marcel's is based.'

'What about giving it to the patients in the Duplessis chapel? I mean…' Assen runs his forefinger along one of the shelves. 'They are in a bad way, aren't they?'

'Most of them will die, yes,' Gérard agrees.

'Then we have nothing to lose. *They* have nothing to lose. If it doesn't work, we've tried everything. If it does…'

'Then you would give it to all the patients in the chapel?' Gérard says, rubbing his chin.

'Not at first. We would have to give it to those – I don't know – facing south, say, and see if they fared any better than those facing north.'

A little smile plays on Pierre's lips. He coughs. 'Dr Broussard moves them around all the time.'

'What?'

'The patients. If he thinks the direction they're facing is ailing them, he shifts them under another window, closer to the fire, the door, more light, less light…'

'I … I didn't notice.' Assen is ashamed he hasn't registered something as basic as patients being in different places. He did wonder last week why he couldn't find Mr Moreau. 'We could keep records. Write down the names of the patients we give—'

'Besides, theriac is out of the question. The ingredients are far too expensive,' the apothecary adds.

Assen lets out a long breath like a pig's bladder deflating. Strolling along the rows of jars, he peers at their contents. A container of white powder labelled 'mercury' catches his eye and he stops and taps his middle finger on the glass. 'What about…?'

He scrutinises the other jars in the vicinity. 'We've got mercury, sulphurs, salts. What else?' He glances upwards and points to the shelves above, his voice rising. 'Look, we also have iron, copper sulphate, lead.'

He spins around to face Pierre. 'The great physician Paracelsus said that—'

'I know who Paracelsus was,' the apothecary snaps.

Assen spots Gérard's stare and continues in a more placatory tone; this is Pierre's domain, after all. 'Of course, of course. Then you'll know he cured the English disease with mercury.'

'I am familiar.'

Resuming his pacing, looking up and down the rows of jars, Assen continues. 'Everything we think of as poisons, even arsenic, can be a cure in the right quantity. And everything we think is safe, like fresh water from a stream, can be deadly if taken in extreme quantities. Didn't Paracelsus say it was the dose that made the poison – or the cure?'

Gérard cocks his head. 'What are you proposing?'

'Back in '34, he cured the plague in Sterzing, didn't he?' Assen says, recalling his old professor Dr Binoche.

'Supposedly. We don't know how.'

'We can guess.'

'Guess!' the apothecary snorts.

Gérard raises his eyebrows.

'We have his writings and discoveries,' Assen says. 'We know his theories – he wrote, "What makes a man ill also cures him." What we need to do is restore balance to these patients. They need salt for the body to help it stand up to the pestilence or whatever ails them. Mercury – in very small quantities, of course – to rejuvenate the spirit. Copper sulphate to strengthen the soul's resolve to prevent them from succumbing to the melancholy that so often follows fever. If we could find the right quantities, the right combination, using very small doses at first... Maybe we can... They might survive, get better.'

'Hmm, you've been thinking about this, haven't you?' Gérard looks at his friend, his eyes bright.

Assen smiles and says nothing.

'I don't know.' Gérard stands beside Assen with his hands on his hips, looking up and down the shelves. 'What about...?' He turns to Pierre. 'Have you noticed if any of these plants, herbs and elixirs have improved *any* patient's symptoms in any way, even a little?'

Pierre shakes his head. 'I only wish they did.'

Gérard sighs. 'Right.'

'We can't do *nothing*,' Assen entreats.

'In small quantities, right?' Gérard offers cautiously.

'Tiny quantities. We'll have to make a list, pick patients. We'll give it to all the patients once we know it works and how much each patient needs.'

'*If* it works.' Gérard folds his arms.

Assen looks at Pierre; he hopes he's done enough to bring the chemist on side. For all his protesting, Pierre has a reputation as an experimenter and for making meticulous observations. 'We'll have to keep strict records of everything – the doses, the patients, their condition.'

Pierre nods.

'Then what?' Gérard asks.

Assen looks thoughtful. 'We compare.'

A loud knock at the door makes the three men jump. It creaks open and nurse Brother Benedict's head appears around the corner. He looks around the room, his eyes settling on Assen. 'Sir, I beg your pardon for interrupting but a message has come from your father. You are needed at home immediately.'

# Chapter Fifteen

A Proposition
North Berwick

Holding her breath, Gelly slowly pushes open the back door. She mustn't wake anyone; they'll ask too many questions. The rest of the household has been in bed for hours.

Mary's left the door open and placed a candle on the kitchen table. Good lassie. The glow is warm and inviting.

Gelly yawns, lifts her satchel over her head and rests it carefully on the table. Tucked neatly into the recess on the other side of the range, Mary snores lightly in the bed box they share. Gelly can't wait to slide in and warm herself from the heat of her ample body.

Mary, the kitchen maid, is a good bedfellow; she doesn't toss and turn and doesn't sound like a hog demanding breakfast. Thankfully she's soft and round, not all elbows and knees like Gelly's sister, Shona. That's the worst of sleeping with your siblings. They do it just to annoy you – stick their knees in your back and steal the blankets. Gelly smiles. This is a great place to sleep.

She unpins her hair and shakes the shawl from her shoulders, then spreads it over the back of a chair. She shivers. The stole is heavy from the rain. She trudges over to the low crackling fire and bends over, letting her long strands of hair dry by the soft glow. Some of the detritus from earlier in the day is still littered around the room, and a heap of scraps is piled at the end of the table. They were supposed to go to the pigs. Mary will catch it from the cook, Mrs Merritt. Gelly resolves to get up early and do it herself.

When she straightens, she looks around and furrows her brow. The tankard of Mrs Merritt still sits at the other end of the table. The master's guests must have stayed late. Cook usually insists everything is tidied away, ready for the morning but not tonight.

After they've served the evening meal and the lassies have cleaned up, Mrs Merritt likes to fill her pewter tankard with nettle tea and add a generous measure of gin. Gelly smiles; even so, they're lucky to have Mrs Merritt, the best cook south of Edinburgh, people say.

Gelly picks up the beaker and looks into it. Empty. Cup in hand, she walks over to the wooden bucket in the corner. There's a little water at the bottom. She washes the tankard, dries it with a cloth she's taken from the pulley above the bed box and places it back on the shelf by the window. The pig scraps can wait. Now bed.

She undoes the knot of her apron string at her abdomen and releases the pinafore, rolls it into a ball and places it on the table. As she reaches for the buttons on the back of her collar, she hears a noise. She freezes, then cocks her head and squints. 'Who's there?'

The door leading to the hall creaks open, letting in a ray of spluttering candlelight. Gelly's heart pounds. 'Who's there? I'll scream if you don't show yourself!'

'Shhh, Gelly, it's only me.' The door slowly opens and Mr Seton stands in the doorway, lit from behind by a sconce in the hall as if exuding an aura.

Her heart sinks and she mouths, 'Sir? Mr Seton, what is it?'

He looks around the room and registers Mary snoring in the bed box. 'Come here,' he whispers, beckoning Gelly into the hall.

Mary rolls over and grunts. Gelly's eyes turn into saucers. *Go away, for Christ's sake.* This is all she needs. 'You'll wake Mary, sir.'

'I need to talk to you about something. Come into the hall.'

Sighing and pursing her lips, she trudges over. Mr Seton lifts his arm and Gelly silently passes under it into the hall. 'What is it, sir? I beg your pardon, but I'm very tired. It's been a long night.'

'Where have you been?'

'To the Thompsons', and I called into the Johnstons' before that. The mistress knows where I've been. She said it was fine.'

'Aye, aye, of course. Little Jennie, wasn't it? Very sad, very, very sad. The minister told me.'

'She's fine.'

'Fine?' He stares at Gelly. 'But Reverend McLaren said final prayers…'

'Aye, well, he was wrong. She's fine now and back at school.'

'Really?' He furrows his brow. 'How? What did you…? Oh, it doesn't matter. Listen, why don't you come into the parlour with me? The fire is still lit, you could dry some of your clothes.'

'No, thank you, sir. I'm nearly dry.'

'Come on. The house is quiet. Mrs Seton never wakes 'til morning. No one'll know. We could … we could keep each other warm. Eh?' He smiles.

A shiver runs from her tailbone to the nape of her neck. 'I can't, sir, I'm sorry. See you tomorr—'

He lunges forward, grasps her waist and pulls her close, his navel pressed against her abdomen. His lips are close to her ear, his hot breath and bottom lip brush her lobe. 'But you like to be warm, don't you?'

Using all the strength she's gained from fetching and carrying pails of water and wrestling with her five siblings, Gelly wriggles her forearms free, presses them against his chest. With all her might, she pushes him away. 'No! Sir!'

'You don't like to be warm?' Mr Seton's bulk stands between her and the kitchen door.

'I have to go to bed now, sir. Me and Mary … we have to get up early.'

'Very well.' He steps to the side, leaving the door handle free. 'By all means. Please go to bed.'

Smoothing down the front of her dress, she walks forward and reaches for the doorknob. But Mr Seton is on her again, grasping her waist, tighter this time so that she is gasping for breath. He places his other palm over her mouth. 'You could come to bed with me. I'd have you up early … very early, in fact…'

He releases his hand from Gelly's mouth and presses his lips hard on hers. She tastes pork mixed with stale tobacco.

A grunt and a cough come from the kitchen. 'Gelly? Gelly, is that you?' Mary coughs again. 'Who's there?'

Mr Seton and Gelly freeze in the predatory embrace. Seizing the opportunity, she breaks away and glares at him venomously. Not taking her eyes off him, she calls soothingly to Mary, 'Aye, aye, it is. I'm coming right now.'

Facing him, the kitchen door now behind her, she fumbles for the catch. It clicks open and she backs through the doorway, not daring to turn her back on him. In the safety of the kitchen, standing before the closed door, she tries to compose herself before going to Mary. Her heart is still pounding and she can't seem to get enough air into her lungs. She rests her palm on the door, the other on her chest.

As she turns, she sees Mary propped on her elbows, staring curiously at her. 'Are you all right? Did I hear…?'

'I'm fine. You were dreaming, that's all. Go back to sleep. I'm just coming in.'

'Are you sure?'

'Aye, aye, I'm fine. It's been a long night.'

'Tell me about it. The minister and the rest o' them dinnae leave 'til gone midnight. Mrs Merritt fell asleep at the kitchen table.'

'Aye? Who was there?' Thankful for something else to think about, Gelly unhooks her dress behind her neck at the collar and lets it fall to the floor.

'I don't know. Some fancy folks from Edinburgh, I think.'

Staring at the candle in her long undershirt, Gelly feels like she is in a trance.

'Are you sure you're all right?' Mary asks.

'I'll tell you in the morning.' She blows out the candle and slips into bed beside her.

# Chapter Sixteen

Too Close for Comfort
Paris

Assen bursts into the large parlour, not waiting for François to open the door. He hastily detaches his cloak, takes off his hat and throws them on the table. François appears, a little breathless after running up from the cellar, and scoops them up.

At the far end of the panelled hall in front of the huge stone fireplace, Assen's father and Dr Brisbois stand silently staring into the furnace. In winter, Assen's father demands the fire is constantly lit. Assen hurries towards them past the long, mahogany dining table with space to seat up to twenty guests, surrounded by high-backed, finely carved, regimented chairs standing silently to attention.

When he reaches the fireplace, he bows to his father, then to Dr Brisbois. 'What happened? What news? I came as soon as... I heard something about... Is it true?' He looks from one to the other.

His father shakes his head and, breathing heavily, says, 'It is here...'

Assen's chest tightens; his doublet digs into his ribs. He is taking little gasping breaths, causing his throat and the space under his collarbone to pump erratically. 'Plague is here? In this house?'

'No, no, son.' Mr Verey clutches his son's upper arm. 'Thanks be to God, not this house. It is your Uncle Manny, Aunt Lottie and your cousins, I'm afraid.'

Heat rises in Assen's neck and ears. He reddens with shame at his first reaction – fear for his immediate family. 'Uncle Manny? Are they...? Is everyone all right?'

'Your Aunt Charlotte is gravely ill. I'm not sure.' He looks at Dr Brisbois. 'It looks – it seems bad...'

'I'll go at once. François!' Assen shouts, though he needn't have. François has remained silently in the corner of the room, fingers interlaced, and is at Assen's side instantaneously. 'Oh. Ah, yes, my cloak, hat – no, make it my coat, the heavy wool, I think, the brown one. Thank you.'

But Mr Verey holds up his hand, stopping François in his tracks. 'No! I forbid it!' Momentarily frozen between the group and the door, François gathers himself, rolling his shoulders back and opening his chest. He bows his head and once more cups his hands in front of him, awaiting instructions.

Mr Verey lowers his voice. 'Son, the area is quarantined. The house is sealed.'

'They'll let me in. I'm a physician – I have the equipment, the robes. I can get what I need at the hospital.'

'They might let you in, but they won't let you out,' Dr Brisbois interjects.

'Listen to the good doctor,' says Mr Verey, struggling to match the doctor's measured tone.

\*\*\*

Over the years Dr Brisbois has learned that listening well, offering sympathy and understanding and not intervening in family disputes are the hallmarks of a good and prosperous physician. Indeed, this approach has ensured he's remained a friend and confidant of the wealthy Verey family for more than thirty years. 'There are other things you can do, Assen. Your father is sending food and wine tonight.'

'Yes, and I am releasing funds for the delivery of daily supplies,' Mr Verey adds. 'François!'

François lifts his head and releases his hands. 'Sir.'

'Come with me to the kitchen. You'll organise everything. Assen, I will see you tonight.'

'Yes, Father.'

Assen and Dr Brisbois stand gazing into the fire. Dr Brisbois is playing with a small clay pipe, turning it over and over. 'It is good to see you.' Assen says.

Dr Brisbois looks up. He has always thought of Assen as a good child. True, the boy doesn't always listen and is often away in a world of his own, but, like his mother, he has a kind heart.

In some ways Assen was a peculiar child, quite different from the others Dr Brisbois cared for in infancy. He cherished the oddest things – the ducks at the chateau and those piglets and –

what else was it? Ah, yes, those frogs. *Those damned frogs*, Theo, his father, had said.

Dr Brisbois smiles, twiddling his pipe. Assen is a lot like his mother, Bahdeer. A young woman with long raven hair pops into his mind, walking gracefully across an immaculately manicured lawn with a little boy in tow.

But in this instance, young Assen's impulsiveness may lead him into making a rash decision with horrendous consequences.

\*\*\*

'There's got to be something I can do. I've been learning… I'd like to try something…' Assen says.

'Oh, yes?' Dr Brisbois pulls his eyes away from the flames and focuses on him.

'I have to get theriac, of course.'

'Of course,' the older doctor agrees.

'And … maybe … things that…' He stares intently at Dr Brisbois. 'Maybe things that the great Paracelsus did.'

Dr Brisbois's eyes twinkle. 'You are a devotee?'

Assen nods. 'Ye-es, and I know you have been a practitioner of the great physician for many years.'

'That is true.' Dr Brisbois sighs. 'But alas, I find the circle of people, even among our fellow physicians, versed enough to discuss the writings and methods of Paracelsus is small, very small indeed. But—' he raises his eyebrows '—I sense a kindred spirit?'

'I think his work has a great deal to offer,' Assen replies.

'Then we have much to talk about,' Dr Brisbois says brightly. 'Perhaps there's something I can help with. Shall we be seated?'

Assen is about to move two chairs closer to the fire when François enters. 'François, help me to move these,' he says, and they slide the chairs across the floor, positioning them on either side of the fireplace.

'Would you like me to build up the fire, sir?' François offers.

'No, thank you. You can leave us now.'

Bowing to each gentleman in turn, François leaves the room.

Dr Brisbois leans back and tucks his pipe back into the breast pocket of his shirt. 'Now, tell me about your ideas.'

# Chapter Seventeen

Discovered
North Berwick

Sleep evades Mr Seton. He's gone through the accounts three times with the same result each time: their debt is increasing instead of decreasing. His wife's inheritance should be coming soon with her father passing in the last three weeks, but he dare not ask her again about it.

He looks out of the window. The moon is high; it must be gone two. Did he hear the kirk bell strike? As he gazes over the garden he doesn't see the sundial in the centre, nor the path skirting around and down to the forest and the bridleway beyond. He sees numbers and his fine dining-room chairs being carried out by the bailiffs.

But wait, what was that? He glimpses something out of the corner of his eye. Something moved just below his window, and he hears stones crunching under someone or something's tread. He stands back, squinting into the garden, now giving it his full attention.

The clouds part for a fraction of a second, allowing a sliver of moonlight to illuminate the meandering path. A shadow glides down the trail towards the woods. *What the Devil?* His heart leapfrogs into his throat. *An omen!* He'll get Mr Gilchrist to set the dogs on the spectre.

But wait a minute. He comes closer to the window. The dress, the build, the way *she* walks, runs, almost floating... He knows that figure. 'Well, well, well. Gellis Duncan,' he whispers.

Exactly what would make a serving maid sneak out of the house in the middle of the night? Nothing wholesome, that's for sure.

'We'll see about that, Gellis Duncan.'

Although he wouldn't admit it, Mr Seton is relieved to have a distraction from the household finances as he considers all the questions he will ask her when he sees her next. He'll seek her out in the parlour tomorrow and get to the bottom of this.

He climbs back into bed; he hadn't realised how cold he is. Curling an arm and a leg around his wife, he nuzzles his cheek into her hair and pulls the covers over his shoulders. He feels warmer already.

Awake early, he opens his eyes and sees the fair hair of his wife tied in a plait. The smell of rose oil and peaty smoke reaches his nostrils. He breathes it in.

The bedroom door slowly opens. He shuts his eyes again and listens to the light footsteps pad across the floor to the fireplace. Opening one eye, he sees the plump figure of Mary carrying a bucket of peat and logs. With minimal noise, she places them to the side and stoops to light the ready-prepared fire. It crackles and bursts into life, flames curling around the logs. She looks at the fire for a moment, turns and leaves the room.

Mr Seton throws the covers back and sits on the edge of the bed. He will take a full breakfast in the hall. But there is something he wants to do first.

He'll catch Gelly alone. Where would she be at this hour? The parlour. He makes his way downstairs. Stopping outside the door, he sees her through the crack kneeling at the fireplace. He swings the door open and coughs.

The girl freezes in mid-stroke; a tiny, hunched figure, dwarfed by the large, plain, stone fire surround as high a man's shoulder.

\*\*\*

Goosebumps rise on the nape of her neck. Gelly resumes her work, focusing even harder on the ash and debris, sweeping with greater vigour, the bristles of the brush digging deeper into the flagstone.

'Go away,' she hisses under her breath. It's been a long night with so many things to think about. Her stomach growls. If she hurries, she can get this done, feed the pigs, clean the last of the dishes from the Seton's evening meal and settle down with Mrs Merritt and Mary for breakfast. Spurred on, she brushes the detritus faster and scoops it into her shovel, stirring up a plume of ash and dust.

'Ah, Gelly. How are you getting on?' Mr Seton asks neutrally.

*Oh, God, what does he want?* 'Beg your pardon, sir?' She sits back on her heels and takes in the room. Two tall, black-stained oak chairs with rich, padded, dark-red velvet seats and backs sit on either side of the fireplace, with another one in the middle. They've been moved.

She bites her lip; three people must have huddled here last night. How late were they up? Her eyes flit to a fourth chair by the window, angled towards the lower garden and forest.

'You've not been with us long, have you?' He doesn't wait for an answer. 'Three months, is it not? Not long at all.' He comes closer to the fire.

Gelly rises to her knees, curls her toes and meets his stare. 'That's right.'

Drawing his eyes away he strides towards the window, looks out at the sundial and path to the woods. 'You've settled in with Mary and Cook?'

Gelly gets to her feet. She needs to stand for wherever this conversation might go. 'Aye, sir.'

'And your mistress, Mrs Seton, she is a God-fearing woman; this is a God-fearing household. Everyone under this roof knows God is watching them.'

'Really?' Gelly can't help laughing.

Turning sharply to face her, he snaps, 'That's why I won't have anyone scurrying off in the middle of the night to God-knows-where and God-knows-whom.'

Gelly's heart thumps against her ribcage, her breathing rapid and shallow. She tries to formulate some plausible story but nothing comes. Her mind won't work, just blankness, nothingness, like being in a trance, a void with no words, no language.

'Where were you off to last night at such a late hour? Who were you meeting? Well? What do you have to say?'

The cogs in Gelly's mind begin to turn. 'No one, sir. I was meeting no one. I … I … felt ill, sir, the kitchen, the smell – it gets hot sometimes. I felt queasy. I just wanted a bit of air. I went for a walk to the bridge.'

It was the truth, sort of. Gelly did in fact walk to the bridge, though that was three nights ago, but it is all her panicked brain could come up with. Someone once told her the only way to tell a convincing lie was to tell the truth about something that had actually happened.

'The bridge? Hmm. I did not see you return. What could have taken you all that time?'

'I can't say, sir.'

'I won't allow it in *my* house, among *my* servants,' he explodes. 'I warn you, Gellis Duncan. Now, get on with your work.' He clasps his hands behind his back and struts off into the hall.

Her heart still beating irregularly, Gelly turns back to the fireplace, purses her lips and releases the breath she's been holding. Clinging on to the stone surround, she lowers herself once more to her knees. Her shoulders sag. As she takes up the brush and pan, her arms feel ten times heavier. She can do nothing in this house without someone watching her.

She sits back on her heels, closes her eyes and imagines the little cottage and stream she's been dreaming about all her life. Her shoulders soften and she begins to rhythmically brush out the debris of last night's fire.

The rest of the morning goes smoothly enough for Gelly. It's always nice having breakfast with the cook and Mary. Jack pops in, too, with a rabbit for supper, and Mrs Merritt says she'll cook it with parsnips and potatoes tonight.

Everything seems normal. Apart from the scene with Mr Seton, the day falls into its daily rhythm. Gelly and Mary make the beds and collect the bedpans. With one in each hand, they head out of the kitchen door and down to the cesspool about a thousand yards from the house. The master specified the distance when it was first dug out, and every housemaid is schooled in the toileting rules. But sometimes, when it is cold or raining and Gelly and Mary are out of sight of the house, they toss the contents into the woods closer by. They often joke about how big the shrubs and bushes are growing in that spot. They rinse out the potties in the burn then head back.

Mrs Merritt is standing sentry-like in the kitchen doorway, her arms folded. 'Ladies,' she says with a smile. 'For your next amusement, see yon pile of plates?'

'Ha, ha.' Gelly likes Mrs Merritt. She works the lassies hard because she has to, but she looks after them too, making sure they are well fed and warm, and that they sleep together out of harm's way.

'Mary, take the piss pots upstairs first. Gelly, you can get started on the dishes.'

Gelly laughs. 'I always got told I'd live a charmed life!'

When Mary leaves, Mrs Merritt nods to the door. 'They've got someone coming again.'

'Who's got someone coming?' Gelly says, looking out of the window and imagining her whitewashed cottage with climbing roses around the front door.

'Them! The master, mistress.'

'I didn't know that.'

'Me neither. I hope they're not expecting refreshments or I'll have to send out.'

'Do you know who?'

Mrs Merritt shrugs. 'Minister, I think.'

Gelly scoops up an armful of dishes, cradling them like a huge, brittle baby. Ushering her, Mrs Merritt opens the back door with a mock flourish.

Gelly holds her chin aloft with a 'Thank you, Mrs Merritt', and heads towards the huge table in the back courtyard. Thank goodness they've got a pump. She places the crockery down with minimal clatter; she doesn't want anything docked from her wages, skinflints that they are.

After reaching for the pail under the table, she seizes the handle and carries it to the pump. She has to pump several times for the water to flow. It splurges out – splat, splat, splat – like it's clearing its throat. She fills the bucket three-quarters. *Jings. Is it getting heavier or is it just me?*

Mrs Merritt leans against the doorframe, watching. 'You'll do yerself a mischief. I've told you half full,' she says, shaking her head and pushing herself away from the post. 'Come here.' She joins Gelly and together they lift the pail onto the table. 'There, ya daft lassie,'

Gelly smiles. 'Thanks, Mrs Merritt.'

She takes a cloth from the many dangling around her waist and plunges it into the pail. With her other hand, she takes the first plate and wipes it with the rag, rinses it in the bucket and puts it to one side. Cook is already back at the kitchen door.

Gelly looks up at the sky – a fine day, still cold though. She might head into the village later if Mrs Merritt sends her to the Stockwells' farm. She hopes she will. She'll have to watch her time, though, not be too long.

She likes doing the dishes. It gives her a chance to quiet her mind and dream. Soon all the plates are stacked on the other side of the bucket. She looks inside the bucket – still half full – then at the back door. She can easily lift that; they can use it for the pots later.

As she picks it up, she hears 'Gelly!' She drops the bucket on the bench with a dull thud and splash. 'Aye?' she says, looking up and wiping her forehead with the back of her hand.

It's Mary. 'You're wanted upstairs.'

'Me?' Gelly furrows her brow.

Mrs Merritt pushes past Mary, taking up the doorway. 'Come on, come on, don't keep them waiting. Mrs Seton wants to see you.'

Gelly struggles to pull her apron over her head. 'What does she want?'

'Now, let me see… Mrs Seton and me are that close that I'm privy to all her confidences.'

'Are you?' asks Mary incredulously.

'No, I'm bloody well not! Gelly, upstairs. They're in the parlour. Wait!' Mrs Merritt pulls out a rag and spits on it. 'Hold still.' She cups Gelly's chin, gently guides her head to the right and wipes her cheek. 'That's better. On ye go.'

# Chapter Eighteen

A Doctor Calls
The Latin Quarter, Paris

What will be waiting for him, Assen wonders? The wind stings his cheek as if someone has just slapped it. He draws his coat tighter against the bitter cold and quickens his pace, clutching his portmanteau. The afternoon went well – very well – at least as far as Dr Brisbois' support is concerned. The patronage of a high-ranking court physician will open many doors, especially at the hospital.

Assen has always had a soft spot for Dr Brisbois. A 'proper family doctor', Uncle Manny likes to say. The type of physician who always has a kind word and sits on your bed and listens to your complaints, then gets up, pats your legs and tells you you're going to be just fine.

One time when Assen had a fever, the doctor sat up every night alongside his mother. Each time Assen opened his eyes, Dr Brisbois was sitting in the chair opposite. 'Sleep a little more, my boy. You'll be fine when you wake up.' He had made Assen drink that awful stuff, too; he can still taste the tangy rancid flavour, like lemon mixed with sour goat's milk. Assen shudders. They wouldn't use it now.

But the good doctor's confidence was always reassuring. Had it helped him get better? Probably. Gérard thinks it did, saying the doctor's job is to distract the patient enough to let the body heal itself. *What about Mother? Nothing saved her.* Assen shakes his head. *Stop it. Get on, now.*

The streets are surprisingly busy. He didn't expect such bustle, given the plague is only streets away. What will he find in the 5th arrondissement? What about at Uncle Manny's house? He pushes the thought from his mind. He is a physician; he will act like a doctor – objective, detached and reassuring.

Straightening up, he strides confidently through the throng. He knows these back streets and alleyways well. He can't count how many times as a boy he sneaked out of the house and dashed over the bridge and down these lanes to his uncle and aunt's house.

He loved being with his cousins. There was always warm bread and sweet camomile tea, and, more often than not, sweet treats. Aunt Charlotte would shake her head and say, 'What am I going to do with you, hmm? You'll get us into trouble, too!' She'd put her arm around his shoulders and ruffle his hair.

It was true: many times he'd come home to his father, arms folded, standing in front of the parlour fire. 'What do you think you are doing?' he'd said sternly. 'Anything could happen to you. Someone like you, ransomed! You will only go to your cousins when Gabriel has no other duties and can take you, and you'll ask us for permission. Is that understood?'

It was understood well enough but not always – well, almost never – obeyed. Yet thinking back, his parents must have been worried. A pang of regret spreads across Assen's chest.

He sees his mother sitting with her hand resting on the arm of a chair. 'I know you want your freedom, darling, it's in your nature, But listen to your father. It's only for now.' Back then, 'now' felt as though it would stretch forever. 'In time you'll be able to look after yourself and anyone else you need to,' she'd added.

*I can look after myself now*, he had thought but never said.

He stops and looks around. Has he gone past it? No, it's up ahead. A sign hangs across the narrow alleyway: *Allée des Cerisiers*. Peering down it, Assen sees it is just as he remembers: no broader than the span of a man's shoulders and one outstretched arm. He proceeds through the dark tunnel and emerges into a small courtyard, concealed from the busy streets surrounding it. Not many people know about this place. It is a relief to be out of that biting wind. His neck and shoulders soften a little.

He places the bag at his feet and bends over to open it. First, he unfurls the long leather gown and holds it at arm's length, then he removes his coat, haphazardly crumples it into the bag and pulls the gown over his head. It fits well. Next, he takes out a mask with a long, crow-like beak and fits it to his face, pulling the attached hood all the way over his head and securing it with a tie. Finally, he draws out a wide-brimmed leather hat and pulls it firmly down onto his head. He grabs his bag, hurriedly stuffs in his hat and muff, then goes back down the alley and out into the busy street.

Not far now. The entrance to the 5$^{th}$ arrondissement is at the end of the next turning on the right. The street has almost emptied and carts are strung across the entrance to the district. Two men casually lean against one of them.

Assen takes off his hat and mask and walks over; he is immediately aware how much better he can breathe. Meanwhile, a well-dressed man has approached the two carters. Assen stops. The man says something to them and points to the door of a house on the other side of the barricade. One of the men nods and moves away. The well-dressed man must be in charge.

'Excuse me, sir.' Assen tries to sound official yet casual. 'I'm here to make a house call to the home of Mr Verey. Mr Emanuel Verey.'

The gentleman looks him up and down. Assen nervously runs his fingers through his hair. 'You are an authorised physician?' the man asks, eyeing him closely.

'Yes.'

'What is your name?'

'I am from St Marcel's.'

'Really? They have sent you this far?'

'They are short of doctors and asked for our help.' Heat rises in Assen's neck and a pebble-sized lump lodges in his throat. The collar of the gown feels constricting.

'You'd better pass, then. Do you know them well, the Vereys?'

'Yes.' Assen nods, loosens his collar then puts his hat and beak back on.

'This way.' With a sweep of the hand, the gentleman steers Assen to a gap at the end of the line of carts close to the wall of what used to be a binder's shop. It is eerily quiet on the other side, just the muffled cries of the carters shouting to each other from inside the dwellings.

White crosses in the shape of crucifixes mark many of the doors. One is open, with a cart parked in front. Two men appear in the doorway carrying a shrouded figure and, with a pendulum swing, throw it onto the cart. Cloths cover their noses and mouths. They head back inside and quickly return with another shrouded figure. They go inside again. Assen shivers, turns away and hurries on.

Soon he emerges into a wider road where the houses are set back from the street. It is deserted. Each residence is fronted by a low wall the height of a man's thigh, topped with iron railings that rise at least three feet above Assen's head. He stops on the threshold of a fine house about halfway down the street. The gates are closed. All the times he's visited his uncle's house, he's never seen the gates closed.

His chest tightens as he pushes the gate open and walks up the short path to the front door on which a large white cross has been painted. His heart thumps irregularly. Is he doing the right thing? What if he catches it? Is he putting everyone he knows in danger – his father, Dr Brisbois, his patients?

Cradling his bag, he looks around. The poles and tongs in his portmanteau jingle and jangle as he sets it on the step. He won't wear his mask, not at first. He still has on his long robe; that'll do for now.

He raps loudly at the door. Silence: there is no movement, no signs of life. He shifts his head closer to the door, his ear touching the wood as he holds his breath. Wait. Was that a noise? Faint, but something. Shuffling footsteps, perhaps?

He stands back and looks up at the great door towering above his head. 'Open up!' he shouts. 'Marie! Jean-Pierre! Open up! Where are you?'

The footsteps from inside are now unmistakable, the soft tread coming closer to the door. 'Who is that? Who's there?' a voice barely above a whisper calls.

'It's Dr Assen Verey. Tell your master his nephew, Assen, the physician, is here to see him. Open up.'

The door slowly opens a fraction as the person struggles with the weight of it, their breathing laboured. Assen carefully pushes the panel of the door with his palm to aid the opening. As he does so, he comes nose to nose with an older dishevelled man peeking round the corner.

Assen jumps back. For a moment he doesn't recognise his uncle. 'Uncle Manny?' he asks, flabbergasted.

His uncle seems just as surprised. 'Assen! Good God, boy, what are you doing here? It's not safe. Go. Go now. Does Theo know you're here?'

Assen hardly hears him. Why is Uncle Manny answering the door himself? Where are the servants? 'Where is Marie, Jean-Pierre, Mich—'

'Gone.'

'Gone?'

'All gone. All our servants fled except Agathe. We sent her away.'

'You sent Agathe away?' Assen can't believe it. Agathe has been in the family since forever, like a precious heirloom passed down from generation to generation. His father told him she had looked after him and Uncle Manny when they were little. 'Let me in, Uncle Manny. I'm a doctor, I can help.'

'No one can help us. Go! I'm sorry…'

Uncle Manny is about to close the door when a cart containing large baskets of food stops outside the gate. Keeping his palm on the door to hold it open, Assen shouts to the carter, 'Come through! The gate is unlocked.'

He turns back to the door. 'Please, Uncle Manny. I have brought food, see?'

The cart rolls to a standstill behind Assen. The driver jumps down and begins to unload two baskets of food – vegetables, bread and a large pot of soup.

Uncle Manny is still guarding the threshold, his fingers curled around the edge of the door. 'Thank you, Assen. You are a good boy. I will take the food gladly, but I will not allow you to cross the doorway.'

'But I've already had the pestilence!' Assen blurts out. 'I had it two years ago when I was studying in Italy. Remember when I was in Padua?'

Uncle Manny's attention is drawn to the piles of food placed neatly at his front door. 'Uh-huh…' he says.

Assen is grateful for the distraction. His jaw has locked and his buttocks have clenched from lying.

But Uncle Manny soon turns back, studying his face with curiosity. 'I do remember your time in Veneto. Theo was very proud. But...' he looks down and frowns '...he didn't tell me... He didn't say you were ill. If I'd known...'

Flushed, Assen turns away and tries to focus on something – anything – except his uncle's face. A crow glides down, settles on the gatepost and folds its wings. With his eyes locked on the bird, Assen thinks of his friend Gérard and what had happened to him in a remote alpine village. 'I kept it from my parents – they never knew. When I was ill I could barely talk in French, let alone Italian. Word never got to them and, when I was better, I didn't see the point in worrying them. I work at St Marcel's now.'

'You work at the hospital for the poor and destitute? Theo never said.'

'Many doctors who've had the plague work in such hospitals.' Assen doesn't know if this is true but thinks it should be.

He hears a polite cough behind him. 'Beg your pardon, sir. All your supplies are here.' The coachman points to the food then glances nervously at Uncle Manny.

'Thank you.' Assen reaches into the pocket of his pantaloons, fishes out some coins and drops them into the carter's open palm. The man jumps back onto his seat and, with a flick of the reins, the cart rolls off.

'Let me take these inside,' Assen pleads.

Seconds tick by as Uncle Manny clings to the door and Assen determinedly holds his ground. Sighing, his uncle releases the door and drops his arms to his sides. 'Thank you.'

Assen breathes out and stoops to pick up the pot of soup and bread.

Uncle Manny joins him on the porch and lifts one of the baskets. Laden, they walk into the dark hallway. Assen waits for his eyes to adjust; even though it is not particularly bright outside, the contrast seems stark. The entry is as grand as he remembers but far gloomier. Perhaps houses get sick too, or maybe it's just his frame of mind.

'I'll heat this up in the kitchen. Where are Aunt Charlotte, Émile, René, little Joséphine?' Assen tries to keep his voice upbeat, as much for his own benefit as Uncle Manny's. The rock in his stomach is like a dead weight.

Uncle Manny leads him through the parlour to the kitchen, a place in which neither of them has spent much time. 'Upstairs. They cannot ... come down. Émile's not so bad, but my Lottie has been in delirium for two days.' He swallows and blinks several times, brushing the side of his eye with a fingertip. 'I fear she ... she's ... going to... She might not... She is very weak, Assen. I don't know what I'd do without...'

'Don't worry. I'll go to her now. I have theriac.'

Uncle Manny brightens. 'Really? You have theriac?'

'Yes. I have plenty for you all, and I'm going to make more.'

'Praise God. Dr Sauveterre said he couldn't get any. He tried, but he couldn't find all the ingredients. He said the whole of Paris society was clamouring for it. I thought it was all gone.'

'I have all the ingredients and I can get more. There's enough for everyone. Now, heat the soup, Uncle Manny,' Assen says gently. 'Eat some, and then come up.'

Assen leaves Uncle Manny eating the soup. Taking his bag, he re-enters the hall and stops at the foot of the opulent staircase. There is a huge stained-glass window above the quarter landing where the stairs turn. It depicts the archangel Michael, a touch Aunt Charlotte had insisted on, saying, 'He will give all who come here love and protection.' The angel is triumphant, his arms outstretched and his wings unfurled, a halo of bronze hair cascading around his head and shoulders, yet he also manages a look of complete serenity. How clever artists are, Assen muses.

He places his hand on the banister and mounts the staircase. The crack of the wood under his feet echoes in the hall.

All the doors are firmly shut in the upper hallway; save for Assen's footsteps, it is silent. Stopping, he listens for the sound of Émile and René arguing, or little Joséphine giggling and talking to her dolly. Nothing.

The third door has a small table outside with a vase of dead flowers. He strokes the wood with his fingertips; he'll remove the flowers later. Raising his fist to eye level, he knocks at the door. No reply. He tries again, louder. Surely someone will hear. But no one stirs.

He slides his hand to the handle and gently eases open the door. 'Aunt Charlotte, it's Assen,' he whispers and tiptoes in.

Still no reply. His heart flutters like a butterfly trapped in a bell jar, making him gulp. He breathes in through his nose then holds his breath at the end of the exhale. When he can't hold it any longer his breathing reflex kicks in and the air rushes into his lungs like a torrent flooding a millpond. It is a trick Gérard showed him to calm his palpitations.

Looking around the room, he notices a figure in the bed. Holding the edge of the door, his eyes fixed on the figure, he freezes.

*You're a doctor, for pity's sake.*

The room is stuffy and the ruff around his neck is tight. He loosens it to free his throat and pulls it away from the back of his neck, then strides further into the room to a window. Once it is open, a light breeze blows in.

The figure stirs. Assen walks to the bottom of the bed so his aunt can see him. 'Aunt Charlotte,' he whispers, then says more loudly, 'Aunt Lottie!'

His aunt stirs. 'Are you an angel?' she exclaims, her eyes round with wonder.

'No, Auntie.' He laughs joylessly. 'It's me, Assen, your nephew.'

'Assen? I'm not dead, then?'

'No, no, you are not dead. You're going to be just fine. I have something for you.' He rummages in his satchel and pulls out a small phial.

'What is it?'

'Medicine. Strong medicine. It will make you feel better.'

'I think you *are* an angel.' She smiles weakly and tries to sit up.

'Dear Aunt Lottie.' He wants to come closer to the bed, sit on the edge and hold her hand.

Uncle Manny appears in the doorway carrying a bowl of soup.

'Here is Uncle Manny. He has brought you something to eat. See? Broth.' Assen walks to the cabinet and places the phial in the centre then steps away and stands under the lattice window. 'Uncle Manny, please give Aunt Lottie all of this with a little soup, if she can manage it.'

His uncle nods, lays down the bowl and picks up the phial. He looks at it then at Assen.

Assen nods. 'Go ahead.'

Not taking his eyes off the phial, Uncle Manny holds it as if it were a holy relic, walks gingerly to the bed and takes a seat beside his wife. Placing it reverently on the small round table at the bedside, he lifts Aunt Lottie under the arms and props her up. She winces but smiles gratefully.

With one arm behind her back to support her, Uncle Manny reaches for the phial, brings it to his mouth and spits the cork from it. 'Try to drink some of this, Lottie.' He raises it to her mouth and her lips wrap around the rim. She tips her head back and her throat bobs up and down.

Assen looks on, relieved. *More, Aunt Lottie. Try to drink it all.* She drains the bottle. He blows out and swallows. 'Good.'

Uncle Manny gets up, sets the phial back down on the cabinet and picks up the bowl of soup. 'Right, my sweet Lottie, just a few mouthfuls and then you can go back to sleep.' He sits back down on the bed and lifts the spoon to her mouth. Their eyes lock, holding each other's gaze until she's finished half the broth.

'Enough. Please, I'm tired,' Aunt Charlotte pleads.

Uncle Manny looks at Assen, who nods, then he takes away the bowl and wipes its rim with a cloth. Aunt Charlotte flops down and falls back into a deep slumber.

The two men tiptoe out. In the kitchen, Assen stands opposite his uncle, the large wooden table an island between them. He peels open his satchel, takes out several phials and sets them down one by one.

'This is all the theriac I have made.' He pushes one phial then another and another to the centre of the table. 'Take one in the morning and one in the evening. The same for everyone, except little Joséphine. Give her half – half in the morning, half at night before bed. You will remember?'

Uncle Manny stretches over and lifts each bottle until they are neatly assembled in front of him. 'I will do exactly what you say. It will make us well again?' he implores, searching Assen's face.

His jaw rigid, Assen looks fixedly at his uncle. 'Yes. Take one now.'

Uncle Manny picks up the phial closest to him, flicks off the cork and swallows the dark-green liquid in one gulp.

'Are you sure you'll manage to give everyone their dose? I can stay and help,' Assen asks. Maybe he should go around the household; it would give him a chance to see how everyone is. The new patient he's supposed to see later in The Marais, whom his father introduced, can wait. He'll say he was held up at the hospital. They'll understand – if not understand, his father will grudgingly tolerate it.

'No, no,' Uncle Manny replies firmly. 'You have other patients to see. We will be fine now we have these.' He looks at the table. 'But how did you get them? It is so hard to get, the ingredients so rare. The cost? We must repay you.'

Assen dismisses his uncle's offer with a wave of his hand. 'It is nothing.'

'No! It is *something*. It is a *great deal*,' Uncle Manny says steadfastly. 'Look at me, Assen. You've saved us. Thank you, dear, dear boy. I owe you everything.'

'You would do the same, you know you would.' Assen begins to pack his satchel back into his case. 'I have to go now.' But when he reaches the kitchen door, he stops. 'There's something else I'm going to … I'd like to try to make,' he adds haltingly, turning back to his uncle. 'It's new. I think it will help. It may take me all of tomorrow to make it, but I'll come as soon as I can – the day after tomorrow. Can you manage? Do you want me to stay? I can have my still brought over. Maybe it's best if I do…'

'No, no, please,' Uncle Manny says. 'Do what you have to do. I will see you in a day or so. We'll be fine with what you've given us. We'll all be up and running around the next time you're here. Just wait and see.' He smiles, the lines etched deep into the corners of his eyes and his cheeks.

'Very well. I'll see you in two days, I promise.'

# Chapter Nineteen

The Accusation
North Berwick

Gelly is outside the parlour. She touches her hair and smooths a strand behind her ear. The door is open a fraction. Dusting down the front of her dress, she takes a deep breath and hears a low murmur of voices from inside the room.

'Come on, Gelly lassie, let's get this done,' she whispers to herself as she taps on the door.

'Enter!' barks Mr Seton's voice.

Her stomach sinks. She could run out the front door and never come back, but where could she go? *He* couldn't help her. He'd want to, but he couldn't. She knows that ... she's always known that.

Instead, she pops her head around the door and quickly takes in the scene. Mrs Seton is perched on one side of the fireplace and the minister, Reverend McLaren, is on the other. The fire's just been stoked up and is sparking and popping in the grate. Mr Seton stands by the window, looking out.

'Come in, girl!' Mrs Seton snaps and looks up at her husband enquiringly.

Gelly steps further into the room, glancing warily at the reverend.

'Minister McLaren wishes to talk to you,' Mr Seton says, spinning round to face her.

Until now, Reverend McLaren had seemed like an ordinary, run-of-the-mill Presbyterian minister with his black skull cap pulled down over his ears, exactly like the one worn by John Knox in a painting over at the Moffat manor at Gullane where Gelly had worked with her cousin. In his late forties, with his long black robe topped with a stiff white collar folded over at the neck, he looks like any other minister of the Kirk.

'Me?' Gelly exclaims.

'Yes, girl. And close your mouth,' Mrs Seton chastises 'Come pay your respects.'

'Yes, ma'am. Beg your pardon. Good day, Minister McLaren.' Gelly curtsies. What does he want? Her stomach flips as if a tiny acrobat just did a backward somersault. Something's amiss. She looks at Mr Seton who has turned back to the window.

'Good day, Gelly. Are you well?' Reverend McLaren is almost jovial.

'Aye, sir,' she replies.

'Good. That's good, Gelly. I'm pleased. Now, we don't want to take up too much of these good people's time.' He looks at Mrs Seton who smiles and gives a little nod. 'So let me get to the point. I've been hearing reports—'

'Reports? What reports?' Gelly bursts out. She hates gossips. People talking behind her back makes her blood boil. 'Who's been talking?' She shoots a glance at Mr Seton.

A little startled by her exclamation, Mr Seton pulls himself from his reflection to face the room.

'Has somebody been spying on me?' she demands.

'Gelly! Do not interrupt the minister!' Mrs Seton says, looking mortified.

The minister forms his index fingers into a steeple, which he gently presses to his lips in contemplation. It's something she's noticed him do before when he talked about fairness and justice in his sermons.

'There have been repor— er ... comments—' he coughs '— that you've been curing people. Some might even call them ... umm ... *miraculous* healings.' He pauses, pushing his palms on the armrests to lift himself higher.

Mrs Seton, stock still, stares intently at him.

'For instance,' he continues, 'the Johnston child was about to meet the grace of God. It was agreed among the good clergy and best physicians that she, angel that she was, was about to depart to our dear Lord Jesus Christ. But you stepped in and stopped it. Can you tell us why?' His tone was gentle, as if they were having a conversation about preparing food for the next parish fete.

*What is he getting at?* Gelly's chest tightens and her throat is as dry as a pumice stone. She sees Agnes sitting by her fireside, saying, 'People don't like miraculous healings. Don't let them call them miraculous. Play it down.'

Gelly swallows. 'I just wanted to help. Mrs Johnston begged me. She was desperate…'

'Desperate, eh?' Nodding, the reverend turns to Mr Seton. 'Would have agreed to anything, then?'

'She loved her child – she didn't want her to die. She asked me to help. That's all.'

'And how did you help?' Reverend McLaren presses.

'I had herbs and some dried flowers, roots, leaves, an old remedy my grandmother gave me. I made a soothing tea. It usually helps if a person is burning up, if their chest is bunged up.'

'Aha. From your grandmother, eh? Would that be your Grandmother Duncan?'

'No, McLeod.'

'From the north. Is that not so?'

'Aye. Aye, it is.' *What's he driving at?* She is not ashamed. Her Highland folk were strong, clever, righteous people.

He changes tack. 'And where did you prepare this tea?'

'In the kitchen. Mrs Johnston's kitchen.'

'And did anybody see you?'

*What's he trying to get me to say, to admit to?* She turns to Mrs Seton. 'Please, ma'am. I don't know what this is about. Honestly, I haven't done anything.'

'Just answer the minister's questions, Gelly, and then you can go. The good Lord loves honesty,' Mrs Seton says, looking at her husband for approval.

'Quite true, Mrs Seton, quite true,' the reverend continues. 'Now, Gelly, this tea. Did anyone see you?'

Gelly's neck stiffens. 'Aye… Mary, the eldest.'

The minister nods. 'Aye, she said that right enough.'

'You've been to the Johnstons'?' Gelly gapes at the minister then at Mrs Seton, who quickly looks at her hands clasped in her lap.

Ignoring the outburst, Reverend McLaren proceeds in an even tone. 'Now. Old man Hunter. He was ready to meet his maker as well, was he not? And you stopped him. Do you not want people to be with God?'

'Not before their time!' Gelly says with a nervous laugh, prickles of fear crawling up her spine. 'I try to make them feel better, that's all.'

'So you don't deny these miraculous healings.'

'Deny! What is there to deny? I don't deny I helped people, gave them a soothing remedy, and they got better. I don't deny that!'

'Hmm. You do know only our Lord Jesus Christ can perform miraculous healings. All else is the work of the Devil…'

'It wasn't a miracle!' Gelly cries, looking at Mrs Seton.

Mrs Seton stares at her husband, alarm flitting across her features.

# Chapter Twenty

Too Late
The Latin Quarter, Paris

*They must be better now, surely*? Assen hurries towards his uncle's house. It is several days since his last visit, much longer than he'd hoped it would be. Distilling the theriac was anything but straightforward. The first batch was ruined because the heat was too intense; it made the compound unsteady, and he'd put in too much mercury.

'Remember, you're trying to cure your patients not kill them,' Dr Brisbois had joked.

No matter. He's nearly there, with more theriac and something new to try. He instinctively pats the satchel he's holding close to his chest. Following the same streets and alleys as he did a few days ago, this time his head is light and clear, his shoulders not hoisted around his ears; even his stomach is soft. He has a plan and everything he needs. He'll attend to Aunt Lottie first, then Joséphine, maybe the boys next and Uncle Manny last. This time he'll stay.

He's almost there.

'Morning, Dr Verey,' a man says, leaning against a cart, a piece of cloth covering his nose and mouth.

'Good morning,' Assen replies politely.

'Good day, Dr Verey.' A woman waves cheerily as she passes on his left-hand side.

Like the carter, Assen has no idea who she is. A shawl shrouds her head and shoulders and is pinned back across her face so only her eyes are visible. He notes the shawl is frayed at the edges – a servant, perhaps. Hastening past, he wonders how they recognise him in his plague-doctor disguise.

As he rounds the next corner, he comes into full view of the square and Uncle Manny's house standing majestically at the opposite corner. The gates are open and there is a cart parked outside the front door. He stops. What would a cart be doing outside Uncle Manny's house? His intestines knot into a pretzel, then he has a thought. Of course, the food has arrived. Good. Quickening his pace, he hurries across the square.

Reaching the gates, he removes his hat and mask; he'll take his chances. The protective garb is too scary for the children – heck, he'd probably frighten Aunt Lottie to death as well. He ruffles his hair and shakes his head. Glad to be free of the garments, he stuffs them into his bag.

'Right, let's do this,' he coaches himself, breathing in and puffing out through puckered lips as if blowing a silent whistle.

Then he sees him.

A figure appears in the doorway, looking just like he did moments earlier. The man is covered from head to foot in a leather coat, with a wide-brimmed hat and a beak-like mask.

A wave of rage swells in Assen's torso. No one else has the right to be here. *He* is treating the family. It is *his* family; *he'll* decide what they get. He seizes his bag and marches towards the figure, his chest constricting as if an invisible hand is squeezing his heart.

'Good day, sir. What is going on?' he asks haughtily. 'You have made a mistake, doctor. These people are my family, and I am taking care of them. My name is Dr Verey.'

The plague doctor slowly removes his hat, lifts the mask to reveal Gérard. He wipes his forehead. 'Gérard!' Assen exclaims. 'What – what are you doing here?'

'I'm sorry, Assen. Your father asked me to look in yesterday.' Gérard brushes some invisible dirt off his hat. 'I didn't know where you were.'

'He did?'

'We thought you were at the still, making the theriac. He sent François, but he couldn't find you.'

'I had to go to Tessier, the apothecary, because I'd run out of cinnamon and crocus. I have it here.' He digs into his satchel and pulls out a phial of dark-green liquid. 'I also have something I made up from the recipes of Paracelsus. Mercury and sulphur, only in minute quantities, of course, but I really think it will do the trick.'

He rummages again and draws out a package, wrapped in linen and tied with twine. 'We'll start with Aunt Charlotte and little Joséphine.' He looks up. 'How did you find them?'

'I'm truly sorry, Assen. My deepest—'

'What?' Assen stammers. 'What are you talking about?'

Gérard sighs and looks at the ground. 'I'm really sorry.'

'I don't understand. I was here a few days ago… I–I brought food – there's plenty of food. They had theriac… I made it, I made it for Uncle Manny – the best, the finest opium, wine, balsam from Peru, lavender honey, red ochre, everything. I prepared it to the letter. They had plenty. I have more here. I have these. See, I have these.' He looks at the phial and packet in his open palms. 'It was going to make them better. I don't understand…'

Another cart piled high with baskets of provisions rounds the corner of the square and advances towards the house. The carter pulls up, jumps down and approaches Gérard and Assen.

'Where do you want these?' he demands in a thick Bordeaux accent.

Gérard shakes his head sadly. 'We won't be needing them, thank you.'

'They're all paid for, sirs.' The man looks from Gérard to Assen.

'The food, Assen. What do you want…?' Gérard asks gently.

Assen's head is buzzing as he stares blankly at the haulier.

'Take it to St Marcel's', Gérard says, 'for the patients and the poor,' He drops a few coins into the man's palm.

'Thank you, sir – sirs. Sorry for your loss.'

'That was all right to do?' Gérard asks.

Assen pulls his gaze from the cart and nods, though he hardly heard what his friend said.

Two men appear in the grand doorway carrying a shrouded body wrapped in beige linen. 'Assen, this way.' Gérard gently guides him so he is standing clear of the door and the pillars supporting the portico.

As the men load the body onto the cart, Assen's legs give way. He drops down and hunkers on his heels. 'I don't understand. I just don't understand,' he says over and over again.

'It happened very quickly.' Gérard's voice is soft and reverential. 'They went downhill fast. When I got here, your Aunt Charlotte had been unconscious for days, maybe since you left.'

'That can't be! She had the medicine, the compound! I watched her take it!' Thoughts tumble through his mind like the contents of a barrel that's been pushed down a steep, rugged hill. Aunt Lottie, comatose since he left? He'd left them to die. He'd failed. He thought he'd saved them but really he'd failed them. His treatment didn't work. He is a poor doctor. His mother would be ashamed of him.

The carters appear lugging another shrouded figure. Assen springs to his feet, seething. 'Where are you taking them?' he explodes. His hands roll into fists; he wants to punch the carters, punch God, punch someone – anyone – senseless. He knows this is grief coming out as anger in the face of impotence to change what's happened, yet he cannot quell the rage surging through his body.

'It's all right, Assen.' Gérard's eyes are gentle. 'They must go to the grounds prepared for plague burials, but they have their own plot and it will be marked. It has already been prepared.'

Assen's stomach lurches and his tears overflow. He blinks and more come. 'It has?' Nothing is making sense to him except that he has let down his Uncle Manny who always looked out for him.

The hauliers emerge once last time, each carrying a small, shrouded figure, and load them onto the cart.

Assen falls back against the wall on the shrivelled ivy that encases the house. 'What now?'

# Chapter Twenty-One

Uninvited Guests
North Berwick

There's still a dead weight in Gelly's stomach from the minister's visit. She'll ask Agnes what to do, she'll know. But for now, she breathes heavily, most of the household tasks that can be done have been done. She looks out of the kitchen window; the sun is low in the sky. It won't be long until it dips below the horizon over the Stockwells' grazing lands. Turning, she drops into a chair at the kitchen table, and glances over at Mrs Merritt and Mary clutching their beakers of barley tea, whisps of steam spiralling upwards.

'It's good to sit down.' Mrs Merritt stretches, crosses her legs and reclines in the high-backed chair.

Mary copies her. 'Aye.'

They've still to do the supper, clear the parlour and set upstairs properly for bed, but none of that needs to be done right now.

The back door opens. It's Douglas: he tends to the garden, looks after the horses and mends the cart. He looks at the trio around the table. 'Must be nice living a life of leisure,' he quips.

'I'd know precious little of that, ya cheeky monkey,' Mrs Merritt bats back. 'Gelly, pet, get Dougie tea and some o' that stew in the pot.'

Gelly gets up and walks to the huge fireplace, the top of which towers a good head above her. Cloth in hand, she pulls the warming pot of stew that dangles from an iron arm towards her. She looks around; a ladle is hanging from the hook by the side of the fireplace.

'Here,' Douglas says, handing it to her together with a wooden bowl.

'Thanks.' Gelly fills his bowl. 'There.'

He pulls up a chair next to Gelly and she places a tankard of tea in front of him. He nods. 'That's appreciated, lass.' He leans back in his chair. 'There's four, maybe five – I didn't get a proper look – horses tied to that hitching post just past the gate.' He takes a sip of barley tea. 'Ah, now, that's good.'

'Really?' Mrs Merritt narrows her eyes. 'The master's not expecting anyone.'

'Maybe it's not for the master,' Dougie offers while chewing a tough bit of beef.

'And who else would it be for? Who else is around here?'

He shrugs.

Gelly gets up and stretches. 'I'll get started on the veg.'

'Aye, well, I suppose…' Mrs Merritt looks into the drained contents of her tankard and places her palms on the table to push herself up when there are three loud bangs at the front door. The four look at each other and Mary's eyes widen.

'You go,' Mrs Merritt instructs her. Mary looks terrified.

'I'll go' says Gelly.

'No. Mary, you go, love. Put your pinny on.'

Mary gulps, her voice quivering. 'Yes, Mrs Merritt.'

\*\*\*

Mary stops in the hallway to straighten her pinny. She notices a stain and twists it to the side, hoping whoever's at the door won't tell Mrs Seton. The front door is heavy and the catch often sticks, which is why she hates answering it – that, and because she never knows how to greet Mr Seton's fancy guests even when Mrs Merritt's told her a million times.

'You've to say, "Good evening, gentlemen, ladies. The master and mistress are waiting for you in the parlour. May I take your cloaks?" Have you got that, Mary?'

Mary would nod but when the time came, she'd just stare wide-eyed and simply say, 'Mr Seton's in the parlour.'

But this time the master is not in the parlour; he isn't waiting for them because he isn't expecting anyone. She resolves to say, 'Good evening, I'll get the master.' Yes, that should be fine.

Heaving open the door, she comes face to face with five men. She recognises the minister, Reverend McLaren, but she's never seen the others before. One is a handsome gentleman, with his head slightly turned looking at the garden. Mary has never seen the like of his clothes, not anywhere, not even on Mr Seton, not even at the schoolmaster's wedding feast.

The man is wearing a beige doublet cinched at the waist and trimmed with gold at the shoulder cuffs and edges where the jacket sits on his plush, dark-blue pantaloons. The sleeves of his shirt are a paler shade of azure, making a pleasing contrast. Small, matching white ruffs poke out of his collar and cuffs. The ensemble is topped with a petite black-velvet hat that sits jauntily on the side of his head with a thin cobalt blue ribbon tied around the rim and a matching feather protruding from the back.

She can hardly take her eyes off him. Not much older than twenty-eight years, with an immaculate pointed beard, he is everything Mary imagines is aristocratic or even royal. She gulps. 'G-g-good day, sir. Yes, sir?'

The gentleman turns to face her, looking somewhere above her head. 'Is your master at home?'

She doesn't recognise the accent. 'Aye, sir.' Her fingers are firmly gripped around the door frame.

'Let us in, girl. We have business with him.'

'Yes, sir, o–of course, sir,' she says, as if waking from a dream. She opens the door wider to admit the group. 'Please come in, sirs. I'll get the master.'

'Tell him Commissioner Baxter, Sheriff MacKay and the Reverend McLaren are here to see him on the king's business.' He doesn't introduce the other two men flanking the trio, attired in matching plain black waistcoats with brown breeches and sturdy black leather boots. They look ahead impassively, their gaze unwavering.

'The king's business?' Mary gasps.

'Yes, yes. Stop standing with your mouth hanging open. Go get your master. Now!'

Mary runs off, leaving the men stranded in the hall.

\*\*\*

Commissioner Baxter takes the lead. 'Reverend McLaren, you have been here before?'

'Certainly. If you'll permit me, gentlemen.' Reverend McLaren walks past the sheriff and Commissioner Baxter to a door at the end of the hall and turns the handle. 'I'm sure that Mr

Seton, the master of the house, would want his guests to be made comfortable in here.'

The commissioner enters first and takes in the furnishings. Well-to-do, middling countryfolk, he surmises. The surroundings are comfortable but neither lavish nor fashionable.

The reverend heads to the cabinet at the back of the room where there is a decanter and glasses. He is about to offer them refreshments when Mr Seton bursts into the room, a little breathless. He looks from the minister to the sheriff to the commissioner and the guards. 'Gentlemen, you are welcome. I– I wasn't expecting such guests. I–I have little to offer.' His eyes lock onto the minister's enquiring gaze. Reverend McLaren gives him a little smile.

'Forgive me, Mr Seton, but the king's business can be dangerous work. Traitors, Catholics, the Devil, you know.' The commissioner paces into the centre of the room as if it were a stage.

'Catholics?' Mr Seton stutters.

'The Devil,' the minister adds. 'We must all be on the lookout.'

'Aye, I suppose that's true,' Mr Seton stammers.

The commissioner turns to the minister. 'Perhaps the good reverend might honour us with introductions.'

'Commissioner.' Reverend McLaren steps forward and bows. 'Mr Seton, may I present Commissioner Robert Baxter.' The commissioner inclines his head to the host. 'Commissioner, may I present Mr Seton.'

'I am pleased to make your acquaintance, sir. Welcome to my home.' Mr Seton nods respectfully, his hands folded over each other in front of him.

The minister continues, 'And you know Sheriff MacKay.'

'Indeed. Good afternoon, sheriff. I am glad you are here. I have something for you.' Mr Seton walks over to the bureau at the window and opens a drawer. He takes out a thin scroll and hands it to the sheriff. 'I think this should settle the dispute.'

***

The sheriff accepts the document. 'Thank you, Mr Seton, and good afternoon. I am sorry for troubling you at such short notice.' The sheriff is a tall man in his late thirties with thick fair hair.

Having been the local lawman for just over five years, he's mainly attended to settling petty misdemeanours and neighbourly squabbles, usually over land and disputed boundaries. Nothing like this.

He is respected for being objective and fair-minded, and famous for never once having taken a bribe. Unlike other sheriffs, his presence is usually highly desired among disputing parties because he puts both sides at ease. He is very conscious of how he dresses and the impression it conveys. He doesn't want to look too lavish, so that he can show some camaraderie with the ordinary folk. Yet he cannot appear too common, as this would suggest there was no distinction.

On this occasion, he has chosen a finely woven black-woollen doublet capped at the shoulders and pulled in at the waist with a black leather belt. The sleeves of his linen shirt are beige with grey horizontal stripes. Although he wears a ruff around his neck like the other gentlemen, it is far smaller than the commissioner's and only just peeps over his collar.

'You are welcome, sheriff. Anything I can do to help an officer of the law,' Mr Seton replies. 'Please, gentlemen, be seated. May I offer you refreshments? A little claret, perhaps?'

He is about to head out the door when the reverend interrupts. 'Please, let me see to it. If you'll permit me, Mr Seton, I'll attend to the beverages to ward off the chill in a moment.'

Mr Seton sits back down.

'Now,' says the commissioner, 'we've had disturbing reports about a serving lass of yours.' He sits back in his chair and gazes levelly at Mr Seton, his expression blank. 'Naturally, as the head of the household it is only fitting we ask you some questions first.'

Mr Seton stiffens. 'What sort of questions?'

'There have been reports of miracle healings,' the commissioner says with a piercing stare.

Mr Seton shoots the reverend a look. 'Aye, well, the minister, Reverend McLaren here, came and asked Gelly a lot of questions…'

The commissioner smooths the front of his doublet. 'He wasn't satisfied.'

'She didn't deny it. In fact, she was quite … unrepentant,' the reverend adds.

'Where is she?' enquires the sheriff. Before this day Sheriff MacKay had never met Commissioner Baxter, but heard he was an ambitious young man with the ear of the king.

He gives the commissioner a sideways glance. Why is this dandy so interested in the mutterings of this little corner of Scotland? Why is he so cagey? Where the conversation is heading the sheriff doesn't rightly know, but something akin to a cockroach crawls in the pit of his stomach.

'I am not sure,' Mr Seton says. 'There are chores to be done… In the kitchen, perhaps, upstairs – or she may be in town on an errand. Mrs Merritt, our cook, is in charge of the lassies.'

The commissioner interlaces his hands and places them on his abdomen. 'You can send for her presently but first, Mr Seton, tell us about this Gellis Duncan. How long has she been in your employ?'

'About three months.'

'And what sort of employee has she been?'

'She is a hard worker and I believe very helpful in the kitchen. Mrs Seton seems happy with her service,' he says cautiously.

'Has there been anything that's … mmm … that's perhaps concerned you about her behaviour?' The commissioner raises his eyebrows. 'Anything odd or unusual?'

'No, well… I–I … can't think…' Mr Seton stumbles.

The minister jumps into the conversation. 'John, if I might address you as a friend.'

The sheriff's shoulders tighten and his right hand forms a fist. The room is silent, except for the crackling and occasional pop of the fire.

'It might not be prudent for anyone close to Gellis Duncan to hide something that … that, well, turns out later to be … incriminating. Do you see?' Mr Seton stares blankly at him. 'She could be part of – part of a large network of…' The churchman glances at the commissioner, who, with the tiniest nod, signals his approval. The sheriff looks from one to the other. The reverend continues, his eyes locking on to Mr Seton's. 'Witches.'

'Witches!' Mr Seton jumps up and the sheriff steps forward.

'Let's not jump to conclusions.' The commissioner holds up his hand and continues in a more placatory tone. 'We don't know, do we? That's what we're here to find out.'

Taking his cue from the commissioner, Reverend McLaren resumes evenly, 'We don't know who might be implicated – neighbours, friends. It is such a terrible business, witchcraft.' He shakes his head, sighs, looks at his hands in his lap. 'His Grace, God bless the king...' The others join in, 'God bless the king!' Bowing his head respectfully, McLaren continues '...has given us his full authority. He is taking a personal interest.'

'The king?' Mr Seton says breathlessly.

A mass like a pebble from the beach catches in the sheriff's throat making him cough.

'Quite so.' Commissioner Baxter says. 'So if there has been anything unusual in the maid's behaviour, it would be best if you spoke of it. Perhaps some brandy would help.'

# Chapter Twenty-Two

An Arrest
North Berwick

The reverend pours a goblet of brandy from the decanter in the cabinet and hands it to Mr Seton. He takes it, twisting the stem, the brown liquid glowing amber with red and gold flecks from the firelight. He gulps it. His throat and gullet are on fire but his stomach has strangely softened.

Staring past the commissioner, he sees his own reflection in the window and the shadows of fir trees encircling the gardens beyond. Should he tell them? Should he say he saw her running down the lane in front of the house into the woods in the middle of the night? Would it get his household tied up in something? But if he didn't tell, would it be worse? If it came out later, they'd all look guilty, be implicated.

'Mr Seton.' The commissioner's voice brings him back.

'Well … one night…'

The commissioner and minister lean forward.

'I couldn't sleep. It was a bright moon…'

The sheriff stands next to the window, looking out.

'Please continue,' the commissioner gently encourages him.

'I heard a noise, like someone quietly closing a door, like they … like they were…'

'Sneaking out,' Minister McLaren interjects.

The sheriff turns back from the window. 'Reverend, please. Let Mr Seton tell it in his own words.'

The minister leans back and rests his hands on his lap.

'It is as the reverend says,' Mr Seton continues, breathing out. 'As if they were sneaking out, aye. I looked out the window and saw Gelly – Gellis Duncan – running down the front path and into the forest.'

'What time was this?' the sheriff asks.

'Around two.'

'How do you know?' the lawman wants to know.

'The moon was bright. I saw a shadow fall across the lunar dial.'

'And you confronted her?' the sheriff presses.

'Aye, I did that.'

'And?'

'Said she was feeling sick, went for a walk to the bridge.'

Reverend McLaren lets out a 'humph'.

'When did she get back?' The commissioner squints, rubbing the tip of his finger along his lower lip.

'She never returned... Well, I didn't see her.'

Commissioner Baxter leans forward. 'Where could she have been going in the middle of the night? What business could she have had? This is a serious affair, Mr Seton, very serious indeed, what with the threats to His Grace's person.'

'The king?' Mr Seton notes it is the second time His Majesty's name has been mentioned, but he cannot fathom why one of his servants could in any way be implicated with doings remotely connected to His Majesty King James VI. 'I'm sorry, sir, but I really don't understand. What can Gelly Duncan possibly have to do with His Grace?'

The commissioner opens his mouth as the door creaks open. Reverend McLaren jumps then leans over to brush an invisible speck of dust from his hose. Two figures appear in the doorway: Mrs Seton and her companion, Miss Simpson.

Mrs Seton grabs her friend's arm to steady herself and places her palm under her collarbone. The men stand.

\*\*\*

She looks around the room. The reverend she knows well, the striking sheriff she knows in passing, but the finely dressed gentleman wearing the height of the capital's fashion is unknown to her.

Mrs Seton has planned a cosy tête-à-tête before supper with Miss Simpson. Her companion has some intriguing news about the Foresters – Mr Forester, to be precise – and Mrs Cunningham. But that will have to wait.

'Oh ... good day, gentlemen. My apologies, I did not know we had company.' Still in the doorway, she looks uncertainly at her husband. 'Good day, Reverend. Good day, Sheriff.'

The sheriff steps away from the window. 'Good day, Mrs Seton. We are sorry to arrive unexpectedly.'

'That's quite all right, Sheriff MacKay.' She searches her husband's face for guidance. 'May I offer you some refreshments. Barley tea? Something stronger? Please be seated, I beg you.'

'Thank you,' Commissioner Baxter says, sitting back down. 'But we are here on business. We may partake of refreshments after our business is concluded. The ride from Edinburgh was arduous and our horses need attention.'

'Of course, gentlemen.' Mr Seton quickly gets to his feet.

'But that can wait for a few more moments. Let us conclude our business here first. Now, if you'll permit—'

'Business?' Mrs Seton asks, frozen in the doorway.

Mr Seton walks over to his wife, unwinds her arm from her companion and guides her into the room. 'Forgive me, dearest. This is Commissioner Baxter, an official of the royal court and Privy Council.'

Her palm once again springs to her chest. 'Royal court! My goodness. Good day, Commissioner Baxter. If I had known you were coming—'

'That's quite all right, dear.' Mr Seton pats her arm reassuringly.

'Good day, Mrs Seton. It's a pleasure to make your acquaintance,' Commissioner Baxter says, rising. 'The nature of our business required that we were not able, alas, to give notice.'

Reverend McLaren coughs. 'Is Gelly – Gellis Duncan – in the house?'

'Gelly? I think so.' Mrs Seton squeezes her husband's arm.

'We'd be obliged if you could send for her.' The commissioner remains standing and rubs his finger along the ledge of the fireplace.

'You have business with Gelly?' she asks, gawping.

'The king's business,' the reverend exclaims.

Mrs Seton's knees almost buckle. 'The king's business!' she gasps.

'All right, Reverend,' the sheriff snaps. 'Mrs Seton,' he adds gently, 'if you would please send for the maid.'

'Of course, Sheriff MacKay.' Taking hold of the door handle, Mrs Seton prepares to leave but in turning around she almost treads on Miss Simpson's foot. 'Good grief, Susan! My apologies,' she says to the room and ushers out her friend. 'I would take it as the greatest favour if you didn't say a word of this to anyone,' she whispers when they reach the hall.

'Of course, dearest. I am the soul of discretion.' Miss Simpson looks at the closed door. 'I will be as silent as the grave.'

Mrs Seton sighs: it'll be all round town by sunset, then.

A small movement catches her eye: it is Mary at the foot of the stairs, staring, open-mouthed, wringing her hands. She must have been here all this time. 'Mary, what are you doing there?' Mrs Seton says, irritated. 'Oh, it doesn't matter.' She waves her hand. 'Tell Gelly she's wanted in the parlour. Now.'

Mary still doesn't move.

'Now, Mary!'

'Yes, ma'am. Sorry, ma'am.' Mary takes off down the hall in the direction of the kitchen.

'So hard to get good servants, isn't it?' Miss Simpson says, looking after her.

'I'm beginning to think so, Susan.'

\*\*\*

Carrots, turnips, potatoes, apples and oats now replace the beakers and bowls on the kitchen table. Gelly stands chopping the vegetables into wedges and cubes. Mrs Merritt is bent over the fire, stirring and inspecting a pot of stew. Her nephew, Tom, a boy of six or seven years, sits by the edge of the table closest to the fire.

'Here.' Gelly tosses him half an apple. He bites into it with a loud crunch. She smiles to see the juice dribbling down his chin.

Mary bursts into the room like a typhoon. 'You're wanted in the parlour!'

Gelly looks up. 'Me? Why?'

'I don't know. But you've to go now, right now!' Panic is rising in her voice.

Mrs Merritt stands up. 'Wait! Who was there, Mary? Did you hear what they said? The master never has visitors at this hour.' She goes to Gelly and stands beside her.

'No... Well, a bit, aye,' Mary replies, wringing her apron.
'The reverend and sheriff are there—'
'The sheriff?' Gelly's heart jolts. 'Mrs Merritt, why's the sheriff there? I haven't done anything! I haven't done anything wrong, honest!'
'I know, love, I know. Mary, who else is there, and what did they say?'
'Well, there was another gentleman – I don't know who he was. He was posh, Mrs Merritt, I mean, really posh, said he came from the king – the king's business or something!'
'The king's business!' Mrs Merritt stares at Gelly. 'Right. Gelly, put that knife down. Wash your hands and go. Watch what you say. Don't say anything.'
Little Tom's lips have formed an 'O' and the juicy apple he was enjoying a minute ago is suspended in front of his mouth as if his arm has petrified.
Her heart pounding, Gelly shoots Mrs Merritt a nervous look. She tries to think of anything she might have done, any little transgressions she could apologise for, promise she'll never do again, but she can't think of any ... except ... except for that night.
A few moments later, Gelly is outside the parlour door. What if she dashed out of the front door and never came back? She could do that. No, it'll be nothing. She'll just apologise and keep putting her pennies away, like Agnes.
She blows all the air out of her lungs, wraps her fingers round the handle and opens the door. As she steps through, she stops when she sees the men Mary had spoken of – the reverend sitting by the fire and a man in fine clothes opposite him. Mrs Seton is seated between them. The tall man by the window is probably the sheriff. Maggie pointed him out at a fair last year, but Gelly has never actually met him.
She is vaguely aware of two guards standing at the back of the room some ten feet apart. She feels the warm, hard door handle in her palm behind her, her fingers gently clasped around it. She could still run, couldn't she?
'Come in, Gelly,' says Mr Seton.
Gelly steps in a little further but leaves the door ajar. She senses little Tom behind her; he must have followed her up. With

her palm still behind, she spreads her fingers as if to push him away.

The commissioner looks her up and down. 'So you are Gellis Duncan?'

'Gelly, this is Commissioner Baxter, officer of the Privy Council to His Grace King James,' Mr Seton begins. 'You know the Reverend McLaren.'

'Yes, sir. How do you do, sir.' She curtsies to the minister and commissioner.

'And this is Sheriff MacKay. I don't believe you are acquainted.'

'No, sir. Good day, sir.'

'Good day, Miss Duncan,' the sheriff replies politely.

The commissioner stands. 'Miss Duncan, there have been some serious accusations against you.'

'I… I… I'm sorry… I don't know… There's been some mistake.'

'Gelly, just listen to the commissioner and answer his questions truthfully. Remember, God is watching you.' Reverend McLaren raises himself higher in the chair.

'You were seen sneaking from this house in the early hours of the morning on Candlemas Eve. Mr Seton saw you hurrying down the lane and into the forest and you didn't return before daybreak. Where did you go? Whom did you meet?' the commissioner demands.

Gelly tries to get her mouth and brain to form some words. 'I … I … was sick.'

'Really? We'll see if you have more to say at Tranent gaol,' the commissioner announces, tightening his belt and crooking his finger to the guards at the back of the room.

The sheriff turns his head sharply.

Mr Seton stands too. 'Commissioner, is that necessary?'

Gelly's head swims and her knees threaten to buckle. She stumbles forward but recovers before the guards reach her. They position themselves on either side of her. Still clinging to the edge of the door, little Tom's eyes have grown wide like plates of black jet.

Mrs Seton gasps for breath and places her palm on the centre of her chest, her upper ribcage heaving up and down. She lists slightly to the side like a grand sailing ship caught momentarily off guard by a sudden swell. Mr Seton rushes over, takes her other hand and starts to pat it vigorously. But the Reverend McLaren remains calm, gazing levelly at the commissioner as if the gathering were enjoying a little light conversation after dinner. He cradles his hands in his lap.

'Gellis Duncan.' The commissioner faces her. 'I arrest you on behalf of King James VI of Scotland on the charge of witchcraft, of consorting in a coven with the Devil to instigate the downfall of His Grace and perpetuate the evil that stalks this country. Come with us.'

One of the soldiers taps Gelly's elbow. She looks at it uncomprehendingly as if it were no longer part of her body but a curious foreign object. She hears a soft gasp escape. Was that her? She looks down. Wee Tom's face is alabaster and his eyes dark pools ready to overflow. 'Get help,' she mouths.

***

Slowly and silently, Tom edges his way from the doorway, unnoticed by the rest of the adults. He runs like an arrow down the hall, through the kitchen and towards the back door.

'Tom!' Mrs Merritt calls as he flies past.

'Can't stop, Aunt Janet! I've got to get… She told me to … as fast as I can … 'cause I'm a fast runner … if anything happened…' He dashes out the door.

'Wait! Who told you? Tom! Tom!' Mrs Merritt shakes her head.

But he is already on the lane leading to the woods, running as hard as he can along the river bank. He is one of the best runners at the parish school; in all the races he always comes first or is beaten by a much older boy.

He stops at a junction where the path meets an overgrown track heading into the thicket. Breathing heavily, he takes several deep breaths before running up the dense track that takes him away from the river. In the distance he catches a glimpse of the cottage through the trees. It looks like a patch of white.

As he draws nearer, a real construction comes into view, large stones piled one on top of the other, with two small square windows cut into the thick walls that let in a little light but, more importantly, keep out the cold. Topped by a thatch of twigs, reeds and an assortment of grasses, the house is well hidden even though it is in a slightly elevated position.

Tom's thighs are beginning to burn as he races up the path to the sky-blue door, but before he can lift his fist to bang on it, he stops, gasping. Bending over, hands pressed against his thighs, he takes in several deep breaths, blowing out through pursed lips, a technique Mother Sampson taught him when he was feeling jittery.

He straightens, allows his juddering breath to become more even and shouts. 'Mother Sampson! Mother Sampson! Mother Agnes!'

Agnes appears from the side of the cottage. 'All right, all right, I'm coming.'

'You've got to help her, Mother Sampson.' He is trembling and on the verge of tears.

'Tom, what is it? Come in and sit down. I'll make you a soothing brew.'

'They've taken her away.' He sniffs. 'They've taken her away. The men!'

'They've taken who, Tom? Who's taken who?'

'Gelly! Miss Duncan!'

'Gelly? What for?'

'Witchcraft. Con ... consor... Playing with the Devil!'

'Oh, dear God.' Agnes drops the twigs she's cradling. Tom rushes to pick them up. 'Leave them,' she says, recovering. 'Where is she, Tom?'

Tom shrugs. His eyes well up and his arms hang limply by his sides.

'It's all right, Tom, you did well. You did right. Wait there.' Agnes goes inside and retrieves her shawl. 'Let's go.'

# Part II

# Chapter Twenty-Three

No Going Back
The Latin Quarter, Paris

'I am so sorry, Assen. I know how close you were, how much you loved your Uncle Manny, your aunt … and your cousins. I'm really very sorry.'

Gérard and Assen are standing outside a medieval church not far from Uncle Manny's house, the church where he and Aunt Charlotte were married, and Émile and little Joséphine were baptised.

Assen has the vaguest of memories of the wedding; he must have been four, maybe five. There was endless sitting down and standing up while a man talked to his aunt and uncle at the front, just under the *altar*, as his mother called it. She also told him to stop fidgeting, but he'd been so bored.

He'd seen his friend Robert across the aisle a few rows behind. Pulling faces to each other had relieved some of the boredom but also resulted in several snorts of laughter, at which his father had given him a withering stare of disapproval. In a fierce whisper, Mr Verey warned, 'Assen! Eyes forward. Behave, or straight to bed when we get home.'

Assen had turned forward, sighed and folded his arms, but not for long. Looking up and down, he'd noticed the intricate carvings and detail around the church. His eyes settled on a stained-glass window; he knew that was Jesus. Jesus was going up a hill and there were two boys behind him. Who were the two boys? He would ask Mother: she would know. He was just about to tug at her sleeve, when…

'Assen? Assen? Are you all right?' Gérard is staring into his friend's face.

Assen is leaning back against the wall, gazing at the churchyard, looking past the detailing on the headstones and simple wooden crosses. Other people begin to stream out, shielding their eyes. It isn't a particularly bright day but the daylight is a stark contrast to the gloom inside.

'Yes, yes, of course.' He shakes himself, scattering his memories.

'The mass was beautiful,' Gérard says. 'Will you visit the graveside? I will come with you, if you like?'

'What? Oh, yes ... yes, I'll go. I tended to them when they were living, and I'll tend to them now they are dead. But please, good friend, don't come. It is not safe. Please, only go where you must. It seems strange that their earthly bodies cannot be present here in the church for the funeral service.' He gestures back inside. 'But,' he continues, 'must be in the ground days before it.'

'It's just the times, Assen, the pestilence. They have to do that.'

'I know, I know. It was a beautiful mass, wasn't it? Aunt Lottie would have... It was her favourite...' A lump the size of a small apple lodges in his throat. How can a wedding, baptisms and a funeral have come so close together?

Assen's father is one of the last to come out, hat in hand. Blinking, he stands on the steps of the chapel. Gérard steps forward and bows deeply. 'Mr Verey, I am sorry for your loss. A great loss for the city.'

Putting on his hat, Mr Verey acknowledges him. 'Thank you, Gérard – Dr Xavier.' He looks at Assen but says nothing and walks on.

Gérard raises his eyebrows. 'We had words,' Assen says with a half-hearted laugh. 'He thinks I defied him, went against his will.'

'He's just scared, scared he'll lose you as well. I've noticed that fear often comes out as anger.'

Assen's head drops.

Gérard continues. 'There was nothing more you could have done. You did everything you knew how to.'

'I could have done more, I'm sure of it.' Every night since that day, Assen has gone over every detail as he goes to bed, checking and double-checking the ingredients and the amounts for each phial. He is sure he followed the recipe to the letter, but did he miss something? There must have been something else, but what? And so, the wheel tumbles on as he wracks his brains each night.

As if reading his mind, Gérard pats him on the back. 'No one knows why some people live, and some don't. There isn't a magic elixir or Holy Grail,' he says softly.

\*\*\*

A vision of a tiny village high in the mountains close to the Swiss border forms in Gérard's mind. A dramatic landscape of mighty firs and white-tipped peaks beyond, creating the illusion of a theatrical backdrop.

But there was more to his time in Switzerland than stunning scenery; something happened there he's told no one about, not even Assen. He glances at his friend. Would it help him now? Would he even believe him?

\*\*\*

Assen continues, his mind whirling. 'I want to know! They shouldn't have gone. I … we … we physicians should have saved them – our medicine *should* have saved them! There was something else. I know there was something else.'

'We are not gods,' Gérard says.

Assen doesn't hear. 'We just need the right medicine, something that works for everyone, that cures everyone of this pestilence.'

Gérard raises his voice and breaks into his monologue. 'No! That's not how things are!'

Assen looks up for the first time.

His friend is looking straight at him, his eyes burning. '*We* don't cure; we *can't* cure,' Gérard continues emphatically. 'The patient has to cure himself. You support him, you help, you encourage. But you give yourself and our profession too much credit … *and* responsibility … and … and you give them no hope when there's nothing you – we – *medicine* can do.'

'We'll see.' Assen fastens his cloak.

'Where are you going?'

'To find the Holy Grail.'

'Oh, Lord.' Gérard shakes his head and looks up.

# Chapter Twenty-Four

The Gathering Tempest
North Berwick

Agnes bursts through the back door, bringing a squall of wind and rain like the goddess of thunder. Little Tom is bedraggled in her wake. Mrs Merritt, Mary, Douglas and another male servant, Ian, are sitting round the farmhouse table talking excitedly about the events of the last hour.

She just catches Ian saying he's never seen anything like it in all the years he's been in service. He's worked all over Scotland for the highest echelons of the aristocracy, as well as in the homes of merchants and sea captains in Edinburgh. 'You should have seen it!' he is saying animatedly as Agnes appears. 'The mistress's gone to bed with a headache. She won't be out before dawn.'

'What happened?' Agnes asks, trying to catch her breath as she places both hands on the table and leans over.

'They took her away like a criminal,' Mrs Merritt's voice trembles. 'Poor wee lass.'

Douglas gets up, his chair scraping along the floor, and walks to a chair next to Mary and Gelly's box bed. It is strewn with drying kitchen cloths. He picks them up, sets them down neatly by the fireplace and draws the chair in towards the table for Agnes. 'Thank you,' she says gratefully and sinks into it. 'Why?' she asks as she looks around the table.

Mrs Merritt shakes her head, her hands clasped around a tankard of cold tea.

'Witchcraft, they said. In league with the Devil.' Ian had been heading back to the kitchen from attending to the horses – someone said a fox had been prowling around – when he'd heard the commotion. Hiding in a dark corner under the stairs, he heard everything. 'It's the healings, as well. Folk calling them miracles and all.'

Agnes looks at the table. Mary has just placed a hot beaker of camomile tea in her hands. She twists it around, her heart racing. 'Did they ask about anyone else?' How far has this gone? How far will it go? Is it just for show, to show how far the rule of law can reach in the countryside? A slap on the wrist, a warning to others, and yet—

Agnes's stomach churns. It reminds her of... No, she can't think of that now.

Ian shrugs. 'One o' them asked where she went tae in the middle of the night, who she met.'

'Aye?' Agnes's throat tightens.

'Folk should keep their mouth shut,' Douglas barks.

Agnes smiles. Douglas has always had a soft spot for Gelly. 'Aye, I ken. Where did they take her?'

'Tranent.' Ian rubs his chin.

'They'll let her go, won't they, Mrs Merritt?' Mary implores, her eyes red and puffy.

'Not if they think the Devil has a hand in it. They'll try and get it out of her,' Ian says authoritatively.

'How? How will they get it out of her?' Mary wipes away a stray tear.

'Hush now, pet, that's enough. It'll be all right.' Mrs Merritt sweeps a stray strand of Mary's hair behind her ear and wipes her cheeks with a cloth she's retrieved from her apron pocket. 'Agnes, will you stay for supper?'

Agnes frowns. 'No, thank you, Mrs Merritt. There's someone I have to see.'

She bids them good evening and heads out the back door, around to the front of the house and down the lane through the woods to the village. It isn't long before she's hurrying along the path by the old stone dyke at the Forbes' place. She's no time to call in; she'll have to see Goodwife Forbes this evening or maybe tomorrow. She wonders how long it will take for the news to spread.

Up ahead, the schoolhouse stands on its own on the edge of town. She bites her lip, there's late schooling tonight and the boys will still be here. The small medieval hall is also used for village celebrations, feasts, festivals and weddings, although there are not so many holy feasts now that the old ways have been swept away. But when there is something to be thankful for, the villagers have been known to have a high old time within the four walls. But not today: there is school today.

***

Eight boys are seated on benches along two long tables, four in front and four behind. One boy is standing at the front, reading from the Bible. The other boys and the schoolmaster, John Fian, his elbow resting on the lectern, are listening quietly.

Most children have an education nowadays, even girls, except perhaps those that live on the farthest flung farms. The church demands they learn to read and write so they can read the Bible for themselves to guide their thoughts and actions. No need for priests to hand down the words of God; ministers are there to make sure their congregations have interpreted scripture in the right God-fearing way.

'Be subject to one another out of reverence for Christ,' the child proclaims. 'Ephesians 5.21,' he confirms. '"For in Jesus Christ you are all children of God through faith… There is neither Jew nor Greek, male nor female, slave nor free, for you are all one in Christ Jesus." Galatians 3: 26 to 28.' The boy stops and looks up.

The schoolmaster stares into space, his eyes unblinking. The rest of the class look at each other, the silence alive with tension. The branch of a tree taps persistently at the window.

'Sir?' A voice cuts through the fog of John's thoughts.

He emerges. 'Very good, Duncan, very good. Thank you.'

Duncan hovers, rocking from one foot to the other, looking at the empty space that was his seat. Meekly he ventures, 'Sir?'

'What? Oh, yes, yes, you may be seated.' The master draws himself up from his elbow. 'So, what are we to make of this? We were studying Aristotle last week, were we not? What does Aristotle have to say on this subject?'

A fair-haired boy in the front row shoots up his hand. 'Sir!' John Fian nods and the boy stands. 'The worst form of inequality is to try to make unequal things equal, sir.' He sits back down.

'Sir!' The hand of another boy shoots up.

'Go ahead, Matthew.'

Getting to his feet, the boy says, 'Equality exists in the same treatment of similar persons, sir.'

He is about to sit down when the schoolmaster enquires, 'Ah, but what if the persons are not similar? What does the Bible say…' Out the corner of his eye, John Fian glimpses a cloaked woman hurrying along the path towards the school. There is an urgency in her steps, and he knows exactly who she is. He has to get rid of the boys.

'Boys, I'd like you to think about how our Lord Jesus Christ guides us in behaving towards our family, neighbours *and* strangers, and how this differs from the advice of Aristotle. You may leave now to ponder this further and be ready to discuss it in detail tomorrow.'

The boys turn to each other and chat excitedly. They've never known school to finish early.

'Gather your things. Be back here bright and early tomorrow morning with your answers,' he says.

They scoop up their bits and pieces and make a mad dash for the door. 'Boys! Single file! You are not a herd of cattle!' John shouts.

A calmness descends on the children, a subconscious awareness they may be called back if they don't leave in a more orderly fashion. They file past the hooded figure entering the hall, barely acknowledging her.

Once they're gone, the woman pulls down her hood and unties her cloak. 'You've heard?' Agnes begins.

'Aye.'

'She hasn't told them.' She runs her fingers along the pupils' bench.

'No?' John steps away from the lectern and faces her.

'She said she felt queasy and went out for a walk. I don't think they believed her – I *know* they didn't.'

'I'll go to McLaren.' John walks past her and lifts his coat from the row of pegs by the door.

'And say what? Add adultery to witchcraft? You'll be nae help to her if you get arrested as well. She needs a lawyer, a minister, someone tae speak for her, someone they'll listen to – someone they'll *have* to listen to.'

'Aye. Aye … you're right.' He sighs. 'I'll go to Edinburgh right now. Brodie's a good man – mind that poor soul at Dirleton?'

'You need to hurry.'

# Chapter Twenty-Five

A New Treatment
St Marcel's Plague Hospital

Assen walks purposefully into the great hall of St Marcel's. It is exactly as he left it. Patients are still lying in beds along its two walls, with its tall, narrow windows towering above, yet everything feels different, foreign, as if he's just returned from years abroad. But it's only been a week; strange how grief warps time.

A light flashes inside his head and he reaches for the pillar to steady himself.

Gérard is seated in the middle of the hall talking with a patient under one of the great windows. As Assen approaches him, a look of surprise and concern crosses his face. 'Assen, dear friend.' He gets to his feet and pats the patient on the hand. 'You're looking much better, Mr Milne. You'll be out of here in a couple of days and on the next ship home by the end of the week. You've done very well. Do you understand?'

The man nods. 'Yes,' he says in a strong Scottish accent.

Gérard cocks his ear and looks at him uncertainly. 'Good ... good.'

He steps away from the bed and takes Assen by the elbow, out of earshot of the patients. 'He's a merchant from Scotland, Aberdeen, I think. Took ill at the dockside, made a very handsome donation to the hospital. Speaks good French, but his accent is strong.' He studies his friend. 'What are you doing here? I thought you were taking some time off. You should rest, you know.'

Assen looks at the vaulted ceiling. 'I've rested enough,' he says emphatically. When he closes his eyes, it's always the same. *What else could I have done? I should never have left. If I had been there, could I have saved them? No! It was this evil pestilence; no one could have saved them. And yet, maybe I should have made the theriac more concentrated.* And on it goes.

It is better for him to work, to think about other things and other people. 'I don't need rest, I need to do something.'

He sees that Gérard is studying him. This morning Assen had caught his reflection in the mirror as he left the house and a haunted version of himself stared out from the Venetian glass. There were dark shadows under his eyes and his cheeks were hollower than usual, making his cheekbones look even sharper. But at least he has trimmed his beard to its usual angular shape and his clothes are clean. Maybe that is enough.

'Well…' Gérard relents. 'You'd do more good if you rested first, but you're not going to, are you? Well, you could maybe help with… I mean, it would be some light duties.'

Smiling, Assen takes out two pieces of paper. 'I've seen Pierre.'

'Our apothecary?'

'We're going to do it like we arranged before.' He pauses, shakes his head as if trying to dislodge something. 'I've adjusted the doses according to the patients' height, weight and constitution.' He hands the list to Gérard. 'Mercury, copper sulphate, salt…'

'I was hoping you'd forgotten about that.'

'We'll start off with minute quantities, just as we agreed—' Assen's eyes twinkle '—until we see what dose makes the difference. I don't think I gave Uncle Manny enough, or I gave them too much – there was so little time. I can be more meticulous now. It'll be different this time. We'll make it different.'

'You were meticulous, Assen. You know you were,' Gérard says sympathetically. 'Listen, I don't know… I've been thinking about it and—'

'I have Paracelsus's notes on his discoveries.' Assen takes out a tattered, yellowing manuscript from his satchel. 'Dr Brisbois found it in the Faculty library. It was in a cupboard tucked away in the founders' room, under heaps of astrological charts from fifty, sixty, maybe even a hundred years ago. Anyway, you know the strides he made against the plague before he died. Who knows what else he could have done? What I'm proposing is we do the same as Paracelsus did but in ever smaller doses.'

'For how long?'

'If they show signs of improvement, say, after two days, we maintain the dose until they leave.'

'If they don't?'

Assen looks uncertain. 'I guess we stop.'

'Is two days enough?'

'I don't know, but we have to start somewhere. We'll need to make sure they're very closely monitored. If there are no improvements within a week, we'll stop the whole thing.'

Gérard moves one ear towards his shoulder, then the other, and cracks his neck. He looks from side to side. 'All right. I'll get nurse Brother Benedict to see to it.' As he walks off, he turns. 'You do have Dr Broussard's permission, don't you?'

Assen says nothing.

'Assen?'

# Chapter Twenty-Six

Imprisoned
Tranent Tolbooth, East Lothian, Scotland

'Come in, Miss Duncan, come in. We have been waiting for you,' the commissioner says in a flat, matter-of-fact tone. 'Do you know where you are?'

The gaoler pushes her further into the room and she is surprised to see a spacious hall. She'd thought she'd be thrown into a tiny damp hole. She doesn't know what's worse. 'I … I… It's…' she splutters, her throat tightening.

'It's Tranent Tolbooth, of course. Only the most serious cases, the most dangerous prisoners, come here.'

Iron implements lie scattered around on benches and on a long table at the back below a small, high, rectangular window. For a fleeting moment it reminds Gelly of a farrier's, with a fire glowing in the corner and a hood and flue drawing the smoke and flames upwards. But the stench of burning, iron, urine and excrement binds her intestines like a Celtic knot and stabbing pains shoot across the top of her abdomen.

'There's been a mistake,' she spits out. 'I haven't done anything.'

'In that case,' the commissioner resumes in the same reasonable tone, 'we can clear all this up very quickly after you've answered some questions. Then we can all go home to our beds. Is that not so, Reverend McLaren?'

Gelly hadn't noticed the minister or the other three men. How has she missed them? They're standing to the side of the huge table in the middle of the hall. There is a tall thin man dressed in black, and a large muscular man wearing a leather apron, his rolled-up sleeves dirty with splatters of black and brown. A little apart from the pair, the sheriff is leaning against what appears to be a printing press, at least what she imagines one would look like.

Sweeping his arm across the room, the commissioner asks, 'Do you know what happens here?'

'I... I...' Gelly shakes her head.

'This is where, sometimes...' He walks in front of the table and runs his fingers along the surface, then draws them back sharply as if he's been burned. '... Sometimes the good officers of the law reluctantly have to bring people. It's where we eventually discover the truth, where – how shall we put it? – the guilty eventually relieve themselves.'

'In more ways than one!' the muscular man says with a sarcastic laugh.

'That's enough, Birkett,' the sheriff cuts in, turning to Gelly. 'Where, as the commissioner says, they relieve themselves of their burden if they are burdened.'

'People must admit to their sins if they are to get to heaven,' Reverend McLaren adds. 'If they die telling lies, or not answering truthfully questions put to them by their elders and betters, the fire of hell is waiting for them.'

Searing anger courses through Gelly and she tightens her fists into little balls by her side. She looks at him with pure hatred and contempt. He is behind this; he must be.

The stranger in black steps forward and looks at the commissioner as if asking for permission to speak. He is a tall, thin man of perhaps thirty years, but it is difficult to tell: he could be older or maybe even five years younger. His attire looks a little old-fashioned, not at all like the modern dress the well-off Edinburgh gentlemen were wearing when she was there last.

She'd gone with Agnes to the market under the castle. What a few days that had been. Agnes had told her to always keep her hand on her purse, and more than once Gelly had felt little fingers rifling her pockets. But it was exhilarating, and they'd stayed with an aunt of Agnes's a little way out from the town. Bruntsfield, that was it.

There was a pleasant common across the way and a lovely wee burn that cut through it. She and Agnes would sit on a flat rock by the grove on the opposite side to their lodgings and dip their toes in the water, Agnes far away and Gelly imagining her 'butt and ben'. How she wanted that wee cottage.

But, come to think of it, this gentleman in front of her looks nothing like the gents in Edinburgh or the ones around here. His hair is fair and longer than most men's. His black hat is taller than any she's seen and the brim wider, with no adornment or colour except for a band of faded black. The rest of his clothes are similarly plain: a simple black tunic tied at the waist, brown-black hose and sturdy boots that look as if he has walked great distances.

He comes a little closer to Gelly. 'Of course, they could have been led quite innocently by other people – evil people.'

'Ah, you have not met Mr McPherson,' the commissioner interposes. 'Aye, we've had to draw on the services of Mr McPherson, a most accomplished witchfinder, in this serious and sad matter.'

Gelly looks from the commissioner to the witchfinder. Alarm stretches her eyes wide, a steady drum pulsates in her ears. She tries to swallow but her throat feels like tinder for the fire. 'Are you not going to give me a lawyer?'

'Of course, of course.' The sheriff steps further away from the group. 'We will go through all due process, according to the law.'

'But we don't want this to be a long drawn-out process. You would make your lawyer's job far easier,' the commissioner says evenly, 'and it would go better for you, if you would… You're a young lass and have the weakness of mind seen in many of your sex. People would understand – a court would understand – if you have been led unknowingly. In all probability, they would be lenient.'

Taking up the commissioner's lead, the witchfinder adds softly, 'Let us help you. Perhaps you could tell the commissioner where you went in the middle of the night when your employer saw you sneak off—'

'I didn't sneak off!' Gelly cries. 'I told you I wasn't feeling well. I went for a walk to get some fresh air.'

'Aye, of course, but did you meet anyone? And the healings – we're very interested in those. How did you do them?' The witchfinder brings his index finger to his lips.

Gelly's head is spinning and her legs feel like jelly fresh from Cook's mould. 'It doesn't happen all the time, just sometimes. We do our best … but—'

'We?' The reverend raises his eyebrows. 'Who is "we"? The other members of the coven?'

'What?' Gelly's head is about to explode.

'Did you secretly meet and call up the Devil? Is that where you were going on that moonlit night? Is that who helps you with these so-called healings? Who is the coven leader, Gelly? Is it—'

The commissioner holds up his hand. 'Now, now, Reverend, please. What Reverend McLaren means is that we would like to avoid any – unpleasantness. The good reverend has not the stomach for it. So, if you give us the information we need to capture the coven, it bodes well for you. On the other hand—' he looks over at the man who has been polishing several iron batons, hooks and clamps and placing them neatly on the great table '— Mr Birkett is one of those people who takes great pride in his work. Is that not so, Mr Birkett?'

The man at the table smiles and nods as if they're discussing his last round of golf.

'Think of your soul.' The reverend stares sternly at Gelly.

Unflinchingly, she stares back, her eyes narrowing with contempt.

'Right.' The commissioner slaps his hand on the table. 'Think carefully about our discussion or the next time we meet might not be so … agreeable. Sheriff MacKay, if you would.'

The sheriff opens the door. 'Mr Bryce,' he calls to the waiting guard, 'take Miss Duncan to her cell.'

# Chapter Twenty-Seven

Overwhelmed
St Marcel's Plague Hospital

A bowl slips from the monk's hand and crashes to the floor. The sound reverberates around the hall, the clatter like a dropped pewter collection plate above the din of shouts, screams and moans. St Marcel's is packed, every bed taken, though at least no one is sharing at the moment. The monks and nuns rush to and fro with basins, blankets and cloths.

A young monk stoops to pick up the shattered fragments.

'Don't do it like that, you'll cut yourself. Get a brush from the store and take this.' An older brother hands him a bit of material. Seeing the concerned look on the young monk's face, the older man adds, 'Don't worry; it happens all the time. Don't want to lose another pair of hands, that's all.'

The novice smiles and gets up. 'Yes, Brother Francis, thank you.'

The older brother smiles and shakes his head. It was not so long ago he'd come fresh from the farm, dropping things all over the place – even patients. The abbot would have killed him if he'd known, but he soon got the hang of it and now – well, he wouldn't be anywhere else or do anything else.

He looks around. Dr Verey is tending a patient, a young man. The patient's condition doesn't look good: he doesn't know who he is or where he is, and there is a yellowish tinge to his skin.

Dr Verey doesn't look much better. Brother Francis takes in the dark circles under his eyes and the stubble on his chin. The young doctor looks dishevelled, like one of the pedlars who hang around outside the church.

The monk crosses himself. *God bless them and keep them, and may we be blessed with enough alms to share with them.* Dr Verey is normally immaculately groomed, but who can blame him? These last two weeks have not been easy. Dr Xavier has told him more than once to go home, rest and come back refreshed. But he won't. He's stubborn, Dr Verey. Soon they'll need a bed for him, too. Brother Francis shakes his head.

Looking at the altar, hands cupped in front of him, he bows and then ambles over to the next patient. 'How are you today, Mr Anouilh? Your colour is much better. You'll be out of here in no time.'

Mr Anouilh smiles, his eyes creasing in the corners. 'I'm doing better for seeing you, Brother Francis. Do you have time to read to me?'

'Of course! I have all the time in the world. Now, where were we?' He stoops to pull out a box from under the bed and retrieves a heavy tome from inside it. 'Ephesians 4:3, was it?'

\*\*\*

Two monks enter the hall carrying a stretcher, with two more stretchers behind. 'Where do you want these patients?' one of the stretcher bearers shouts into the hall to no one in particular.

Assen looks up then turns to his patient. 'I'll be back in a moment. I have something else for you. It will make you feel better, but just rest now.'

A weak smile plays on the young man's lips and he closes his eyes. Assen purses his lips and, with a sharp intake of breath, hurries over to the monks with the stretchers. 'You can't bring them in here. There's no room. We're barely able to attend to the patients we have – we can't take any more,' he says, sweeping his hand around the hall.

Gérard rushes forward and places a firm, reassuring hand on Assen's shoulder. 'Take them into the Duplessis Chapel,' he says, taking charge. 'There are blankets in the store and a pot of hot water in the kitchen. Do what you can to clean these unfortunates, then go to the Sisters of Mercy. Tell them we need their help.'

'Thank you, Dr Xavier,' the first stretcher bearer replies. 'This way,' he adds, half turning to his companion behind. He leads the procession in a straight line past the altar, through the great oak door and into the Duplessis Chapel.

'Our experiments aren't working. It's completely random.' Assen runs his hand over his hair. 'It makes no sense. I don't know why some are getting better and so many are not. Maybe you were right.'

'About what?' Gérard says, taking out a scroll of parchment, the apothecary's list, from his doublet and studying it.

'Maybe it's just God's will.' Assen sighs. 'Maybe there's nothing we can do. Maybe everything we learnt, all the money that went into our education, was wasted and we can't help anyone. Maybe it was God's will that Uncle Manny, Aunt Charlotte, Émile and little Joséphine all died,' he says bitterly.

'No … no … wait,' Gérard says haltingly, placing the list back in his pocket. 'We've been looking in the wrong places. I've seen people get better. I've seen them recovering from the plague. Some did … some *do*. Good grief, *I* did!'

Assen's rage recedes like a wave drawn back out to sea, replaced by curiosity. 'What did you do exactly? What did you take?'

'Nothing to speak of. Nothing in our texts. Remember I was in a remote village on the Swiss border. The villagers left me teas, hot soup, food on the doorstep … you know. But while I was lying there, whenever I woke up staring at the beams, I just… I thought I had so much left to do, so much I wanted to do. I couldn't die … I couldn't die before I did that … and…' He bites his bottom lip. 'Don't laugh.'

'I'm not laughing.'

Gérard's face flushes. 'Look, I know we're educated physicians, students of the famous Paris Faculty of Medicine, trained in method, history-taking, astrology and anatomy. We're not back-street healers and sorcerers, and yet…' He swallows. 'I prayed, fervently…' Laughing nervously, he continues, 'I promised I would devote my life to the sick if I ever rose again. And the dreams I had … the places I went. I've seen things, wonderful things.' He draws himself up. 'It must have been the fever, but it changed me.'

Assen searches his friend's face. 'Are you saying it was your prayer, your own will, that healed you?'

'All I'm saying is that getting better is about a lot more than taking potions and pills.'

'Hmm.' Assen draws his hand from his chin and strokes his neck.

'Look out!' Gérard whispers.

Assen turns. 'Shit!' Dr Broussard has entered the hall through the door at the back, clutching sheets of parchment. Brother Benedict is at his side, listening intently and nodding.

Dr Broussard looks up from the pages and spots the two young physicians. He slams the sheets onto Brother Benedict's chest, almost knocking him over. 'Finish the rest of this.' He marches several steps up the aisle, stops and turns back to the monk. 'The moon will start to wane on Thursday. The procedure can be done then.'

He swivels on the balls of his feet and steams forwards, his face red with fury. 'What in Christendom's name is the meaning of this?' he bellows as he reaches Gérard and Assen.

'We had an influx of patients in the night, sir. The brothers have taken them to the Duplessis chapel,' Gérard offers in a level tone.

'Not that!' Dr Broussard snaps. 'I have been speaking with the apothecary, Mr Coutelle.' He wheels round to Assen. 'He tells me *you* have been treating my patients! Is this your list?' He waves a sheet of parchment in Assen's face.

Assen opens his mouth but Dr Broussard is apparently in no mood to listen. He ploughs ahead like a farmer late with planting. 'Are these your treatments? You have gone too far, far too far. If it wasn't for your … your blo— I won't blaspheme in the house of God, but if it wasn't for your connections, you'd be out this instant!'

He holds up the sheet, rips it up and tosses it to the floor. 'This experiment is over! One more misstep, Dr Verey… I warn you…You are suspended for seven days.' He turns to Gérard, glowering. 'Did you know about this?

'I—'

'If I find out… Oh, you are lucky, Dr Xavier. We can't afford to lose two doctors. But if I find out… Just get back to work!'

'That's true, sir.' Assen steps forward. 'We are full. There are so many patients, we need everyone.'

'You should have thought about them before your ego! It is because of you some of these unfortunates will not be treated! Good day!' Dr Broussard sweeps off in full sail, leaving the two physicians stranded.

Gérard blows out and looks at Assen. 'Don't pay him any mind. His pride is dented. He sees this place as *his* hospital, *his* patients.'

'I know. But *you* don't think I'm being selfish, that I'm doing it for me, my pride, my reputation, do you? I'm doing it for the patients, for Uncle Manny. Well, I thought I was, but maybe ... maybe he's right and I am doing it to lighten my conscience.'

'Of course you're not! You care, that's all!'

'That's all that matters, right? We'll get it right this time. We'll make some tweaks, just a few adjustments.'

'What? Assen, you're not thinking clearly. Take this time off and rest. When you come back, everything will look different.'

But the last thing Assen needs is rest. Besides, his brain stubbornly won't rest even when he wills his body to lie stock still. No, he must occupy his mind to distract it. If he throws himself into the work and helps people, maybe the cacophony of accusations will subside. 'It wasn't strong enough,' he asserts.

'No, Assen.'

'We were far too conservative, gave the bare minimum. That's why it didn't work! The dosage was wrong!'

'Maybe it just doesn't work.' Gérard sighs. 'We did our best. That's all we can do.'

'We'll see.'

'What do you mean?'

# Chapter Twenty-Eight

An Audience
Holyrood Palace, Edinburgh

Never could Reverend McLaren have imagined being in the presence of the king, let alone being favoured by His Majesty. He clasps his hands behind him and tries to supress a grin as he looks from Commissioner Baxter to Sir William Balfour, no less, in an antechamber of Holyrood Palace.

'His Grace is most concerned,' William Balfour says gravely. 'His dreams grow ever more turbulent. Our blessed Queen Anne has endured fever after fever. The Devil is at work, galvanising his minions in the war he is waging on our king, God's emissary on Earth. His Grace is determined to root it out! He fights a courageous war. His subjects must be as resolute, as unwavering in their support for the king as His Majesty is for God.'

Rubbing his chin, the reverend nods sagely and furtively glances around the room in awe. It is a small room by Holyrood standards, an outer receiving room, but no less sumptuous. Luxurious tapestries spun with gold, red, green and blue threads of all hues hang in vertical panels, each three feet wide, covering the four walls save for the doorway and fireplace. Each panel is an integral part of a scene from the Bible or of classical origin. One depicts King Solomon imparting judgement on two women fighting over a baby. The reverend makes a mental note.

The hangings stop on either side of the fireplace, flanking a painting above and a hearth below. The painting is a more modern affair portraying the king astride a handsome white stallion out hunting with his dogs. He stares majestically at the gazer, commanding him to avert his eyes.

Behind the monarch is what appears to be Sir William on a smaller steed. The minister screws up his eyes. Yes, it looks like him. He'll have much to tell his parishioners when he returns home. He imagines being welcomed into the best drawing rooms in the parish and avidly asked for every detail of the visit. He tries to take it all in to make sure they can pick over every morsel.

The centrepiece is the rich, dark-oak throne with a luscious red-padded seat and back. William Balfour stands in the favoured position on the right-hand side. They have been waiting for half an hour. Little butterflies settle then take flight in the reverend's stomach.

At last the handle of the door in the far corner rattles and the door swings open. All heads turn. An attendant in fine livery marches into the room, his head held high as he looks at some distant point far above their heads. 'His Grace, King James of Scotland,' he cries, side-stepping as the monarch glides into the room.

After bowing deeply, hat in hand, almost touching the floor, the servant surreptitiously takes up his position in a corner of the room. The reverend notes the young man is a good head taller than the king and as broad as he is long. Although the youth is graceful and handsome, he has the build of a palace guard.

The group choruses, 'God save the king!'

King James waves his hand. 'All right,' he says, sitting down heavily on the throne.

'Your Grace.' William Balfour bows then addresses Commissioner Baxter. 'What news have you? I believe you have one of them. Is that so? Has she confessed? Give us the facts. Who are her conspirators? How many? How far and wide does this go? Who is the coven leader? His Grace is anxious to know whom he faces, who is in league with the Devil, who in his kingdom rallies against him.'

The commissioner and Reverend McLaren look at each other. Proceedings in North Berwick have not moved as quickly as they wanted. 'We are interrogating a serving lassie, Gellis Duncan,' the commissioner answers.

'We are aware of that,' Sir William snaps, mirroring the king's tetchiness. 'Has she confessed? Named others?'

'Not yet, sir. But she will,' the commissioner says confidently.

'Why not?' Balfour barks.

The king shifts in his seat and leans on his elbow. 'The security and morality of this nation is at stake,' he says. 'My dreams have shown me hideous hags transforming into grotesque wolf-like creatures, snarling and salivating, ready to devour anything in their path. I am chosen by God to do His bidding on Earth. You must do everything in your power to serve me in this task. You will root out this coven. You will find its leader. Is that clear? Disturb me not until you've done this.'

'His Grace grows ever tired. The Devil plagues his dreams,' Sir William says.

'That's enough, Balfour.'

'Sire.' Sir William bows deeply.

King James waves his hand and rises. 'Return when you have news.' Flanked by two guards, and with another behind, the monarch sweeps out of the room.

Turning to the commissioner and the Reverend McLaren, Sir William reiterates, 'Come back when you have *good* news. You may take your leave.'

A young male servant, who has been standing silently by the door through which they entered, slides forward, grabs the handle and opens the door. The young man's handsome features have a feminine quality and the reverend notices a pink tinge to his cheeks and cherub-like lips. Perhaps what they say about the king is true.

As the door closes behind them, the commissioner grimaces. 'We have much to do. We need a confession and the names of the co-conspirators – and the sooner the better. This is the biggest threat His Majesty has ever faced, and from the Devil himself. Imagine…' he glances over his shoulder '…how grateful His Grace would be if we could help him to defeat Satan's minions? This close to the divine power of God's ambassador on Earth. Think of the work we could do. But first…'

A warm satisfying glow cascades through the reverend's abdomen. 'I am at your disposal.'

# Chapter Twenty-Nine

A Favour
The Marais, Paris

'Your note sounded serious. You wanted to discuss an urgent matter?' Dr Brisbois asks as Assen strides into his drawing room.

'Congratulations on your new appointment,' Assen replies, taking off his hat and cloak.

Dr Brisbois gives a little shrug. 'It's nothing. Everyone else passed away in the natural course of things, so there was no one else. They had to pick me.'

'That's not true, and you know it. Everyone knows you're the best physician in Paris – all of France, probably. Your appointment as chief physician is richly deserved.'

Dr Brisbois places his hand on his heart and gives a little bow.

Although the doctor has only recently moved into this newly built grand house in the 4$^{th}$ arrondissement, Assen tries to spend little time looking around. But at a glance he registers almost every bit of wall space, from waist height to the vaulted ceiling thirty feet above, is covered with exquisite paintings, old masters and newer Dutch pieces.

With more pressing matters, he barely registers the footman hovering by his side waiting for his hat and cloak. 'Please,' Dr Brisbois says, and Assen relinquishes his garments to the servant.

'Forgive my abruptness, Dr Brisbois, but yes, I have something I must ask you.'

'Is it about Ivry? Terrible news. I've spoken with your father; we could scarcely believe it – the Duke's forces defeated! Overrun, the news was. But I said to Theo, he won't march on Paris; he wouldn't dare.'

'What? The Battle of Ivry? Henri of Navarre? Yes, yes, I've heard. But it's not about that.' Assen looks up and a painting of St Joan of Arc catches his eye; her sword is held aloft with legions of soldiers behind her disappearing from view beyond a hill. 'Prince Henri believes himself to be the true king of France, so maybe he thinks he's entitled to march on Paris. But no, I agree with you. They'll negotiate with him. The league will ... they'll make peace.'

'If it's not about the battle, what did you want to discuss?'

'I have been attending St Marcel's, as you know,' Assen begins.

'Your father is not best pleased.' Dr Brisbois pours two glasses of brandy from a silver jug resting on a silver tray delicately engraved with entwined vines and Romanesque wine jars. He hands one to Assen.

Assen takes it and cups it in his hands like a chalice. 'We have been doing experiments...'

'Oh, yes?'

No doubt Dr Brisbois already knows about his efforts. Precious little about Paris medicine probably escapes his attention, especially now he is chief of the Faculty.

Dr Brisbois settles back in his chair, clasping his hands across his middle.

'They're not working.' Assen takes a sip of brandy and places the goblet onto the table next to him. He leans back, too.

'What have you tried?'

'Salt, mercury, copper sulphate...'

'Ah, a good combination to fortify the body's resistance, give the spirit strength. But I would add a hint of antimony as a further purge.'

Assen nods. Of course, that would purify the body in preparation for the right balance of chemicals.

Dr Brisbois eyes Assen closely. 'There's something else?'

'The preparations we gave them weren't strong enough. We were too conservative. We didn't have the proper equipment to extract their essence and combine them properly. We gave them the bare minimum. It did nothing.' He rummages in his pocket and fishes out a piece of paper. 'This is my calculation for the maximum dose we can give to a man, and this for a woman.'

He hands the note to Dr Brisbois, who wrinkles his brow. 'You're sure of this?'

Assen nods enthusiastically and points to the paper. 'Look. Weight, height, age, constitution. We can vary it for each person, adjust each dimension.'

'Well, I can't deny it,' Dr Brisbois looks at the sheet. 'You've certainly been meticulous in your calculations. You've done well. You'll want my apparatus, then? But didn't Paracelsus also mention the patient's unique astrology?'

'Yes, but we don't have time to do charts for all the patients. Besides, most of them have no idea when they were born.'

'Hmm. Well, the Faculty is keen to expand its philanthropy. This could be its first act of charity under my humble leadership.' Dr Brisbois narrows his eyes in thought. 'Very well, I will arrange for a still to be brought to St Marcel's. You need supplies, too?'

Assen hesitates then nods. 'Thank you … yes.'

'Is there something more?'

Assen stares at the painting of St Joan again. He might as well tell the truth. He's never been good at bending a story to suit himself; the tell-tale signs of deception always show on his face. It is his eyes that give him away; that's why he gave up lying when he was six, except…

The image of Uncle Manny holding the edge of his front door, ready to close it, comes into his mind. *I've already had the pestilence! I had it two years ago, when I was studying in Italy. Remember when I was in Padua?* The story was true, except it hadn't happened to him. He inwardly shakes his head, dislodging the scene.

'It's Dr Broussard, the head physician at St Marcel's…' Assen blurts out.

'Let me guess. He is not favourably disposed to Paracelsus – or zealous young physicians?'

'You know Dr Broussard?'

'Of course. I've made it my business to know all the eminent doctors in Paris. Dr Broussard and I have sparred – in a gentlemanly fashion, of course – many a time over the table in the Faculty boardroom.'

Glad to be telling the truth, Assen feels his shoulders ease. 'He's already reprimanded me for interfering in the treatment of his patients. I fear he will throw me out.'

'I remember another young zealot.' Dr Brisbois drains his glass and puts it on the tray. 'Not a doctor but a young advocate who locked horns with a magistrate over some contentious point of common law. Your father was a principled young man, too, hankering to change the world. Like father, like son, eh? I might have known – newly qualified and already a troublemaker!' He laughs affectionately. 'Very well. I will take care of it.'

# Chapter Thirty

Help Arrives
Tranent Tolbooth

Gelly lies curled up on a pile of straw on the uneven stone floor. Staring ahead, she is neither asleep nor awake. Alone in a dank, dark cell, she cannot let herself think; madness lies one thought away.

Keys jangle in the lock. She sits bolt upright then springs to her feet. The door creaks open and every fibre of her being tenses; her intestines form a trinity knot like the ones carved in stone down by the ruined kirk near Kingston Woods.

A man steps into the dungeon holding a candle above his head. Gelly doesn't recognise him. His face turns towards the door as if he is waiting for someone else. She pushes herself further into the corner, pulling her meagre shawl tighter around her shoulders as if it might shield her.

The man places the candle in a sconce in the middle of the cell wall and the flame casts a yellow halo against the granite-grey stone. A stab of pain pierces behind her eyes, which are already unaccustomed to even the meagre glow of a single flame. She shields her gaze as she looks up. As quickly as it materialised, the knot in her stomach dissolves and the tension evaporates from her neck and shoulders. 'John!'

Schoolmaster John Fian looks down as Gelly staggers forward then throws herself at him like a bullock charging a gate. She wraps her arms around his waist and lays her head on his chest.

'John, John ... thank God. Thank God. Oh, God, help me. Please help me!' She looks up at him.

\*\*\*

John stiffens. He knows she hasn't noticed the other person sliding in behind him. Nervously turning his head a little to see if the man is watching, he finds the gentleman has looked away and is studiously examining a piece of limestone as if it were the most interesting thing in the world.

John looks at the top of Gelly's head; her lovely hair is matted and thick with dirt. The schoolmaster would rather not have a witness to such a passionate embrace, but these are not normal times and he cannot push her away; he doesn't want to push her away. Affectionately, he pulls her close, recalling their embraces in the small antechamber of the schoolhouse and the cabin along the river, down by Ingles' wood. Resting his cheek on the top of her head as he's done many times before, he closes his eyes. If only it were one of those times; if only he had agreed to run off with her when she'd pleaded instead of teasing her.

Reluctantly he raises his head, takes her by the shoulders and looks earnestly into her eyes. 'My sweet Gelly. I have brought a lawyer, an advocate, Mr Thomas Brodie, of The Cowgate, Edinburgh. He's one of the best in Scotland.'

'Please, Mr Fian. Ah claim nae fancy titles. Ma clients decide fur themselves,' Mr Brodie says firmly in a thick Edinburgh Old Town accent.

John laughs. 'Good man. Quite right.' He pats the lawyer on the back.

\*\*\*

Gelly steps back, shocked. She hadn't even sensed his presence. Has the ordeal robbed her of her gifts?

She regards the lawyer closely. A short man of about forty-five years, wearing a soft black hat with a wide brim, black robes, a white-linen collar folded over his tunic, and white cuffs. She smooths her hair, brushes down her dress and says in her best servant accent, which she finds most genteel folks expect, 'Pleased to meet you, sir.' She bobs a little curtsey. 'Will you speak for me?'

But, as John Fian explains, Thomas Brodie is not genteel. 'Gelly, my love, Mr Brodie here is the very person you'd want on your side in a tavern brawl!'

Brodie puts his hand out to Gelly. 'Pleased tae meet you, Miss Duncan. Aye, I'll speak fur ye, if you want me tae.'

'Aye, sir, I do, sir. Thank you, sir.'

'Good, aw right then.' Brodie sniffs and takes out a crisp white handkerchief. 'But first, we'll huv less o' the "sirs".' He lightly wipes his nose and places the hankie back in his pocket.

'Yes, s— Right … aye. Aye.'

Gelly and John look at Brodie expectantly as he fishes around in his breast pocket and pulls out two pieces of paper. 'Mr Fian – John – has given me the details of the case. You are charged with witchcraft, summoning up the Devil to help with your healings, and conjuring storms to destroy your enemies.'

He folds the sheets carefully then places them back in his pocket and pats it. 'I won't lie, it's not going to be easy. But … ye huv a good reputation and you've helped a lot of people – influential people – and they'll speak fur ye.'

Gelly looks from Brodie to John, who smiles and nods reassuringly.

'We'll huv tae show yer a guid, God-fearing lass,' Mr Brodie continues. 'A regular attender at the kirk…'

John and Gelly look at each other.

'Ye dae attend the Kirk?'

'Aye, but if somebody's sick or needs me, I'll go.'

'So, ye've missed services?' Brodie confirms, apparently making a mental note. 'Hmm … absence fae church could be construed as huving an irreverent attitude, but ye wur daeing guid work … daeing God's work, if it comes tae it.'

Gelly looks uncertainly at John. 'Aye…'

'Right, well, Ah'll start building yer defence. We must show these healings o' yers are no miracles. Ye've just used yer auld fashioned remedies, and it wis God's will and God's will alone that decided the fate o' every soul you treated.'

Gelly nods. 'Aye, of course. Of course it was, s—'

John puts his arm protectively around her. 'What chance do you think she has, Thomas?'

'I'm no gonnae lie, it'll be tough. But it's no' the first witchcraft accusation Ah've defended. And the witness statements make nae sense, they're completely inconsistent. Ah'd say wi good testimonials we've a chance. I cannae say more than that.'

# Chapter Thirty-One

A Promise
St Marcel's Plague Hospital

A large table dominates the centre of the room where fading light is cast from the tall, thin lattice windows high above. Assen rubs his eyes and pinches the bridge of his nose, blinking. The church bell peals. He counts seven. So he has been here for thirteen hours, though it doesn't feel like it. But he needs more light.

'Brother Francis! Brother Francis!' he calls down the dim corridor.

A monk sticks his head out of a door further down the hallway. 'Yes, Dr Verey?'

'I need more light in the distilling room. Can you bring candles from the store? As quickly as you can, please.'

Brother Francis silently closes the door behind him and heads down the hallway.

Assen is grateful to have exclusive use of the antechamber adjoining the apothecary, where ingredients are often mixed and potions brewed away from the main shop. Placing his hands on his hips, he studies the distilling apparatus on the table and scrutinises the beakers and phials of liquid gurgling over the flames. A smile playing on his lips, he looks at the sheet in front of him.

The door swings open and there is a cough from the doorway. Assen turns from his calculations to see Brother Francis cradling half a dozen long, thick candles. 'Do you think these might be enough?' he asks.

Assen laughs. 'Yes, thank you. Please...' With an upturned palm, he gestures around the room. The monk begins to place the candles on the benches pressed against the walls and the shelves, careful to sweep scrolls and pieces of parchment to one side.

Assen's doublet is discarded on the trestle table by the door. He can't imagine how he looks to the monk. His shirt is open to the chest and he hasn't attended to his grooming for five days or more. As he rubs his jaw, the rough stubble prickles his palm. Never mind. This is the happiest he's been for weeks. At last, he's doing something useful, something that might make a difference.

After placing the last candle on a high shelf, Brother Francis takes in the still.

'A fine piece of apparatus, don't you think?' Assen says, putting down the sheet and arching his back. 'I borrowed it but I hope to have my own one day.'

The monk smiles. 'What does it do?'

'See the liquids bubbling over the flame? The green one here, the amber over there and the clear one just here?' Assen says, walking around the still and pointing at the different phials and flasks. 'They have more than one constituent – different parts. When we heat them, we can separate the parts and distil the substance down to its essence. We make it purer, if you like – stronger. We can make it just how we want it. See that pot over there?'

He points to an iron container, its lid vibrating over a high flame. 'We're refining mercury from the cinnabar, the ore in the rock.' He picks up a rock the size of his palm from a small pile at the end of the table. 'We still need help from the farrier, but—'

'Amazing!' the monk exclaims, bending to examine the pot and the still. He opens his mouth to ask another question when there is a gentle knock at the door.

Gérard's head appears and his eyes dart around the room. 'Ah, Brother Francis. You're needed in the kitchen. Assen, may I come in?'

'Of course.' The monk leaves and Assen asks Gérard to close the door. He turns his attention back to the sheet and leans over the table.

'Is it ready yet? Are you sure about this?' Gérard asks, gripping the edge of the bench.

'Nearly. Just two more phials. You have the patient list?'

Gérard pulls a sheet from his breast pocket. 'We agreed these patients are deteriorating fast and, if our experience is anything to go by, they'll die soon anyway. They have little to lose, right? This might save them. And if it does—'

'If it does,' Assen says, 'we could use it throughout the hospital and other hospitals in Paris.'

'*If* it does,' Gérard adds under his breath. 'Pray to God it works.'

'Right, help me. Let's get the last few ready.' Assen pours the dark-red liquid into empty phials.

'Broussard is apoplectic. He's making all sorts of threats. I ... don't think they're just threats.' Gérard passes across two phials.

'I can't think about that now – I need to concentrate. Right, here we are.' Assen looks at the phials. 'Help me get them to the bench.'

They move the containers over to the counter to join other trays of salts.

Assen sweeps his palm over his hair and picks up the sheet again. He has been meticulous in his calculations but he checks them again. 'We'll give them the strongest dose we can before—'

'It kills them.'
'Before it is fatal, yes.'
'You can do that?'
Assen frowns. 'I think so.'

The door bursts open, banging against the thick stone wall. The trays of phials clink alarmingly. 'For Christ's sake, watch what you're doing!' Assen spins around. 'Who told you to come in, don't you—?'

Dr Broussard is framed in the doorway, his lips drawn in a tight line. For what seems like an eternity, he stands motionless. Then, hands behind his back, he walks slowly into the room, prowling around the still and taking in the little piles of salts on the trays. He ignores Assen and turns to Gérard. 'You have patients to see to.'

'Yes, Dr Broussard.'
'You may close the door when you leave.'

'Yes, Dr Broussard.' Giving Assen a furtive look, Gérard closes the door quietly.

Dr Broussard faces Assen and says in a menacing tone, 'You may have friends in high places, Dr Verey, but this is by no

151

means the end. I will see to it you never practise medicine again. You will be known as a charlatan. If you kill any of my patients, I will see you hang. That's a promise.'

# Chapter Thirty-Two

The Net Tightens
North Berwick

'Please.' Reverend McLaren gestures for his guest to sit in one of the sumptuously upholstered chairs on either side of the fireplace. The red-and-gold detailing on the seat and back pads stands out against the room's dark-wood panelling in the soft amber firelight.

'Some refreshment?' he adds, indicating his best pewter tankards on the table between them. 'I took the liberty of ordering camomile tea when I received your note. This is a great honour ... most unexpected ... but a great honour to have you visit, Reverend Henderson. And all the way from the General Assembly, too. It is most gratifying that the highest office of the church is taking an interest in our little misfortunes out here in North Berwick.'

He notices Reverend Henderson looking around, his eyes settling on the simple but fine mahogany dresser in the corner and the writing desk under the window. A quill protrudes from the inkpot on the bureau and a pile of papers is heaped under a smooth round stone adorned with a painted white rose. An extinguished candle stands sentry over the stack.

Reverend Henderson lifts the mug. Reverend McLaren does the same, the heat warming his hands. He looks down at the whisper of steam curling towards the tip of his nose.

The visiting clergyman coughs. 'Indeed, Reverend McLaren, we are interested in all our presbyteries, especially when, as you say, some ... misfortune, something untoward, befalls the congregation. But I think, Reverend,' he continues slowly, 'you have understated the tribulation that you – indeed the whole country, including His Grace – faces. Is it true what they are saying – that evil, the Devil, lurks in this township? That the dark arts are being practised? His Majesty's life threatened? The palace is full of rumours.'

'I fear it is true.' The minister lifts his tankard too and swirls the contents.

Reverend Henderson shakes his head solemnly. 'This was expected, given the reports circulating in the Assembly and the court, but we needed to check with our local man, as it were. You know you are doing vital work for the Kirk in these dark times, Reverend McLaren.'

Reverend McLaren inclines his head. 'I do my best to serve.'

'We've been watching you – your service, your self-sacrifice. We're expecting great things. A place at the Assembly may even be free in due course, should things turn out… Should the crisis be averted.'

Reverend McLaren's heart thumps in his chest.

'But as the Kirk's representative, for this to come to pass, you must make sure you play a leading role in any witch trial that comes about. Witchcraft,' the senior churchman wags his forefinger, 'is an area in which the Kirk must have ultimate authority, even above His Grace. *We* are the authority on the Bible's teachings and what constitutes godly action. You must be involved in *every* stage of the investigation. Do you understand?'

'Yes, Reverend Henderson.' The minister straightens his back and looks levelly at his superior. 'I will serve the church faithfully and to the best of my ability according to my vows, and ensure the Kirk is at the centre and held in the highest esteem by all entangled in these unfortunate events.'

'Good.' Reverend Henderson leans back. 'You have put my mind at ease and we will leave this in your capable hands. Should you need any guidance or assistance…' He stops, frowns. 'Young Minister Campbell is available to help with any paperwork you need.'

'Thank you,' Reverend McLaren answers quickly. 'I don't think that will be necessary but I am grateful for the Assembly's interest and kind offer.'

Reverend Henderson shrugs. 'You know, I think some good might come from all this. It'll reassure your flock that their faith will protect them – that *only* their faith will protect them – from evil and misfortune.'

He drains the last of his tea and sets the beaker on the table between them. 'Happily, it will keep the Bible's teachings at the heart of their everyday lives and the rule of presbyteries central to discipline. Not a bad thing, given the turbulence of the last few years. What do you say?'

'Indeed.' Reverend McLaren smiles and places his tankard beside the older churchman's.

As Reverend Henderson gathers his cane, coat and hat in the hall, the doorbell clangs. He looks enquiringly at Reverend McLaren. 'I'm expecting the king's commissioner, Commissioner Baxter, to discuss the progress of the case,' the reverend states with a satisfied smile. He had been hoping the commissioner would arrive before the Assembly's representative left.

'The king's commissioner?' Reverend Henderson repeats, raising his eyebrows. 'I'd better let you get on, then.'

'Well?' the commissioner asks impatiently, once the clergyman leaves.

'This way, please.' Reverend McLaren leads him into the parlour. 'Pray be seated.' The two chairs sit untidily by the fireplace, illustrating their recently vacated status. The commissioner takes the one furthest from the door.

The minister retakes his seat, feeling the warmth on his back. A serving lass pops her head around the door. 'Is there anything you need, Reverend McLaren?' she asks uncertainly, her eyes flitting from the minister to the commissioner.

'Aye, Isabel. Clear this away.' He indicates the spent beakers. 'And bring brandy. Something to warm you after your journey, Commissioner.'

Reverend McLaren sits back as the door clicks shut and the maid's footsteps retreat down the hall, then he leans forward, pressing his fingers together as if about to pray. He's been thinking about this, even before the promise of a seat on the General Assembly.

'They – that is the maid Gellis Duncan and the other witches – must meet near the sea to conjure up such storms as could thwart the king,' he suggests. 'St Andrew's Auld Kirk in North Berwick would be the obvious choice. It looks out over the sea and no one else would go there in the middle of the night.'

A plain silver salver, a present from the Setons and a glass decanter with two glasses of brandy have appeared on the table between them. The reverend picks up a glass.

The commissioner leans forward, too. 'The king wants more details. Sir William is demanding the particulars of how we're planning to thwart the conspiracy.'

'Well, they secretly meet there in the Auld Kirk in the dead of night…'

'The coven?'

'Aye, the coven, and … and they are presided over by the Devil himself!' The reverend places his brandy back on the platter.

The commissioner folds his arms. 'It is as His Grace surmised – Old Nick challenging him on his own ground, in his own kingdom. If the rumours around the palace about his night-time terrors are to be believed, he will be grateful for any knowledge and righteous action that will aid him in the good fight. God protect and keep him.'

The reverend nods. 'Quite so, Commissioner. The Devil's fiendish plan is to destroy his greatest enemy on Earth.'

'Our good King James.' Commissioner Baxter looks into the fire.

'Good King James indeed.' The minister continues, getting into his stride. 'It started when the coven whipped up storms to stop His Majesty from carrying our gracious Queen Anne home from Denmark to prevent—'

'Heirs.'

'Precisely. Heirs, the bloodline … future saviours of Scotland. A diabolical plan.'

The commissioner picks up his glass, toys with the stem then brings it to his nose. Emulating him, the reverend lets the aroma infuse his nostrils. There is a light undertone of peat – or it could be the fire. He swallows a good mouthful which burns his throat, then he warms in the pleasant afterglow as the brandy descends.

'But is the threat sufficient for the king to want to be directly involved in the proceedings, maybe even the trials?' the commissioner muses. He places the glass down and claps his hands. 'It is treason, after all, yet we have no proof! Just one serving lass who hasn't confessed. We need her to confess,

Reverend, and to name others, to confirm His Grace's fears are right – that danger stalks the land, that a network of witches is conspiring to destroy His Majesty and all his descendants. How many do you think there are in this coven?'

'Who knows?' Reverend McLaren leans back and smooths his gown over his thighs. 'But there are several in the parish I can think of.' He shakes his head. 'Women whom men don't seem to have much control over, women who have little or no respect for authority. There's one in particular the others seem to look up to. A midwife, a so-called healer.'

'Go on.' The commissioner sits forward in his chair.

'No one knows where she came from, she just arrived here one day – what, thirty years ago? Said she was a widow or some such nonsense. Said her young husband had died at sea.'

The commissioner clasps his hands in front of his mouth and rubs a thumb along his lips, studying the minister intensely.

Holding his gaze, the reverend senses this may be the perfect opportunity to settle that he is the man to lead the crusade in North Berwick; that he, the Reverend McLaren, deserves to be the king's representative, with the king's authority over this town. 'But, as you say,' he continues slowly, 'the Setons' maid will have to confess and name others.'

'We have been slow,' the commissioner says. 'The sheriff has been pedantic about procedure and evidence, but if we could show the danger is imminent and His Majesty's life could be taken at any moment, things could move a lot faster.'

'If you put it like that, Commissioner, I feel it is my moral duty to name…' he picks an invisible thread from his sleeve, choosing his word carefully '…the conspirators.'

He has been waiting for this moment, carefully considering the names he would put forward. It'll give them a fright, show them who's in charge. He'll have no trouble at the kirk now, no sniggering behind his back; everyone will be in their rightful place once the troublemakers have gone.

He remembers as a lad seeing a young woman with a round belly holding out her palm and a woman wrapped in a grey woollen shawl dropping a small brown bag into it. The young woman had turned to him. 'It's all right, child. Just some herbs and pods to make me feel better.'

He shakes his head. He needs to concentrate on getting this done.

'Gelly Duncan is close with the midwife and healer, Agnes Sampson,' he says slowly. 'They look up to the schoolmaster, John Fian, a radical who preaches equality, everyone being a child of God or some such nonsense.' He purses his lips. 'There's been concern about him for some time, his teachings, what he puts in the minds of bairns and the simple.'

'Like these women?'

'I've seen them conversing with him many a time. Jannet Blandilands, she's another with a scold's tongue.'

'And maybe more, Reverend?'

'Aye, maybe more ... a lot more.'

The commissioner pinches his lip between his forefinger and thumb, pulling it forward. 'Hmm. As I've said before, we could be saving His Majesty from a massive network of witches. His favour on such an occasion would be like the sun shining on a land of eternal darkness.'

'His Grace is most generous.'

Reverend McLaren sits back and takes up his brandy once more, staring contentedly into the fire. It started long ago, and it will finish soon.

# Chapter Thirty-Three

A Mistake?
St Marcel's Plague Hospital

Moans and groans, shouts and screams echo around the great hall of St Marcel's. Nurse brothers and sisters are rushing to and from patients with basins and bowls. The hospital is in chaos, with every bed taken and more patients arriving. It is on the verge of being overwhelmed by the wave of humanity pressing on its doors. All staff are in full-length leather robes, with hoods and masks covering their faces.

Assen stands at the head of a male patient; the young man is scanning his mask, searching for his eyes. Aware the patient will ask questions as soon as he locks on to them, Assen prepares himself. *Will I live?* – the inevitable first question. If the answer is no, the second question will be: *Who will take care of my wife, my children?*

Assen pulls his eyes away and nods like a marionette. 'Of course you will. You're strong, you can fight it and you will.' His intestines knot. 'Eat as much broth as you can – there's mutton in it – and take the medicaments. Mass is being said day and night; listen to it. All this will help you get better.' Out of the corner of his eye he sees Gérard approaching and moves away from the young man.

'Barreau is gone,' Gérard states.

The band gripping Assen's abdomen turns into a vice. Barreau was a young apprentice, not yet wed. 'You can't mean Alain?'

Gérard nods.

Assen forces himself to remember what he's been taught: be practical, deal with the immediate problem. Emotions, grief, regret and self-recrimination must be put to one side. Easy for a crusty old professor to say in medical school, not so easy when your patients are dying around you.

'Are the collectors here?' he asks, his voice trembling. Annoyed with himself, he swallows hard.

'Yes.'

'How many have we lost?' His voice is steadier, even though his fingers are quivering by his side. He makes a fist then stretches his fingers and clamps his hand to his thigh.

'Nine … no, ten.'

'Are there many outside?' Assen wonders if this is the point where they should accept, give up, surrender to the pestilence and allow it to pass through, trust that humanity will somehow survive. *I will not give up! Do you hear, God? I refuse!*

'Too many.' Gérard picks up the discarded rods and tongs from beneath a patient's bed. 'I'll have the beds cleaned and fresh blankets put on.'

'Burn the old ones.' No sooner are the words are out of his mouth than Assen realises they were unnecessary: Gérard is far more versed in dealing with the plague than he'll ever be. 'Sorry, Gérard, of course you've…'

Gérard replies without offence. 'Done.'

'Thank you. Move the dying into the chapel so they can better hear the prayers. And have the collectors come to the side door tomorrow morning.'

'You'll have to see Dr Broussard. You can't avoid him.'

'I'll see him when this is over … when it's under control.'

Gérard looks around the packed hall, at the patients too close together, some shivering and calling for blankets, some burning up, reaching out to some invisible rescuer. 'Yes, it will be over,' he says. 'But it won't be because we controlled it … maybe because we rolled with it. It has a natural progression, a pattern, I think.'

\*\*\*

Something occurs to Gérard, something he learned in Italy from an old woman he encountered on Mount Ciarforon. He often wonders how she got there, so close to the summit, with her thin shawl, plain walking stick and simple peasant dress. It had been spring, but snow was still piled high on the peak's ridges and ravines with no signs of it melting in the weak sun. But it was fresh and wonderful to be on top of the world.

Yet he can't remember how he got there either, where he had set off from or why he had decided to go alone. But there he was with this elderly lady who told him something, something important, something that would be useful right now, here in St Marcel's, if only he could remember it.

\*\*\*

'Where is Dr Verey?' a voice bellows down the hall. The cacophony of screams and shouts of delirious patients falls silent as if God himself commanded it. Brother Benedict pauses mid-sentence, his lips parted, and Gérard, momentarily suspended, holds the poles and pincers out by his side like some prehistoric bird.

In the hush, Dr Broussard marches down the central aisle towards Assen. Like a hare caught in the sight of a hunter, arrow drawn back, bowstring taut, Assen locks eyes with Broussard. He is unable to move.

'It hasn't worked, has it?' Dr Broussard bawls, looking pleased. 'Your little experiment? I think it's making things worse. I think you are actually killing your patients, Dr Verey!'

Gérard comes to his friend's defence. 'That's not fair! The whole district is overwhelmed – our sister hospitals are the same.'

Ignoring Gérard, Dr Broussard continues his tirade. 'I think your days as a doctor are over, Dr Verey. Perhaps a man of the cloth would be more your forte, dispatching your patients to their maker as quickly as possible. Well, maybe you'll be joining them.'

'What does that mean?' Gérard says, deep lines appearing between his eyebrows.

'If that's all, we have much to do,' Assen says levelly, despite the anvil in his stomach.

Dr Broussard turns to Gérard. 'If you need me, you know where I am.' He heads back down the aisle and out of the side door. As it slams shut, the hubbub restarts. Two monks at the front of the hall carrying basins and blankets whisper to each other.

'Don't mind him. He's still angry,' Gérard reassures his friend.

'But what if he's right?' Assen looks up at the huge figure of Christ on the cross. 'My patients are dying, maybe even quicker than before. What have I done? I don't know how to treat them. I don't know how to save them.' He lets his arms drop by his side and hangs his head.

'I've told you before, you are not God. You are not here to save people, you are here to help people save themselves.'

'Save themselves?' Assen draws his head back up. 'Right. We have to keep going.'

# Chapter Thirty-Four

A Dilemma
Tranent Tolbooth

'She denies all knowledge of it – the coven, meeting at the Auld Kirk.' The sheriff steps out of Gelly's cell, lowering his head to avoid the lintel above the door. The commissioner is waiting in the dank hall.

The guard pulls the cell door shut with a dull thud and locks it with three turns of a filthy iron key the size of his hand. He fixes it back onto the hoop hanging from his belt.

The sheriff recalls at one time they only had great iron snibs on the outside of the doors, with no lock and keys. But no one stayed in gaol for very long, thanks to a bribe here and there, and a snib would be left open. Easy money for the gaolers and visitors. His old sergeant had said you might as well take the prisoners out after you arrested them and let them go on the common.

'You offered her a pardon and safe passage south if she named her accomplices?' The commissioner takes a handkerchief from his breast pocket and presses it to his nose.

'Aye,' the sheriff replies. 'She said she didn't know what I was talking about, she's never been to the Auld Kirk, that it's not used anymore and no one goes there. I'm inclined to believe her. Who witnessed these goings-on, anyway? Who made the complaint?'

'It is of no consequence. She knows what will happen if she doesn't cooperate?'

'She's had no sleep these last two days, precious little food and rotten ale… She understands it's only going to get worse.'

'Very well.'

'She's asking to see Fian and the lawyer again.'

'Not until she confesses.'

'She does have the right...' The sheriff frowns. 'All prisoners have the right to a defence and a proper trial before a magistrate, if it comes to it. And there has to be evidence. Where is the evidence? If we don't follow the letter of the law, the people won't obey it. Remember how it used to be? We can't let that happen again.'

The commissioner looks the sheriff squarely in the face. 'There are no rights when it comes to treason and witchcraft.'

Unfazed, the sheriff holds his gaze. 'It has not been proven. We do not have evidence other than hearsay. Where are the witnesses, the complainants?'

'They'll come. I have assurances.'

'What do you mean? I am the sheriff of the district – if you have information about the prisoner, I need to hear it. I need names of the witnesses then I will question them in accordance with our stated procedure.'

His neck and spine tingle as if something is crawling up them. Behind his back a great web is being spun; every now and then he senses the vibration of a huge body moving around. He stares at the corridor's fusty stone illuminated with the glow from a candle in a sconce. It gives off a muted yellow, oppressive light. Dampness penetrates the seams between the slate-grey jagged stones.

A spider has spun a web that spans the ceiling where the light cannot reach; a single thread bridges the expanse from the roof to the bracket holding the torch. How clever, silently and ceaselessly it spins its net; it is almost invisible unless you look for it. His eyes search the corner. There it is: the motionless beast waiting for some poor moth to stumble into its meticulously constructed snare. Such is nature! He shakes his head and feels his hair tickle the back of his neck. He needs a haircut; he'll ask Mary.

The commissioner is talking with the gaoler and slips some coins into his hand. 'Have the cellar prepared. Call Mr Birkett. We'll have a confession before the night is out.'

'Sir, with all due respect.' The sheriff feels his shoulders and neck stiffen; he can't let this happen. 'We do not have the evidence to pursue such a course.'

'We will find it. Have the Seton house searched and get the witchfinder. That is an order. I trust he has a woman to examine her person for the usual deformities – the marks of the Devil?'

'A trained midwife will conduct the search,' the sheriff answers stiffly.

'So be it. The Justice Ayre has been notified of an impending witch trial.'

'The Justice Ayre! But ... nothing is certain. This may just be petty squabbles and jealousies, spurned suitors – a case of adultery, nothing more. It's too early to involve the royal court, surely? And I know they are due in Perth, Stirling and Elgin, so couldn't we ... sir ... get to the bottom of it ourselves before we involve the circuit court, the Justice Ayre?' The sheriff's upper abdominal muscles tighten as if a thick belt has just been pulled taut around his middle.

'On the contrary. The king's dreams tell us that his life is under threat and the realm is in imminent danger. The court has determined we are its first stop. So, you see,' the commissioner continues with a satisfied expression, 'we must use every means at our disposal.'

The sheriff rubs his cheek and chin. So that is the way of things. What defence can a soul have against the spectres that haunt His Majesty's dreams? He lets his head fall back against the stone, hoping His Grace dreams no more.

# Chapter Thirty-Five

Which Way Will It Go?
St Marcel's Plague Hospital

The Duplessis Chapel is silent except for the monks whispering and tiptoeing from patient to patient, mopping brows and carrying away chamber pots. The atmosphere is in marked contrast to the chaos and mayhem of the great hall next door. Here beds are spaced further apart; they line both walls with the high altar at the end. The altar has a table covered in white linen with a spectacular brass crucifix in the centre that draws the eye and is flanked by two ornate brass candlesticks. In front is a large, foolscap, medieval Latin Bible open on a lectern as if the priest has just finished saying mass. The colourful pages display gleaming gold embellishments, cobalt blue, yellow swirls and varying hues of green and red flourishes that adorn the black lettering, perfectly centred and executed.

Assen lies in one of the beds in the middle of the row along the south-facing gable wall, furthest from the hall next door. His eyes hurt as he looks at the vaulted ceiling. It is so high, so very high. *Where am I? Where is this place?*

He tries to turn his head but it won't budge. He opens his mouth but all that escapes is a raspy croak. The blankets feel tight around his shoulders and legs as he tries to wriggle his arms and shake his feet. The effort makes him gasp.

Somewhere in the hall, a tiny bell tinkles. There it is again. He strains to hear. Shaking free of the blankets, he props himself precariously on his elbows, tries to steady his head and focus. There are other people here, too, in beds next to him and across the aisle. *But why am I here?*

The scene swims around as if he is underwater. He hears deep, distant, echoing voices. A statue of an angel – no, the Virgin Mary – slowly comes into focus then blurs. People are whispering … wait … praying … yes, saying prayers … and chanting... People are chanting. He's in church! Hah! A church somewhere! He doesn't remember going to church.

Wait, there's Gérard, his friend Gérard. He is at the front next to the altar, speaking with one of the nurse brothers. *Good old Gérard.* Assen breathes out; his upper chest deflates and his shoulders drop away from his ears. *Thank goodness.* Gérard has a sheet of paper in his hand and is pointing towards the back of the room. The monk nods.

As Gérard gives the monk the paper, his eyes catch Assen's and stretch wide. Smiling, he approaches. Assen wonders why Gérard is walking as if he is on the deck of a ship and how he can stay upright with so much swaying. His stomach churns and he looks away.

'How are you?' Gérard asks gently, his voice echoing like he is in a cave a great distance away.

'Where am I?' Assen asks.

'At the hospital, St Marcel's. How are you feeling?'

Assen looks around. Most of the patients are either sleeping, unconscious or talking quietly with someone or something only they can see. 'Why am I here?'

'You are being looked after,' Gérard offers.

'Am I going to die?' He smiles inwardly at the question.

His friend takes a deep breath. 'I'm going to be honest. That's up to you.'

A wave of heaviness sweeps through Assen's body, pulling him further into the bed. 'I'm tired,' he says, and flops down.

'Sleep now. I will see you when you wake. All right?'

Assen nods gratefully. 'All right.'

*As his eyes close, the sights and sounds of the chapel are replaced by a churning fog. Bit by bit this starts to clear and he finds himself floating above a bed, looking down at a body. It is his body. He must be dreaming.*

*The floating sensation is enjoyable though. He can see the nurse brothers working around the other patients. Some are sitting quietly reading the Bible to them, others are rushing to and fro with washbowls.*

*Assen is amazed at how calm he feels, as if it is the commonest thing in the world to hover in mid-air some fifteen feet off the floor. He thinks of the other doctors – Gérard and Lucas – and* wonders where they are. As he does so, he materialises in the main hall next to Gérard, who is talking to a monk about a patient a few beds away.

'He should be fine to leave in the morning,' Gérard says. 'We'll give him another night, but it looks good, Brother Francis. You've done well.'

'It is the good Lord we must thank, Dr Xavier. But thank you.'

'Of course. Now, Mr Dubois.' Gérard heads off down the central passageway with Assen falling into step beside him.

'Gérard, Gérard! See, I'm perfectly well. I can help now,' Assen calls excitedly.

But Gérard doesn't answer and continues walking down the hall to another patient who is sitting up in bed. 'Mr Dubois, how are you feeling today?' he asks cheerily.

Assen tries again. 'Gérard, it's me...' But Gérard carries on talking to Mr Dubois, asking how his sons are and if they are looking after the shop well. Perhaps he's done something to offend Gérard. But his friend has never been so petty before, and it really does look as if he can't see him. But how could that be?

Assen thinks of another doctor, Lucas. Instantly he is inside the apothecary's office watching Lucas pick up a phial. Staring at it, Lucas asks Pierre Coutelle, 'You think it will quell the chills?'

'Yes,' the apothecary advises. 'Give it after a little soup and, if that is tolerated, after the evening meal. You should see an improvement by the end of the day.'

Lucas turns as if to leave, then stops. 'Was there something else?' Pierre enquires.

'No... Well, actually, I have a friend in the Duplessis chapel.'

'I've heard about Dr Verey. I'm sorry.'

'What?' Assen shouts. 'Lucas! I'm here! I've never felt better in my life! See, I'm fine.' But no one hears.

'Perhaps there's something we've not tried?' Lucas asks.

Pierre regards him with sympathy. 'Everything's been done, that can be done. It is in God's hands.'

'Of course.' Lucas sighs. 'Thank you.' Taking the phial, he gives Pierre a weak smile.

'There is to be a mass?' the apothecary asks.

'Yes. This evening.'

Lucas gathers his wares and carries them to the door. As he touches the handle, the apothecary calls, 'I will pray for him.'

'Thank you.' Stepping into the cool corridor, Lucas rolls his neck in little semicircles and takes his shoulders forward and back. They feel stiff and tense; he hadn't realised he'd been straining them. The body is a truthful messenger of how you are really feeling and what you've been thinking, Lucas muses, seeing all his medicaments on the shelf of his raised bed at home.

Assen looks closely at Lucas; he didn't know he needed medicine. What is wrong, dear friend? Maybe I can help, maybe we can find something. It doesn't seem at all strange to Assen that he's just heard his friend's thoughts. Growing ever more frustrated, he tries one more time. 'Lucas, for goodness' sake, I'm here! I'm fine! I've never been better!'

'They can't hear you,' says a voice that Assen recognises – but surely it can't be?

'Uncle Manny?' he splutters.

The corridor around him, its thick stone walls that have stood strong for four hundred years with the fluttering flames in the sconces and the crucifixes dotted along the walls high above, begins to fade.

The scene is replaced by a picturesque garden; it reminds Assen of the pretty cottage gardens he saw in the south when he was visiting his grandparents. Sweet little houses in the centre of the village with frontages straight onto the street, and huge wild grounds stretching far out the back.

He looks around, awestruck. He's never seen so many colours, some he didn't know existed. How can that be? The meadow flowers appear to be growing in a wild yet curated way, as if to show them at their very best and display their true essence.

An ancient stone fountain sits at the centre of the garden, two-tiered with a wide round base that Assen estimates must be knee-high. The rim is ornately decorated with intertwining grapevines and flowers, reflecting those in the garden. He's never come across such a fountain before: it feels organic, alive, as if it knows what you're thinking.

Lilies are floating on the surface of the pool, all perfect in their uniqueness. The top tier is shorter in diameter but equally ornate, with delicately carved birds, seraphim and cherubs. The water cascades over its edges yet barely disturbs the surface of the mirror-like pool below. The sun is shining; it is a beautiful day, a perfect day.

Assen breathes in deeply. He is alive; he can breathe. He looks closely at Uncle Manny, who looks decades younger, perhaps the same age as himself. There is a vitality, an energy to his uncle. 'Do you live here?' Assen asks.

Uncle Manny smiles and nods contentedly. 'Mm-hmm.'

'It's beautiful. Is this heaven?'

'It is my heaven.'

Assen wonders if he can stay. Hearing his thoughts, Uncle Manny replies, 'No, you have to go back.'

Turning his back on the fountain, Assen sighs. 'I don't want to go, Uncle. I'd rather stay here with you. It is so peaceful and beautiful. And I miss you.'

'I know, my dear Assen, and there is nothing I would like better, but it is not your time. There are things you want to do ... that you have chosen to do.'

'I have chosen? I don't remember.' Yet something stirs at the back of his mind. There was something, wasn't there?

He senses something vaguely familiar about why he wanted to be a physician in the first place. What was it? He can feel it in his chest, except he hasn't got a body. He's almost got it, this thing he wanted to do, what he wanted to finish. If he could just reach out and grab it, have a good look then discard it and tell them he's changed his mind. 'I'd like to stay,' he says firmly.

On the other side of the fountain, a woman is ambling towards them. She is wearing a long cream robe tinged with orange, gold and blue. Her hair is shoulder length, thick and black, and her skin a smooth, glistening nutmeg. Like Uncle Manny, she looks in her early thirties and has a glow around her.

She glides towards Assen. 'Are you arguing with your uncle again?' Her voice is soft yet deep.

Never, even with all the Bible's teachings or the philosophy, astrology and the humanities he's ever learned, did Assen think he'd hear that voice again.

'Mother,' he whispers. He clutches at his heart – or where it should be – and is astonished to feel the locket he never takes off

in the other earthly life clasped in his hand. A cascade of emotions sweeps through him. His heart feels so big, as if it has expanded several feet beyond the boundaries of his body.
His mother laughs. 'You still have your token. Even here, you'll always have it.'
'Of course, Mother. I always wear it.' Mirroring him, she makes a fist in the centre of her chest. 'And your mother always keeps it close to her heart. You are always in her heart, every day. You know that, dear son, don't you?'
When she removes her hand, he sees the locket just as he remembers it – big and oval, identical to his except for one detail: he has an 'A' on the underside of his pendant, while she has a 'B' for Bahdeer.
'Yes, Mother, I do. I really do.' His heart swells even more. Never could he have guessed it could grow so big; he thinks it will burst! He senses what this feeling is: gratitude. Awestruck with sensations that threaten to overwhelm him, his knees begin to buckle. He wants to drop to the ground in veneration.
'Mother,' is all he can say.
She smiles and stares into his eyes. She sees into his soul – he can feel it. She knows who he really is, his true essence; he can hide nothing from her. But as she places both palms over her heart, an intense wave of heat and energy emanates from her chest towards him, searing through his heart then his entire body. He falls back. He's never felt anything like this, anything close. So is this love ... real love?
'Your uncle is right. There are things you still have to do...' She lets her hands drop, cupping them in front of her. '... and in Beaune, you will find the answer.'
'Beaune? To what?' he asks, perplexed.
She places her forefinger in the centre of his chest. 'To the question that has been locked in here.'
Once more, a velvety energy flows into his heart and courses around his being. If it had a colour it would be the rose pink of a winters' sky as the sun sets and merges in the grey haze of a fading day. Something, an image, flutters into view, like the ghost of a butterfly. Then it vanishes.
But how can he go back with everything in chaos and worse than before? 'I've made such a mess. I haven't helped anyone –

I've maybe even made it worse. Wouldn't it be better if I stayed with you?'

'You will find a way,' she says simply. 'All you have to remember and take with you, my dearest boy, is that you are loved beyond anything you can imagine.'

A strong fresh breeze blows through the garden. It is different from any wind he has felt on Earth. It feels like the energy that flowed from his mother's heart but stronger, a thousand times stronger if that were possible. It is like the greatest wave there has ever been in the ocean but made of love and compassion. Is this the love of heaven?

Dumbstruck, he knows he cannot argue with God. This is meant to be. 'I must go back,' he says with a sigh. He looks at the fountain and wonders if he can take a walk around the garden before he returns.

'Of course,' his mother answers.

He laughs. So nothing is private here, he thinks.

Uncle Manny adds, 'If you choose it to be, it is. All decisions and choices are respected here.'

'Even the wrong ones,' Assen ponders regretfully.

'There are no wrong decisions, Assen, only ones you learn from and resolve not to repeat,' his mother says.

'You decide to do something else, something different, when you are faced with a similar situation,' Uncle Manny explains. 'In this way you change, advance. Do you see? You progress, evolve.'

'There are no wrong decisions?'

'No,' Uncle Manny says. 'And there are some things you could not have changed because it was not in your power to do so. It was someone else's decision, someone else's choice about what they were going to experience.'

'I see – I think.' Assen feels something heavy, like a boulder, lift from his chest. He becomes aware of voices whispering in the background. 'What is that?'

'Prayers,' Uncle Manny answers. 'They have been there all the time but you didn't notice.'

'People are praying for you,' his mother adds.

'Really?' Assen drops his head and listens. 'I can feel them,' he says excitedly, his body tingling. 'It's like ... like ... being tickled inside!' He laughs but then turns serious. 'But I don't know what I'm supposed to do when I go back. What do I do?'

'As you are advised to do. Leave the hospital and go to Beaune,' Uncle Manny says.

'Travel light ... and learn,' his mother adds. 'Seek out the healers in every place you shelter. Be humble, for you know little.'

'Go to the House of God,' Uncle Manny says.

'The House of God?'

'There you will find shelter – and you will need it,' his mother explains. 'You will offer your services. Let your heart guide you on your journey. Trust it and be true to it. All your questions will be answered.'

'It is time.' Uncle Manny gently clasps Assen's upper arm.

A breeze blows through the garden once more and the scene fades, leaving the three facing each other as a mist swirls around them.

'Will I see you again?' Assen asks.

'Yes,' Bahdeer reassures him. She steps forward and wraps her arms around him. A tear rolls down his cheek. 'Be brave and trust,' she whispers.

He closes his eyes and is back in the chapel, floating above his body. He knows what he must do.

Like a slate falling from the roof, he slams back into his body and wakes with a gasp.

# Chapter Thirty-Six

Found!
Tranent Tolbooth

The sheriff watches the commissioner, who is behind the large oak table, scribbling away at documents with a long quill. Its brown, beige and white spines forming a tapered diagonal from nib to tip. An eagle, the sheriff thinks. No, that would be too decadent even for the commissioner, too fine a bird for an ink pot. A pheasant, perhaps. The musing takes his mind off contemplating what's happened and what may happen.

The commissioner dips the plume into the jar and jots, the scratching amplified in the quietness of the room. His assistant, Grant, who is standing behind him, points out items on the sheet and gestures to the other papers scattered on the desk.

The sheriff looks out of the small window to the courtyard below. It must be around noon. The stable lads are loading the overhead baskets with hay ready for the advance party from Edinburgh. Tranent is a well-kept gaol, all things considered.

He sees his and the commissioner's horses side by side, their heads nodding over the half-stable doors, stretching to blow into each other's nostrils. One of the lads gives them handfuls of hay and a bit of carrot, if he's not mistaken. The horses are well looked after and so they should be; without them, it wouldn't be possible to cover the distances necessary to keep law and order.

Sheriff MacKay looks back into the room at the crackling fire. He tugs his collar away from his neck and stretches his chin. The reverend sits contentedly in a high-backed chair by the flames, a glass of port at his side. Three short sharp raps at the door interrupt the sheriff's chain of thought.

'Enter!' the commissioner shouts.

A prison guard enters, bringing a blast of chilled air from the corridor. He holds the door open for an older woman, who glances nervously around the room.

'Ah, Goodwife … umm…' The commissioner looks down at the document, searching.

'Strachan, sir,' the sheriff states. 'Goodwife Strachan.'

The commissioner looks up, shifts his papers to the side. 'Of course. Goodwife Strachan. You have conducted a thorough search?'

The woman is in her mid-fifties. Her hands are pressed so tightly together that she looks as if she might drop to her knees in prayer at any moment. Wearing a plain, dark-brown dress, with an off-white linen apron tied at the waist that reaches to her shins, she looks like any other goodwife of the middling sort, wife of a tenant farmer, perhaps. A brown cap covers most of her hair with little grey curls protruding at the ears.

'A thorough search?' Reverend McLaren asks.

The sheriff glares at him.

The reverend continues quickly. 'These things can be well hidden … *very* well hidden. Gelly – Gellis – Duncan is a mischievous young woman, unmarried, sneaking out at all ungodly hours, and the power to bewitch… Mrs Bryce noticed…'

'With due respect, Reverend McLaren,' the sheriff cuts in, 'this is an official investigation. We are not here to indulge in neighbourhood tittle tattle.' The sheriff has heard too many tales of proceedings descending into hearsay and being used to settle old scores and land disputes. He determines it will not happen on his watch.

Mrs Strachan looks uncertainly from the sheriff to the reverend. 'I … umm…'

'Please continue, Goodwife Strachan,' the commissioner intervenes. 'You have conducted a thorough search of the suspect?'

'Aye, sir, I have.'

'And you've found something?' he presses.

'Aye, sir. I have, sir.'

The commissioner leans back and places his palms on the table, sweeping them across it as if smoothing out the wood. He turns his head to his shoulder and addresses his assistant who is still hovering behind him. 'Mr Roberts – Grant – get the goodwife a chair and perhaps some ale. Cook has pie left?'

'Aye, sir. She does, sir,' the young man answers as he rushes for a chair.

'Please sit, Goodwife Strachan, and tell us all you have found.'

Mrs Strachan sits, nodding her thanks to Grant as he positions a plain pine seat beneath her ample bottom.

The pie and ale arrive. She takes a sip, then another, and bites into the pie. The reverend and Commissioner Baxter look on eagerly, but the sheriff stares at her like a fox intent on its prey. She finishes chewing and swallows. 'I found the Devil's mark, sir.'

'I knew it!' the reverend bursts out, clapping his hands.

'Go on,' the commissioner instructs.

She takes another mouthful. 'It's on her neck, just under her left ear. There's no mistaking it. It's red and mauve, where the Devil's kissed her.'

'That's why she wears that scarf all the time.' The minister drops his hands to his lap as if the verdict has been decided.

'Are you sure it is not a bruise?' the sheriff asks, unconvinced.

The goodwife nods. 'Yes, sir, it is permanent. I've seen it before. The witchfinder, Mr Hart at Banff, sir, a very respected gentleman and man of the cloth, showed me what to look for.'

'And you've seen it on other witches?' the commissioner asks.

'Aye, I have, many times – and we were right! They were all convicted, so we must have been right.'

The commissioner leans back, rubbing the arms of his chair. 'That's all we need, gentlemen. Mr Roberts, if you would assist the goodwife,' he instructs, pointing to the tankard and half-eaten pie. 'Goodwife Strachan, you have been most helpful … most helpful indeed. Mr Roberts here will see to your fee and expenses. Now, perhaps you would be more comfortable supping in the kitchen.'

She gets up. 'Yes, sir. Thank you, sir.'

Grant leads the goodwife to the door and gently but firmly closes it behind them.

The commissioner turns to the sheriff, his face stony. The candle flickers, causing grotesque shadows to dance on the wall. 'I want a confession from Duncan and the names of every member in her coven. I want warrants issued before the night is out!'

# Chapter Thirty-Seven

A Journey
St Marcel's Plague Hospital

Assen wakes with a gasp and his eyes flick open. He huffs and coughs, his breath stuck in the upper part of his ribcage. His body writhes as if underwater, desperately trying to get to the surface for its next breath. Before he would have panicked, but not now. He knows he will not die; this is not how it is going to end.

A technique he learned to soothe anxious patients pops into his mind. He lets the panic from his gut rise and course around his body and watches it curiously. Pursing his lips, he blows out as far as he can and holds his breath for as long as he can, then lets his body take over. The air rushes through his nose and goes deep into the lungs. He does it again, and again. The air reaches almost to his abdomen. The panic subsides, disappearing as quickly as it rose; he feels his stomach muscles soften and his shoulders slacken. His head flops back onto the pillow, and his brain is clear and calm.

Looking at the vaulted ceiling, he marvels at the craftsmen who made the structure, how they smoothed and curved the beams and carved the little adornments they added to their base, even though no one would ever be up there to see them. He props himself on his elbows and looks around.

Yes, St Marcel's. That's right. As if on cue, the bells chime. One, two, three ... he counts to ten. It must be mid-morning. He hears faint sounds from the kitchen: pots and pans plopped on tables and hearth.

An older gentleman and a young boy occupy the beds on either side of him. Both are either sleeping or unconscious. Weak sunlight streams through the tall window opposite, casting a corridor of light on the sleeping child. There is a young woman sitting on the edge of the boy's bed. Strange: he hadn't noticed her before. He didn't think female visitors were allowed at this hour.

Almost closing his eyes, pretending to be asleep, he takes a closer look. She is wearing a long cream robe from head to foot, edged with a cobalt-blue trim. The boy wakes, sniffs and rubs his eyes. Seeing her, he starts to chat excitedly. Good, he is awake; the boy will live. They'll put him back in the great hall or maybe let him go home.

What else is going on? He turns his head. Gérard is standing at the front of the chapel by the altar, talking with a nurse brother. The monk nods, takes a sheet from Gérard and heads next door.

For a moment Gérard remains transfixed below the altar, flanked by two enormous brass candlesticks and the magnificent brass crucifix rising above his head. He scans the chapel and his gaze eventually settles on Assen's row. A look of amazement and puzzled delight crosses his face as Assen gives him a little regal wave.

Hurrying down the aisle with a broad smile, he nearly breaks into a run. 'Assen!' he says, a little breathlessly. 'You are recovering. I can't believe it, dear friend. Praise God!'

'Yes, praise God, for I *am* recovered. But I must go. I have work to do … real work. I must learn. I don't know everything… I must be humble—'

'What? Wait a little, Assen. You've been ill. You need time to recuperate, to settle and think clearly.'

'I am thinking clearly,' Assen says with a laugh. 'I've never thought so clearly!' He looks around again, and his eyes rest on the young boy now sleeping peacefully as if he had never moved. The young woman is gone. He looks up and down both rows; there is no trace of her, just the brothers going about their business. 'Where is…? There was a young woman talking with the child. One of the nuns? She was here a minute ago. Which order? I didn't recognise her habit.'

'There was no one here, only you. Besides, females cannot come in here during washing. These times are reserved, as you well know.'

'But the boy was talking to her. You'll take him back to the great hall today, yes? Is he to go home soon?'

'It's in God's hands, dear friend. The child was given the rites this morning; he has not woken since yesterday afternoon.'

'But I saw him; I saw her,' Assen protests. 'They were chatting and laughing. He looked fine!'

'You must rest. You've been through a lot.' Gérard pats his shoulder. 'Are you hungry? I'll bring you a little broth, then you should sleep to recover your strength.'

'I am quite well. Where are my clothes? I must get dressed ... wash... I have a journey to make.'

'You won't get far if you don't eat.'

'Perhaps you're right.' Assen knows Gérard is talking sense. Although he is bursting with energy, it wouldn't do any harm to build up his reserves for he doesn't know how long he'll be on the road or where he'll next find shelter and food. 'Where can I get dressed and washed?' He swings his legs over the bed, his nightrobe settling on his calves.

'I'll have a cell prepared for you.' Gérard regards him enquiringly. 'Where are you going? You said a journey?'

'Beaune,' Assen replies, using the heels of his hands to propel himself forward. 'I'm going to the House of God. Laugh all you want.'

But Gérard remains serious, sensing a shift in his friend, as if he has found the lost piece of a puzzle. 'I'm not laughing. I'm curious.'

'All right. I've seen... I went somewhere. I ... I saw Uncle Manny ... my mother... She was beautiful ... young. I felt such— You'd never believe...'

'Try me.'

Of course, if anyone will believe him it is Gérard. Assen breathes deeply and lets his body sink back into the bed. 'It was just ... love, the whole place ... the flowers, the fountain, the water, mother, Uncle Manny. They ... it was all just pure love ... that was *it*... They told me to go to Beaune, the House of God.' He looks at Gérard. 'You think I'm mad?'

'I think you're saner than I've seen you for a long time. It is what you must do.'

Encouraged, Assen hurriedly continues. 'I am to travel off the main bridleways, take the old roads and seek out healers, the old women, those to whom people turn in need, in sickness, strife. I am to learn what I've lost.' He stops, leans back and looks up into his friend's eyes. 'What I dismissed.'

'Are you, indeed? Listen,' Gerard says seriously, 'Dr Broussard thinks you are dying, maybe already dead. It is best he continues to think that.'

Assen is confused. 'Why?'

'He ... umm... Look, there's no way of coating this in syrup. He wants you tried for murder.'

'What? Is that a joke?' Assen plants his feet on the cold stone floor, the icy chill seeping through his soles into his ankles and calves. Getting to his feet, he is surprised to find he is quite steady. Good. He needs to be grounded, firmly connected to the earth if he is to follow his calling.

'The patients who died,' Gérard says slowly. Assen recognises the slow, clear manner for imparting troubling information they'd learned at medical school. 'He's saying it was your potions that killed them, not the plague.'

'I'm getting dressed. I must speak with him.'

'No!' Gérard says firmly. 'It's not the time. You should go. You *have* to go. Besides, you have been told, have you not? Your mother told you, didn't she?'

Assen nods. He lifts his head and takes several steps towards the aisle. 'Shall we?'

Skipping around the bed to join him, Gérard lightly takes his elbow, but seeing his friend is quite stable, he lets his hand drop. They walk side by side down the passageway.

Assen looks up at the crucifix. 'I didn't kill those patients, did I?'

'Of course not! It was the plague. It took more than half the patients in the hospital, in *all* the hospitals. You did everything you could, you were here day and night. Heavens, you got the plague yourself! Everyone knows it. Broussard has always had it in for you.'

'Hmm.' Although Assen knows Gérard is speaking the truth, doubt gnaws inside him. Could he have done something he didn't do, or not done something he did? 'You really think Broussard will...?'

'I think for now you should go somewhere far away,' Gérard says gently but firmly.

'Yes.' All the people he most loves in this world and the other want him to go, so it must be right. 'It is decided,' he says as they reach the altar. The words feel good, steadfast, ready for anything. 'Where are my clothes?'

Gérard laughs. 'You can't wear them!'

'Why not?' He looks around, wondering what else he needs. If he is to avoid the main road south out of Paris, he'll have to find the lesser-known paths and bridleways deep in the countryside. He doubts there are any maps.

'You'll attract the wrong kind of attention,' Gérard says, interrupting Assen's mental journey.

'Ah…' The penny drops. His clothes, which he'd never given much thought to, could be a beacon of wealth, status and opportunity. He would be the target of every ruffian, a maiden or two who would wed a gentleman no matter how down on his luck, or even a lady with a less permanent arrangement in mind.

'I'll find you something. The cell next to Brother Francis is free. I'll meet you there.'

Assen looks down at his new old clothes. Gérard has done well. He rotates his arms inwards, checks the sleeves. Definitely more befitting of a tradesman than a gentleman. Did he not see a scribe once, wearing something similar? A plain brown tunic, longer than is currently fashionable, reaching mid-thigh, brought in at the waist with a brown leather belt; breeches all the way to his ankles, and hose to keep him warm.

Everything smells fresh and clean. He wonders how many people have worn these clothes and who their last owner was. He shakes his head. He mustn't think about that. The boots are sturdy, just what he needs for the long journey.

Gathering up his bundle and the bag of food Gérard has prepared, he makes his way to the small side entrance of the chapel. Gérard is already there. 'Well, friend,' he says, pointing to a horse with a thick white coat tied by the reins to a large metal hoop in the wall, 'your steed awaits.'

Assen laughs. 'Has she been waiting here all this time?' He takes Gérard firmly by the shoulder and puts out his hand. Gérard clasps it and they shake resolutely; it is a custom Assen brought back from England several years ago. They've used it when kissing on the cheek fell from favour during these last few years of intermittent plague.

'Well ... umm, listen, Gérard... I ... if it wasn't for you...' Assen wants to tell Gérard how much he has helped him, how he wouldn't have survived medical school without him. How he saved his life and how he might not see him again.

'I know. But it is best you leave Paris. You made the right decision – and you have providence on your side!' But as Gérard drops his hand, a shadow crosses his face. 'Actually,' he adds quietly, 'it would be best if a lot of people left Paris.'

'What do you mean?'

'Nothing. Get on your way, good friend.'

'What are you not telling me? Be true, good friend.'

Gérard's shoulders sag. 'It is just talk, hearsay. It'll blow over, I'm sure.'

'Tell me.'

'They say the prince is amassing more soldiers.'

'You think he'll attack Paris? I'm not going, then! It's decided.' Assen starts to take off his satchel.

'No! It is just talk – he'll never get in. No army could. Look at the walls, the defences. No one would even try. Besides, they'll negotiate ... they'll come to an arrangement. They always do.'

'Y-e-s, but the Catholic League said they'd never accept a Protestant king. They said Paris won't have it,' Assen says uncertainly.

'He'll convert. Your father and Dr Brisbois are certain of it and they're usually right. It'll all blow over. But for some reason you are meant to go to Beaune. Assen, you *have* to go to Beaune.'

Assen replaces his satchel. 'You're right. Gérard, will you promise me something?'

'Anything.'

'If something happens, will you get my father out?'

'You have my word.'

Assen hugs him. To hell with disapproval. 'Listen, if you need to get in touch, I will go by the name of—' he looks to the side, thinking '—our good friend, our Limousin pig at the chateau.' He takes out a crumpled piece of paper. 'This is where I think I'll be going.' He gives his friend a final pat on the arm, crosses the street towards the white horse and unties the reins. He jumps on.

*This is it.*

He steers the mare around and nods to Gérard, who returns a cheery wave.

'*Allez!*' Assen gently taps the mare's withers with his heels and gallops off, leaving Gérard in a little cloud of swirling dust.

# Chapter Thirty-Eight

A Confession
Tranent Tolbooth

A fire burns heartily in the grate in Commissioner Baxter's office at Tranent Gaol as they wait for news. It is three in the morning. Sparks pop and leap up the chimney; others occasionally land next to the reverend's crossed feet.

Sitting opposite the fire in a high-backed, dark-oak chair, he is glad of the new blood red plush seat cushion. He twiddles his thumbs; what is taking so long? How long have they been waiting?

The commissioner's assistant is slumped over the table, quill still in hand, documents spread in front of him. Perhaps a bit of fresh air would revive him. The commissioner is asleep in the chair facing him, chin on his chest, occasionally grunting and jerking but never quite waking. Reverend McLaren walks to the window and opens it outwards. An icy gust cuts through the oppressive heat and stale smells of pork, cabbage and sweat.

The change stirs the sheriff who is leaning against the opposite wall, arms folded. He pushes himself upright and scans the room. 'Commissioner, sir,' he clears his throat, 'do you think we should not perhaps—'. Then he notices the commissioner is asleep and he sighs and leans back against the wall.

The reverend pulls the window back and fastens its catch.

A loud knock at the door makes them jump. The commissioner sits bolt upright and looks around, eyes glazed as he grips the arms of the chair. No one moves; the atmosphere is alive with static.

The minister looks from the commissioner to the sheriff to the young assistant who is on his feet, a look of terror on his face. The young man sways slightly and places his fingertips on the table to balance himself.

'Enter!' the commissioner barks.

Mr McPherson, the witchfinder, strolls in, with Mr Birkett behind him. He is wiping his hands with an old rag as if he has been working on a cart or at an anvil.

'Well?' demands the commissioner.

'It's done,' Mr Birkett says matter-of-factly, as if he's just replaced a broken wheel.

'She's confessed. They met in St Andrew's Kirk, right enough,' the witchfinder adds.

The reverend purses his lips. So, his instinct was right. He thought there might have been a coven, imagined it even, but in the wee small hours, he'd had doubts, a gnawing in his gut, a wave of dread and a cold sweat. He'd asked himself if it was it the right course and prayed for guidance. On several occasions, he'd even resolved to talk to the commissioner and suggest they settle the matter in another way.

So much had depended on his knowledge of the congregation and the mutterings of goings-on at the Seton House and the schoolhouse, but now there is a confession, which settles everything. He was right after all. Thank goodness. He can rest easy; he was right from the start. He heaves a sigh of relief. He *is* doing God's work, wherever it might lead.

'She's named others?' the commissioner quizzes.

The witchfinder nods. 'She has.'

The sheriff looks troubled but says nothing.

'Tell us!' the minister demands.

Mr McPherson takes out a piece of parchment from a pocket in his long coat, unfolds it and begins reading. 'Agnes Sampson, John Fian, Agnes Thompson of Edinburgh, Barbara Napier, Jannet Blandilands, Francis Stewart, the Earl of Bothwell—'

'The Earl of Bothwell!' the sheriff exclaims. 'How in heaven does a serving lass know the Earl of Bothwell! He's the king's cousin!'

The witchfinder exchanges a fleeting glance with the commissioner.

'They meet together in the coven,' the reverend explains, his conscience now clear.

'How many?' the commissioner asks. The greater the number of arrests, the stronger the case for the presence of the royal court and the king himself, especially if the conspiracy can be traced to the highest echelons of society.

Mr McPherson considers the parchment. 'So far eleven, but likely many more if you allow me a little more time with her. The size of this conspiracy is beyond anything I've encountered. And once we question the co-conspirators and the leader, who knows—?'

'The leader? She has named the leader?'

'John Fian!' the witchfinder states definitively.

'I knew it!' Reverend McLaren claps his hands. *I'll must write to the General Assembly this instant.* This is news Commissioner Baxter can take to His Majesty – the name of the Devil's right-hand man in Scotland. He can tell his grace he has the Devil's general in custody. *Now we're getting somewhere.* The minister sighs contentedly.

The commissioner turns to Grant, his assistant. 'Issue the warrants! Raise the guard! I want every one of them in custody before the morrow. Mr Birkett, what do you need?'

'More men … with strong stomachs.'

'See to it. Call on the reserves,' the commissioner instructs Grant, who is busy scrambling papers into an untidy pile.

The reverend gets up and walks to the window. Taking out his handkerchief, he dabs the corner of it on the tip of his tongue and wipes a peep-hole in the grimy window pane. He peers out.

Hooves are soon clattering on the wet cobbles of the gaol courtyard and court buildings. Orders echo in the enclosed space as the men mount the horses. They form into two groups of four and each man grabs a flaming torch. The horses don't flinch; a well-trained mount is a prerequisite for imposing the rule of law in this wild country.

It is still several hours before dawn and clouds hang low, dark and forbidding. Each group speeds off in a different direction, one thundering along a bridleway like an approaching storm, the other cantering on a well-trodden path deep in the forest.

# Chapter Thirty-Nine

A Chance Encounter
Vézelay, France

Assen rides along the banks of a river, dozing in the saddle. He has been riding for days and the gentle, rocking motion of his horse, Esther, has had a hypnotic effect.

*He dreams he is with Gérard and Dr Brisbois in a carriage upholstered in purple velvet when a strange man gets on. Assen has never seen anyone dressed like him before, in a long black coat and tall hat. The man makes him nervous. His two friends chat amicably while the stranger looks on. They are talking about how to treat the sleeping sickness; Dr Brisbois is hopeful an elixir of mercury and antimony will do the trick. Then it comes to Assen in a flash, pops right into his head, a revolutionary new cure – and it is so obvious.*

He wakes with a start as Esther trips over a tree root, poor girl. He will stop soon. If only he could remember it, the cure. What was it again? Esther's gentle swaying once more rocks him into a slumber.

*He is back in the carriage, but this time it is only him and the stranger. The man sits opposite and speaks for the first time. He has a foreign accent that Assen can't quite place. 'Only Jesus Christ cures the sick. Owt else is the work o' the Devil.'*

'Pardon?' Who is this man, and why is Assen sharing the carriage with a religious zealot?

*'Those that assist the Devil will burn and their mortal remains will be scattered to the four winds for the beasts.'*

A wave of terror sweeps through Assen, and his stomach lurches as he falls forward, slides down Esther's neck and lands on the grassy verge of the river. Startled, he jolts his head up to see Esther's muzzle dipped in the water. Thank goodness she picked a soft landing for him, but he wishes she'd given him a little more warning; she must have known he was sleeping up there.

'Did you do it deliberately?' he asks, wiping down his arms.

She turns towards him, blinks and shakes her head, her mane flapping.

'Hmm,' he tuts.

Never mind. It is a fine day and perhaps this is the perfect spot for respite. Looking around, he sees a tree close by, sloping away from the river, a prime spot to rest his back and watch the river go by. The water is calm, almost like a mirror, but with a gentle undercurrent. Bits of straw and little twigs float by. Where will they go? Snag around the next bend or float all the way to the sea? The Mediterranean!

He once had an uncle, his mother's brother, who travelled all round the globe to the lands on the far side of that great sea, even to terrain where there are no maps – the Orient. His mother had told Assen that his uncle was a real explorer, very brave. Unfortunately he had died when Assen was young, so he'd never known him. That was a pity because he sounded fascinating, and the ingredients and spices he would have been able to get to make medicines... Oh well. People die young, but Assen wishes he had known his uncle even for a little while.

Perhaps a rest is in order. He settles down and closes his eyes. Heavenly. He breathes out a long satisfying breath.

'Hello.'

'Huh?' Assen blurts out, feeling for his sword. Where is it, damn it? He's left it on Esther. Ten days out of Paris and he's forgotten everything Gérard told him.

Shielding his eyes with one hand, he looks up, the heel of the other braced on the ground, ready to propel him to his feet.

'Have you come far, sir?' A boy of about eight or nine years is looking down at him.

'Umm ... yes... Well I...'

He looks down at his clothes, sensing he must look a bit unkempt. Rust-coloured dust clings to his worn, black-leather tunic from the bone-dry tracks he's been navigating since Paris. Mud from where he crossed the Seine is still splattered liberally on his black linen and leather breeches. He brushes the backs of his arms to dislodge some of the detritus and gets to his feet.

Dusting down his trousers and smoothing back his hair, he hopes he looks better. The boy doesn't seem frightened, so he can't look that bad.

He might as well ask; his next stop can't be far away. He rummages in his pocket, pulls out a piece of paper and looks at it, then at the boy. He coughs. 'I am looking for the village of Vézelay and the midwife and healer named Madame Lambert.'

'Good day, sir. My name is André.'

'Forgive me. I am long on the road and have left my manners there. My name is Doc— I mean, my name is … Alain …. Alain Durand. Pleased to meet you.' He bows his head.

The boy bows too. 'How do you do, sir.'

'André, can you tell me how to get to Vézelay and—?'

'Yes, sir. I can take you there,' André replies brightly, clearly pleased at being able to help a poor, worn-out traveller. 'Would it be alright if I tell Papa when I get home that I helped someone less fortunate than himself?'

Assen supresses a laugh. 'Yes, of course. That is most kind of you. Is it far?'

'No, we can walk or … if you want, you can ride your horse. I don't mind.' He stops, biting his lip. 'Are you sick or poor?'

'Uhmm, no, no, I'm not.'

André furrows his brows. 'Papa says we should try to help people who are sick or poor.' He looks Assen up and down. 'I'll help you anyway.'

'Thank you, I am much obliged and I think a walk would be good. My trusty steed needs a rest.' Assen smiles, places his hand between Esther's ears and smooths down her forelock. She looks at him steadily then gives a jerk and a nod of her head. He laughs and winks at her. 'For both of us. Lead on.'

André turns and heads up the trail away from the river. It is steep in places and Assen has to use his hands and feet to scramble over the top of the gorge to reach the path leading to the ancient Burgundian village of Vézelay perched majestically on a hill.

As they round the corner, the trees thin out and Assen gets his first glimpse of the town. It looks magical, like a place in the fairy tales his mother used to tell him. 'Once upon a time,' she'd say, 'there was an old cobbler who lived and worked in a tiny workshop in a faraway town perched on a hill. Day in, day out, he made boots for the townsfolk, and nothing ever happened until one day a stranger arrived.'

'Uncle Galib?' five-year-old Assen would burst out. Stories about his uncle's adventures were always the best.

'That's right, Assen.' His mother would laugh. 'Until Uncle Galib arrived!'

Assen would settle down under her arm, his eyes wide.

Now it is his turn to be the stranger. He hopes the inhabitants of Vézelay won't be as weird and stand-offish as some of the places his uncle stumbled upon. He doesn't think he has quite the same aptitude for adventure as Uncle Galib had.

They head up the narrow path towards the village square. The church sits at its pinnacle on the far side of the quadrangle, its tall, majestic spire soaring high above the other buildings. There are fresh flowers in vases adorning the front of the chapel, and the steps leading to the vestibule are so worn and bowed they look like mellow crescent moons. He wonders how many feet have stepped on them. It leaves little doubt about the place of faith in Vézelay.

André leads Assen down the side of the church along some cobbled alleyways that eventually open onto a wider thoroughfare. He stops outside the door of one of the tall narrow houses lining the street. 'This is where Madame Lambert lives,' he announces.

'Is it?' Assen takes a deep breath.

What would Uncle Galib do? Well, there's no time like the present. He strides forward and raps on the door rather more loudly and confidently than he feels. He digs into his pocket; he mustn't forget to reward André. Without his help, he could have wasted a lot of time. Besides, he is in no doubt he will need the boy's services again. He feels the cold surfaces of the coins in his pouch and fishes one out. 'Here … here's a penny for your trouble. I'm sorry it's not much.'

'That's all right. Kindness is its own reward,' André replies, looking pleased.

'Well, that's true. Where did you learn…?' Assen beams, a little surprised.

'Papa always says that. He told us the story of the Good Samaritan.' André looks down thoughtfully. 'Am I like the Good Samaritan?'

'Yes, you are!' Assen answers, patting the child's shoulder. 'I'm very grateful.'

The sound of a chair being scraped along the floor echoes from inside. They turn to face the heavy oak door as someone pulls it open with some effort. Assen suppresses the urge to help the person by giving it a push: it might not be well received.

When it finally opens, he comes face to face with a woman in her mid to late thirties, possibly seven years or eight years older than he is. She has shoulder-length, thick dark hair and dark eyes, and she is attractive – very attractive.

Embarrassed at his unbidden thoughts, he stutters, 'I... I...' This is certainly not what he has come for. He is here to study, to learn from this woman about the art and craft of healing. The best midwife and healer around, he was told by the wives of several merchants, and the most highly regarded.

In some ways she is not at all what he expected; in others she is exactly what he thought she would be. Dressed modestly, although not poorly, in a plain dark-turquoise dress, with a tiny glimpse of cream at the rim of the collar and cuff, she exudes authority and earthiness at the same time.

She looks from Assen to André. 'Good morning, André. You are not in the grove yet?'

'I was being the Good Samaritan.'

\*\*\*

Madame Lambert regards Assen, quickly taking in his olive skin and dark collar-length hair. He stands out as not being from anywhere around here. His hands look smooth and uncalloused, so he does not labour for a living. And yet, his clothes suggest someone who earns their living in a workshop. They look dirty – wait, no: they are dusty. So, he's travelled a distance. In the past, she's had reason to size people up quickly.

'Were you?' she says softly to André.

\*\*\*

'Yes. This is Alain. He was looking for you and he was lost.' He looks up at Assen. 'Weren't you?'

Assen swallows, 'Y-e-s, yes, I... I... I was looking for you... That is to say...'

'Were you indeed, Mr...?' she says quizzically, looking him square in the eyes.

'Durand... Mr ... Mr ... Alain Durand,' Assen responds.

'So, Mr Durand, you have business? Someone is ill? André, your papa will be wondering where you are. Thank you for your help.'

'Yes, Madame Lambert. You are welcome, Madame Lambert. Can I tell Papa I helped a stranger in need?'

'Of course you can. He'll be very proud of you.'

'Bye, Mr Durand.' He gives Assen a big smile.

Assen remembers being that age. 'You can call me Alain.'

André beams. 'Alain.'

'Bye, André. And thank you again.' Assen gives a formal bow.

The boy heads off, then turns and waves to Assen and Madame Lambert. They cannot help but break into broad smiles mirroring André's.

When he is out of sight, Madame Lambert faces Assen and lets the smile fall from her lips. Pulling her shawl tighter around her and folding her arms, she enquires, 'Now, Mr Durand. What is it that you want?'

Assen senses he has one chance. This woman has been appraising him with a sharp-eyed intelligence and something indefinable, as if she already knows the story of his life. But that's stupid, and yet he knows he must be as honest as he can.

'Please forgive me and my poor introduction. I am from Paris. I am travelling to the House of God in Beaune... I am to learn healing ... and to offer my assistance.' There, he's said it, and it is true.

He rubs the back of his neck with one hand, then the other, elbows pointing forward. He blows out, releasing his hands and letting his arms and shoulders hang. That's better. It's like he has laid down a heavy bag.

'You are a brother?' Madame Lambert says slowly, eyeing him curiously.

'No, a scribe.' It pops out before he's had time to think. He has no idea where it came from and hopes he hasn't ruined everything.

Madame Lambert looks him up and down. 'You don't *look* like a scribe.'

'I have been in the saddle for many days and slept not too well along the way. My horse, Esther, needs a stable.'

'Esther!' Madame Lambert bursts out laughing, 'You have a horse called Esther?'

Assen stiffens. 'She is a fine and loyal steed.' He sounds like a hurt child.

'Is she, indeed?' Madame Lambert teases. 'But you have still not answered my question. What is it you want?'

'I wish to learn from y—'

'What is it you *really* want?'

Flustered, caught in her keen stare, he blurts out, 'I had a … dream.'

'Go on.'

He caresses the back of his neck again. This is it. Well, he tried; he can always say he tried. 'I had a dream where I saw my … dead mother and my Uncle Manny in a garden. They said I must leave my place of work, my home in Paris, and travel to the House of God in Beaune.'

He brings his palm to his throat, gently massaging it as if coaxing out the truth. 'They told me to seek wisdom, the knowledge of healers – traditional healers in the villages I pass through…' Acutely aware of how odd it all sounds, he adds, 'It was very vivid.'

'It must have been!' A smile plays on her lips. 'Have you eaten breakfast?' she asks, opening the door wider.

'Um … no,' he says uncertainly. He has never felt so wrong-footed.

'Hmm, I thought not.' She looks him up and down once more. 'Come in.' Standing back, she tilts her head sideways for him to go inside.

Stepping in from the pale afternoon sun, he needs a moment for his eyes to adjust to the dim interior. The room is much larger than he expected, extending around eighteen feet to the rear. Along the adjacent wall is a large fireplace with a plain, ancient, stone mantel. It reminds him of some of the slabs he's seen in old ecclesiastical buildings.

The fire is lit and a large black pot dangles from a hook inside the fireplace. Whatever is cooking smells good. For the first time since last night, Assen realises he is hungry – ravenous, in fact. Saliva rushes into his mouth. A large farmhouse table sits in the centre of the room with several rough-hewn wooden chairs scattered around it. He steps closer.

'Sit, please.' Madame Lambert gestures to the chair nearest the fire.

He sits down gratefully, weariness overtaking him. 'Thank you.'

He watches her take a bowl from a small stack on the bench under the window furthest from the fireplace. After lifting the ladle from its hook, she stirs the contents of the pan before scooping two ladles full into the dish. She places it in front of him and pushes a plate of flattened bread towards him.

He reaches into his pocket for his spoon and knife and retrieves a cloth from the breast pocket of his tunic, which he uses to wipe the utensils. Madame Lambert fetches two tankards, places one for herself and the other by Assen's elbow. She pours steaming camomile tea into them from a small round pewter pot and sits down to face him. 'Eat, please,' she says.

He begins to devour the stew. It tastes wonderful – different from Paris, and no meat that he can find, but bountiful cabbage, artichoke, beans and carrots. Perhaps his ravenous state is enhancing his senses, but he thinks this is the best meal he's ever had.

Realising he has been gobbling the food, he carefully places his spoon diagonally on the dish and leans back, lifting the tankard to his lips. The tea tastes sweet and fragrant. He sighs. He hopes he doesn't look like an oaf.

But she surprises him. 'I have need of a scribe. Do you have much experience?'

'I have a neat hand,' he answers honestly.

She looks at his hands.

He quickly moves them under the table. They are not blackened the way he'd observed the hands of scribes at the medical school were. 'I…' he stammers. *I'll have to tell her who I really am. She'll find out soon enough.* 'Well, you see—'

'No matter,' she says. 'I need a scribe with a tidy, legible hand. Think you are up to it?' She doesn't wait for him to reply. 'If you are agreeable, you can write down the properties of plants and salts as I tell you them. I will show you, then you will write it down neatly and the sheets will be bound in a manuscript. In return, I will teach you. You will have lodgings – not here, of course – and food. You may sup here – but that is all. I cannot pay you. Is that acceptable?'

'Very acceptable.' It is exactly what he'd hoped for. 'Thank you, Madame Lambert. Thank you.'

Madame Lambert gets up, a little smile curling the corners of her lips. 'More tea?'

'Yes, please.'

\*\*\*

Glancing at him sideways, she feels the hairs at the back of her neck rise. 'There's something about you, young man, I know it. There's a tempest shadowing you. I hope it doesn't sweep both of us away.'

She picks up the pot of tea.

# Chapter Forty

### The Storm Rolls In
### North Berwick

The birds fall silent. Seconds ago, their dawn symphony had soared; it had begun with a single, tuneful trill from a soloist and was quickly followed by a chorus of tweets and squawks. But now the birds silently blink, heads turned and cocked.

There is a distant rumbling. Feathers ruffle; something is not right. Some birds rotate on their perch, claws clutching the branch awkwardly. Is a cyclone or inferno approaching?

The rumble is closer now. A band of men on horseback are galloping hard in the noiseless forest less than half a mile away. Time to fly. The birds take off in a murmuration, soaring high above the treetops. Some scatter north but most head south towards the wood at Kingston, passing over the stronghold of Fenton Tower. The medieval graves and ruined Christian chapel lie just beyond and crows with outstretched claws land awkwardly on the listing stones.

The men come to an abrupt halt outside a tiny cottage on the edge of Turner's wood. A stream gurgles at the bottom of the incline towards the back of the dwelling. It is the only sound in the hushed glade except for the stamping of hooves and occasional snort of a horse.

One of the group raises his hand and the other three dismount soundlessly. Some of the horses shake their heads, their manes flapping from side to side, and nod up and down as if they've not decided if they are excited or enraged about being dragged out in the middle of the night.

The leader whispers to the men and gestures for one to go around the back. Looking at the remaining two men, he crooks his finger at the bigger of the two. The man steps forward, lifts his foot and, with an almighty crash, frees the door from its hinges.

***

Agnes wakes bolt upright, heart pounding. *God Almighty. Sweet Jesus. I'm being robbed.*

Impulsively, she looks up at the loose stone above and to the left of the fireplace. It is undisturbed. Whatever happens, whatever *this* is, she mustn't look at it.

She stares transfixed at the doorway. A huge black figure looms on the other side of the threshold; she can see a glint of his sword. He steps out of sight and another man appears. Lowering his head, he enters her cottage and looks around him. 'You are Agnes Sampson, midwife and healer,' he announces.

'Aye... Who are you?' she answers as steadily as she can.

The man comes further into the room. She recognises him: he was at the courthouse in Tranent when Jannet had a boundary dispute with one of the farmers over at Weir's Way. The farmer, the crafty bugger, had moved the cairn stones. Must have taken him ages. Never got away with it, though. Yes, this man was one of the court guards. What is he doing here?

Another man steps through the gaping hole that used to be her door. *How many are there?* 'Nothing round the back, Sergeant,' he says.

*That's right, he's a sergeant at the courthouse. He took Farmer McLeish away to get fined. What is his name again?*

The sergeant turns to Agnes and extracts a rolled-up piece of parchment from a large pocket in the breast of his doublet. 'Agnes Sampson. We hereby arrest you on the charge of witchcraft and consorting with the Devil, and of conjuring up Satan in St Andrew's Kirk in the village of North Berwick to do devious mischief to the king on evenings in the months of November and December in the year of our Lord 1589, and on occasions too numerous to count in the year of our Lord 1590.'

'Wha...?' This can't be happening. She knew Gelly was in trouble, but... 'Oh, my God.'

'Come with us.'

'I–I–I am not dressed,' She must buy time. *Think, Agnes, think!* 'Allow me some privacy to dress, for decency's sake.'

After a brief hesitation, the sergeant concedes. 'Very well.' He indicates the back door. 'That is your only other door?'

'Aye.'

'See to it,' he tells one of the men who is standing where the front door used to be. He turns back to Agnes. 'Make haste!'

The men leave Agnes sitting up in bed. She has to move fast. Leaping out, she makes for the loose stone. Hands shaking, she carefully removes it, flinching as it scrapes along the ledge. Holding her breath, she gingerly takes out the tattered box, wincing as the lose battered lock rattles.

She takes out a pile of papers tied with twine; underneath is a linen bag. She holds the bag, sensing its contents, its weight and shape. Drawing the string back, she peers inside as if satisfying herself that something is still there. Curling her fingers more tightly around it, she clasps it to her chest.

She looks over her shoulder, puts the item in the deep pocket of her skirt then stops, frozen. Hurriedly she takes it back out and returns it gently to the box, covering it with the papers and old cloth. She closes the lid, slides everything back into the hole and slots the stone into place. Gratified it looks like the rest of the wall, she jumps back to face the opposite direction.

'Time is up, Midwife Sampson. Out now!' the sergeant bellows from outside.

\*\*\*

Some miles away on the other side of the village, another four men on horseback come to a sudden stop outside a modest but far grander house than Agnes's humble home. It is double-fronted, with two, tall lattice windows flanking a warm-mahogany door with three sturdy iron hinges holding it in place.

It is an unusual door in these parts and not readily kicked in. It was a gift from a grateful sea captain whose son was educated by John Fian; indeed, he was taught so well, that the lad secured a place in the highest law court in Edinburgh on merit alone. It wasn't long before the young man sailed through the ranks and married into one of the wealthiest families in the city. John had always found him a personable fellow, too, and had waived fees and expenses when the captain lost his ship. A kindness the mariner had never forgot.

As is often the way, Captain McGarry's fortunes soon turned around, and he found himself skippering one of the most majestic ships plying the trade routes between Rotterdam and Leith. On one trip he made his way to Delft to seek out a master carpenter.

At first the carpenter said he was too busy to take up the commission; he had a long list of wealthy clients who'd been waiting months for their dressers, tables and chairs. But the captain had been persuasive and, on his return, the door was ready. He was delighted with it; there was nothing like it in North Berwick or anywhere else in the county. In fact, there was nothing like it in the whole country. It would make a fine wedding present.

With the help of two midshipmen, he left the new door outside the couple's newly acquired house for when they returned after the wedding feast. Kitty, John's spouse, was delighted with the present for it reflected perfectly their place in the community: strong, ornate, but not too ostentatious.

John had married well. Kitty brought with her a handsome dowry, which allowed him to set up the parish school and purchase the house as well as the little luxuries that made his wife more comfortable so far from the diversions of Edinburgh.

He loved his wife, if not faithfully. Gelly had brought out something in him – a passion, and not just a physical one. She had instilled in him a thirst for ideas, and the more he read to and educated Gelly, the more the passion gained momentum. His long-held desire to change the world he thought had been extinguished, was rekindled by their affair.

The men dismount outside his house and crowd around the mahogany door. Two of them hold flaming torches above their heads. The leader raps hard on its timbers. 'Open up! Open up in the name of the king!' He turns to the biggest man. 'Dalgleish, do your stuff. You others, stand back.'

As Dalgleish raises his foot, the door opens and John Fian stares blearily out holding a candle.

'You are John Fian, schoolmaster?' the leader asks.

'Aye, I am. Is there some kind of trouble? Who are you?'

'Sergeant Cox,' the man replies. 'I have a signed warrant for your arrest.'

John's tired eyes widen. 'Signed by whom? On what charges? What is this?'

'Commissioner Baxter,' the sergeant replies.

For all his education and rhetorical skills, John is finding it hard to think. 'Commissioner … Baxter? There must be some mistake… Mistaken identity, that must be it.'

'There's no mistake,' the sergeant says emphatically. 'You are charged with witchcraft.'

'What?' Thoughts tumble through his mind. *Gelly! What have they done to Gelly? Where is Agnes? What have the Setons done?*

The sergeant goes on, 'Summoning the Devil, leading the coven.'

'Jesus!'

'Do not blaspheme!'

John remembers the sergeant is a staunch Calvinist.

'Get dressed and come with us.' The sergeant calls Dalgleish forward. 'Go with him.'

'John, John! What is it?' a woman's voice calls from upstairs. 'What's going on? Who's there?'

'It's all right, Kitty,' John calls, trying to sound matter of fact, but his voice trembles. 'It's nothing. I … I have to go out for a bit. Go back to bed. I'll be back soon.'

'I'm coming down,' she shouts back.

The men look at each other as her soft but hurried tread descends the stairs. She reaches the door, pulls it from John and comes face to face with the posse arranged in a solemn semicircle, the downcast light from the flaming torches sharpening their unshaven, chiselled features.

Kitty looks up at her husband and back to the men. 'What do you mean?' She searches his face. 'Where are you going at this hour? Who are these people? What do they want?'

'There's been a misunderstanding, that's all.' John regains his authoritative, reassuring voice, the one he uses with his pupils. 'I am going to clear it up.' He must keep calm, stay in control, yet he has a sickly feeling in the pit of his stomach that things are far beyond his control now.

His tone does little to placate Kitty. 'Where are you going?' Her voice is shrill.

'He's going to Tranent Gao—' the sergeant begins, then changes tack. 'Umm … we need to talk to your husband at the court buildings in Tranent.' He turns to one of the men and John hears him mumble, 'The last thing we need is a hysterical woman.'

'I don't understand. Why?' Kitty asks, her cheeks reddening.

'It's all right, Kitty. I have to go, but I'll be back.'

The sergeant coughs. 'Mr Fian, sir, if you would make haste.'

John releases the door and heads back into the house.

'Dalgleish! Go with him.'

Open-mouthed, Kitty lets her arms drop by her side and stares at her husband's back.

John stops as he remembers something. 'Kitty, you recall the lawyer in Edinburgh – Mr Brodie?'

'Yes, Husband.'

'Get him. If you can't get him, fetch Mr McGarry.'

# Chapter Forty-One

A Fresh Start?
Vézelay

It had been an odd few weeks for Assen. Most people in the village seemed to have accepted him as Madame Lambert's assistant but others cross the street when he approaches.

'Don't worry, they'll come around', she says.

'I suppose so.' But a dead weight settles in the pit of his gut. It is never good when people see something to fear about you.

He stands in front of the raised bench that spans the back wall of her house. Piles of seeds, leaves, stocks and flower heads lie neatly between him and Madame Lambert. The shutters are open as there is barely a whisper of air. He looks out into the long garden which is efficiently organised in beds of herbs, flowers and vegetables. As far as he can see, she grows almost everything she needs: ingredients for many of the remedies she uses to treat her patients.

Wearing the long sleeves of a scribe, he attempts to flatten the piece of linen he is to write on; it's not as easy as parchment or paper to work with. He dabs his quill into a pot of black ink and carefully scrapes it along the rim of the pot to remove the excess. At the other end of the table, Madame Lambert grinds seeds and corms with a pestle and mortar. The crunching and scraping punctuates the birdsong and occasional buzz of an insect from the garden. Assen finds the whole process calming; he has nothing to think about except the properties of flowers, herbs and vegetables.

'It is not what you are used to,' she says, breaking his meditative state.

'Hmm?'

She points at the linen with her pestle. He places his hands on either side of the sheet, careful not to touch it. 'It is often used in the church by the brothers … the monks,' then he quickly adds, 'so I'm told. Apparently it lasts for generations, hundreds of years, maybe thousands.'

She turns back to her grinding.

'It's just a little difficult to work with,' Assen continues, concentrating on getting the loop of the 'Y' in rosemary to slope the right way. 'It takes a little longer than parchment. Sorry if I'm being slow.'

'Not at all. Speaking of the church, Father Girault is coming to see you.'

'The priest?'

Madame Lambert picks up a length of twine and softens the ends in her mouth. 'Uh-uh.' Using her wooden scoop, she puts the dried petals of peonies, lavender seeds and chopped thyme leaves into a small cloth bag and firmly ties the top with the cord.

'Why?' Assen asks, mildly curious as he focuses on the swirl of the 'J' in juniper.

Madame Lambert laughs. 'Have you ever lived in a small village?'

'No,' he answers truthfully, although he can see the pretty little cottages in the village close to his grandparents' estate. He smiles as he recalls the wood and lake beyond the formal gardens. A picture forms in his head of him holding a duck. He feels its weight in his hands as he gently cradles it, strokes its folded wings, soft and smooth. It wriggles its tail and quacks. Careful not to hurt it, he can almost feel the down, sleek and delicate to the touch. But that can't be right, surely? Yet… He blinks; he must have dreamt it.

'He likes to tend his flock, make sure a wolf hasn't sneaked in,' Madame Lambert continues, tying another bag.

'What? Who?' Assen looks up.

'Father Girault. He likes to make sure a wolf hasn't sneaked into his flock.'

'Me?' Assen almost scratches a diagonal line through the near perfect 'J' he's just created. He puts his quill back into the ink pot and wipes his hands down the front of his full-length apron.

She smiles and shrugs. 'He is like that with everyone. When I arrived, he wanted to know where Mr Lambert was, what had happened to Mr Lambert, why there wasn't a Mr Lambert.'

Assen raises his eyebrows, as intrigued as Father Girault regarding the answer. She catches his look. 'You too?' she states with an intense gaze.

'I'm sorry,' he says hastily. 'It is none of my business.' Picking up his quill, he bends over to resume his writing though his hand is shaking, imperceptibly but even so. Damn. 'Forgive me. I did not mean to offend.'

'You didn't. Mr Lambert is gone … a long time ago.' She looks out of the window.

'I'm sorry.'

'Thank you… Father Girault will report back to the mayor.'

'Why?'

'They run a tight ship – no breaches where the Devil might get in.'

'The Devil!' He sets down his pen again. 'Surely we've left that behind, along with dragons and fairies?'

'You really have never lived in the country, have you?'

No, he doesn't think so … not really… Unless…

# Chapter Forty-Two

The Interrogation
Tranent Tolbooth

'She's here,' someone announces from inside the room. The door is opened a crack and Agnes sees a shadow flit across the gap. A young man appears. The light momentarily sears her eyes. The pungent smell of horses and sweat from the guards on either side of her still assails her nostrils.

The commissioner looks up from the papers he's scrutinising. 'Bring her in.' He places the documents to one side.

The young man steps to the side, allowing the first guard to enter with Agnes and the other behind her.

Commissioner Baxter reclines as if he's just finished a delicious meal and clasps his hands on his stomach. A thin smile stretches his lips. Reverend McLaren looks like he's just woken up and pushes himself higher in his padded seat. Another man, a stranger in black, stands behind him, his hand lightly placed on the corner of the minister's chair.

Agnes clasps her hands firmly to stop them shaking as she walks further into the room. She tries to take a deep breath but it catches in her throat, making her cough. Moving closer to the desk, she notices headings peeping from the untidy pile by the man at the desk's elbow. *Title Deeds*, *Agreements*, *Lands adjoining the Seton estate and Mr John Fian's holding*. She frowns.

The sheriff is looking out of the window. He throws it open and turns to face her. She tries to take another deep breath and this time crisp air cuts through her like a blade. She shivers.

'Wait outside,' the commissioner orders the guards.

The door's hinges grind as it shuts with a thud and a clink, like a cell door closing.

'Come forward,' he commands Agnes.

The men scrutinise her with tired eyes. It looks like they've been here all night.

'Well, well, well. *You* are Agnes Sampson,' the commissioner states. 'I must admit, I expected someone of greater stature.'

'The extent of a person's integrity is not in their height,' she responds quickly, determined not to show the fear churning in her stomach.

'Very true,' the commissioner concedes. 'That's what we are here to examine – your integrity.'

The witchfinder coughs. 'With your permission, Commissioner Baxter.'

The commissioner opens his palm. 'Please go ahead, Mr McPherson.'

\*\*\*

The witchfinder is acutely aware his involvement in this trial could change his life. His livelihood until now has often depended on the whims of gossip and superstition. For a shilling, he would give his verdict on the misfortunes to befall neighbours and communities, declaring it sorcery or not. But now his future could be secured. Never again would he have to ride from village to village offering his services.

Although he has been successful in hunting and identifying witches and witchcraft all over Scotland, and given evidence in many witch trials, never in his wildest dreams has he imagined he would serve the king of Scotland.

From now on, every word will be crucial. He has to place himself at the centre of the investigations, picking up signs no one else notices, showing his expertise is indispensable in detecting the dark arts and critical in gaining convictions.

'How far would you go, Agnes Sampson?' the witchfinder begins, pacing in front of her. 'How far would you go to heal people, to take their shillings, to make them your puppets? That's what you did, isn't it? All these silly lassies and crones are marionettes under your control!'

'Aye, and sup with the Devil in St Andrew's Kirk, while you formed your diabolical plans,' Reverend McLaren adds.

\*\*\*

'What?' Agnes's mouth falls open, and her stomach sinks. It feels like she is falling down a well. 'The Auld Kirk! What are you talking about?'

'All in good time, Reverend McLaren,' the commissioner says with a placatory gesture.

'What's he talking about?' Agnes snaps, anger momentarily overtaking fear. Her heart pounds in her ribcage and white light sears through her brain. She wants to punch the smug vicar in the face.

'Agnes,' the sheriff says slowly, 'you need to tell the commissioner how you go about your healings.'

'Yes, let's start there.' The commissioner picks up a piece of paper. 'Now, there was a Mrs Aird, barren for years.' He turns his head fractionally to his assistant, Grant, who has materialised silently behind his shoulder. 'How long had they been married?'

'Seven years, sir.'

'Seven years and no children – a punishment from God. But I defer to our good churchman. Was that your opinion, Reverend?'

'Indeed, unhappily so,' Reverend McLaren answers with a sage nod and rests his chin on his interlaced fingers.

'Then you give Mrs Aird a potion,' the commissioner continues, turning his attention back to Agnes, 'and miraculously she is with child! She had been to see the good reverend, offered penance, prayed to our Lord Jesus Christ, seen the best physicians, but nothing worked. Alas, everyone agreed – and Mrs Aird herself accepted – that she was being punished for having an impure soul. Then you come along, interfere where good men have failed, and Mrs Aird gives birth to a healthy baby boy. It is a miracle! Reverend, tell me, who performs miracles?'

'Jesus Christ, Commissioner Baxter,' the minister states, releasing his fingers and slapping his thigh.

'And if the miracle were not performed by our Lord Jesus Christ, who else would be responsible?'

'The Devil!' the reverend answers, his eyes twinkling.

'The Devil,' the commissioner says slowly, nodding as he peers at Agnes.

Agnes feels like a fly in the centre of a spider's web: every answer she gives makes her stick faster to its fine threads. She stares unblinkingly at the commissioner. She knows what happens when people start talking about the Devil; she's heard the stories of the witch hunts in Fife. *Tread carefully, Agnes Sampson.* She mustn't mention the word, even if they ask her directly. She mustn't link herself to the one who calls himself Satan. *Dear Jesus, guide me in my answers.*

The commissioner bangs his fist on the table. 'What do you have to say?'

'This is about Mrs Aird?' she says slowly. 'You're asking me about Mrs Aird? She came to me. She heard I was a midwife, a good one; she asked if I could help her. Mrs Aird was highly strung, overwrought. She blamed herself.' Agnes looks at Reverend McLaren. 'She thought she was being punished. Her courses had stopped but there was nothing wrong with her that I could see. I gave her a brew of lavender, camomile and valerian root.'

Grant begins scribbling furiously.

Agnes glances at him and continues, 'These weren't to bring forth a child, just to calm her and help her sleep. I thought if she relaxed, got a bit of sleep, nature might take its course. That's all it was.'

The minister explodes, 'You presume to interfere with nature! God's creation!'

'Please, Reverend,' the commissioner implores. 'Goodwife Sampson is here to explain. Maybe we can get this whole matter cleared up.' He looks directly at Agnes and nods. 'Pray continue.'

She senses a big black beast moving in the web she's caught in - slow, methodical and mesmerising. A lightning strike is imminent. She sways backwards. Any mistake could fasten the noose around her neck. She must be vigilant, watch every word.

In the most reasonable voice she can muster, she continues slowly, choosing her words cautiously. 'I was just helping nature. Doesn't God give us the plants, crops, water, so we can use them to help ourselves?'

'You think you know the mind of God? You think you know more than the officers of the Kirk that you so blatantly disregarded?' the reverend asks.

'No ... no ... I don't. I know the mind of God no more than anyone else,' she says sadly.

The commissioner cuts in once more. 'Please, we are straying. Agnes, you were telling us about how you performed this miracle.'

'I did not perform a miracle,' she says firmly. She cannot allow the questioning to veer into the realm of miracles and magic. 'I just talked with her, calmed her. I told her there was nothing physically wrong with her, she wasn't being punished, and that these herbs were very powerful. Countless barren women who had taken them were now with child.'

'You admit it!' Reverend McLaren jumps to his feet.

'No! No! It wasn't the brew. It was her belief in it!' *What a stupid man.* A stupid and dangerous man. Her fists have turned into little balls of fury clamped by her side. 'Mrs Aird *believed* it would bring fruit to her womb. That's all – it was Mrs Aird herself. When I saw her next, she was peaceable, happier, eating better, and it wasn't long…'

The sheriff tugs his lower lip between his thumb and forefinger and squints as he looks more closely at her. 'So you're saying it wasn't these teas, brews and potions that cured Mrs Aird or Mrs Faulkner, or the Seton girl of her dropsy?'

'They played their part, but it was everything – the talking, listening, reassuring. Gradually, the mind settles, the spirit revives, the body heals. That has been my experience.'

The sheriff rubs his chin, nodding. 'I see.'

'The spirit! You talk of the spirit!' Reverend McLaren jumps in. 'That is not your province!'

'Reverend McLaren, please,' the sheriff says. Turning to the commissioner and Agnes, he continues quietly, 'I would like to hear what Goodwife Sampson has to say – for the sake of justice.'

The commissioner sniffs and gestures for her to continue. 'Go on.'

Agnes folds her arms. 'I have nothing further to say.'

'It may save your life,' the sheriff presses.

She looks at him, and their eyes lock. 'I've seen it many times,' she starts haltingly. 'It is not magic, and it does not always work. It depends on the patient. If they believe … if they believe the medicine will work, if they believe and trust in the healer, and if they want to get better, they often do… Not always, but often.'

'This is getting us nowhere!' The commissioner bangs his fist on the table. 'Ask her about their meetings at St Andrew's Kirk! John Fian's summoning of the Devil.'

'John Fian?' Agnes repeats, furrowing her brow.

The witchfinder strolls along the front of the table towards her. 'Now, Agnes. Have you ever been to St Andrew's Auld Kirk?'

'I have passed it many times, as have others.' She glances at the reverend.

'Could you be more precise? Exactly when have you "passed" it?' he continues.

'On my way to the shore cottages. You have to go by the Auld Kirk to get there. Why? Why are you asking this?'

'You are here to answer *our* questions.' The commissioner sits back, arms folded.

The minister takes up the thread. 'When were you last *inside* the kirk?'

Agnes furrows her brow and looks down. She's been in it, but when?

'Please answer the good reverend,' the commissioner presses.

'I … I… I can't think. It was a long time ago. Umm…' An image bursts into her mind – the whitewashed walls of the interior with posies and vases of flowers on the floor and every surface, and baskets of fruit, berries and apples on the old benches at the front. 'Yes! That's right, everyone was there from all around the place! Aye, I remember… I remember now.' She sighs. 'It was the feast – the whole town was there – for Saint Nicolas and—'

'A festival for a saint!' Reverend McLaren interjects. 'It gets worse! Papist plotting and a coven!'

'What did you say?' Agnes gasps, looking from the minister to the commissioner to the sheriff. 'A *what*?' All this time, she has thought the minister is just pompous, ridiculous and condescending, but now? He is none of these: he is dangerous, extremely dangerous and deranged. How can she disentangle herself from the yarns spun by a madman?

The sheriff cuts in, once more holding Agnes in his gaze. 'I believe Goodwife Sampson has not finished. You have more to say about why you were there?'

She hesitates before speaking. 'Aye … aye…' she replies, swallowing. 'Our sailors still hold Saint Nicolas as their patron and our fishermen take comfort in Saint Peter. It was a feast to give thanks for the lives of all the men caught in that storm on Midsummer's Eve. I don't know, it must have been two years ago. Not one life lost… The whole village and everyone around here celebrated for two days.'

'Commissioner, I have heard of these celebrations,' the sheriff adds. 'They are well known. As the goodwife says, to give thanks. I couldn't attend them myself, I was away on business at the time at Pencaitland – some cattle rustling. But most of the village was there.' He stares at the minister. 'Reverend McLaren, you surely must have been aware of these feasts?'

The reverend purses his lips but says nothing.

The sheriff turns back to Agnes. 'And you've never been in since?'

'No.'

'It has been a long night for us all,' Commissioner Baxter announces, then turns to his assistant. 'Have the goodwife taken to her … accommodation. Oh, and Grant, give her our full hospitality for the next four days.'

'Aye … yes … yes, sir.'

Grant walks from behind the commissioner's chair and stands level with Agnes. 'This way,' he says without looking at her.

With an open palm, he leads her to the door. Just as he opens it, a guard appears. He must have been waiting the whole time, Agnes muses, wondering if he had his ear pressed to the door. It does look a little red.

\*\*\*

When the door is firmly closed, the sheriff shakes his head and blows out.

Reverend McLaren drops back into his chair. 'Well, that didn't get us very far.'

'On the contrary,' the witchfinder replies, reaching into his pocket for a small clay pipe. 'We learned that Agnes Sampson uses magic to bend her subjects to her will.'

A chill runs down the sheriff's back. 'Wh-a-t?'

'She casts a spell over them so they miraculously heal,' McPherson continues, getting into his stride. 'A very serious transgression, I believe, Reverend McLaren?' he adds, with a little bow to the clergyman.

'Yes, yes, of course. You are quite correct,' Reverend McLaren replies with a smile.

McPherson places his hand just below his collarbone, inclining his head in a gesture of humility.

The minister gets up and walks over to the commissioner. 'Sir, we need to find out more about this coven,' he says earnestly. 'This plotting. Exactly who is involved, how far it has spread, what their plans were, how many all told.'

The commissioner holds up his hand. 'All in good time.' He gets up. 'The goodwife is not a foolish wee lassie unlike some. And if she is in league with the Devil…'

'She is,' the minister asserts.

'Then she will be very wily. But I find four days' lack of sleep and a purifying diet of bread and rancid ale is enough to loosen the tightest of tongues.'

'What about the others?' the sheriff asks. 'We have the others below in the cells. What about them?'

The commissioner rubs his chin, gently drawing two fingers across his lips. 'They know they are accused of witchcraft and, if found guilty, what awaits them. We'll let them stew for a bit. All we need is one or two to crack and names will flow like a sluice gate opening.'

'What do you mean "like a sluice gate opening"?' The sheriff bites his lip. 'Just how many are you thinking of?'

'Who knows? Twenty, thirty?' the commissioner says casually.

'It could even be fifty, or one hundred! Who knows how far it has spread!' Reverend McLaren retorts.

'My God!' the sheriff exclaims, dumbfounded. 'You can't be serious! There is no evidence any of these accusations are true. It's all supposition and hearsay. Nothing is in stone.'

'We'll get the evidence. Do not fear on that account,' the commissioner replies. 'You may take your leave, gentlemen.'

The sheriff tries one more time. 'There's never been anything like… There is no precedent.'

Looking steadily at the lawman, the commissioner opens his hands in a sign of supplication. 'We must do all we can to protect

His Grace at this time. It is our duty. And if, during the course of our work, of our investigations, we come across a conspiracy, then we must act. We must do everything in our power to thwart it! After all, to pursue any other course would be ... treasonous, Sheriff. Now, if you'll excuse me.'

# Chapter Forty-Three

A Service
Vézelay

'Come on, come on!' Madame Lambert whispers to herself as she hammers on her neighbour's door again and stamps her feet. 'It's cold out here.' The wind howls down the alley sweeping up leaves in shadowy whirlpools of debris. She shivers. 'Come on.'

Nothing stirs. She looks up. There is blackness behind the windows, no warm glow from a candle of one of the occupants keeping late hours. She hugs her shawl around her shoulders and arms; it offers little cover in the pouring rain. She tries again, this time with more vigour. A dog barks next door, setting off others behind the doors lining the street and in backyards in a disharmonious chorus. *Sod it.*

A flickering light appears in the downstairs window of the house across the street. That's the last thing she needs. It disappears, then the front door creaks open and a robust woman of around forty appears, holding up a candle and looking up and down the street. Madame Lambert feels like a moth caught in the flame.

'Are you all right, Madame Lambert? Do you need help?' the woman calls.

'No, no. Thank you, Mrs Alfonse, I am quite all right. Sorry for disturbing you. I am trying to rouse my assistant, Mr Durand. He lodges here with Mr Canaveri. We have a case to attend to.'

'The dark gentleman?'

Madame Lambert's innards tighten. 'That's right, the dark gentleman. His name is Mr Durand,' she replies with restraint. Mrs Alfonse's probably looking for a morsel of intrigue to pick over for an hour two with her old friend, Miss Houchin, after church on Sunday, she speculates.

'Would you like me to help you?' Mrs Alfonse begins to close her door.

'No, no, it's fine! I think I hear a noise inside,' Madame Lambert lies. 'You have been very kind.' Mrs Alfonse is a good customer with lots of connections among the well-heeled women folk in the locality; her good opinion has brought many paying clients to Madame Lambert's door.

She turns back to the door and bangs so loudly that she worries she has woken the whole village. 'Come on, come on.' Her heart joins in with the thumping, beating erratically against her ribcage.

Finally a light appears, moving behind a crack in the shutters of the window in the storey above, and now she really does hear the soft tread of footsteps coming down the stairs. At last, the door opens and a bleary-eyed elderly gentleman holding a lantern peers out.

A noise above tells her someone is climbing down the ladders from the attic room which faces the back gardens. Soon Assen appears on the stairs behind the older man. Partially hidden in the darkness, he looks over his landlord's shoulder, wary and curious.

'Madame Lambert!' Mr Canaveri exclaims. 'What is it? Come in, come in. You are wet through.'

'I am sorry to trouble you, Mr Canaveri, but my assistant, Mr Durand... I need Mr Durand to come with me to help me with a case. Could you wake him, please?'

Assen emerges from behind the gentleman and opens the door wide, letting in a gust of wind, a few swirling leaves and a light sheet of rain. A sheen quickly forms on his face.

'Alain, I need you,' she blurts out a little breathlessly.

'A case, you say?' calls a voice from across the street. Mrs Alfonse is still standing in her doorway. 'Is it old Mr Picard? I still have some of the brew he's so fond of, which he says helps his chest. I could go and get it.' She is about to head back into her house.

'No, no!' Madame Lambert calls across the street. 'Thank you, Madame Alfonse, it is not Mr Picard,' she says quickly, and a bit too shrill for her liking. 'It is a ... delicate case, Madame Alfonse. A woman of your breeding I know will understand. I would be eternally grateful if we could keep this between ourselves ... a confidence between two women of refinement.'

Mrs Alfonse draws herself up. 'Of course, Madame Lambert. You have my word as a gentlewoman, and please do let me know if I can assist you in any way.'

'Thank you. Your discretion is the greatest gift you have bestowed upon me.'

'Madame Lambert,' she says with a bow of her head.

Madame Lambert does likewise. 'Madame Alfonse.'

Carefully shielding the flame of her candle with a cupped hand, Mrs Alfonse backs into the house and, with one last look, she closes the door. Madame Lambert blows out a breath and the men draw their eyes back to her.

'Come in, come in,' Mr Canaveri entreats once more.

Madame Lambert gratefully steps over the threshold, out of the squall. She hugs her shawl even tighter and trembles. Mr Canaveri darts to the window ledge at the rear where he lights a candle, then finds several others and ignites them, placing one on the rough pine table in the centre of the room and another in an oblong hole above the fireplace. The room basks in an orange-yellow glow.

'Sit down,' he urges, bringing a chair forward and positioning it close to the fire, which is still glowing but showing only minimal signs of life. He carefully criss-crosses a few thick sticks in the centre and blows beneath them. Slowly, flames begin to curl around the frame. He sits back on his heels. 'Please, Madame Lambert, won't you sit?'

Madame Lambert barely touches the seat before making eye contact with Assen. 'We don't have much time. I need you to make up three beakers and bring the dark-green phial, with the tincture. You remember?'

'Is someone ill?' Mr Canaveri asks, his eyes wide with concern.

Mr Canaveri has been a friend to Madame Lambert for as long as she can remember. He'd told her one night that he'd come to Vézelay from Milan with his parents. He must have been around seven or maybe eight; he couldn't quite remember. That was fifty years ago and over the years, he got to know everyone, came to care about everyone. It was in his nature, he'd said, his family were like that – his parents and grandparents always went out of their way to make new friends, especially in a new area.

Madam Lambert had put her palm over the old man's hand. Mr Canaveri has given countless wayfarers shelter, including Madame Lambert. The original Good Samaritan, she smiles, thinking of André, and now he was doing the same for this strange young man.

She glances at Assen. In her early days in Vézelay, it was Mr Canaveri who secured her lodgings with Mrs Alfonse and made sure she ate each night. Like a dog that never forgets kindness, Madame Lambert would go to him about anything, trust him with everything. 'It's the Lafayettes, Paulo,' she answers. 'Mrs Lafayette has childbed fever.'

'May the good Lord protect her and Saint Raphael heal her.'

'Amen,' she replies softly. 'Alain, I need you to prepare as quickly as you can – for the fever – willow bark, oregano oil, echinacea, garlic and raw apple vinegar. Do we have a little honey to sweeten?'

'Yes, there is enough.'

'For the pain … you remember?'

He nods, his curls falling over his face. 'Yes, lavender, rosemary, peppermint and the rest of the willow bark. Right?'

'Right. Good. There is also some vinegar made from witch hazel, thyme and lavender. Bring it too, a lot of it – we'll need it to clean up. Come as quickly as you can.' She looks at Mr Canaveri then back to Assen. 'Paulo will take you to the Lafayette house. I'll meet you there.'

\*\*\*

Assen grabs his cape draped over a nail protruding from the staircase and goes next door with Mr Canaveri to Madame Lambert's house to prepare the ingredients. Stepping out into the storm behind them, Madame Lambert heads off in the opposite direction.

Assen watches her disappear into the darkness and a band tightens across his stomach. He wants to go with her to protect her. Though from what, he doesn't know. Like a loyal animal, he is drawn to be at her side, safeguarding her and surveying the territory. But this is what she asked him to do, and he must see to it.

Determined to follow her instructions to the letter, he follows Mr Canaveri into Madame Lambert's house.

***

Outside, the cobbled streets are slippery from the rain, and Madame Lambert gingerly picks her way down the hill toward the Lafayette house. It stands on its own just beyond the edge of the village, majestically surrounded by manicured gardens on four sides. She bangs forcibly on the door. To her surprise, Mr Lafayette answers. Then she notices their maid, Evette, behind him, holding a large basin and strips of cloth.

'Good evening, Mr Lafayette. I came as soon as I could. My assistant, Alain – Mr Durand – will be here shortly; he is preparing the medicaments. Where is she?'

'This way, please,' he says, stepping aside. 'Thank you. Thank you so much for coming. I'm sorry that we…'

She hears the relief in his voice. 'Nonsense, Mr Lafayette. There is no need for any apologies. I am glad to be here. I'll do everything I can to help.'

'Thank you, Madame Lambert.'

He leads her up the narrow staircase, the glow from his candle surprisingly bright enough to light the entire stairway. Lifting her skirts, she looks up, places her right hand on the familiar plank attached to the wall for support and follows him. When they reach the landing, they face two doors; one is firmly closed and the other ajar, with a sliver of silvery yellow light leaking out. She knows which one is the Lafayettes' bedroom, having attended Madame Lafayette, and before her, Mr Lafayette's mother.

He softly opens the door wider and Madame Lambert tiptoes in after him. The room is as she remembers it: the mahogany bed in the centre, the long dresser under the window, chairs by the fire and the bed.

She's not sure what she'll find, but her father trained her to exude nothing but calmness, control and reassurance. It is important to radiate confidence, he had told her. It reassures people, makes them believe they can get better and that the potion, or whatever you're doing, is helping. It also calms those around them; they like to see someone else is in charge so they can set down their burden, even for just an hour or so.

*What if the person doesn't get better?* she remembers asking.

*Well*, came the reply, *then the passing is generally more peaceful for everyone.*

She looks at Mrs Lafayette, deathly white and sweating in the bed, feverish and barely conscious. Madame Lambert shivers. She has forgotten how cold she is from the rain and east wind.

Taking off her wet wrap, she turns to Mr Lafayette. 'Mr Lafayette, I'm sorry, would you place this somewhere to dry, please?'

'Of course,' Mr Lafayette mumbles, drawing his unblinking eyes away from his wife, as if rousing from a deep trance. 'Please forgive me – you are wet through. Come stand by the fire for a moment.'

The vibrant fire is tempting. Someone must have just put a bone-dry log on it, she muses, but she is only too aware that every moment from now on is precious. 'No, no, that is fine. I will attend to your wife now, with your permission.'

'Of course. Please.'

Stepping over to the bed, she looks at Mrs Lafayette. Beads of sweat glisten on the woman's forehead as she mumbles and tosses her head from side to side. Looking back at Mr Lafayette, Madame Lambert asks, 'Where is …. umm, Doctor… ?' Madame Lambert begins.

'He left … two hours ago, or something like that. Robert has gone to fetch him, but … but … I-I fear it's been too long…' The breath catches in his throat. 'My poor Marie… Madame Lambert, I'm sorry we…'

'There is no need to be sorry, Mr Lafayette, you were doing what you thought was best for your wife. Dr Dévereux has a great reputation. Besides, I do not need to be at the birth of every child in this village. The child … all is well?'

Mr Lafayette nods, looking relieved. 'Yes, thank the Lord she lives.'

'That is good news, good news indeed. You have a daughter. My congratulations. Now, please, go and boil a large pot of water. Do you have salt?'

'We do.'

'Put in as much as you can spare. Bring it up. Oh, put some in a small bowl when it is warm and wash your hands thoroughly in it. Bring one for me too … and a bowl of cold water … and cloths, as many as you can get.'

Madame Lambert scrutinises Mrs Lafayette's pallor, the texture of her skin and her breathing. She is as pale as the finest white Italian marble and her skin is waxy to the touch. Her breath is erratic, with little intermittent movements below the collarbone as her body tries to preserve the life that is left.

'Mrs Lafayette, Mrs Lafayette!' Madame Lambert shouts.

The woman does not respond but continues to ramble feverishly.

'Mrs Lafayette!' Madame Lambert tries again, shouting at the top of her voice. There is a scraping sound downstairs like a chair being drawn back, and she worries Mr Lafayette will come running up the stairs for fear she is murdering his wife. Mrs Lafayette remains embroiled in a conversation only she can hear.

Madame Lambert walks to the window and opens it a fraction. He'll never notice. The room is stifling; the fire is like a furnace and looks as if it has been burning for hours, no doubt a recommendation from the doctor. Why they think stuffy oppressive heat is good for childbirth, she'll never know.

A cool breeze snakes its way through the room, brushes the side of Mrs Lafayette's face and lifts a thin strand of her hair. 'That's better, isn't it?' Madame Lambert says gently as she pulls the covers down past the woman's shoulders.

She'll wait for the salt water to wash her hands before starting the more intimate examinations. It was something her father told her, that he had got from his mother, that she had got from Great-Grandma Pellegrini. They must always wash their hands in salt water before they touched any patient, the old woman had said. Does it make any difference? She doesn't know. Is it superstition? Maybe. But it has become her lucky charm and it differentiates her from the other healers and midwives, which is no bad thing.

A shaft of light comes into the room from the hall. Mr Lafayette appears carrying a tray with two bowls. He sets them on the dresser next to Madame Lambert.

'Thank you.' She takes one of the cloths, plunges it into a bowl, squeezes it and shakes it out. Turning back to Mrs Lafayette, she places the flannel on her forehead.

Assen quietly enters behind Mr Lafayette and places three beakers on the cabinet opposite the bed. 'Here.'

She looks up and is momentarily caught in his dark, penetrating eyes. A heartbeat catches in her throat. Does he know how unusually handsome he is, she wonders. For goodness' sake, she's not a silly girl. This woman needs her help; she's here to help her, not flirt. 'Thank you,' she says, quickly turning away and adding perfunctorily, 'Now, wash your hands, please.'

Assen obediently washes his hands thoroughly in the bowl.

Madame Lambert stands next to Assen. Facing the three beakers neatly stacked in a row, she picks up the middle one. 'She must drink as much of this as possible. Will you hold her up?'

Assen accompanies Madame Lambert to the bed and takes Mrs Lafayette in his arms, holding her upright.

Madame Lambert gently tilts the patient's head back and trickles the yellow liquid down her throat. Mrs Lafayette manages to swallow some, although a little dribbles out of the corner of her mouth. Pulling out a cloth from a pocket in her skirt, Madame Lambert gently dabs the woman's mouth.

'Good,' she says, relieved. 'Let's try the other one.'

Madame Lambert returns to the dresser, puts the mug down and picks up another. 'Right,' she says confidently, going back to the bed. 'Mrs Lafayette, this will help with the pain. Try to drink as much as you can.'

A flicker of comprehension flits across Mrs Lafayette's face and she nods. She takes three big gulps and would have flopped down if Assen were not holding her up.

'That's fine, Alain, you can let her down now.'

Assen gently lays the barely conscious woman back onto the bed. Madame Lambert covers the patient's shoulders and she and Assen look at each other. Quickly pulling her gaze away, Madame Lambert smooths down the blankets and tidies the bed so that the patient looks like a pretty little package. She gets up and returns to the dresser. Assen joins her.

Barely an inch separates them. Madame Lambert arranges the beakers back into a neat row, moving each a tiny fraction so that they are perfectly horizontally aligned. She sighs. 'That's all I can do … all *we* can do… It's all I know. Now, it's…'

'In God's hands,' he finishes, looking at the painting of a bowl of fruit and a wine glass above the cabinet.

Her gaze follows his, she hadn't registered it before. Amazing what you don't see right in front of your nose when your mind is elsewhere.

Normally Madame Lambert would be annoyed at Assen for finishing her sentence, but it doesn't irritate her tonight. In fact, it triggers a warm feeling in her abdomen like gooey treacle and a flash, an image of him and her, old and laughing in a garden she doesn't recognise. *For goodness' sake, woman! Look at him! He's young and handsome. He'll leave, get married, have ten children.*

She glances sideways at him staring at the painting, and she can't help laughing at herself.

'What's funny?'

'Oh, just—'

There is a loud rapping at the front door. Assen rushes to the bedroom door and holds up his hand. They hear raised voices – Mr Lafayette and another man – then a heavy tread on the stairs. Assen steps back, positioning himself between the men who enter and Madame Lambert.

Mr Lafayette steps in, looking concerned. Behind him is a well-dressed man. Taking off his cloak and gloves, the man hands them to Evette, who is hovering nearby. He looks around the room and sniffs. 'I will see the patient,' the gentleman announces, giving Madame Lambert a cursory glance and looking Assen up and down. 'Give me room. I need space to see to *my* patient.'

Madame Lambert turns away from the dresser and faces the newcomer. 'Mrs Lafayette is sleeping, Doctor,' she offers in a tone she hopes will convey respect.

'I can see that!' he snaps. 'Now, if you will all leave, I will treat the patient. You, of course, can stay, Mr Lafayette.'

Mr Lafayette looks uncertainly at Madame Lambert.

Madame Lambert tries again. 'Dr Umm…?'

'Dr Dévereux, Madame Lambert,' Mr Lafayette quickly interjects.

'Oh course.' She bows her head and clasps her hands. 'Dr Dévereux… Dr Dévereux, Mrs Lafayette is not out of danger yet.

I have done all I can, but... I would stay, I would like to give her more—' she turns to take hold of one of the beakers '—to revive her when she wakes.'

'And who might you be?' Dr Dévereux bellows. 'I don't believe we have been introduced.'

'Pardon,' Mr Lafayette says in a placatory tone. 'Dr Dévereux, this is Madame Lambert. She is the village midwife and healer. I asked her to come when—'

'A village healer!' Dr Dévereux scoffs. 'Whatever next? Well, I'm sure you have done what you can and Mr Lafayette is grateful. But I'm here now, so you may leave, Madame ... umm ... Madame...' He waves his hand dismissively.

'Madame Lambert,' Assen growls, stopping Dr Dévereux in his tracks as he takes in the dark stranger.

Madame Lambert feels her cheeks flush with pleasure but is careful to keep her expression neutral. Trying to gauge his reaction, she studies Mr Lafayette's face. He looks helpless and confused. She hears her father's voice: *Take charge!*

'No,' she says firmly. 'With Mr Lafayette's permission, I would stay. Mrs Lafayette needs more ... she needs to drink more of this if the fever is to break.' She raises the tankard.

'Madame! Really!' Dr Dévereux exclaims, his face red. 'You forget your place. You are an uneducated, untrained practitioner of useless charms and—' he gestures to the beakers on the cabinet '—questionable, if not dangerous, potions.'

'I made those potions!' Assen declares in a low snarl.

A picture of a hound she once knew in the countryside just outside Marseilles pops into Madame Lambert's mind. He was a beautiful creature with a sleek grey coat, ears that flopped in line with its jaw and large, intelligent brown eyes. The dog was warm and loving to her and her uncle and cousins but fiercely protective, growling when a stranger approached. How odd that such things pop into your mind at inopportune times.

The doctor glares at Assen.

Unabashed, Assen continues, 'I brewed them from the finest ingredients, as per Madame Lambert's instructions. They have well-known therapeutic benefits and, when combined, their potency is increased many times.'

Although gratified and charmed by his gallantry, Madame Lambert quickly interrupts. 'That's all right, Alain,' she says, gently pressing his arm.

But Dr Dévereux begins to scrutinise Assen more closely. 'And who might you be?'

'I am Madame Lambert's … assistant … a—'

'He is a scribe … a very good one,' she interrupts again.

'Your name?' he commands, still glowering at Assen.

'Alain.'

'Alain who?'

'Durand… Alain … Durand,' Assen stumbles.

Madame Lambert raises her eyebrows and glances quizzically at him.

Dr Dévereux addresses Mr Lafayette. 'Well, it is your home and your wife. If this woman stays,' he says, with a nod at Madame Lambert, 'I'll assume you no longer need my services and I'll take my leave.'

'I… I…' Mr Lafayette looks from the doctor to Madame Lambert.

'Don't worry, Mr Lafayette, I'll go,' Madame Lambert offers, gathering up her tankards and phials. 'Alain, will you help me collect my things?'

'No!' Mr Lafayette shouts, finally finding his voice, then more quietly, 'I would like Madame Lambert to stay.'

Madame Lambert's shoulders drop as she quietly places the glasses back onto the cabinet. Assen remains like a statue by her side.

'Very well. My things,' Dr Dévereux orders, and Evette comes forward with his hat, gloves and cloak. 'I hope you do not live to regret this decision,' he says to Mr Lafayette, tying his cape.

As they hear the front door clicking shut, everyone breathes out. The air feels lighter and fresher. Madame Lambert seizes the opportunity. 'Mr Lafayette, may I open the window wider, please? I think it would make your wife more comfortable.'

'Please do, it's stifling in here. I feel like a suckling pig that's been spit-roasted the whole night,' Mr Lafayette says in a clear attempt to lighten the mood.

'Thank you for letting us stay. I will do everything I can.'

'There's no need to thank me. I'm only sorry I didn't call for you sooner.'

Madame Lambert smiles and turns to Assen. 'You can go now, Alain. Thank you.'

'You don't want me to stay?' he asks, trying to catch her eye.

'It may be hours before she wakes. There's nothing much we can do 'til then. You may wish to take your rest, too.'

'The last thing I'm thinking of is rest,' he says hurriedly. 'I would stay – if you would have me.'

She notes the urgency in his voice and again something flutters in the pit of her abdomen. 'Very well. Thank you. Perhaps you could clear this dresser and bring more hot water and fresh bowls.' She lifts one of the beakers and peers into it. 'We'll try and give her the rest of this when she wakes. This, too, if she can tolerate it,' she adds, picking up a phial.

Assen gathers the bowls; soon the dresser is clean and tidy, with the tankards, phials and bowls lined up. Standing by the cabinet drying his hands, he looks over at Madame Lambert. She gives him a little smile and lets her head fall back against the chair. It is solid and supportive. Nothing they can do for now. Her collarbones rise and fall and she lets her mouth open. Perhaps she could shut her eyes for a few moments. The house is silent, except for the odd creak of timber as the building settles.

*Crash!*

Madame Lambert's eyes blink open and she sits bolt upright. 'What is it? Is she awake?'

'Shit!' Assen stands with a cloth dangling from his hand and a shattered bowl at his feet. 'No... No... I'm sorry, I...' He bends down to pick up the pieces and wipe the floor.

Madame Lambert rushes over to Mrs Lafayette and touches her forehead with the back of her hand. A wave of queasiness rises in her chest. She looks at Assen. 'The fever has not broken. I don't like it. If she does not wake soon we must wake her and try... I have something. I don't normally use it, but if I have to...'

'Isn't it better to... In the hospital, we used to let it...'

Madame Lambert turns sharply, squinting. She knows what he is about to say, that it is better to let the fever burn itself out. 'Normally,' she explains. 'But she burns, and her colour ... it prefigures death. We have to do something now.'

He approaches the bed. 'Right.'

'Wash out that tankard and fill it with tea – tepid peppermint tea.' She reaches into her skirt and pulls out a tiny phial. 'Put one drop – only *one* drop – of this in it.'

'What is it?'

'Wolfbane … essence of wolfbane.'

'Wolfbane! But that's poisonous!'

'Only if you give it in a big dose. I'm not in the habit of poisoning my patients, Alain. One drop in a full beaker should bring down the fever – if it is God's will.'

'Of course,' he mumbles. 'The dose makes the poison or the cure.'

Madame Lambert attempts to lift the patient. 'Help me.'

Taking over, Assen lifts Mrs Lafayette from under her arms to a sitting position.

'Mrs Lafayette!' Madame Lambert shouts. 'Mrs Lafayette, wake up, wake up! Marie, wake up!' Placing her hands on the patient's shoulders she shakes her, gently at first then more vigorously. 'Wake up, wake up! Just for a moment.'

Mr Lafayette bursts into the room, his eyes wide with hope. 'Is she awake? She's all right, isn't she? She's going to be all right?'

'We have to wake her to take more of the remedy,' Madame Lambert says calmly, as she goes over to the cabinet and picks up the middle tankard. 'Her fever has not broken as I'd hoped,' she adds, sitting back down on the bed. 'I won't lie to you…' She looks into the beaker. 'If she doesn't take more of this—'

'I'll wake her!' he cries as he rushes to the bed. He grasps his wife by the shoulders and shakes her so hard, her head lolls from side to side like a rag doll. 'Wake up, darling Marie. Wake up for me, please. Please, please, wake up, for our baby.'

Mrs Lafayette's eyes flicker open, and her lips part as if she wants to say something. Madame Lambert quickly intercedes with the tankard and takes Mr Lafayette's place. He stands back, staring over her shoulder. 'Marie, please drink this, as much as you can. It will make you better,' she coaxes.

Mrs Lafayette looks to her husband, her eyes glazed.

He nods. 'As much as you can, my darling.'

Mrs Lafayette manages three good gulps before Assen gently lays her back down. Madame Lambert pulls the blanket over her shoulders and again gently touches her forehead with the back of her hand. 'Mr Lafayette, would you like to sit with your wife?' she asks, stepping away from the chair by the side of the bed.

'Thank you. I will be with her now.' He sits down heavily.

Madame Lambert returns to the dresser and gathers up the used receptacles and rags. Now they can only wait.

The cockerel next-door-but-one has crowed many hours since. The townspeople are going about their business now, Madame Lambert muses. André will be gathering apples from the far orchard ready to be made into chutney to sell at next week's market. No doubt Madame Alfonse will be supervising her maid as they prepare the afternoon repast for the ladies of independent means in Vézelay and thereabouts. Madame Alfonse has confided in her that there was something she wanted to discuss over their cosy tête-à-tête, something about a small piece of land adjoining the Garnier place, unused for years and overgrown but which would make an excellent herb garden. Madame Lambert wishes she had thought of it first. Oh well, she'll find out later how things went.

She looks around the room. An empty tumbler lies on its side at the edge of the dresser. Mr Lafayette is slumped in a simple rustic wooden chair, a criss-cross of reeds forming the seat, by his wife's bed. Assen sits on the floor with his back against the wall, his head lolling to the side.

Pushing herself higher in her chair, something catches her eye. A mouse, quick as a flash, darts behind the bowls and tankards and spent phials on the cabinet. Its tail clips the upturned cup. She watches mesmerised as the mouse and chalice dive from the dresser in unison. *Clatter*! The tinny sound is amplified in the stillness.

'God's mercy! What in the name of Christ…?' Mr Lafayette exclaims.

Assen leaps to his feet, his right hand searching his hip for his sword.

'What's happening? Why are you blaspheming, Husband?' Mrs Lafayette says calmly. 'Why am I in bed?'

'Wh-a-t?' he splutters, rising from the chair and sitting beside her. Putting his arms around his wife, he rocks her gently. 'Thank God. Thank you, God. My dear, sweet Marie.' He buries his face in her hair.

'Husband—' she draws back, studying his expression, '—what is going on?' She pulls herself up and looks at the window. 'Why am I in bed at this hour? What are you…? Madame Lambert? What are you doing here?'

'Good morning, Mrs Lafayette. You are feeling better? You were a little unwell and I, and my assistant, Mr Alain Durand, have tended to you.'

'Good day, Mr Durand.' Mrs Lafayette swallows and tightens the nightgown around her neck as if it were a collar.

'Good day, Mrs Lafayette.' Assen smiles broadly and starts to gather the used cloths, tankards and phials.

'Now, gentlemen,' Madame Lambert cuts in, drying her hands, 'if you will excuse us ladies. If you will permit me?' she says to the patient. 'I will see to your toilet and ensure all is well.'

As Mr Lafayette heads to the door, Madame Lambert calls after him, 'Mr Lafayette, I will return this evening to check on Marie. I'll bring another two cups. If you could please give Mrs Lafayette what is left in that one before then.' She points her head to the solitary beaker Assen has left on the counter.

'Thank you, Madame Lambert. Thank you, Mr Durand.' Mr Lafayette's voice cracks. 'Words… I cannot say how truly … grateful we both are… This family…'

'Hush now, that is what I'm here for. We're glad to help. Is that not so, Mr Durand?'

'Yes,' he answers, turning from the dresser. 'It is an honour to serve and work with Madame Lambert.'

# Chapter Forty-Four

Breaking Point
Tranent Tolbooth

There is a dank mossy smell. Agnes sways as drowsiness threatens to overtake her, the heaviness of lack of sleep drawing her to the floor. She is aware of the guard watching from a few feet away but she can't help it. She begins to sag, her knees buckling.

'No sitting!' He prods her in the back with a stick.

Her hair hangs in tails around her shoulders, her eyes are heavy and there's a low rumbling in her ears. When did she last sleep? The day before yesterday? The day before that? How many days has she been here? She can't remember. Wait, the tiny scratches in the stone under the grate – one, two, three, four, five: she's been here five days.

When the guard wasn't looking, she'd pulled a flint from a pocket hidden deep within the folds of her skirt and carved a thin vertical line each time the daylight disappeared. It was easy; the warder was bored and he'd been asleep more than he'd been awake these last few days. When she heard him grunt like a pig searching for truffles, her shoulders had relaxed, and she'd let her head fall back against the wall. Her eyes closed, her head flopped and her mouth hung open. Soon she, too, was deep in slumber.

But at this moment her gaoler is wide awake. She hasn't heard the clunk of a metal plate on stone, nor smelt the mouth-watering aroma of cooked meat and fresh bread; his midday meal has not arrived and he is irritable rather than sleepy. So Agnes stands, swaying, her chin bouncing off her chest each time she lapses into sleep. It'll be the floor next time.

There is a noise outside the door, a jangling of keys, perhaps. She lifts her head but it feels like a huge boulder. Hard to imagine one's own head could feel so heavy.

The cell door swings open. 'You're wanted upstairs,' a voice says to the guard.

'Watch this one – she's dangerous,' the guard warns the newcomer.

'I've to come with you.'

'Really?' The guard gets up. 'What about her?' He jabs a thumb towards Agnes. 'We're meant to keep her awake.'

The other man shrugs and Agnes holds her breath.

'Right, well, I suppose we'd better go. Who wants me, anyway?'

They head out, slamming the cell door and turning the key twice. Once she no longer hears the tread of their boots, she lets herself slide down the wall, knees bent and pulled into her chest. Releasing them, she straightens, lets her back rest against the stone and stretches her legs. As she wonders how long she has before he returns, darkness overtakes her. Her chin falls to her chest, and she flops to the side.

'Agnes, Agnes,' she hears, echoing as if at the end of a long tunnel. 'Agnes, Agnes!' she hears again, but louder and closer. 'Are you in there, Agnes?'

She squeezes her eyes open and shut. Where is she? Oh, yes: hell. *Come on, Agnes, you can do this. You've been here before.* She swallows the hard lump in her throat. 'Who's that? Who's there?' she asks.

'It's me, Agnes, it's me. I'm so sorry…'

She knows that voice but it sounds different, a little higher, almost wild. 'Gelly … is that you? Where are you?'

'Over here.' The voice comes from above.

Agnes tries to get up but her first attempt fails and she slides back down the wall. 'Come on, lassie,' she tells herself. This time she uses her right hand to steady herself. Pushing against the wall, she gets past a squat and up to standing. Wavering, her legs threatening to give way at any time, she steadies herself. She can do this.

One foot in front of the other, she walks to the opposite wall in the direction of the voice. There is a small grate high up in the stone wall. Standing on her tiptoes, she peers through and sees Gelly looking up from the next cell. Her clothes are filthy and torn, her hair is in rat's tails and there is a bruise on her cheek. Her eyes are swollen and one is closed.

Agnes looks at her own torn dress, the dirt smeared on her arms and her hair hanging about her shoulders. She lifts her palm to her head; there's no cap. She laughs mirthlessly. She can't look like an oil painting either. 'Oh, Gelly.'

'I'm sorry, Agnes. I didn't mean it.' Gelly's voice is quiet, practically childlike. 'They made me— I'm sorry I told on you.'

'What are you talking about, lassie?'

'They made me—' There's a rattling at Gelly's cell door and a key in the lock. The bolt is drawn back and the door swings open, bringing a gust of cold, stale air. Agnes ducks down.

'You've to come with us,' a man's voice orders.

Agnes angles her head but can't see who it is. The guard, probably.

The hinges creak as the door opens wider. There are light footsteps – Gelly heading out of the cell – then the heavy footfall of the man behind her.

Agnes comes down from her tiptoes and rolls back on her heels. Her cell looks even gloomier than before. She wants to get as far away as possible, even if that only comes through sleep. The sweetness of oblivion. *Pray God I never wake.*

She returns to the far wall and lets herself slump down once more. Sleep comes in seconds.

*It is summer. A warm breeze blows through the reeds next to the duck pond. She feels a hand on her shoulder and her stomach flutters. She smiles. It is like little acrobats are doing back flips in her tummy. She looks up and shields her eyes; she can hardly see his face for the sun, just his broad smile.*

*'I have something for you,' he says, sitting beside her under the tree.*

*They lean back against the trunk and she kisses his cheek. 'What is it?'*

*He turns to face her and firmly plants his lips on hers. She tastes black cherries and a faint hint of tobacco. 'Here.' He reaches into his bag and takes out a wooden box with silver edging and hinges and a key protruding from the lock. When he passes it to her, she can feel the weight.*

*'It's beautiful,' she says in wonder.*

*'I made it myself. You are to keep all your treasures in here.'*
*Touching his thick black hair, she replies, 'I only want one treasure.'*
*He takes her fingers and kisses them. 'Then you shall have it.' He pulls out a knife and shears a lock of his hair. 'Your first treasure!'*
*She grasps the tresses tightly as he turns the key slowly in the lock. Click ... click...*

Drip … drip … drip. Water trickles from the tiny, barred window high up in her cell. Thump, bang, clank. A bolt is slammed back.

Agnes opens her eyes. Where is she? What is this place?

Remembering, she stumbles to her feet. The noises came from Gelly's cell next door. She listens intently, frozen. Two men are whispering, and there is a rustling movement.

'That's that, then,' one says.

'Aye. Job done,' the other replies.

The door slams shut, and keys jangle at the lock. Agnes holds her breath.

Nothing. Silence.

In the distance, men are shouting and a horse is neighing. Nearby there are scratching sounds. She creeps towards the grate, rises on her tiptoes, curls her fingers around the wires and peeks through. Gelly is slumped in the corner like a pile of rags; at least, she thinks it is Gelly. Her heart pounds.

'Gelly. Psst! Gelly! Are you all right? What's happened?'

She strains to hear the slightest whisper from Gelly but instead she hears a scream. It comes from somewhere far off in the prison, or maybe from outside. Just some poor deranged soul given shelter out of harm's way, she tells herself. It was better before, when the poor, sick and feeble of mind found refuge in the hospitals run by the brothers and sisters of the auld church. It is an opinion that many share but few dare voice.

She raises her voice. 'Gelly, child … speak to me.'

The pile of rags starts to move. One rag slides from Gelly's face revealing dried congealed blood under her nose and from her mouth and one eye. The pretty, childish face is almost unrecognisable. She looks up through glazed, unfocussed eyes. Agnes knows Gelly cannot see her.

'Dear God,' she exclaims, pressing her back against the wall with the grate above her. Her breathing is high in her chest: short little explosive bursts just below her collarbone.

Gelly is trying to say something. Agnes jumps up, curling her fingers around the bars of the grille.

'I'm sorry. I told, Agnes...' it comes out in little rasping whispers '...about the Devil ... all the things we did with him ... the evil things ...the bad things ... the coven, lots and lots of people ... there were lots of people there ... at the dances ... kissing the Devil...'

'What?' Agnes's mind races. *What's she talking about? What have they done to her?*

'I shouldn't have let the Devil kiss me on the neck ... that was bad. It was wrong ... it was a sin ... that's why I got the mark,' Gelly is saying, her cadence rising.

'You didn't! It never happened. It isn't real – none of these things are real. They've put it into your mind... They...' Agnes stares down at Gelly who is now rambling incoherently, lost in a made-up world of demons and celestial battles. She knows the girl can't hear her anymore.

When Gelly looks up again, some of her old self flashes in her eyes and for a second Agnes thinks she might have got through to her. But then Gelly blinks and a look of utter incomprehension descends again on her once-exquisite features. She collapses into the pile of rags, excrement and straw.

Agnes draws away from the grille, her head bowed. 'Sweet Jesus, help us,' she whispers as she falls back against the wall.

# Chapter Forty-Five

A Celebration
Tranent Tolbooth

The atmosphere is convivial, practically celebratory. The commissioner, Reverend McLaren, Mr McPherson, the witchfinder, and Grant, the commissioner's assistant, are sitting back as if they've just finished a satisfying meal.

There is a glass of wine on the desk in front of the commissioner, which he draws closer as he leans back in his chair. He takes a gulp. The sweet liquid tastes like the black cherries he'd once gathered as a boy from the orchards in Linlithgow.

The reverend, seated by the fire, holds a smaller glass of port, twisting the stem between his thumb and middle finger while gazing through it into the fire. Sitting in the chair opposite, the witchfinder sups ale from a tankard. Only the sheriff and the commissioner's assistant are not drinking. The sheriff leans against the wall farthest from the fireplace with his arms folded.

Turning in his chair, the commissioner glances over his shoulder out of the small, squared lattice window behind him. Through the blurred glass he sees a tall man in a tall hat carefully place a rolled scroll of parchment inside his coat, mount a large powerful grey mare and gallop northwards.

Commissioner Baxter takes another sip of wine, picks up the sheet of paper by his elbow, scans it and places it down carefully, smoothing the creases. He looks from the minister to the witchfinder to the sheriff, savouring the moment. 'The king, His Royal Grace, will honour us with his presence. He has confirmed the royal court will come here … a few miles from here. The trial will commence in North Berwick!'

'Imagine the king here in our jurisdiction! He'll see our work, our unwavering loyalty!' Reverend McLaren says, his cheeks flushing.

'Indeed.'

'Confronting the Devil on his own ground,' the witchfinder adds.

Sheriff MacKay propels himself forward. 'It is not *his* ground!'

Ignoring the sheriff, the commissioner addresses his assistant. 'How many?'

Grant holds up a piece of paper. 'All told—' he clears his throat '—seventy, sir.'

'Good God! Seventy?' The sheriff shakes his head in disbelief. 'Here!'

'Mostly here in North Berwick, sir.' Grant swallows. 'Some in Edinburgh and down in the borders as well.'

'There might be even more once all the confessions are wrought,' Reverend McLaren chimes in.

The sheriff gasps. 'More?'

'We can't be too careful,' Commissioner Baxter states flatly, taking the sheet from his assistant. 'Let's see. Euphemia MacLean, daughter of Lord Cliftonhall; the porter's wife of Seaton; Robert Grierson, skipper; the smith at Brigge Hallis...'

'Nowhere is safe.' It is the minister's turn to pace. 'My flock must be vigilant. I will instruct them to watch their neighbours, look out for signs.'

'I commend your enthusiasm, Reverend, but let us not spread any more panic than is necessary.' This is the commissioner's first investigation and he is keen to show King James that, while he has been thorough, his approach has also been measured. It is well known the monarch sees himself as a modern-day Solomon so he will want a calm, reasonable stalwart to corroborate his judgements. 'You know how petty these simple country folk can be. We don't want to provide a platform for every paltry gripe, do we? Now, confessions. What do we have?'

'A full confession, sir. A signed detailed confession, sir, from—' Grant looks at the sheet again '—Gellis Duncan, the serving lass of Seton House.'

'Excellent. Read it out.' The commissioner leans back, lifts his glass and rests it on his abdomen, both hands wrapped around its stem.

His assistant, Grant, coughs and unrolls a sheet. His ears turn bright red. 'Gellis Duncan said, "I attended meetings at St Andrew's Auld Kirk in North Berwick in the middle of the night. John Fian summoned up the Devil, and two hundred people came from far and wide."'

'Two hundred!' the sheriff splutters, the colour draining from his face. 'Commissioner… Commissioner… Sir, this is madness! There can't possibly be… If there'd been two hundred people meeting in that wee kirk in the middle of the night, it would have been all over the place. We'd have heard long before now…'

The commissioner smiles inwardly, enjoying the sheriff's reaction.

'It just proves what I was saying – we have to be on our guard, keep a lookout for signs,' Reverend McLaren reiterates in an innocent tone, as if they were talking about farthings going missing from the collection plate.

Grant looks nervously from the sheriff to the minister then back at the piece of paper in his hand. 'Aye, it says "two hundred came from far and wide. We danced in a frenzy with the Devil and … and … and…"'

'Get on with it, lad,' the commissioner barks.

'"…and … we … we kissed him on the buttocks."' Grant lets his hand drop to his thigh with a slap.

'What?' the sheriff splutters.

Lifting the sheet again, Grant reads, '"We kissed him on the buttocks, and I let him kiss me on the neck."'

'Ah, that'll be the mark, then,' the witchfinder adds, rubbing his index finger along his bottom lip.

The minister nods. 'Aye.'

The sheriff walks to the window. Lifting his hand, he lets it rest on the frame, his fingers curling around the casement of the open window. 'And this … this plot against His Grace. Exactly how did they arrange it? How were they able to conjure up the storms?'

Grant searches through the document. 'Ah, here, it says, "I met…"' Grant looks nervously round the room. 'This is Gellis Duncan speaking—'

'We know that! For strewth!' The commissioner shakes his head. 'Get on with it.'

'Yes, sir. It says, "I met with a witch from Denmark and we hatched a plot to conjure up storms to stop the king and his betrothed, Anne, from reaching Scotland. The idea came from the Devil himself, who said King James of Scotland was his greatest enemy on Earth."'

'And what was the name of this Danish witch?' the sheriff enquires.

The assistant searches through the papers. 'It doesn't say.'

'Really.'

The commissioner notes the lawman's tone but chooses to ignore it. 'Most gratifying. His Grace will be very interested. Now, the witch Agnes Sampson – has she confessed?'

'Sir.' The sheriff takes a step towards the desk. 'With all due respect, that has not been proven. She's a respected midwife and healer around here. There's no evidence she ever used witchcraft.'

The commissioner places his hands face down on the table and looks at the witchfinder.

'It will be straightforward enough. I have this.' Mr McPherson pats the tome by his side. '*The Hammer of the Witches*. It has, of course, been updated by our own Presbyterian and Calvinist brethren.'

Reverend McLaren smiles and lifts his glass of port.

The witchfinder continues, 'Aye, we have all the information we need on their cunning ways and how to root them out in our midst.'

'No, sir!' Grant blurts out, looking at the sheet.

Everyone turns to him. The commissioner furrows his brow. 'What? What is the boy talking about now?'

'The witch Agnes Sampson … she hasn't confessed, sir.'

'Sir!' The sheriff tries again. 'Calling someone a witch is a very serious accusation. As I've already said, nothing has been proven. Mr Roberts, you must desist…'

'All right, all right!' The commissioner rises and walks to the front of the table. 'Hmm. If the—' he looks at the sheriff '— midwife and healer Agnes Sampson has not yet confessed, we will progress to other means. Mr Roberts, Grant…'

'Yes, sir.'

'Call for Mr Birkett, if you will.'

'Yes, sir.'

The sheriff leans on the table, his hands spread wide. 'If she has not yet confessed and there is no hard evidence, I'm not sure this is the right course.'

'She has been named and damned by her co-conspirators,' Reverend McLaren asserts authoritatively. 'Did you not hear how she danced with the Devil and conjured up storms to thwart the king's advance?'

'Aye, but under the circumstances…' The sheriff's words sound like a trickle of rain bouncing off parched earth.

'Those not zealous in their pursuit of evil might be taken to side with the malevolent forces raged against the king,' the commissioner growls. No one moves. The minister opens his mouth to say something, then closes it and looks around. 'But, of course, that is no one here; we are all of one mind. Am I right?' Commissioner Baxter adds, returning to his convivial tone.

'Quite right,' Reverend McLaren replies brightly.

'Yes, sir,' Grant joins in.

'No one would knowingly side with evil,' the sheriff ventures cautiously.

The commissioner clasps his hands and brings a bent forefinger to his lips. The sheriff is a man not easily frightened. It will do for now; everyone knows where they stand. 'Quite,' he says, picking up papers from the desk.

Mr Birkett enters the room. 'You wanted me, sir?'

'Ah, Mr Birkett. We have been waiting for you. We have another little job.'

# Part III

# Chapter Forty-Six

Suspicion
Vézelay

Assen sits on the churchyard wall, swinging his legs. A plump polished red apple sits by his hand. He picks it up and throws it in the air, then watches it fall back on his palm. On the third catch, he brings it to his mouth and takes a satisfying bite. It tastes sweet, almost like a raspberry, and leaves juice at the corners of his mouth. Drawing the apple away, he looks at the gash; the interior is rippled with pink-red veins. Nice. He takes another bite.

What a lovely day. He savours the moment, contentedness seeping through his body. He has a roof over his head and eats food – good food – each day. The surroundings lift his spirits as he glances at the pretty little cottages snaking their way down the steep hill and the irregular fields beyond, separated by ancient stone dykes. He is doing work that means something; he is helping people, really helping people. He is learning from a wonderful woman, and to think he found her in a place like this. So, yes, *content* is the right word. Or is it? Is it something more? He takes another huge bite.

'You look like a gentleman of leisure, Mr Durand.'

He turns to see Madame Lambert approaching through the gate at the other end of the wall. A basket is slung over her right arm containing sprigs of rosemary, lavender, tarragon and basil, apples, and something purple, probably carrots. She is wearing a pale-blue dress with different hues of sapphire, and a bonnet of matching shades with a soft pink ribbon etched around its rim. The ensemble is very becoming but he knows better than to tell her that.

Assen stops chewing, the chunk of apple suspended in his mouth. All his thoughts have coalesced into one amorphous pleasing sentiment he cannot quite articulate. He stares straight ahead.

'Mr Durand, Mr Durand,' Madame Lambert says louder, as if she were rousing a drowsy patient.

'Huh?'

'Anyone would think that was not your name,' she says.

Assen shifts, and his face warms. Is she teasing him, or does she suspect? He wants to tell her everything, the whole truth – the patients, the experiments, what he's done, what he couldn't do. But all he manages is 'I ... umm...'

Madame Lambert laughs and looks back across the graveyard. 'Don't fret. We all have our little secrets ... but as long as our heart is true. Yours is true, isn't it?'

She *is* testing him, he determines, and replies earnestly. 'I will always do my best to serve.'

Her eyes linger on his face. 'Yes. I believe you will.'

'Look ... I just wanted to say, the other day ... at Mr Lafayette's house. You were... That is to say, I've never seen anything quite like—'

Madame Lambert waves her hand dismissively. 'It is nothing. It is my work – it's what I do.'

'It is far from nothing,' he says gravely. 'You are a true healer. You actually heal people!

'Don't sound so surprised!' She looks at his earnest face. 'Thank you. But really, people heal themselves. I do everything I can to help them do what they naturally do. Sometimes I just get out of the way. I don't hinder. I give them encouragement. Nature knows how to heal if we don't interfere too much.'

'Unlike modern medicine.' Assen sighs, takes another bite. 'I've learned a lot from you – I *am* learning a lot from you. I wish I'd known you before, when I left the...'

'Go on. Left where?'

'It doesn't matter. Please go on. You were telling me about the art of healing.'

'Oh, I don't know about that. It's just that sometimes physicians intervene too quickly, that's all. They want to try out new things ... they're too zealous. It can be dangerous.'

Assen turns to face her. 'You're right, Madame Lambert. In fact, there's something I want to tell—'

'Oh dear,' Madame Lambert whispers.

'What?' Assen asks nervously.

'Father Girault.'

'Ah, Madame Lambert, Mr … er … er…' Father Girault holds up his hand and barrels across the square towards them. The breeze catches his black cape, making him look like a raven landing unexpectedly.

'Durand. This is Mr Durand,' Madame Lambert chimes, looking mischievously at Assen.

The clergyman catches his breath. 'Yes, of course, Mr Durand. It's good to finally meet you.'

'Is it?'

Madame Lambert shoots him a look.

'I wanted to speak to you both,' the priest continues, apparently ignoring Assen's acidity.

'I'm so sorry, Father, it'll have to wait. I am late for an appointment,' she says, turning to Assen, the corners of her mouth turning up and her eyes creasing. 'I'm sorry, Alain. Can we continue our talk later?'

She glides off down the path alongside the wall that runs north towards the millers' cottages at the edge of the village. After fifteen or so yards, she turns around. 'Oh, Alain, this is Father Girault, our town priest.'

\*\*\*

Assen wonders how he can be irritated and attracted to her at the same time. Is that even possible? Apparently, it is. He shakes his head.

'Well, no matter.' Cocking his head to the side, Father Girault eyes Assen. 'Mr Durand, you were both at the Lafayettes' abode two nights ago.'

'Is that a question or are you making a statement?'

Father Girault clears his throat. 'Let me be clear. I understand that you and Madame Lambert were at the Lafayettes' place two nights ago and the physician Dr Dévereux was also present.'

'Do you want me to confirm that?'

'And the eminent physician Dr Dévereux, who is highly regarded all over the county, was – and I can hardly believe this myself – was asked to leave!'

'No.'

'No?' the priest echoes, confused.

Assen sighs. 'He gave Mr Lafayette an ultimatum. If Madame Lambert did not leave, he would.' He shrugs. 'And he did.' He jumps down from the wall. 'Now, if you'll excuse me, I have an appointment too.'

'Wait! Your glib response might be adequate for wherever you come from but, believe me, it won't make you any friends here. We are not in the habit of treating eminent physicians and other personages with such disrespect when they deign to offer their services. They are accorded the reverence and respect befitting of their learning and status.'

'Really?' Assen says flatly.

'Especially in the presence of... Well, Madame Lambert is... I'm sure she can treat minor ailments that don't require much skill or thought...'

Assen narrows his eyes to slits. 'I would be careful what you say next.'

'What? It is not *I* who needs to be careful, Mr Durand. Your tone might be tolerated where you come from, but it won't get you very far here. Madame Lambert is capable, I dare say, but compared with Dr Dévereux she is an illiterate village midwife who needs someone to write for her!'

Assen faces the priest and takes a step closer so they are scarcely a foot apart. 'How dare you!'

'How dare *I*?'

Assen hears himself shouting but doesn't care. 'That illiterate village midwife

probably – no, almost certainly – saved Mrs Lafayette's life! Mr Lafayette would be a widower now if he'd left that buffoon Dévereux in charge. The doctor left her with childbed fever! God, he probably caused it.'

'That is slanderous!' Father Girault explodes.

The last of Assen's patience evaporates and he knows he must leave before he loses control. 'I have to go.' He starts walking down the hill in the direction of Madame Lambert's house.

'This is not over! I have not finished,' Father Girault shouts at his back. 'We take defamation very seriously in this part of the world!'

Assen turns. 'Then you should have been more careful in what you said about Madame Lambert. Good day, Father.'

\*\*\*

The priest watches Assen stomp off down the hill, veer sharply to the right and along the path that descends to the river. Clasping his hands across his abdomen, he presses his lips together in a thin line, his jaw set rigid.

'Good morning, Father Girault. It is a grand morning, wouldn't you agree?' Mrs Alfonse has been watching the two men from across the square.

'Ye-es, Mrs Alfonse. Indeed.'

'I couldn't help noticing you were talking to Mr Durand, Madame Lambert's assistant. A personable young man, wouldn't you say?' She looks at the priest's clenched fists.

'I… I… Mrs Alfonse, tell me what you know of this stranger.'

# Chapter Forty-Seven

### An Offer
### Tranent Tolbooth

It is pitch black, except for a narrow beam of low light high up at the grate through to Gelly's cell. Agnes's eyes have grown used to the dark, but it doesn't matter; she doesn't want to open them anyway.

Water is dripping, echoing, soporific. She'll focus on that until she falls asleep. Her legs are splayed out before her and her back is numb, rounded against the wall. Her chin drops to her chest. Good. There's no point imagining all that is to come. It will be hard enough to deal with it as it happens, never mind magnifying it. It was always something she told her patients, and it was true. Yet, as is ever the way, she is now charged with following her own advice in the most terrifying situation she could ever imagine.

A horse whinnies in the distance. At the normal everyday sound, her shoulders loosen fractionally. Stretching her neck, she rotates her head in small circles, three rounds to the left and three to the right.

Faint footsteps descend the stairs at the end of the corridor. She turns her ear towards the sound. The tread is coming closer: maybe two people. Placing her palms on the cold, hard floor, she straightens her elbows and sits higher to focus. They are almost here. They stop outside her cell.

Stumbling to her feet, she uses the wall for balance but the room swims. She sways, almost tipping backwards, and her head glances off a stone jutting from the wall.

*Concentrate on the hardness and coldness of the stone*, she tells herself, spreading her palm and fingers against the wall. The wall is icy and dank. It is the advice she used to give patients in pain. 'Bring all your attention to another area of the body where there is no pain, or focus on something outside your body, preferably something natural like a tree or flower.' Ironic that she now has to do it for herself – but it is working. The room stops rising and plunging. *Feel your feet. Feel the hardness of the floor through your feet.* That's better. The room is almost level; she'll not fall over, at least, not for a little while, anyway.

The bolt draws back and the key twists in the lock. The door creaks open.

The guard appears holding a candle aloft as he peers into the darkness. She marvels at how the halo of the candle expands and floods the room with light so bright she has to squeeze her eyes shut. The guard comes further into the room and places the candle in a sconce high on the wall alongside the screen to Gelly's cell.

Another man enters, making the room look and feel two feet smaller. 'Leave us. I'll speak with the prisoner alone.'

Agnes recognises the sheriff's voice. *What does he want?* Goosebumps prickle at the back of her neck.

'Are you sure, sir?' the guard warns. 'She's a dangerous witch, that one. Mr Birkett says so.'

'Aye, all right, all right. I know.'

Is there slight irritation in the sheriff's voice?

He puts his hand in his pocket, takes out some coins and covertly places them in the guard's hand. The guard immediately pockets them. 'Aye, right ye are, sir. Give us a shout when you need me.' He flattens himself against the door as he squeezes out past Sheriff MacKay.

For a split second, Agnes sees a torch burning in the corridor in a holder high on the wall. She homes in on the light – yellow, gold, amber-red, blue, green, white – so beautiful. How has she not detected such colours before? They momentarily calm her, softening her chest and slowing the beating of her heart. She wonders if they light the whole of the corridor and, if she followed the flames, she'd find a way out to the daylight. Her mind is wandering; perhaps she is delirious. *Do not trust anything you see or hear.*

The guard closes the door behind him and Agnes and the sheriff stand facing each other in silence. Agnes opens her mouth to ask him what he wants but the sheriff puts his forefinger to his lips and raises his other hand. They freeze until the gaoler's footsteps have retreated. The sheriff slowly returns his hand to his side. 'Goodwife Sampson. May I call you Agnes?'

She looks at him squarely. 'If there's one thing left to me, it is my name. My friends call me Agnes. I do not count you as one of them.'

'I see. Forgive me.'

'Why are you here?'

'To help you.'

She laughs bitterly. 'Really?'

'Things are going to get worse—'

'I've seen Gelly.'

'Right ... of course... I'm sorry ... that must have been...'

Water gathers in her eyes as she tries to find something to focus on. She looks above the sheriff's head to the candle's flame.

'Look,' he continues, 'they want a confession – *your* confession. The king's court will be here any day now. There's to be a big show trial. Two hundred warrants have gone out.'

'Two hundred! Dear God! What hellish nightmare is this?'

'The point is that the king's favour is a precious commodity. Those who have uncovered this plot and a vast network of conspirators will never have to worry about their livelihood again. They have no interest in the law or a fair trial, only in showing His Grace that they thwarted a plot to murder him. Do you see? They have to get confessions and convictions.'

'Aye, I do see ... now.'

'They'll go to any lengths to get a confession. John Fian has confessed to summoning up the Devil and leading the coven.'

'John?' *The kindest and fairest of men.*

'I'll spare you the details but there is only so much a body can stand. I'm sorry. He'll be executed, and Gelly, too.'

'And me?'

'I think it's very likely...' He exhales. 'Goodwife Sampson, things could get bad, very bad indeed.' He reaches into his pocket and pulls out a small pouch. 'I've brought you something ... if they get... You know, if it gets too much.' He opens his palm and offers the pouch to Agnes.

'What is it?' She looks from the pouch to his face but sees only openness; kindness, even.

He looks over his shoulder before whispering, 'Hemlock.'

'Hemlock,' she repeats. She snatches the pouch and gazes at it, feeling the lightness in her palm. *Can I trust him?* she enquires within. *Yes*, the answer comes back. Her intuition has never let her down before. 'Thank you.' She slips the bag into the concealed pocket of her skirt. 'Will it hurt?'

'I am assured it will be very quick.'

'Aye, I have heard it so. I've never used it before. Some healers do ... but ... but I never have.'

'Goodwife Sampson, I ... I am truly sorry for what has happened. I am sorry I can't get you a fair trial, that I can't get justice for you, John Fian or Gelly Duncan, or any of the two hundred souls facing these witchcraft charges. The whole thing is out of control and out of my hands. There are too many reputations and livelihoods bound up in proving the biggest coven in history is intent upon obliterating the king.'

'Agnes,' she says softly. 'You can call me Agnes.'

'Agnes.' He smiles sadly. 'I am honoured, Agnes,' he adds with a little bow.

'What will you do?'

'What? Oh, I'm leaving... We're going... I'll get a boat.'

'Listen, there's a skipper,' she offers, 'just by St Andrew's Auld Kirk. Williamson – he's a good man. Ferries goods back and forth to the Low Countries. Tell him I sent you, and that Elaine was very well and happy the last time I saw her.'

'Thank you. I will.'

'Where will you go?'

'France. If we can get there.'

She brightens. 'I've been to France. I have... I had a friend, friends, in France.'

'Is that right?' he says encouragingly, as if they were old friends retelling stories, kindly listening and never interrupting a cherished memory in true friendship.

'Aye, I speak French. Not so good now, though. Nowhere ... no one to practise with. But many years ago, I was a maid to Lady Rocheid. They took me to Paris. Can you imagine? I was so young.' She looks past the sheriff's shoulder up at the grate. 'She was like me...'

'Lady Rocheid?'

'What? No. A girl I met there. Same age as me. She was the daughter of one of Lady Rocheid's friends. They were very exotic, from some faraway place. There was always a hint of sandalwood and nutmeg when she walked into the room. I always loved that smell. We would walk together in the gardens. She taught me about plants and flowers and how they could heal ... all the different things they could be used for. She even introduced me to some of her family – a cousin, her brother. They were good people, genuine... There was, I don't know, an honesty to them. That's when I first got interested in healing ... it was useful... I could be of use, not just picking up and scrubbing after some toff. She said I had a talent, a gift. She was kind, not stuck up, treated me the same as any one of her rich friends. I think she preferred my company.'

'Is she still in France?'

'In a manner of speaking. She died.'

'I'm sorry. What was her name?'

'Bahdeer Aldabeh. Oh, wait ... she married, so Bahdeer Verey. If you get to Paris—' her eyes crease '—ask for the Verey family. They are well known.'

'I will, though I don't know if they will let me in. I wouldn't.'

Agnes's smile vanishes. 'Sheriff ... can I tell you something?'

The sheriff nods. 'Of course.' He comes closer.

Time has sped by more quickly than Agnes could have imagined, yet so much has passed between them. The sheriff now knows something she's never told a soul, not even Gelly. But time is pressing on her; she can't afford the luxury of weighing pros and cons or finding the right moment. Her story needs to be told now or it will be lost forever; who would have thought Sheriff MacKay would be the guardian of 'it', the very reason for her existence, so she has always told herself.

Placing her hand on her heart, willing it to slow, she prays to herself. *Please, God, may he be true; may he reach France. Please, God, have mercy.*

They look at each other in the radiance of the candlelight. Funny how even the tiniest glimmers can look like beacons in pitch darkness.

The clang of the bolt being drawn back echoes through the cell. They didn't hear the footsteps approaching this time. How long has the guard been there? How much has he heard?

Agnes swallows but the lump won't go down. She cranes her head forward and tries again, takes a gulp of air. The sheriff raises his hand and gently places it on her upper arm. His eyes soften. 'Agnes Sampson, your story is with me now. It is safe. I will keep it for you. I will carry it and I will deliver it. Trust me.'

She nods and her body slackens. 'Thank you.' Now that her treasure is safe, she can face what she must endure.

The cell door opens and a guard stands on the threshold. 'The commissioner wants to see you.'

'Right,' the sheriff says, still looking at Agnes. 'Goodbye, Agnes.'

'Goodbye, Sheriff MacKay.'

'It's Gordon to my friends.'

'Goodbye, Gordon.'

\*\*\*

Walking out of the cell, Sheriff MacKay knows something momentous, even historical, has passed between them. His body is heavy yet light. The heaviness in the pit of his stomach is from the responsibility he bears for the destiny of another soul, and the lightness in his breast is from knowing he has done the right thing.

He treads along the dank corridor towards a spiral staircase. Each step is worn, sagging in the middle, testifying to the footsteps of all those who have stepped down into the stink and blackness. How many were innocent? How many climbed back out into the light?

He looks up. There is a chink of light far above his head, with so many twists and turns in between. He steadies himself, places a palm on the cold, damp outer wall and takes one step after another, relishing the sweetness of not thinking or feeling, just stepping.

At last he climbs out into the courtyard and a wave of nausea engulfs him, making him dry heave. Putting both palms against the wall, he braces himself until the queasiness passes. As he prepares to walk across the courtyard, the witchfinder steps out from a nearby pillar.

'You have been to see the witch Agnes Sampson?'

'That's still to be proven. I'll thank you not to refer to anyone as a witch before the trial.'

'I don't think there's any doubt. What were you talking about?'

'I just wanted to see if I could get any more out of her.'

'And did you?'

'No.'

'Does the commissioner know you've been speaking with her?'

The sheriff looks warily at him. *So, that's the way of it.*

Gazing straight ahead, Mr McPherson continues, 'You know, people who are friends with witches, or the people who accuse witches, tend to get tarred with the same...'

'Are you threatening me?'

'Of course not,' the witchfinder says quickly, apparently thrown by the sheriff's candidness.

'Well, I have business to attend to. Please excuse me.'

# Chapter Forty-Eight

Deceit
Vézelay

'You made quite an impression on Father Girault.' Madame Lambert grinds the pestle hard into the mortar, the marigold seeds crunching under the pressure.

Autumn is still some time away but leaves from the orchards and the oak are congregating in the corners of the herb beds.

*I wonder when he'll leave.* Madame Lambert grinds the seeds a little harder.

Assen lifts a phial from the bench and holds it to the light, gazing intently at the liquid. He puts it down, brushes away the dried flecks of ink and starts writing. Other phials and flasks gurgle on distilling apparatus, and neat piles of dried leaves, seeds, roots and petals sit in rows.

'Father Girault's an ass,' he replies, still writing.

She laughs. 'You have little respect for authority. I like that.'

'Authority is earned, worked for, deserved. Or it should be.'

'I don't think many would agree with you. They say you're born with it. There is a divine order with some at the top…'

'And some at the bottom.'

'Most at the bottom.' She tips the mixture from the mortar into a small linen bag.

'He was insulting.'

'Hmm? Oh, you need a thicker skin.' She carefully picks up a phial using long wire tongs and a cloth wrapped around her hands. 'This should do the trick.'

'It wasn't about me.'

'Uh-huh?'

'He made some comments – about you.'

'Ah, probably not the best comments anyone's ever made, but I dare say not the worst.' She pours more seeds, pods and buds into the small clay bowl and begins to rhythmically grind.

*He cares what people say about me. Defending my honour. Oh, for goodness' sake, how can you even entertain such a notion? He's just a kind young man. He'd do it for anyone, even for Mr Canavari, his landlord. Although...*

'They're so entitled.' Assen seemingly hasn't noticed Madame Lambert's attempts to keep her eyes fixed on the bowl of decimated seeds.

She tries to sound casual. 'What? Who is?'

'Bloody priests, physicians, so-called gentlemen...' he almost shouts, slamming down the quill.

She looks up.

'Sorry. But they really have no idea of the work of people like you, what healers – true healers – do. You get to know people, don't you? You want to know what their hopes are, what troubles them.'

'I find it helps. Why does it bother you so much?' Her heart is now in her throat.

'Medicine has great potential if ... if they'd condescend to learn from people who've been doing it for years, for generations.'

'On that we can agree. You should go into medicine. You are a quick learner. Perhaps we could get you a patron. Maybe things would change then.'

'They didn't.'

'Excuse me?'

Assen moves his quill and linen out of the way and faces Madame Lambert. 'I was – that is I *am* – a physician. I trained at the Faculty in Paris. I treated the highest ... the wealthiest... I also worked in a plague—'

'You are a physician?' she bursts out.

'Yes.'

'A physician?' she repeats in a whisper. 'I don't understand.' Slowly, she pushes the bowl to the centre of the table; she is still holding the pounder in her right hand. 'A physician!' she spits, glaring at him. 'Oh, I see. It was a game, huh? A little distraction for you? Let's go and spy on the stupid illiterate village midwife? That should be good for a laugh to entertain your fancy friends in Paris.'

'What? No, no! Of course not!'

'I've met your kind before! You think I haven't? Pretending to be ordinary and kind …and … and … just *observing* us, our strange ways, superstitious beliefs … village idiot—'

'That's not fair! It's not like that at all.'

'I bet you and Dr Dévereux had a good laugh. You're probably drinking companions!'

'You're not making any sense.'

'What? Because I'm a stupid bloody country midwife?'

'No. Because you're angry. I should go.'

'Yes, you should.' She slams the pestle on the counter, almost shattering it.

Assen rubs his mouth. 'Look there's something. There's something I need to tell you—'

'Just go.'

# Chapter Forty-Nine

Standing Firm
Tranent Tolbooth

'Damn it! Why hasn't that woman confessed yet? The king will be here any day!' The commissioner gets up with a screech of his chair, scattering papers across the desk.

'They usually do,' Mr Birkett says, his face set.

'Usually? Usually is not good enough.'

'She's a tough one,' the witchfinder joins in.

'Tough! She has the Devil by her shoulder.' Commissioner Baxter marches to the fireplace. 'Birkett, just do what it takes. Get that confession.' He returns to the desk and picks up the quill, drawing the dispersed sheets to him.

'Um, sir, it could kill her. It's been four days already.' Birkett coughs. 'It wouldn't look good.'

'A confession would be better, sir,' the witchfinder adds.

'What? Aye, right.' Commissioner Baxter knows they are right. But the delay has already cost him credibility in the eyes of some Privy Council members, although not in the eyes of the king, as yet. So far, His Grace has been pleased with the scale of the investigation and how it has reached into all levels of society. It is unparalleled. But his tolerance for delays will stretch only so far. 'Do I have to do everything myself? Right, take me to her,' he orders Birkett.

'Aye, sir. This way, sir.'

Grant dashes to the door and opens it for them.

After descending the spiral stairs, they reach the bowels of the gaol. It is pitch dark except for the sconces spaced unevenly along the wall of the corridor, each facing a cell door.

They reach the last one. A guard is seated outside the door, a torch directly above his head high on the wall casting a halo effect. The two men are almost upon him before he stands. Most likely asleep, the commissioner notes, but no matter: there are more pressing matters. The gaoler is a lucky man – this time.

The commissioner transfers his weight from one foot to the other as the guard fumbles through the gigantic ring for the right key. Looking around him, Commissioner Baxter can see very little, but the stench is overpowering. Wrinkling his nose, he reaches into his breeches for a posy pouch, brings it sharply to his face and inhales deeply. Lavender and rose oil fills his nostrils.

Heaving a sigh of relief, the guard separates one key from the rest. He slots it in the lock, turns and pulls back the snib. Stepping back, Mr Birkett is just about to enter, when the commissioner places his hand lightly on his arm. 'I'll speak with her alone.'

Mr Birkett's deadpan expression breaks only fleetingly to betray mild surprise, but he steps back to join the gaoler under the sconce.

At first, the commissioner sees nothing even though a candle still burns in the holder next to the grille. As his eyes become used to the gloom, he notices what he thinks is a pile of rags and strips of bleached wood in the corner. The rags stir.

\*\*\*

Agnes, through her stupor, senses someone in the room. She raises herself onto her hands, straightening her elbows. Something is covering her head, around her ears, under her chin. She tries to say something but her tongue won't move; she can't open her mouth. She shakes her head from side to side. The metal in her mouth feels cold and rough.

\*\*\*

'What is this?' The commissioner has never seen such a contraption before. Maybe it is for her own protection to stop her banging her head off the walls to become senseless. He has seen that happening once at Edinburgh Castle; the prisoner even tried to escape through the bars he'd worked free. The man got as far as climbing down the cliff face on knotted blankets but they found his body in the Nor Loch the following spring.

'It's a scold's bridle, sir. She has a terrible mouth on her,' the guard explains. 'The Devil's words can make a person go crazy.'

'Get it off!' Baxter snaps at Birkett.

Birkett walks past the commissioner and kneels beside Agnes. The commissioner notes he is surprisingly gentle as he removes the bridle. She coughs, probably from the weight of iron lifting from her tongue. Leaning forward, she rubs her jaw and mouth, reclines and looks up at him.

Now he sees it. She is completely bald, and her shoulders and arms are also bare. There are patches of purple, blue, green and yellow on her upper arms and wrists, and rivulets of blood as if she has been bled by a physician. He draws his eyes away but notices how short her skirts are; his eyes rest on her calves. The visible flesh displays a rich palette of indigo, jade and pus-darkened hues.

'You did this?' the commissioner enquires, indicating Agnes's bald head.

'The witchfinder, lookin' for marks, ye ken.' Birkett shrugs.

'I see. Leave us now.'

Birkett withdraws. 'I'll leave the door open.'

'Close it. I'll shout if I need you.'

Stepping deeper into the cell, the commissioner wipes an imaginary speck from his sleeve and cups his hands on his belly. 'Do you know who I am?'

Agnes looks up, eyes glazed. Now free of the harness, her head swings. 'The orchestrator?' she retorts in a husky voice.

'What?'

'No.' She shakes her head. 'That's the king. Good King James.'

'Things can only get worse.'

She laughs bitterly.

'Birkett has ways of drawing things out so that you don't actually die, but you'll want to, you'll really want to. You'll scream for him to kill you, for anyone to put you out of your misery. But if you confess, Agnes, and ask for God's forgiveness, we can make things quick, painless, much easier.'

'Ah, you can make the end quick and painless, can you?'

His words are not having the desired effect. Perhaps she really is in league with the Devil. Of course she is; that's why she's here. 'It's either that or slow strangulation before the final burning.'

'Right,' she nods, composed. 'What do you want?'

*Now we're getting somewhere.* 'I have your confession written up. You just have to sign it.'

Agnes raises her head and catches his eye. He quickly looks away. 'If you just sign here ... see...' He points to a blank space below pages of writing.

'So...' she begins slowly. 'You want me to confess for the king ... to help him sleep easier ... quell his demons, the things he's done ... the things he wants to do...'

'Have a care.'

'No *woman* can do that. You know that ... and you have your answer.'

'You'll regret this.'

'I regret many things. This is not one of them.'

'Birkett! Birkett!'

The cell door flies open, and Birkett appears in the doorway, obscuring the light from the torch behind him. 'Put that thing back on,' the commissioner snaps, gesturing to the scold's bridle.

Birkett picks up the jumbled straps and metal, untangles them and bends down to Agnes. As he slips the leather hood over her bald head, she does not resist.

# Chapter Fifty

Coming Clean
Vézelay

Madame Lambert sighs and pushes away the plate; she's hardly touched her supper. It's been two days since their quarrel and she hasn't seen or heard from him. Well, she did tell him to go. Was she too harsh? No. He'd lied to her – not a small lie, but a big one. What else did he lie about? It's better he's gone. Things can get back to normal, the way they've always been.

She gets up wearily, takes the plate and stacks it with the others on the bench under the window.

'Damn!'

There is a soft knock at the door. 'God, I hope they haven't heard me.' She picks up her old woollen shawl that is draped over the chair by the fire and wraps it around her shoulders. It's not very becoming but at least it's warm. She needs some comfort; the air has grown chillier in the last few days. The gentle rap comes again.

'All right, I'm coming.'

She has learned to intuit the sound of knocking: this one isn't urgent, but it is important. It helps her prepare her demeanour as she opens the door.

He has his back to her at first and is looking up and down the street. He spins around at the squeak of the loose hinge. 'I want to explain,' he says gently. 'Will you let me in?'

*I've already let you in.* Madame Lambert is frozen, her hand on the edge of the door. His oval brown eyes are soft and pleading, and the tightness in her chest releases a little. Opening the door wider, she steps back and he passes pensively into the warm room.

'May I sit?' he asks, keeping his coat on.

Madame Lambert indicates a chair – not her best one, but the one closest to the fire, the one she first offered him. 'Would you like some tea?'

'Yes, please… Thank you…'

'You'd better take your coat off unless what you have to say will take no time.'

He hurriedly pulls at his sleeves, catching the shoulders at his elbows and cuffs. Wriggling free from the garment, he throws it on the back of his chair. 'Thank you.'

Madame Lambert places two beakers on the table then carries over her blackened pot from the fire. As she pours, steam rises from the stream of hot water. She pushes a tankard to Assen and draws another to herself. The scraping of the pewter on wood is amplified in the hush.

He takes a sip. 'Peppermint. Thank you.'

'Well?'

'It's true, I was a physician. But I didn't do any good. I thought with the latest discoveries, the new elements and chemicals, we could cure – well – everything, anything, even the plague. I thought we just needed to discover … to uncover something … refine it, and people would take it and be cured.'

'Like magic?' She wipes an imaginary stain from the table with her palm.

'Something like that.'

'And you were wrong.'

Lifting his head, he locks on to her eyes. 'I was wrong. My uncle, Uncle Manny, he supported me all through my training, but it was not just money. We, that is the Vereys – that's my name – we were … we *are* very wealthy. We didn't need the money, you understand. It was the support he gave me, the encouragement. He encouraged me, praised me. He loved me.'

He hangs his head, staring into the abyss of the beaker. 'I loved *him*, you know.'

'I know,' she whispers.

'Plague came … the whole family, Uncle Manny, Aunt Lottie, Émile, René, little Jo. I thought what I'd learned in medicine – the new medicine – could make a difference.'

'It didn't?'

'They all died.'

'I'm sorry,' she offers, releasing her hands from the table.

'Do you know what I remember?' He stares into space. 'A man with a soiled apron carrying a tiny shrouded figure under his arm coming out of Uncle Manny's house.'

Assen swallows, and grabs the tankard swigging back a mouthful of tea. The smell of peppermint wafts across the table. His hands tremble as he sets the vessel back down. 'I've seen it, the plague. Sometimes – actually, most of the time – it doesn't take everyone in the household. Usually some people are spared in a family. Uncle Manny was the least ill, you see. When I was there, he assisted me, he tended the others.'

'You saw them? You were in close contact with the plague?'

'Yes. I brewed my own theriac with the finest ingredients,' he continues, head bowed. 'I worked at the still all night ... but I left them. I shouldn't have. I thought it would be all right, just a few days, but it wasn't. It was too long, too late... I shouldn't have left. I made a mistake. I've made lots of mistakes... I didn't... I didn't... I didn't want this to be a mistake, too.'

Madame Lambert takes him in, head slung low, staring into his cup. 'Alain, listen to me. Sometimes you can't help. You're just a small part, a cog. You think you have more power than you actually have. Some people get better, that's true, but often it has little to do with the doctor. Maybe they had a stronger constitution, they breathed in less miasma, it wasn't their time ... or God had a different plan.'

'It spared me,' he looks down.

'The plague?'

'Yes. I worked in a plague hospital on the edge of Paris. I felt strange one day, different, sweating, fever. I couldn't keep my eyes open. I don't remember much about it, but I saw... I had a dream... I–I ... I had this dream.'

'Ah. The dream,' she says. 'The dream that brought you here?'

He hears his mother's voice. *Come what may, truth will lighten your heart. You have a courageous heart.* He lifts his head and leans back in the chair.

'I left this world. I went to a garden. Uncle Manny was there, and my mother. She was so beautiful and kind. She had the thickest black hair – wiry, they call it. And the love in her eyes –

I can't tell you. There was just love, nothing else. It overwhelmed me. I was overwhelmed, that's it, overwhelmed. The whole place was overwhelming – the flowers, the plants, the fountain, and when the wind blew, it was like…' His arms dangle as he looks from side to side, as if trying to find the answer. 'I know you'll think I'm mad…'

'I won't,' she says gently but firmly.

'It was like… The wind was like a force, a power, but a gentle power. It was pure love … intense, uncomplicated … undiluted… Just love … purely love. I don't know how else to describe it. They – Uncle Manny and my mother – told me it wasn't my time. But at the same time, it was *my* choice. I remember that. I *could* go with them if I wanted to, but there was something I had promised myself I would do with this life.

'They said if I chose to go back, I must leave the hospital and wander through the villages of Burgundy until I reached the House of God in Beaune. I was to learn everything I could from the healers along the way, and only then would I find what I was looking for. I was to be humble and understand I knew very little about healing. I was to watch, help and learn.'

Madame Lambert leans forward, her elbows on the table and her chin cupped in her hands. *You are such a strange and beautiful man, Assen Verey.* 'And have you learned?'

'I've learned about people and what they… We need to be healthy and to heal, but sometimes, it's not in the person's destiny to heal, and that can be right … even beautiful, too.'

Reaching forward, she places her hand on top of his. 'You *have* learned.'

He quickly turns his hand upwards and squeezes hers, curling his fingers around the fleshiest part. Pressing back, she looks into his earnest eyes. Their fingers still entwined, she gets up and circles the table to sit on the chair next to him. Scrutinising his face, she lifts her free hand and touches his full deep lips. He cranes his neck to kiss her fingers.

There is a tingling in her navel, the soft fluttering awaking something dormant, something primeval. She brushes his cheek with the back of her hand, running the pad of her thumb along his cheekbone. Neither has blinked and she lets her hand fall to her lap. He lifts his and slides his thumb along her lips and rosy cheeks, flushed from the fire.

'Is Madame Lambert your real name?'

She throws her head back and laughs, her hazel eyes effervescent in the firelight. 'My name is Thérèse Segal.'

He laughs too. 'It's a beautiful name. Thérèse Segal,' he repeats, rolling it around in his mouth. 'Where are you from? If I may ask.'

'I was born in Marseilles.' She waves her hand dismissively. 'But you don't want to hear about that.'

Taking up her hand again, he urges, 'Yes, I do. Please.'

'My father was an apothecary.'

'Oh?' He raises one eyebrow.

Enjoying his surprise, she carries on. 'They had no other children. My mother was a seamstress, and a good one. I had a comfortable, happy childhood.'

'Sounds idyllic.'

'Hmm, I suppose it was. Funny how we don't think that at the time, don't really appreciate it. I helped my father and learned ... shelves and shelves of medicines, powders, seeds, elixirs. I thought they were magic potions. I learned accounts and kept the inventories.'

He furrows his brows. 'You can write? Then why did you get me to…?'

'Why does anyone do anything?' She shrugs. 'For the adventure!'

Assen chuckles. 'And is it?'

'I'll let you know.'

'Why did you leave Marseilles?'

'The plague. We are defined by it, you and I. I was sixteen and my parents died. They had little property to leave – they had rented the premises, the house. But I had plenty of marriage proposals. I was young and pretty.'

Scenes from Marseilles sail across her mind: its busy streets and the docks; the grand opulent residences of the merchants who brought the finest medical ingredients to France's shores – cinnamon, the purest opium, agarics and other rarer fungi. They were also, incidentally, her father's most lucrative clients.

'But I saw myself year after year in childbirth, worn out in ten years. I couldn't do that to myself if there was another way. I'd learned a lot from my father, and I had treated people and advised them. I had an instinct... I listened... I found I could help, say the right thing. I sold as much from the shop as I could and also what was left of our possessions. I kept my mother's best dresses. I needed to look respectable. I invented Mr Lambert, a gentleman who had died tragically not long after we were wed, and travelled as a widow and a gentlewoman healer.'

'You travelled from village to village ... a young woman? Isn't that dangerous?'

'If you're not careful, I daresay. But I dressed like a nun, stuck to travelling during the day and always employed a guide. I became known as a healer, a gentlewoman healer. I earned my keep, which was a relief.'

'And you stopped here?'

'I passed through many times and always thought that when I had the money to settle down, I'd do it in a place like this. I'd buy a house and have a room where I could prepare my remedies, and all the villagers would know where to find me. They'd tell strangers in need, "Go to the house of Madame Lambert. She will help you."'

He smiles. 'And then I passed through.' He takes her hands, kisses them and looks penetratingly into her eyes.

Her heart jumps into her throat, making her gasp. She takes a deep breath through her nose to coax it back into her ribcage where it pounds for a little longer.

'So, there is no Mr Lambert or Mr Segal?'

'There is no Mr Segal, unless you count my father, and there is no Mr Lambert. There never has been.'

Gently removing one hand from their interlaced fingers, he places it on the back of her head and draws her towards him. 'I'm glad,' he says.

She smells the peppermint, sweet and fresh, through her parted lips, and feels the warmth of his breath. Releasing his other hand, he puts it around her waist and pulls her close. She wraps her arms around him, their faces almost touching, a sliver of air between them. The gentle warmth of lip on lip, breathing in each other's exhale. He presses his mouth hard on hers; she presses back as hard, every instance of attraction distilled into this moment, a heady, potent mix.

After a long moment, they release and look at each other. The slightest word would break the spell. Thérèse stands, takes Assen's hand and leads him to the staircase. Holding his hand, she guides him up the stairs.

# Chapter Fifty-One

Beyond the Veil
Tranent Tolbooth

'Who's there? Who is it? Show yourself? I'll die before I let you go further.'

Agnes is slumped in the corner on some filthy straw, covered in stained blankets and rags from all the other guests who had the misfortune to cross the law, or the church, or a landlord. All the diseases of humanity are wrapped around her shoulders; she shudders at their collective suffering. Her skin is clammy; perhaps she'll die before dawn. A good thing because there will be no sin of self-murder to account for on Judgement Day. She wonders if she can will herself to death.

At least the bridle has been removed. She chews her tongue, trying to produce saliva. Her mouth is as dry as driftwood baking in the sun. But at least she can still speak, if a little hoarsely. Things need to be said. They will allow her, won't they, if she makes it to the trial? But how long can she hold out for?

*Don't sign the confession whatever you do, Agnes.* But wouldn't it be quicker and easier? Aye, for them.

Heaviness once again pulls her head backwards and lolls it to the side. Darkness, the texture of thick, black molasses, begins to pour through her, consciousness retreating as it goes.

There it is again! 'God's truth! What's that?' Something moved in the corner of her cell.

'Don't come any closer. I swear, I will end my life now. God save me!'

'It's all right, Agnes. It's me.' An oddly familiar voice softly echoes around the room.

'What? Who? Show yourself!' Agnes pulls herself up straight, pinning her back against the wall. She braces her palms on the floor ready to propel herself forward, her eyes searching the inky blackness where granite-grey and coal-black shapes cut through the darkness.

One shape begins to form into a human silhouette and steps out from the shadows. Agnes inhales sharply as someone who looks like Gelly – but different – appears. The young woman is wearing a long cream robe with lilac garlands spiralling down it to her feet, which are bare and clean and the colour of Mrs Merritt's butterscotch pudding. There is no dirt, tears, patches or blood staining her attire. Her dark-blonde hair hangs long and luscious around her shoulders.

Agnes has never seen Gelly look so bright, healthy and beautiful; so incredibly beautiful. There is even a glow surrounding her.

*Agnes Sampson, you are either going mad or this is the Devil's work. Which is it?* And yet ... and yet ... there is a warmth, a gentleness, a kindness emanating from the figure in the corner.

'Gelly! I thought you were... I thought you were done ... that they'd...' Something round and hard lodges in Agnes's throat. She tries once, twice, but she can't swallow it. In a trembling, squeaky voice, she adds, 'You looked terrible.'

'I know, Agnes, but I'm well now. I'm happy. You can see.'

'Did they let you go?'

'I have been released, yes.' She opens her arms to reveal more lilac garlands around her wrists.

'You're not injured?'

'I have to recuperate from this ... what happened here.' She looks around the cell in a detached manner.

'Recuperate?'

'We need time and care to recover, you and I. We picked a difficult path.'

'What? What do you mean?'

'I think you know.'

Something in Agnes's half-conscious, half-dreamlike state feels familiar, like they've had this conversation before. 'Aye,' she replies, blinking and fleetingly looking down. 'Are you going away, somewhere else, to ... heal ... to recuperate? Will you come again?' She lifts her head sharply, her eyes pleading.

Gelly looks down, her gaze soft. 'I will be somewhere else *and* right here. I am always here, and I will see you again soon. We are waiting for you. No matter what happens here, Agnes Sampson, everything will be all right. It will all pass very soon. Let your heart guide you. Let the natural feelings in your heart lead the way. Speak your truth for no other reason than to be true to yourself, and you too will be released soon.'

'Will I?' A wave of relief and gratitude washes through Agnes. Her chest and shoulders soften, her pharynx opens and moisture returns to her throat.

'Yes.'

Behind Gelly something else shimmers and long vertical lines appear, like a transparent flickering curtain. Agnes braces against the wall, banging her head. Two tall figures come forward from behind the veil – a woman in a long dress like Gelly's in shades of pale green and pink, and a man with long dark-brown hair wearing a robe of white and pale blue.

'Who are *they*?' Agnes cries, attempting to scramble to her feet.

'It's all right,' Gelly reassures her. 'They are here to help us. They are healers.'

'Oh.' Agnes slumps back down.

'I have to go with them now, to recover.'

'Where?'

'A beautiful place. I have a cottage with a stream at the bottom of the garden.'

'Really, Gelly? The little cottage? You're going to the little cottage you dreamed of?'

Gelly smiles and her whole face lights up, like the sun is shining through her.

In awe, Agnes sees little flares of light emanate from the young woman's body and dance in the air around her. 'And me, Gelly? Will I go there? If I…?' She squeezes the little pouch in her pocket. 'If I make things easier? If … if I do it, will I … will I still go there?'

'Aye. You'll join us. You are loved and we are waiting for you.'

'Soon?'

'Soon.'

# Chapter Fifty-Two

Afterglow
Vézelay

The sunlight, weak but welcome, streaks between the gaps of the shutters. It falls across Assen's sleeping features in diagonal lines. Thérèse smiles and studies his features: high cheekbones and two or three days of stubble, dark against his olive skin. Apparently conscious of being gazed at, he opens his eyes. She extracts her hands from under the blankets and touches the coarse hairs on his cheek.

Enveloping her hand, he squeezes her fingers, drawing the pads to his mouth and kissing them, then gently running his tongue along the fleshy mounds. 'I could lie here forever.'

She laughs. 'I'm not sure the good people of Vézelay would be very happy.'

'Hang the good people of Vézelay.' He runs his fingers through his hair and rests his head on his arm shaped in an upside-down V.

'Assen! That is not you!' A smile tugs at the corners of her mouth.

'I want to get to know you. Everything about you.' He turns onto his front and props himself on his elbows, his gold locket dangling from the long gold chain around his neck.

Thérèse looks at it for a moment. 'I think you know a good bit about me now.'

'You know what I mean. What about … what about a picnic! This Sunday, after church, down by the river. We could have it under Joshua's oak tree. What do you say? I'll bring everything.'

'All right. But I'll bring the bread and olives. And if the weather turns, we can have it here.'

'Good.' He rolls over again.

Thérèse sits up, turns and sweeps her palm over his chest, taking the locket in her hand. It covers her entire palm. She gauges its weight, similar to a large smooth pebble on the beach.

'This. It was your mother's?'

A shadow crosses his face, and she adds quickly, 'I do not wish to pry,' then places the locket carefully back on his chest.

'No, no. It's fine. Yes, it was my mother's. She gave it to me when I was three or four. She has – she had one the same. Look.' He opens the adornment and inside is a rose-coloured stone carved into one half of a heart. 'She has…had the other half. I was always to keep it close to my heart; she was very insistent about that. The court jeweller Moreau made the locket to house it. It was designed to her exact specification. It would remind me of her, she said, and keep her close to my heart wherever I might go.'

'That's beautiful.' Thérèse studies it more closely. 'A rose stone … for eternal love.'

'Hmm. I remember when she first gave it to me, and then when…' He stops, furrowing his brow.

'What is it?'

'It's just … well, she never… It's nothing. Never mind.'

Thérèse smiles and settles into the crook of his shoulder. He kisses the top of her head and rests his cheek on it.

'Assen.'

'Uh-huh.'

'Don't you have to go?'

'Not yet.'

'You know what I mean. The dream. Your mother. The House of God at Beaune?'

\*\*\*

His abdomen tenses. Leaving Vézeley and Thérèse is the last thing he wants to think about. 'Maybe they sent me on this journey so I could find you.'

'Do you believe that?'

'Hush. Let's not dwell on that now.' A vision of his mother, standing in a long flowing robe with her lush coal-black hair draped around her shoulders forms in his mind. The flowers circling her wrists and arms, the scent of sandalwood, spicy, warm and sweet, and the breeze blowing through his body.

*'Go to the House of God,'* her words echo. *'There you will find sanctuary, and you will need it. Let your heart guide you in*

*your work, in all you do. Be true to it. Your truth will only be revealed in Beaune.'*

Rising onto his elbow, he stares down at Thérèse. Her eyes are closed. He drops his lips to hers, gently presses them open, then glides his tongue over her teeth and deeper into her mouth.

She blinks open her eyes, presses his shoulders and forces him firmly onto his back. She climbs on top of his torso as he cradles her pelvis, his hands warm and kneading.

# Chapter Fifty-Three

The Escape
North Berwick

Moonlight fleetingly lights up the sea wall before the next cloud plunges the edifice into darkness. Fishing boats and other crafts anchored in the natural harbour creak and rock from side to side, bobbing up and down in constant movement with the energy of the tide and spasmodic breeze.

At the end of the harbour wall, a bigger merchant ship is secured by heavy ropes attached to iron rings grafted into the stone. Silent shadowy figures move around its deck, unfurling the sails and pulling on rigging.

From the gap between the clouds, the moonlight illuminates another three silhouettes – one small and two taller – hurrying along the sea wall towards the ghostly ship. When the spectres reach their destination, the tallest figure, a man, calls out. The other two, dressed from head to foot in dark cloaks, stay back in the shadows against the wall.

'Ahoy, ahoy. We are expected,' the man calls. 'Captain Williamson has assented…'

'Weesh. Have a care. Who goes there?' a voice calls back.

'It is I, MacKay. We have an agreement with Captain Williamson,' the sheriff returns, lowering his voice.

The hatch lifts and scrapes open, and another figure climbs out, jumping nimbly and silently onto the deck. He stands next to the crew member. 'Aye, all right, don't wear my name out,' he commands. He steps onto the dock and studies the sheriff. 'Yer early.'

'We didn't want to be late.'

'*We?*' The captain looks around, squinting into the shadows. 'We never said anything about a *we*.'

'You know my wife, Elspeth. We are recently wed,' the sheriff says quickly, his heart pounding.

'Aye, of course. Congratulations.' The captain's keen eye has already picked out the smaller figure under the overhang, flattened against the sea wall. 'Ye've someone else wi' ye?'

'It is the Johnston girl, young Jennie.'

'What?' His voice is a mixture of rage and concern. 'You'll have us all at the end of a rope.'

*Tell the truth, son; ye'll not go far wrong.* The sheriff hears John Fian telling him how a second right goes a long way to atone for a first wrong.

A vision of a yew tree forms in his mind. *He is standing beneath it in the school grounds, apologising to a boy for stealing his book of prayers and hiding it in a tree. He hands back the volume, which the boy accepts, saying, 'I forgive you, Gordon MacKay.'*

*The schoolmaster looks on. 'Good lads,' John says. 'Now, what have you learned?'*

*Young master MacKay begins hesitantly. 'I've learned that telling the truth and owning up makes you feel better. And ... and ... if you've done something wrong, and you make up for it – you do something good – that's good, and it makes you feel better too.'*

*The master smiles. 'Aye, lads. It's called "atoning". It is the right thing to do because it feels right. It feels right here.' He puts his fist at the centre of his chest.*

The sheriff lifts his head. 'Look, Captain Williamson. Jennie's parents – you know Robert and Mary – they begged me. Ye ken what's been going on… Gellis Duncan, you heard what happened to her. The thing is, Gelly treated Jennie, gave her some – I don't know – something to drink, and she got better.'

'So?'

'The witchfinder's been round asking about Jennie. Is there anything different about her? How's she's been behaving? Does she like to go off on her own? The other children are saying they're scared of her. Robert and Mary are frightened. You know what it's been like. There's two hundred warrants, anyone could be… Agnes Sampson's a good woman, just a midwife.'

The captain sighs. 'Aye, I ken.'

Sheriff MacKay takes a deep breath. It's now or never. 'There's one more thing, Captain.' He motions to his wife,

Elspeth, to come forward. Stepping out, she looks fearfully at her husband. 'Go ahead,' he says softly. She opens her cloak to reveal a baby tightly swaddled to her chest. As if it knows it is being introduced, the infant gurgles and hiccups.

'Jesus Christ!' the captain blurts out. 'A bairn! No way. Cannae do it.'

'Her name is Hope,' the sheriff says quickly. 'John and Maggie's child. They were … they were executed at the same time as Gelly.'

'I heard.'

'We had tae take her – we couldn't leave her. She's nobody in the world to look after her. I've got more money, I'll give you more money.'

'Keep your money. God Almighty. All right, all right. May God protect us from this madness.'

'Amen,' Elspeth says under her breath.

'Get on board.'

The sheriff takes the baby from Elspeth and Captain Williamson reaches down to pull her on first. Baby Hope is passed from man to man, then to Elspeth, where she settles in the crook of her arm, burbling contentedly. The sheriff offers Jennie his hand, and a seaman stretches down to help her on board.

Sheriff MacKay is last to climb onto the ship. Jumping onto the deck, he puts out his hand to the captain. The captain takes it, and they shake firmly. 'Thank you,' the sheriff breathes out.

'France… Well, I'm told it's a nice place to live out your days. A man could get lost in the towns or maybe the countryside. Hope you've brushed up on your French, Sheriff MacKay.'

'I hope *you* have, Captain Williamson.'

# Chapter Fifty-Four

Strangers
Vézelay

*It's going to be a beautiful day*, she thinks, as she lifts her face to the sun and takes in the heady smell of lavender outside Mrs Dupont's cottage. Thérèse makes a mental note to place some outside her own back door and bedroom window when she gets back. Many years ago, when she'd first arrived in Vézelay, an old village healer told her that if she planted the shrub at her doors and windows it would keep out those pesky tiny whining insects that are so common after the summer rains. The old woman warned that the flies' bites caused the marsh fever that afflicted so many travellers who passed through.

Thérèse sighs and breathes in the sweet odour again. The memory vanishes and a vision of Assen's hand on her stomach replaces it. She feels his warm palm move around to cup her buttocks, gently but firmly caressing. The smell of peppermint once again fills her nostrils as he presses his moist, hungry mouth on hers. She shudders. *Come on, Thérèse, get a hold of yourself. You're not a silly maid, for heaven's sake.*

As she turns into the square, she notices Father Girault standing outside the church talking with two gentlemen. She hopes he hasn't seen her. She wants to stroll along the riverbank on her way to the Lafayettes' and watch the unhurried flow of the current, and maybe catch the sun glinting on the water's surface. Pulling her wrap over her head she turns quickly, but not quickly enough.

'Madame Lambert! Madame Lambert!' the priest shouts. 'Please. These gentlemen would speak with you.'

Her stomach sinks. Her daydreams will have to wait. Taking time to compose herself, she meanders over to the trio. 'Yes, Father Girault. How can I help you? Is someone ill?'

'No, Madame Lambert. Let me introduce you. Madame Lambert, may I present Mr Noiret and Mr Fauvergue.'

She knows they are not from the village or any of the surrounding towns: the quality of their shoes gives them away. It's always the first thing she notices about people. You can tell a lot from a person's footwear – whether they come from a town or a village, the countryside or a big city, whether the shoes hail from the finest workshops in Paris or the back streets of Marseilles. Theirs are from Paris, she'd swear to it. But what are these well-heeled fellows from Paris doing here, wanting to talk to a simple village midwife? Something feels off. A rock settles in the pit of her stomach.

'Good day, gentlemen,' she says, brightly, swaying nonchalantly.

Both men give a little bow in acknowledgement.

'Good day, Madame Lambert,' Mr Noiret begins. She regards him more closely. A mature gentleman in his early fifties, or late forties, perhaps? He is of medium height with a sturdy, lean frame, and is wearing a rich black velvet doublet embroidered with black adornments of an even deeper hue with matching jet-black pantaloons. In Paris, his attire would be seen as understated and sombre, befitting a gentleman on serious business. But what business might that be?

'These gentlemen are from Paris.'

*I knew it!* 'Oh, yes?' she says, feigning surprise.

'They are looking for someone … a man.'

The rock gets bigger. 'I don't see how that has anything to do with me. If you'll excuse me, gentlemen. I have business to attend to.' Drawing her head away, she notices André across the square, talking with his friend Pierre.

'I'm sorry, Madame Lambert,' Father Girault interrupts, 'but their description sounds very like that scribe of yours. Alain, isn't it? He is from Paris, is he not? The good Dr Dévereux told these gentleman that a ruffian very much like the fugitive they are hunting was assisting you in your … umm … practice. Most gruff and threatening he is, the good doctor said.'

Madame Lambert spins around to face the three men, looking from Mr Noiret to Mr Fauvergue. 'What is this all about?'

Mr Noiret fishes in his doublet and pulls out a piece of paper. 'A fugitive, a former physician called Assen Verey, is wanted for questioning. I have a warrant for his arrest.'

Her heart almost escapes her ribcage and she fears they will notice her discomfort. 'I'm afraid there must be some mistake. I really don't see what this has to do with—'

'The charge is murder,' Father Girault exclaims triumphantly.

'What?' Her stomach churns and her throat narrows as she tries to take in a quivering breath. Her mind races. *He could never – he would never – he wouldn't! But where did he come from? Why is he here? Come on, girl, calm down. You know where he comes from; you know why he's here.*

She gulps in more air and her breathing begins to slow. When has she ever been wrong about people? She takes a breath through her nose. It feels better. Her neck is still tight but her head is clear.

'It was brought by his superior,' Mr Fauvergue says, picking up the thread, 'the eminent physician Dr Broussard, a most highly regarded professor. The fugitive is described as a man of twenty-eight or so years, of some refinement – distinctive, dark, a Moor. Very noticeable, unmistakeable, in fact.'

'Part Moor,' Mr Noiret corrects him.

Bowing, Mr Fauvergue continues, 'Quite so. Such a man would stand out if he travelled along the southern route from village to village.'

'And we believe such a man has, according to fellow travellers and simple country folk around here. Of course, it may be a case of mistaken identity, as you say—' Mr Noiret eyes settle on Thérèse, taking in every twitch and flicker in her features '— but we could clear all this up in a few minutes.'

'So,' Mr Fauvergue resumes. 'If you could tell us where this ... scribe ... Mr ... um...' He glances at Father Girault.

'Mr Alain Durand,' Madame Lambert cuts in. 'His name is Mr Durand. He is not here at the moment, I've sent him to get supplies in Dijon. It'll be four or five days, maybe a week, before he is back. I've told him to rest, take his time.'

'You are not in a hurry for the supplies?' Father Girault asks.

Locking eyes and giving him a withering look, she replies, 'No. They are to top up our stock before the winter, things I can't make and grow here.'

'Very well,' Mr Noiret concedes. 'We will wait.' He signals to Mr Fauvergue. 'Send two men on to Dijon. The rest can relax ... for now.'

'If you'll excuse me,' Madame Lambert says, sensing an opportunity to escape. 'I have patients to see.'

Hurrying away, she stops herself from breaking into a run. The cobbles are slippery and uneven underfoot and she feels off balance in a way she never has before. Imagining the men scrutinising every step, she slows down, lifts her head and lets her basket swing by her side. Rounding the corner, once she is sure she is out of eyeshot, she falls back against a wall. When did breathing become so hard? Right. She needs to act fast.

*Think, Thérèse! Think! Wait, there's a saying that the English – or is it the Scottish? – are so fond of: 'Act in haste, repent at leisure.' Calm down first, get control. Breathe. My God, this dress, these stays.*

Her bodice is tight against her ribcage. She tries to breathe in some air but it only reaches her collarbone: rigid, unforgiving, the corset won't budge. She'll never wear this damn thing again.

*Stop panicking, Thérèse Segal.* If she could slap her own face hard, she would. At last, the breath finds its own way. The stone wall presses against her back, chilling but solid. She lets her palms rest on it, absorbing its strength.

'Right.' Pushing back against the wall, she stands upright and looks around.

*Where is he?* She saw him a minute ago. She relaxes at the sight of André in his calf-leg breeches, swinging a long stick and chopping the heads of dandelions as he goes, whistling that tune he picked up from a vagrant at the fayre in the summer. She smiles as a warm blanket of comfort descends over her. Everything will be fine. André is normal, everyday, with little to distract him from the exquisite chores of everyday life.

'André! André!'

He looks up brightly, a smile cracking his face.

'If you are not too busy, I have something I'd like you to do for me. But it is very important you tell no one. Do you promise?'

The smile falls. 'I promise. Cross my heart.'

'That's all right, André. You're a good boy; your promise is good enough.' Her fingers scramble in her basket, searching for the cold flatness of coins. Clutching them, a little too tightly, her nails press into her palms. 'Here are *two* pennies for this very important task. Think you are up to it?'

André nods, mesmerised, as the coins drop into his open palm.

# Chapter Fifty-Five

The Trial
Tavistock Hall, East Lothian

It should have been a dark and foreboding day for the trial of Agnes Sampson, with low gloomy clouds hanging over Tavistock Hall. Instead, it is a bright, crisp, sunny morning, with thin wispy clouds stretched across a cornflower-blue sky.

The hall is already packed and the Justice Ayre— the circuit court for any serious trial south of the Forth, have just arrived, followed by the entire royal court. A buzz of excitement sears through the crowd. The court are seated at a long table at the far end of the hall, together with local barons, the commissioner and the Reverend McLaren. The royal household stand out in their finery, wearing fine velvet hats adorned with lavish, brightly coloured feathers of peacock green, turquoise, rose pink and red.

'They get them from the Far East,' Mrs Wilson says, nudging her husband.

'Get what?' He rubs his arm.

'Those plumes.' She tilts her head to the top table. 'The merchants, the ships from Edinburgh, they go out to the lands at the edge of the world and get them there.'

'Do they?' he says, craning to see the door behind the table of dignitaries.

'Burnett says the king will be arriving at any moment,' a neighbour behind joins in.

Mr Wilson half turns. 'Who's Burnett?'

'You know, over there.' His neighbour points to one of the guards at the other end of the hall next to a small door.

Mrs Wilson nudges her husband again. 'The plumes, Husband! At the end of the world, furthest east, where they don't have any day and it's always night. Aye, Mr Wallace told me that's where they get them.'

'Well, it must be right, then,' he says with a sniff.

'Everyone's here!' she adds, rubbing her hands and looking around. 'Aren't those the two lairds from East Linton and Haddington? Remember we saw them at Lammas last year, with their wives and—'

'Where?'

'There, in the middle, just to the left of the minister.' She nods her head at Reverend McLaren who is seated at the end of the top table, deep in discussion with two other clergymen, one of whom is shaking his head. 'And aren't they the two magistrates from that case over at Prestonpans? What was it again? Cattle? No ... it was poaching, that's it, poaching. Wasn't it over at Lethington?'

Mr and Mrs Wilson are seated on the public benches. Every seat is taken. People have come from as far as Dunbar, Dalkeith and Coldingham. It is as if the carnival has come to town. Those who didn't arrive two hours early, like Mr and Mrs Wilson, have to stand at the back or down the sides. Some people have brought their own stools, as they do for church, so they can sit when nothing much is happening. Most are also dressed in their Sunday best and chatting excitedly.

'Mr Paton says they'll start with the witnesses, then they'll let the witch talk at the end,' announces Mr Maxwell, a farmer from Gifford.

'How does he know?' asks his companion, a miller named Mr Cochrane.

'He saw it over in Fife.'

'Really?' Mrs Wilson exclaims, swivelling around, while four others turn similarly to face the farmer.

But there is a heavy silence among the patients and friends of Agnes Sampson; their dress is sombre and subdued. Mr McPherson, the witchfinder, sits among them at the front, dead centre.

At the worthies' bench, the commissioner glances from left to right, shuffling his papers. He notes Reverend McLaren's contented demeanour and signals his acknowledgement with a diminutive raise of his glass.

A large, gilded, throne-like chair sits at an angle to their table, and behind it two royal guards stand on either side of the double doors. One door opens and a finely dressed gentleman enters carrying a manuscript. The people in the public gallery elbow each other to shush. Those talking stop in mid-sentence, some with their mouths hanging open; through osmosis, a hush descends on the court.

Transfixed, they watch as the gentleman sits down and nods at the standing dignitaries to sit. Two court officials face the common folk and, with splayed hands, look as if they are bouncing a giant invisible ball as they indicate for everyone to sit or stand back.

The commissioner gets to his feet and cues the sergeant-at-arms, who is standing with an ornate staff and towering a good two feet above Baxter. The sergeant-at-arms lifts the staff and brings it down with a dull thud, once, twice, three times.

'Bring the prisoner in!' the commissioner roars.

The small narrow door at the back of the hall screeches open. All heads turn, some with excited anticipation and morbid curiosity, a few with stomach-churning dread.

A crumpled, dishevelled, emaciated figure in a scold's bridle staggers in, flanked by two guards. Her dress is short – wantonly short – barely covering her knees. No decent woman would allow herself to look so immodest and licentious, lacking the chastity required of decent God-fearing women folk in the local community.

Some look on with contempt and disdain, while others seek out the ground in place of the spectacle of a respected practitioner reduced to an object of denigration. Some men stare unashamedly at her bare legs; they reason that they are on show and it would be against a man's enquiring nature not to look. They have plenty to attract their attention, for her shoulders are also naked, adorned with a complex pattern of purple, yellow, green and blue.

\*\*\*

Agnes stumbles forward, one step in front of the other. The ground is spongy; it is like walking on a thick mattress. Next it disappears, and she free-falls through space, slipping between the hands of the guards. *Thud*! Cold hardness slams into her side.

A gasp rings out from the public gallery. The gaolers grab under her arms and pull her upwards, but her feet can't find the floor and she hangs like a rag doll between them. They half drag, half prop Agnes until the trio are standing in the epicentre of the hall.

She can't see much through the slits in the mask except a hint of red velvet on the table twelve or so feet in front of her and her filthy bare feet. But perhaps that's Mr and Mrs Johnston in the crowd?

'Sweet Jesus,' Mrs Johnston whispers to her husband, shaking her head.

Putting an arm around her he says, 'Hush,' and looks about him.

'Remove the contraption,' the commissioner orders one of the guards.

The guard tugs at the straps and Agnes lets her head be yanked this way and that. As the bridle releases over her head, the air feels cool, a delicious tingling in the ears and scalp. There is a large intake of breath when the crowd see Agnes's bald head. In some ways, she is gratified. It is they who have allowed this; it is they who will live with this.

'Agnes Sampson,' the commissioner reads. 'Widow, formerly midwife. You are charged with witchcraft, summoning up the Devil and plotting to cause the death and destruction of His Glorious Grace, King James VI. How do you say?'

She hears the words, her name. *Is he talking to me? About the king? The Devil? Witchcraft? How did this happen? Wait! Be calm, Goodwife,* she counsels herself. Through her clothes, the tiny pouch of hemlock is soft against her thigh. She can leave any time she wants. Her shoulders release and her neck loosens. *I'll make them wait.*

A voice she doesn't recognise as her own, dry and croaky, barely more than a whisper, answers, 'Not guilty.'

'What? Speak up. The court cannot hear you,' the commissioner barks.

'She needs something to drink!' a voice in the crowd calls out.

'What's that?' The commissioner scans the public benches. Reverend McLaren leans in to the commissioner and whispers, 'Commissioner, we may hear her better if she has some ale.'

'Very well.' He motions to one of the guards. 'See to it.'

The court is silent save for a cough or two, the shuffling of feet and shifting in seats. The guard returns with a metal beaker and places it firmly into Agnes's shaking hands. Her body doesn't seem her own any longer. The tepid liquid infuses her mouth and throat but doesn't quench the aridness. She gulps again then slows down, drinks steadily. The weak ale mixes with the gravel that seems to coat her gullet. With a wave, she passes the cup back to the guard. He steps back, leaving her exposed.

'May we proceed now?' The commissioner starts again, sheet in hand. 'How do you say to the charge of witchcraft ... summoning the —'

'Not guilty!' she interjects, her voice low but clear.

'Do not interrupt an officer of the king!' he retorts.

'I heard you the first time. I was dry, not deaf.'

A titter goes round the public gallery.

Commissioner Baxter glares at the communal benches. 'This is a serious business,' he growls. He turns back to Agnes. 'You are in serious trouble. Do not make it worse.'

'Worse!' she splutters before succumbing to a coughing fit. The room undulates; the commissioner looks like he's on the bow of a ship, bobbing up and down. She sways and only just keeps herself from falling over. 'How could it get any worse?'

'Oh, it can. Believe me, it can. Ask John Fian ... oh, that's right, you can't. No one can.'

A lump the size of a large plum stone lodges itself in her throat. *Do not think on this, lassie*, she directs herself. *Do not imagine the unimaginable.* She sighs and fleetingly brushes her palm down the side of her dress, over the stitching of the hidden pocket and soft rise of the purse. 'Not for me,' she whispers defiantly. 'Not for me.'

Three loud bangs ring out from the double doors behind the high table. Everyone looks. This is it. The two royal guards, as still as portraits, spring into action. They grasp the iron rings and pull open the doors.

A finely attired debonair gentleman with an air of authority and importance, struts into the hall and positions himself in front of the high table. 'All rise for His Royal Grace King James VI of Scotland!'

People glance at their neighbours, some with little wry smiles. They get to their feet. The atmosphere is charged.

But the earth is still moving for Agnes. She sways and reaches out for the back of a non-existent chair. She imagines the warm hardness of mahogany under her palm, steadying her. *That's better. The king here, for me. Has the world turned upside down?* Gelly's words float around her head like playful butterflies: *You'll be with us soon.*

King James strolls in flanked by two elegant young men. Some people are on their tiptoes in the public gallery, craning to see, necks stretched and chins uplifted. Not so for the witchfinder, who is a good head above those around him.

But he is not what Agnes expected, this king, oscillating before her eyes.

There is no sunlight around him, no hallowed glow to show he is the mouthpiece of God on Earth. She looks at him with the same curiosity she might have when encountering a new herb, trying to seek out what properties it might possess, what its essence might be. He is shorter, plainer, more ordinary than she expected under the bejewelled finery. His eyes are drooping – sad, even. What could *he* be sad about? His hair is a muted reddish brown, as if it has faded, and his moustache and chin beard are of a reddish, fair hue and finish in a point. His skin is the colour of pale magnolia; it reminds Agnes of the cream Mrs Merritt uses for puddings.

King James and his two companions walk unhurriedly towards the throne-like chair. One man unties the king's cloak from behind, removes it and drapes it over his elbow. The other offers an arm and the king places his hand lightly on it. King James steps up, turns and sits, and his two assistants position themselves on either side of him.

Everyone is agog, seemingly holding their breath. Later, people will say that even the birds stopped singing in reverence.

The king nods to the debonair gentleman in front of the dignitaries' table. The fellow steps forward and calls out, 'Court be seated! Court is in session,' then retreats to his place at the end of the bench closest to the king.

The commissioner saunters over to take the vacated place, parchment in hand. Peeling one sheet back, he opens his mouth, But at that moment Agnes's legs turn to aspic and she crumples to the floor. Her cheek strikes the cold but strangely comforting earth. She tastes the dirt in her mouth; it is tangy, with a hint of iron – or is that blood?

'This is not a pantomime!' Commissioner Baxter explodes, then quickly regains his composure. 'Your Grace, apologies.' Waving dismissively to the guards, he orders, 'Pick her up.'

They hook an elbow under each arm and pull her to standing. The earth feels cold and firm under her feet, and she smells stale sweat and tobacco from the men beside her. They keep her braced like the towers of a bridge, then slowly unhook their arms and place their hands on her shoulders and elbows to check the stability of the edifice. She remains still. They detach and step backwards.

King James turns his head towards one of his attendants, William Balfour. Balfour leans over, cocking his ear. 'The witch?' the king asks.

'Aye, sire.'

'What ails her?'

'Exhaustion, sire.'

His majesty nods. 'Ah.' Opening a magnanimous palm to the commissioner, he instructs, 'Proceed.'

The commissioner gestures to the guards to move further back, leaving Agnes tottering precariously in the centre of the hall.

'Agnes Sampson, you are charged with—'

Again, she drops like a stone.

The commissioner slaps the document by his side. 'If you refuse to stand, Goodwife Sampson, you will be made to stand in a cage!'

'She can't stand, for sanity's sake!' a disembodied voice hails from the crowd.

'For pity's sake!' another calls.

'Silence! A stool,' the commissioner instructs one of the guards.

They place it behind her knees and, with a hand on her shoulders, push her roughly down. She feels a jolt through her seat bones as she hits the cold, rock-hard surface. Shifting, she tries to find the fleshy part of her bottom.

The commissioner snaps his fingers at his assistant, Grant, who rushes over and places a sheet in his hand. 'We have signed statements from witnesses that you, Agnes Sampson, were seen on numerous occasions conspiring with Gellis Duncan and John Fian, and Maggie the smith's wife to use the dark arts against His Grace.'

The king arches an eyebrow and leans forward.

'The executed witches, sire,' Balfour explains.

Agnes stares at the commissioner. 'Maggie, too?'

Ignoring her, he signals to one of the court officials. 'Call the first witness.'

The official stands and cries out, 'Call the Reverend Ignatius McLaren.'

A snigger circulates around the public benches like an infection.

'Silence!' the commissioner thunders, scanning the faces of the throng. 'Or you will be ejected from this court!' He bows to the king. 'With Your Grace's permission, of course.'

King James beckons his counsellor, Balfour, with a crook of his finger. 'Tell them to get on with it,' he says, irritation crisp in his voice.

'The king permits you to continue ... and—' he glances back at the monarch for the blink of the royal eyelid '—and to remove forthwith to the town gaol any townsperson who disrupts this most serious session.'

The reverend walks to the middle of the hall and stands mere yards from Agnes. She eyes him with curiosity. It is like watching a play unfold, and she wonders what's going to happen next.

He seems unremarkable, this clergyman, dressed sombrely in his heavy long black robe, with a modest ruff at the neck and white lace protruding from the cuffs. The small black skull cap sits snugly at the back of his head, circled by streaks of grey hair peeping out at the ears and forehead. He is resting his hands, one cupped upon the other in front of him. What is he thinking? What could have driven him to this?

The court official steps forward to face the reverend. 'Do you, Ignatius McLaren...?'

The commissioner glares at the public gallery.

'Do you swear by God, His Grace the king and your country that you will tell the truth?'

'I will… I do.'

The commissioner takes over the questioning. 'On Sunday, April seventeenth of this year, you were giving a sermon to your congregation.' He sweeps his hand in a semicircle around the public benches. 'Many of the good people of the town sitting here were present.'

Several people look at each other, furrowing their brows.

'Can you tell His Grace and the court what your sermon was about?'

'It was about natural order, divine order. God the highest, then His Divine Grace—' the reverend bows to the king, clutching his own wrist '—the head of the country, the head of every man, and then every man being the head of every woman, a husband the head of a wife, a father leading the mother and children. I talked about the most honourable place for a woman … all women, the state of grace of motherhood. I quoted Timothy verse 2:12, which proclaims—'

King James quotes, '"I do not permit women to teach or have authority over a man; she must be silent."'

This elicits nods of approval among the notables at the high table. It is well known the king is an authority on the Bible and takes a keen interest in all things ecclesiastical, much to the chagrin of the new Church.

'Your Grace,' Reverend McLaren acknowledges. 'And Verse 14—'

'Yes, yes – Eve was the sinner, not Adam. She was a weak vessel, easily led,' the king adds impatiently. 'That's why most witches are women. This is a well-known fact. Where is this leading?'

'Sire,' the commissioner explains, 'his sermon was disrupted by the woman you see before you! When he got to the authority of God and God's representatives, she couldn't stand it!'

Agnes screws up her eyes to see if it might help her to remember the church services she'd been to in the last year. Nothing specific comes into view, just a mishmash of Gelly laughing and looking sneakily at John Fian, then Maggie saying, 'Well, that's a couple of hours I'll not get back.'

The townspeople on the public benches continue to look from side to side at each other. Many shake their heads; some shrug their shoulders.

'What?' Agnes asks searchingly, squinting from the commissioner to the minister.

But the king, now enthralled, sits up and leans forward. 'Proceed.'

'I heard a noise at the back of the church. She was screeching with laughter, egging others on around her. Talking about what comes out the Devil's ... arse,' Reverend McLaren rushes on.

'She said what?' the king exclaims.

William Balfour leans in, brings his lips to King James's ear and is about to explain when Agnes hauls herself up. Laughing incredulously, she shakes her head at the minister. 'So that's what this is all about? Women laughing at your sermon? You did all this because you were mocked?'

'Mockery! By her own mouth.' The commissioner slams down his fist.

But the king waves his hand as if batting away a particularly annoying fly. 'Mockery is wanton, I'll grant you, but it is no crime. Where is the evidence?'

'Sire, it shows her character, her intent,' the commissioner presses. 'Disrespectful of authority, of God's natural representatives on Earth, of righteous society.' He casts his eyes to the base of the throne, where they linger for a moment. 'Only hours later, that very night, she met with her coven at St Andrew's Auld Kirk on the harbour to conjure up storms and mayhem, all the forces of hell against His Grace. I have the signed confessions of Gellis Duncan and John Fian.'

The king holds out his hand. William Balfour snatches the sheets from the commissioner and gives them to the king. After scanning through the documents, the king leans back. 'I see. Continue.'

Agnes squeezes her eyes shut then opens them several times to see if she might wake up. It is like someone has written her into a story where she has no knowledge or control over the unfolding of the plot.

'With Your Grace's permission,' Commissioner Baxter resumes, 'I will call the next witness. Thank you, Reverend McLaren. Your testimony has been most enlightening.'

The minister lets his arms drop to his sides and stares at the floor, giving the impression that a great weight has been lifted from his shoulders. Returning to his seat with his eyes cast downward, he looks every inch a pious, God-fearing man of the cloth,

'Bring in Mr Powell.'

Mr Powell takes the minister's place and all attention turns to the nervous-looking young man in the centre of the hall. Agnes knows him, of course, but she hasn't had much contact with him or his family. The Powells, with their two healthy boisterous boys, never really had use for her services and Mrs Powell was born of a long lineage of ruddy, robust herring wives. He looks very well presented; better than she's ever seen him. She wonders if the hat is new. It is a pleasing shade of turquoise, soft and round, with a peak in front. His calico shirt is spotless, as are his leather waistcoat and breeches.

'Tell the court your occupation and where you live,' the commissioner coaxes.

He takes off his hat and clutches it in front of him. 'Yes, sir. I am a carpenter and I live in one of the harbour cottages, across from St Andrew's Auld Kirk.'

'You have a good view of the kirk, is that correct?'

'Yes, I do, sir.' He coughs, says, 'Excuse me, sir,' and shifts from one foot to the other.

'Please tell the court what you saw on the night of the seventeenth of April this year.'

'Well, sir, I heard a noise,' he rushes, twisting the cap in his hands. 'It was late. I don't know what time. There was a full moon. I heard whispering … people talking, quiet-like. I looked out the window and saw folk all covered up, creeping along the wall in front of St Andrew's. Then the kirk door opened. It was lit up inside…' He pauses, running out of breath. 'John Fian was standing at the door, waving them all in.'

Gasps emanate from the public gallery as Powell's eyes dart over them and back to his hat.

'Go on. Who did you see going in?' Commissioner Baxter asks encouragingly.

'Well ... there was Gelly Duncan, Maggie, the smith, Agnes Sampson ... Jannet Blandilands...'

Agnes stares at him, transfixed.

'And is this Agnes Sampson anywhere in the court today?'

'Aye, sir, that's her there.' He points at Agnes and she catches his eye.

'How much did they pay you?' she asks softly. He gulps and looks away.

'Silence! One more word,' the commissioner warns Agnes. 'Ready with the bridle!' he adds, addressing one of the guards behind her.

The gaoler picks up the harness, lets the straps dangle from his hand but does not move. 'The next time another word is uttered,' the commissioner cautions.

But Agnes whispers softly so that only Mr Powell can hear, 'However much it was, it won't be enough.'

'What happened next?' presses the commissioner, glancing at the throne.

The king leans forward, his chin turned to the carpenter and his eyes narrowed to slits.

'Well, sir. They all went inside and there was a lot of singing and dancing.'

'How do you know, Mr Powell?'

'Well, sir—' he coughs again '—when they all went inside, I went across and looked through the keyhole.'

'That was brave of you! Weren't you afraid?'

'Aye, sir, I was. I saw John Fian in the middle, and the others all round in a circle, holding hands. They were chanting some horrible incan— incant— um ... incant—'

'Incantation, Mr Powell. Is that what you were trying to say? It must have been very disturbing for you, very frightening. Take your time.'

'Aye, that's it, an incan ... ta ... tion. Then this smoke came up in the centre—'

'Of the circle?'

'Aye, in the circle, and there was flames, too. Then the Devil appeared … and they were all laughing and clapping. Aye, rejoicing, they were! That's right, they were rejoicing!'

Some onlookers in the hall clasp their hands to their heart; others shake their heads and mutter to their neighbours. This time the commissioner allows the hubbub to exhaust itself. As the room once again falls silent, he takes up the questioning.

'What did he look like, the Devil?' Nearly everyone sits forward in their seats with unblinking eyes.

'He had legs like a goat, sir, long, with hooves at the bottom. Spindly arms with claws, glowing red eyes, and horns on the top of his head. Horrible! It was horrible! I was scared out ma wits. Then they got a cat … and … and…'

A racket once more erupts in the hall.

The commissioner holds up his hand. 'Quiet! Quiet! Yes, Mr Powell, they got a cat. Please go on. But you seem a little distressed. Perhaps you should sit down.'

'Aye, sir. I'd like to sit.' Mr Powell's hat is wrung out in his hands. A guard positions a three-legged stool behind him and he flops down.

'But please speak up, Mr Powell, so the good people can hear you.'

'Well, they got this dead cat—'

'Speak up, please.'

'They got this cat…' he shouts. 'They went to the graveyard first … and dug up bodies … and then … they chopped the bodies up… And they – and John Fian – tied the arms and legs to the cat and … and they tossed the whole thing into the sea, and the sea began churning and the sky went black, like being in a cellar. And … the wind was screaming, it was like old crones screeching, like no storm I've ever seen, sir.'

The king shifts in his seat, crossing his legs and smoothing his throat with his fingers.

Casting sidelong glances, many onlookers murmur their horror to each other. 'To think that was happening just around the corner from us and we never saw a thing. Makes your blood run cold,' Mrs Wilson breathes to her neighbour, Mrs Ramsey.

'I've heard witches can put a spell over you so you sleep through anything. That's probably why we never saw any of it,' Mrs Ramsey replies.

'What? They put a spell o'er the whole toon?' Mr McTaggart chips in from the back. 'I cannae see that.'

'Well, I've heard some witches can whip up storms, giant waves, thunder and lightning, and send the poor souls out at sea to the bottom of the ocean,' Mrs Ramsey states triumphantly.

Agnes's stomach turns to lead. Are they really going to believe this? She hears Granny McLeod's voice: *People believe what they want to believe and it can be to your advantage or disadvantage.* This time, Granny, she thinks, the untruths and fantasies people tell each other to help them sleep at night have allowed them to stand back while unspeakable torture is inflicted on their neighbours, acquaintances and even people who have served them all their lives.

She stumbles to her feet. 'For pity's sake! If he was so scared out of his wits, why did he spend so long looking through the keyhole?' Scanning the first three rows of the public benches, she says, 'Wouldn't you have run? Wouldn't you have run for the sheriff or the minister as fast as you could? Besides—'she sighs, taking her head back '—John Fian couldn't have been there.'

The commissioner's fingers tighten around the sheets he's holding. 'Silence! Guard, put on the bridle!'

'Wait!' The king holds up his hand and addresses Agnes. 'Why do you say that?'

The effort has sapped the last of Agnes's strength and her bones feel like jelly. She drops onto the stool, the hard surface jarring her tailbone. 'Because he was somewhere else, that's why, and there are people in this hall who will swear to it.'

The townsfolk look at their neighbours and the people around them.

Agnes's back is rounded and she lists wearily to the side. 'John Fian was at the Browns' – Mr and Mrs Browns' – for supper. They wanted to talk about wee Ian. The schoolmaster had to stay over because the storm came in quick that night. Quicker than any of us thought. He couldn't have been at the Auld Kirk.'

All heads turn to a couple seated in the third row. Mrs Brown's face is frozen in horror, while her husband's normally tanned weather-beaten face has turned a light shade of taupe.

'I see.' The commissioner's fingers relax on the sheet. 'So, Mr and Mrs Brown had John Fian, the coven leader, over to their house where they conversed. Presumably discussed various things over dinner and into the night. Is that right?' He looks down at Agnes. 'To your knowledge, was this a regular occurrence? Were Mr and Mrs Brown friendly – good friends – with the witch leader, with the tried and convicted witch leader?'

Agnes sits bolt upright, eyes wide open, and stares into the faces of the couple.

'I think, then—' the commissioner swats a tiny buzzing insect from his paper '—we might perhaps ask Mr and Mrs Brown some questions, too.'

# Chapter Fifty-Six

Flight
Vézelay

It is pitch dark except for the fat moon fleetingly appearing between the thick clouds. If only it would show itself for more than a few seconds. Thérèse sees the path in front of her veering to the right towards the undergrowth. She catches a glimpse of the hawthorn: good, she's managed to stay on track. The river gurgles. It smells fresh, cool and mossy. Her skirts brush the feather-like ferns that overshoot the path.

She was careful as she left the village. There were no lights on, as far as she could tell. She hopes no one saw her. But even if they did, they'd assume she was off to deliver a baby somewhere on the outskirts of the village. She's noticed most babies pop into the world in the early hours of the morning. Old Midwife Valentin used to say it was the best window for souls to find their receptacle for their next life on this planet.

A twig snaps. She freezes, fingers clenched around her skirt as she holds it in mid-air, not daring to breathe out in case whatever or whoever broke the branch pounces. She can't tell how long she's been standing statue-like, but it's enough time to convince her it was either an animal uninterested in her, a simple flexing of nature growing and cracking, or a human who is not ready to spring. Either way, she must press on.

*Come on, Thérèse, you've been through worse than this*, she tells herself as she pushes through the undergrowth.

Somewhere ahead, the path will veer upwards. She's traversed it so many times in the daytime, she could do it with her eyes closed. *Well, now's your chance, village healer!*

The recalcitrant moon makes another appearance, lighting up the path for a fraction of a second. The track looks as if it stops dead, swallowed up by the dense foliage, but Thérèse bends her head, steps down two invisible stairs and clambers underneath the canopy and up the steep rise on the other side.

She has only climbed a few feet when something tugs at her dress, pulling her back towards the river. Her heart pounds. 'God help me!'

The wild pumping of her heart catches in her throat and every sinew of her body tenses. She is ready to fight for survival like a wild animal. Pulling hard, she yanks her skirt upwards; the material rips and she falls sideways into a tangle of vines and fallen branches. Her dress has caught in a thicket of brambles and wild raspberries and now a long strip of muted turquoise dangles in the mess of thorns.

'Damn!'

She has to retrieve it. She shakes herself free from the lesser twigs clinging tenaciously to the hem and brushes her sleeves and her skirt, trying futilely to make them smoother so as not to catch on anything. She stretches an arm over the top of the bush towards the scrap of cloth but her fingers can't quite reach. She inches further into the thicket and feels tiny sharp needles scraping her hands and face.

'Ouch!' A thorn pierces her upper arm through the material. She shakes herself free again; she'll have to leave it. No one will pass this way. Few people, even in the village, know about this trail.

Not far now. Used to the darkness, her eyes make out the rosehip bush near the top. From there she'll have a clear view of the gorge, the waterfall and the cliffs beyond. To strangers the cliffs look like an impenetrable rock face with tenacious trees clinging to the sides and standing sentinel at the top, but a closer look at its craggy lines reveals a thin black vertical fissure: the entrance to Ossian's Cave.

She wonders if he's here yet. He'd better be!

As she edges nearer, the narrow cleft opens into the mouth of a cave that is surprisingly cavernous. She squints into the inky blackness, straining to pick up the slightest sound or tiniest movement. 'Alain… Assen, Assen,' she whispers. The soft echo returns her words. 'Alain… Assen…'

He appears out of the darkness and little butterflies take flight in the pit of her abdomen, swooping and diving in a warm, fuzzy murmur, but concern is etched on his sharp features. She pushes him back inside, looks around and presses her forefinger to his lips. He lets himself be pushed back and waits for permission to speak. She removes her hand.

'What's going on, Thérèse? André was so insistent. Poor child – I thought he was going to cry.'

'Never mind that. You have to leave – now! Go to Beaune as you planned, go to the House of God. And may God forgive you.'

'Forgive me? For what? I want to marry you, you know that!'

Momentarily caught of guard. 'What?', she says. 'You—you want to… ?' *For goodness' sake Thérèse focus.* 'No, no, it's not that. Two men came today asking questions about you.'

'What sort of questions? Is it my father? It's my father, isn't it? Is he ill? The siege – he didn't make it out!' He takes two strides to the mouth of the cave but she grabs his arm.

'It's not that,' she says quickly. 'Your father's fine – well, I think he is. You had that letter from your friend, remember?'

'Gérard?'

'Yes, yes. You told me your father had gone to the chateau before it began. You had a letter from him there, remember? He got out before the bombardment. The siege is over, you know that. There is peace in Paris now. They made peace and all of that is over. It's not about that, it's about you. The men from Paris, they have a warrant for your arrest.'

'What? For me? What for?'

'Murder.'

'What? Is this a joke?'

'You think I would joke about such a thing?'

'Of course not. It must be some mistake! They've got the wrong person.' This time, he pushes past her. 'I can clear this up right now!'

But she clasps his forearm again, her grip vice-like and urgent. He stops and looks at her pale hand. 'They said a Dr Broussard raised the charges.'

He creases his brow. 'Dr Broussard! Huh … he really does hate me. Right, I'll go with them. Two men, you said? I have witnesses too – Gérard, Pierre, Lucas.' He takes Thérèse by the shoulders and makes her look into his eyes. 'I did not murder anyone. I tried to help. I was foolish, brash even, but the plague … it was so random and we had too many patients. I wouldn't kill anyone – I couldn't! You know that, don't you? You surely know that about me?'

She raises her hand and lightly brushes his brow with her fingertips. Of course she knows that; she wouldn't be here if she didn't. She wouldn't have taken him to her bed. 'Yes, of course I do,' she answers, sweeping aside an irreverent curl from his forehead. 'But you must go to Beaune. Now.'

'No. I will clear my name.'

'No! Your dream told you to go to Beaune.'

'What about you? Us?'

'They say in a far-off land there is a flower that blooms only once a century, but when it does those who see it are changed forever. Few people are that fortunate. We have been fortunate.'

'Once in a century? Fortunate? No. This is not how it will be. I will come back for you.'

Assen moves his hands from her shoulders. Placing one firmly on the small of her back, he pulls her close to his chest. His heartbeat is steady and fast. She looks up to meet his gaze, tilting her head and parting her lips. Breathing out, he brings his lips onto hers. They are soft and warm, with a hint of peppermint tea. She'll never forget his smell, his taste.

'You smell of lavender,' he says.

She laughs.

Breaking free, he sighs wearily and trudges deeper into the cave. Presently, he appears with Esther, his horse, and leads her out. 'How will you get back to town?'

'I'll be fine. Go!'

Assen grabs the pommel and mounts, then pulls the left rein around for one more look. 'I will stay if you want me to. I will meet this challenge – I will account for myself. I do not choose to leave you.'

'Go. I *want* you to go … please.'

With a kick and a tongue click, he speeds off.

Thérèse sighs. Her tiny intestinal butterflies have turned into sludge, tugging her downwards. 'Come on, Thérèse, old girl,' she chivvies under her breath. 'It was the right thing to do. You'll get over it. Get on with your work. No distractions.'

\*\*\*

High on the hill above the cave, a man is standing by a tree, looking down. As Assen rides away, the man turns from his viewing point, unhitches his horse and mounts, then heads south in the direction of Beaune.

# Chapter Fifty-Seven

### The Verdict
### Tavistock Hall, East Lothian

'No! Wait! Wait!' Agnes cries. She cannot pull the others into this cesspit with her. The truth must wait, and anyway John is gone now, God rest him. 'I'm sorry… I was mistaken. John Fian was not at Mr and Mrs Brown's that night or any other night.'

She turns her gaze to the couple, her eyes soft. Even now, her desire is to heal. She mouths 'sorry'. 'I was wrong. Forgive me,' she adds, turning back to the commissioner.

Mrs Brown crumples and slides down her husband's side, her fingers almost scraping the earth floor. He catches her and pulls her up, his muscular arm encircling her like a brace. They stare at Agnes.

'Right. If we might continue.' The commissioner separates the top sheet of paper from the stack in his hand and places it underneath. His eyes flit over the top line of the next page. 'If we can address the next point—'

King James holds up his hand and looks down at Agnes. 'Are you sure you were mistaken?'

'Aye, I'm sure.'

'Aye, I'm sure *what*?' demands the commissioner.

Drawing her eyes from the commissioner to the king, she rasps, 'Your Grace,' her head hanging like a rag doll.

'Mr Powell,' the commissioner says, pacing in front of the witness, 'aside from that night, did you ever see the accused enter the Auld Kirk?'

'Aye, sir, I did, sir.' He gives his hat another twist.

'Go on.'

'Last November, sir, late, sir, in the middle of the night. Loads of them. She was there, plus John Fian, Gelly…'

'Yes, yes,' the commissioner encourages.

'They were all singing and dancing, and the kirk was all lit up in a horrible red light. Then there was this storm – the worst I've ever seen! Lightning! Sheep were falling from the sky into the harbour. I never seen anything like it.'

Agnes is bent forward, her head hanging heavy like a ripe pumpkin waiting to be smashed.

'Exactly when in November was this occurrence?'

'It was the middle of November, sir.'

'Middle of November? Around the time His Grace was returning from Denmark with his new bride, Her Grace Queen Anne?'

'Yes, sir. There *was* talk of the king coming home with his new bride, sir. Her Grace Queen Anne, sir, yes, Queen Anne. There was to be feasts and celebrations.'

'Feasts and celebrations? Here in North Berwick?'

'Yes, sir. We were looking forward to it.'

'Were you, indeed? And so you should. But it didn't happen, did it?'

'No, sir.'

'No, sir, it didn't.' The commissioner strides past Mr Powell and walks in front of the public pews. 'It didn't happen because something else happened instead. Well, thank you, Mr Powell. You may return to your business.'

Mr Powell lets a long breath escape through his pursed lips and walks towards the double doors, one held open by a stony-faced royal guard. He passes through into the sunlight.

The commissioner rocks back and forth on his heels. 'Our little corner of Scotland has seen the biggest witch trial of the century! Perhaps in entire history! This small but mighty nation and her glorious king will go down in history as the "Hammer of Witches", His Grace, the most fervent adversary of Satan there has ever been!'

'Wait!' the king commands, laying both hands on the arms of the throne. 'It is enshrined in law – my law, Scotland's Law, and it is God's will – that the accused may answer all charges brought against him. So...' His eyes drop to Agnes. 'What do you say?'

She looks up. She's heard tales about King James's Solomon-like wisdom and fairness. Could it be true? No: the carnage that has already been dealt out in his name says otherwise. What can she say? The die is cast. It would do her little good now to speak in her defence.

'Right. Let's move on.' The commissioner tosses his sheets of parchment on the table beside the reverend and picks up another. 'On the charge of using the black arts to—'

A voice rings in Agnes's ear. *Speak thy truth, Agnes Sampson. Be true to yourself; it will free you.* 'Wait!' she yells, struggling to her feet. 'Though I know it will not save my life – this body, this vessel, is doomed – it would do my soul good to speak. I would speak.'

The commissioner flattens his lips in a thin line and glances at the king. King James sits back and opens his palms to the ceiling.

'Very well. Proceed.' The commissioner clenches his teeth.

Agnes turns her back on the top table and settles her gaze on the public arena, scanning every face, row after row. 'I will tell the truth and it is up to you to decide whether you know the truth when you hear it – whether you're ready to hear the truth. The crimes of which I am accused, of which John, Maggie and Gelly were accused, were contrived, fantastical, scary stories like those you tell children when you want them to behave. No one, not one of you, has ever seen St Andrew's Kirk lit up at night or heard screaming, chanting and singing, have you? *Have* you!'

Some shake their heads in agreement while others fix their eyes determinedly on the floor. 'When have I ever killed someone with my herbal remedies? Hmm? All Gelly ever did was cure people, help them. Some of you wouldn't be here if Gelly hadn't given you her teas – the recipes she learned from her grandmother and her grandmother's mother. What is our crime? We're too good at what we do? Because we do better than the physicians, apothecaries, learned men? But we're *only* women, so the Devil must have helped us; the Devil must be controlling us.' She searches the faces in the crowd. 'Do you really believe that? In all honesty?'

Her arms hang limply by her side and a weight as heavy as a boulder lodges below her collarbones, pushing into her throat. 'And yet ... maybe the Devil has been at work...' Her voice is barely above a whisper. People move to the edge of their seats. 'Would the Devil not want the good destroyed, the kind decimated, the gentle trodden on? Those restoring peace put to the sword, those mending broken hearts, bodies and souls destroyed?' She turns to the top table. 'I don't know. Maybe it's not the Devil, just ... just the evil that men do.' Her eyes flit from the commissioner to the reverend, then to the king.

With the commissioner firmly back in her sight, she continues, 'Power, getting close to power, can be an irresistible temptation. But how to do it? Huh? Make up a threat – a deadly threat – that the king, the realm, is in imminent danger and no one is safe. Scare people enough and they'll believe anything. They'll *do* anything. Every action is justified. Any non-compliant, non-believer is a fair target. A high price for high stakes – wealth, status, power – to be part of the inner group, to be special, to be close to the ruler ... a heady mix, intoxicating. Far more dangerous than anything Gelly or I could come up with.'

The commissioner bangs his fist on the table. 'Damn you!'

The king's fingers curl around the ends of his armrests.

'Sire, my deepest apologies.' The commissioner sweeps off his hat and bows, his head nearly grazing the floor.

'It is not I you should be apologising to, but you are fortunate. Matthew 12:31–32 says every blasphemy will be forgiven against men, but blasphemy against the Spirit will not be forgiven. I counsel you to moderate your language.' The king sits back, resting his hands in his lap.

'I'm sorry, Your Grace. This witch and her words are enough to drive a man mad. With your permission, sire, we'll fit the bridle and get to the end of this trial.'

'I have the right to speak!' Agnes's voice is loud and clear, her fists tight balls by her sides. 'It is my birthright even as a woman. I have the right to be heard! I have that right!' Her toes dig into the dirt, and a cold, damp energy rises through her legs and torso connecting her to the earth.

The king rests his forefinger on his lip then releases his hand and opens his palm towards her. 'The floor is yours.'

'I am sorry for your bad dreams, Your Grace, but I did not cause them. Neither did Gelly, or John, or Maggie. Whatever thoughts, visions, creatures, people and wanton, salacious acts you see are in your mind. It is not the Devil who targets you. You are at war with yourself. You are not the first king to be different, and quite probably it is only because you are the king that you are not standing where I am now.'

There is a general intake of breath as the great and the good at the top table look straight ahead, steely-eyed.

'Yet the very ones you condemn are not the people who would condemn you for your thoughts … your desires.' Her fingers relax. 'Nature has variety and grace. It is a wonderful thing. Love is not wrong however it shows itself.'

The king's jaw twitches and a little nerve jumps under his eye.

Agnes turns back to face the public gallery. 'What has driven all you good people to go along with this? Fear?' She points at the long table. 'Is it because they are educated, well read, clever? The minister, a royal commissioner, the Justice General, the king – if they say it's right, it must be. You don't have to think. They'll tell you what to do and it'll keep you safe. But what if they are wrong?'

'Have you finished?' Glancing at the king, the commissioner gets to his feet. The corner of the monarch's mouth is turned down and his eyes are fixed on a distant point.

'One thing more.' Agnes claps her hands. 'I freely forgive all of you for what you are about to do … and may God forgive you too.'

She closes her eyes and lets her chin fall to her chest. It is done. A vision of Gelly – beautiful, young, vibrant and healthy – hovers in her mind. The beings with her friend also come into view. What were they? Angels?

Agnes looks up, thumps her fist on her breast and says in a low voice, 'And I pray I go where Gelly is.'

'Do you not think it is you who should be asking God to forgive you?' the king interrupts.

The bigwigs at the top table nod furiously. 'Hear, hear.'

Agnes holds the king's gaze. 'I ask him every day.'

She drops to the stool and closes her eyes for a moment. When she opens them, the commissioner, members of the royal court and Reverend McLaren are huddled together whispering. Discussing her fate, she supposes. She strains to hear but only picks up a burble, as if she is underwater.

The group breaks, and some of the men lean back, nodding. The commissioner goes round the circle. 'Aye,' the first man accords. 'Aye,' agrees the second, until every man has concorded. A younger gentleman on the end of the table scribbles a note, gets up and takes it to William Balfour who is standing by King James.

Balfour's eyes dart back and forth across the sheet, expressionless. Agnes wonders if his countenance would be the same if he were deciding on the price to pay for a flock of sheep? He bends over and whispers into the king's ear. King James leans back and gives a single nod.

On straightening, Balfour looks at the commissioner. 'You may proceed.'

Baxter lifts the thick mahogany stick from the table and holds it horizontally at shoulder height. Facing the king and the public gallery, he turns it vertically and brings it down three times. The muted thuds match the dull light in the hall; the sun is now only just above the horizon.

All is quiet except for a gust of wind and a lark singing. Agnes looks up; it seems she alone can hear it. She hopes it is high above the hall, beyond the clouds, in the sapphire sky where Gelly is.

'Be upstanding, Agnes Sampson.' The commissioner brings her back to the cold earth. 'It is the decision of the royal court gathered here today that you are guilty of witchcraft, consorting with the Devil, and with evil, malicious intent, conjuring storms with your master, Satan, to murder His Grace, our saviour on Earth, and his most precious issue.' Murmurs of 'Amen' circulate around the worthies' table.

Getting to her feet, Agnes feels numb, detached, as if she is watching the proceedings from a distance like an uninteresting play. Bone-tiredness oozes from her scalp and drips down her jaw, shoulders, arms, chest and abdomen, pulling her legs and feet further into the earth. How comforting it would be to be swallowed by Mother Nature, back into her womb.

A voice whispers, 'It will soon be over.' She looks around. Did anyone else hear it?

She tries to focus on the commissioner, who is still speaking. 'The Bible, Exodus 22:18, says, "Thou shalt not suffer a witch to live." We now act in accordance with God's word. In view of such malign crimes, where you and your kind have put the whole country in mortal danger, the court has no option but to sentence you to death by strangulation and fire. Seven days hence you will be taken to Gallows Point where you will be strangled and your body consumed by flames.'

Gasps and sharp intakes of breath resonate around the public benches. 'God bless you, Agnes Sampson,' a woman's voice calls out.

A wave of lightness and relief washes through Agnes's body, the unaccountable release that comes from certainty, from knowing what will happen next or, crucially, knowing *you* can decide what happens next. She glides her palms over what is left of her skirt, feeling the miniscule bulge deep in her pocket. *I will choose when and how I die.*

A sharp pain bursts between her shoulder blades as the guard pushes his baton into her back. 'On yer feet.'

She takes a few faltering steps, like a newborn fawn, then stops and pulls her head up. *Come on, Agnes lass. This is your last act. Get your head up and walk out of this building as the respected midwife and healer you've fought so hard to be.*

# Chapter Fifty-Eight

Journey's End?
Beaune, France

The sun is high overhead; Assen has been riding all night. His lower back aches, and every plodding shift in Esther's gait sends a spasm through his pelvis. Her head rocks from side to side. Poor old girl; she is as weary as he is.

In the last half hour, the countryside has transformed into a row of higgledy-piggledy cottages, kiosks and taverns snaking its way to the centre of town. Assen's chin drops to his chest and his head lolls from side to side in the same rhythmic motion as Esther's. A crow perched on a hitching post eyes them and, when they are level, it screeches. Instinctively, Assen grabs the hilt of his sword, his heart racing.

Pulling Esther up, breathing in short bursts, he looks at the dwellings on either side. A woman is shaking out a rug at a front door and beating it with a huge stick. Next door an elderly man sits outside, smoking a pipe. They don't seem to have noticed his discomposure, or they are ignoring him. Perhaps the inhabitants of Beaune are used to dusty, dishevelled strangers making their way to the alms-house.

He hopes he will find it soon and, more importantly, they will let him in. He wonders what they'll make of him. Looking at his dust-laden leather breeches, he can only imagine what his over-jacket must look like. No matter; if it's anything like St Marcel's, the brothers will be far more concerned about spiritual matters and cleaning out chamber pots.

His head feels as heavy as a cannonball and it takes effort to keep it upright. Rubbing the back of his neck, he sees it. It is unmistakable, exactly as he has been told, exactly as he imagined: the Hôtel-Dieu. With a glance at the sky, he whispers, 'Thank you, God.'

He stops to take it in, with its distinctive roofs of brightly coloured geometric patterns and the tallest of its spires reaching high above the town.

'Come on, old girl, nearly there,' he coaxes Esther and she looks round at him with disdain. He laughs. It is the first time he has felt heartened since leaving Thérèse.

'All right, I know, less of the old. Let's move forward then, trusty steed.'

Esther nods several times, shakes out her mane and tramps onwards. When they reach the outer wall of the Hôtel-Dieu, Assen slides off and his legs almost buckle. 'Jehovah! A night in the saddle and I've forgotten how to walk,' he mumbles. He hears his father's voice: 'Do not blaspheme!'

Feeling contrite, he brushes down his clothing and smooths his jaw, which has more growth than he expects. There is an iron ring on the wall opposite. Taking the reins, he sweeps Esther's forelock from her eyes. 'There, girl, hang on. I'll find out about food and shelter for us both.'

Crossing the road, he notices a small boy with a bucket by the church. The lad is collecting water from the spout on the church wall, the bronze tap encased in an exquisitely carved lion's head. Some of the water splashes over the pail and there are beads of sweat on the boy's forehead. He puts it down with a thump and more water splashes on the ground. He mops his brow with the back of his hand.

Assen hurries over. 'Excuse me. Good day.'

The boy blinks and looks around him.

'May I ask, what is your name?'

'Jules, sir.'

'My name is Ass— Alain. my name is Alain. I would be grateful for your assistance. Actually, may I offer you my assistance first?'

The boy looks down at the bucket.

'Where are you taking it?'

'Over there.' Jules points to a cottage at the end of the street. 'My aunt needs it. My cousins are coming from Lyon.'

'Is that so? Here, let me carry it for you.' Assen feels pressure in his lower back as he lifts the pail; it is heavy, even for a man. Or maybe he's just been in the saddle too long.

They walk side by side. 'Perhaps you could assist me, too?'

'Yes, sir!'

'See that white horse tied to the wall by the doorway to the smith's workshop?'

'Yes.'

'She is my horse, Esther. She is very gentle but she is tired and hungry like me. We have been travelling all night. If I give you the money, can you find her a place to rest, and some food and water?'

'Yes, sir! My uncle has stables just around that corner – see, over there.' The boy points to the far corner of the church where there is a narrow gap between the buildings and more workshops beyond.

'Thank you, Jules. I am in your debt.' They arrive outside the cottage and Assen carefully places the bucket down. 'Here is some money for Esther's lodgings, and here are three pennies for your trouble.'

'Thank you, sir!' A smile engulfs Jules' face. 'Aunt Louise, Aunt Louise! I have to look after this gentleman's horse and take it to Uncle Maxime!'

'Oh, yes, and what gentleman is this?' A woman appears in the doorway, wiping her hands on her apron.

'Look! He gave me this!' The boy opens his palm.

His aunt looks down and nods in satisfaction. 'Well, you'd better take the gentleman's horse to the stalls, then.'

'Yes, Aunt Louise!' Jules runs off.

She eyes Assen with curiosity. 'You've come to the Hôtel-Dieu, sir?'

'Yes.'

He is aware of how he must look – dusty from the road, in the saddle for days, mud caking his boots. But she must see many like him pass by on their way to the alms-house. He sees her looking at his ear and instinctively covers it with his hand, the gold loop earing cold against his palm. He draws a curl forward.

'You'd better get on, then,' she says.

'Y-e-s. Thank you.'

He feels her eyes bore into his back as he crosses the street to the great oak door of the church. Blowing out, he presses his thumb into his palm. Glancing over his shoulder, he sees her turn away, pick up a broom and retreat into the cottage. Releasing his arms and straightening, he raises his hand to the large iron knocker, lifts it and lets it crash down three times.

Bringing his ear closer to the door, he homes in on the light footfalls echoing within the church, and strains to distinguish the inner sounds from the clattering outside. The footsteps stop, then start, then stop, and it seems an age before the soft tread reaches the door.

Assen stamps his feet. 'Come on.' Catching himself, he mumbles reprovingly, 'Be patient, humble. You are here to learn. You are here to fulfil your destiny, whatever that might be.'

He inhales deeply, guiding the breath to the knot in his gut, where it begins to unravel. His jaw softens and he clicks it from side to side, his chin in the heel of his hand. The footsteps inside have reached the door. Assen hears the person fumbling with what sounds like chains and the giant handle begins to turn. Slowly the door creaks open.

The head of an elderly monk appears, squinting up at Assen and around him from side to side, as if looking for someone else. He opens the door wider. 'You are ill, sir? You have brought someone…?'

'I am not ill. I have come to offer my help … if you'll have me? Yes, I would like to help … and to learn.' Assen realises he has no idea why he is here except for the dream, and he is not ready to share that yet.

'Your help?' The brother raises his eyebrows.

'Ye-e-s, I am … Doc … umm… Brother, yes, Brother. Brother Assen.'

The monk smiles. 'An unusual name.'

'My mother was a Mo—' How much should he say about himself? 'My mother named me Assen, and when she died—' his neck burns at the lie he is about to tell '—when she died, I asked to keep it.'

'I see. Your abbot allowed this?' The monk's eyes are soft yet piercing.

'I–I–I, well…' His throat is suddenly as parched as straw under the August sun. 'I was a corporeal brother in Paris. I've tended the sick. I've also learned something from local healers, the healers in the villages I passed through.' He meets the churchman's penetrating gaze. 'I can help.'

'Well…' The monk rubs his chin. 'We do need all the help we can get.' He opens the door wider. 'Another pair of hands would be warmly welcomed by Brother Thomas. He runs the corporeal brothers. Come in. I'll introduce you.'

The monk heaves the door wide open and Assen is unsure whether or not to close it behind him. He does so, then hurries after the elderly brother who seems to be moving much faster than when he came to open the door.

They enter a large hall with dark-brown stained rafters rising forty feet or more above their heads. The beams draw Assen's eyes upwards.

'Come.' The brother beckons.

The room is flanked on both sides by sizeable bed booths. The beds look comfortable and clean, and there are rich, red-velvet curtains drawn back across most of the cubicles. Each bed has clean white sheets topped with blankets; many are occupied. Assen has never seen anything like this in an alms-house; it is warm, welcoming and even luxurious.

Presently, another brother enters the hall and walks down the central passageway with a large warming pan. Heading to an empty booth, he pulls back the sheets and begins warming the bed.

The elderly monk notices Assen's captivation. 'Come, I'll show you around,' he says, waving his hand slowly around the hall. 'This is the room of the poor. No one is turned away. People from all over bring in those they can no longer care for.'

'To die?'

'No … well, sometimes. We give them food and warmth, and remedies from the physick garden. We read to them, soothe their minds with passages from the Bible. Many get better and leave.' He smiles. 'They come back with donations, alms, to give thanks.'

Looking at the bed booths and the sisters and brothers gliding around with warming pans and bowls of delicious-smelling hot soup, Assen's mouth salivates. 'But that can't be where you get all your funds.' He quickly wipes his lips with his handkerchief.

'It is all donations. We do have sizeable legacies but many, many small donations from people all around the region.'
'Really? It's ... well ... amazing.' Assen grins.
The monk laughs. 'It's been a lot of hard work. Ah, here's Brother Thomas.' Another monk approaches carrying blankets.
'Abbot,' the monk replies with a little bow.
'Oh!' Assen exclaims. 'I'm so sorry, Abbot. I did not know ... I did not know you were the abbot when you opened the door yourself.' He runs two fingers inside his collar to loosen it.
'I told you we were short-handed.' The abbot winks. 'Brother Thomas, this is Assen. Brother Assen—'
'Really? Huh, Brother Assen?' Brother Thomas casts his eyes over Assen's dusty breeches and worn leather tunic. His gaze rests on the hilt of a small sword on Assen's hip. 'I'm afraid we do not allow such weapons in the House of God, Brother.'
'I was wondering when you were going to notice that,' the abbot says convivially. 'Yes, Brother Assen, if you could leave it with Brother Francis in the store, he'll make sure it is locked away. You can have it when you leave.'
Assen reddens. 'Of course. I am sorry, Abbot, Brother Thomas. I have been on the road; there are many dangers ... it is purely for defence. I don't think I could ever use it, it is just to show ... to make a thief think twice...'
'I know, my son, to give one a chance to get out of a situation, get a bit of a head start, eh? But these things have a habit of getting out of hand, and before you know it blood is on your hands and forever on your soul, or your life is cut short in a pointless skirmish. My advice is to give the robber everything you have and watch him go. Leave it in God's hands. Life has a way of balancing out justice.'
'You're right.' Assen unbuckles his blade and hands it to Brother Thomas.
'Good.' The abbot pats Assen on the arm. 'Now, Brother Thomas, Brother Assen here is a corporeal brother and has come to offer his services.'
Brother Thomas offers his hand and they shake. 'Don't worry,' he says conspiratorially, 'he's always like this. So, you've come to offer your services. Have you any experience?

Actually, it doesn't really matter.' He sighs and looks at the abbot. 'Another pair of hands, right?'

'I worked in a plague hospital in Paris.'

'Really? Which one?' The abbot turns to face Assen more fully.

Assen looks at his feet, curls his toes upward then turns back to the abbot. 'Umm ... St Marcel's.'

'Ah.'

'This place knows something about plague, too.' Brother Thomas stares into space.

'It is why it was built in the first place. Where there is war and famine, disease, plague and death soon follow,' the abbot adds.

'And the townspeople built it?'

'A wealthy benefactor put up the funds. He had a dream about healing the sick and treating the poor, and he founded this.' He spreads out his arms, sweeping them from side to side.

'It is wonderful.'

'It is! You could say this is what happens when you follow your dreams. Hmm? But, for now, there are chamber pots to be emptied. Am I right, Brother Thomas?'

'See what I mean?' Brother Thomas winks at Assen. 'Come on.'

Assen follows him down the centre of the hall. 'Hold these, please.' He wraps several blankets around the crook of Assen's arm. 'The sisters look after the female patients. They are really in charge – they run the place. We just assist with the male patients.'

Assen looks more closely at the goings-on in the hall. Several nuns and monks sit on chairs and stools by the bed booths, reading to patients. Others walk briskly to and fro, fetching bedpans, basins and sheets. 'You have a physician?'

'We have several attached to the alms-house, including one who oversees the treatment when needed. There's also an apothecary and a herbalist; we cultivate our own physick and vegetable garden. We're very lucky.'

Brother Thomas stops beside a booth where a man is sitting in a chair next to the bed. He is thin and pale, and there are shadows under his eyes. 'This is Mr Picard. He will be staying with us for a little while. Mr Picard, this is Brother Assen. He will be looking after you. Be gentle with him – he is learning.'

Mr Picard offers a weak smile, and the monk pats him on the shoulder. 'There, our new brother is going to look after you and get whatever you need. How does that sound?' Brother Thomas turns to Assen. 'Undress Mr Picard and assist him in any toileting requirements. If he can manage some broth, there's a big pot in the kitchen. Chamber pot and spewing pan are under the bed. When you've done that, come back to me.'

Brother Thomas walks halfway down the central passage, turns and walks back to Assen. He unhooks the blankets still hanging from Assen's arm. 'I'll take these. Oh, and remember to wash your hands after contact with the patient's body and its … excretions. There are bowls and a spout in the yard.'

'Of course,' Assen replies, recalling Madame Lambert's strict instructions.

When Brother Thomas is out of earshot, Assen bends down to Mr Picard. 'Now, Mr Picard, you have not been feeling too well? Let me help you get ready for bed.'

'Will you read to me?'

Assen hesitates. 'I … I'm … I'm sorry, the spiritual brothers usually read … they'll read the Bible for you. I'm not supposed to. I'm just a corporeal brother. I see to your body, that's all.'

'I don't want the Bible. Causes too much trouble.'

'Oh? Are you able to stand?'

Mr Picard struggles to his feet and Assen removes his overshirt. 'Well, if you put it that way… What would you like instead?'

'How about the adventures of Madame Gantillon, the Happy Countess?'

'Hmm. I don't think the church library houses such a volume, unless it's under the abbot's desk.'

Mr Picard laughs as Assen slips the nightshirt over his head. 'There.' Gently holding his elbows, Assen guides Mr Picard to the bed, sweeps back the sheets and tucks him in. 'Would you like anything else?'

Mr Picard ponders. 'How about *The Cloud of Unknowing*?'

'Good choice. I'll see what I can do.'

Assen doesn't know how long he has been reading but it must have been for some time for the bones of his rump are numb and his eyes keep blinking shut. He thinks he might slide off the chair at any moment. But no one seems to need him. They've probably forgotten all about him. Mr Picard, on the other hand, is sitting up as bright as a button.

Assen stretches his back and takes a deep breath in an attempt to waken his brain. Opening his eyes wide, he continues, '"All creatures, angels and men, have a power called a loving power. These loving souls know God insomuch as they comprehend God in themselves..."'

Something strikes Assen and he pauses; he is not quite sure what it is. It feels familiar, yet it is slippery and he can't quite grasp it. Is it a memory? Was it something in his dream?

A picture begins to form and he is back... to where? *The sun is streaming in from a window high above and its' rays are deliciously warm on his face. He oozes with contentment. Someone is singing, a woman with a soft sweet voice. Is it a lullaby? Something moves, a shimmer of olive and lilac cloth floats towards him. Excitement tickles his stomach. He can't wait to see...*

'Are you all right?' Mr Picard sits up and stares in alarm.

Assen smiles and lets the serenity settle in his torso. 'I've been on the road for many days.'

'Do you want to be in here? Perhaps you should find a cell to sleep in. You can read to me tomorrow, if you like.'

Assen laughs. 'It's nothing, Mr Picard, just a chill.' He starts reading again. '"This is the endless, marvellous miracle of love; the working of which shall never end... The feeling of this is endless bliss."'

Assen can't remember how long he's been here now – several weeks, or months, even. Mr Picard is still here but will be ready to leave soon. Assen enjoys their late-afternoon study sessions; they are a welcome respite from cleaning bedpans, scrubbing floors and doing endless laundry.

Today he has brought *Utopia* by the English martyr, Sir Thomas More. They are going to discuss whether an egalitarian society can ever work. After taking his seat and drawing it closer to the bed, he opens the pamphlet and takes out the marker. '"From whence I am persuaded that till property is taken away, there can be no equitable or just distribution of things, nor can the world be happily governed…"'

Mr Picard lifts himself higher; he is listening intently. 'Read that bit again about happiness.'

'Umm, let's see. Ah, yes, here it is. "Nobody owns anything, but everyone is rich – for what greater wealth can there be than cheeriness, peace of mind, and freedom from anxiety."'

'But you can't be free from anxiety if you're poor. That's what makes you anxious! How are you going to eat? Where is your next meal coming from?'

'I think he means after all that is taken care of. Look.' Assen points at a paragraph, bringing the book closer to Mr Picard's face. 'Here he says, you must first—'

The main door crashes open, and six men are framed in the doorway, four carrying sheathed swords. Previously a hive of activity, the monks and nuns freeze, bedpans and bibles in hand.

Assen stands and the volume slides from his lap. His right hand reaches for his left hip but the space is empty. In that split second, he knows what he must do.

# Chapter Fifty-Nine

Farewell
A Hill Overlooking North Berwick

The sky is powder blue with a whisper of candyfloss clouds stretching across the expanse. There is a 360-degree view from the top of the hill. In one direction, across the tranquil sea reflecting the baby-blue sky, there is the island of Craigleith and the Bass Rock in the distance; in the foreground, the anchored fishing boats rock from side to side in the bay. Inland, in the other direction, the outlook is uninterrupted for miles over the lush green latticework of flat fields dotted with cattle, sheep and the occasional copse.

But today is different. A long wooden pole with the girth of a child's waist protrudes from the apex of Gallows Hill, and a crowd is snaking its way up from the village, following the meandering path. Three figures are in front, separate from the group: one is small, flanked by two larger forms towering a good head above her. As they near the peak, the lone pole comes into view; twenty feet away there is a pyre with a stake in the centre.

Agnes stumbles as her leg plunges down a rabbit hole. With her arms tied behind her back, she trips over stumps of grass and burrows. Each time Mr Birkett hauls her up, lifting her off her feet.

He and the guard grip her under the arms and half drag, half carry her closer to the summit. The trio stop at the thick pole and the crowd forms a semicircle, facing the bay. Among them are the commissioner, Reverend McLaren and the witchfinder.

Stony-faced, the commissioner addresses Mr Birkett. 'Proceed.'

Mr Birkett prods Agnes in the back and pushes her towards the pole. The blow almost knocks her off her feet and pain sears between her shoulder blades. She gasps, staggering. Gelly promised it would soon be over, but was that real? Did she really see Gelly? Did she imagine it? The breath catches in her throat as if the rope were already around it, squeezing the air out of her. Her head spins and the crowd becomes a whirl of greys, blacks and browns.

'Breathe, lassie, breathe!' a voice whispers close to her ear, the tiny vibrations tickling her lobe. 'Don't resist what is. This will soon pass.'

She turns her head but no one is there, only Mr Birkett three feet away with his baton.

It was real. It was *real*! She swallows. *Thank God.*

Lifting her head, she takes a deep breath; the air is fresh, clean and sharp. *This is it, Agnes Sampson. Trust. It is in God's hands. You saw the angels and Gelly. Trust, trust, trust. Put one foot in front of the other. Nothing more.* Her body obeys.

The stake comes closer and closer, looming larger and larger, until she could reach out and touch it if her hands were not tied. Mr Birkett loosens the rope binding her. *Now! Do it now!* Agnes swings a hand to her mouth with such force that she slaps her face before swallowing the pellet.

Mr Birkett positions his thickset frame between her and the crowd, concealing her act.

'What's going on there? What's she doing?' The commissioner cranes his neck to see. He glances at the king's representative, William Balfour, who is staring straight ahead, lips pursed and arms folded. 'Everything will follow the letter of the king's law, Sir William. We will be rid of this scourge, and His Grace and his subjects will sleep safely in their beds again.'

'Your loyalty and perseverance do you credit, Commissioner Baxter. These proceedings have shown your devotion to the Crown and your service in defending the royal lineage.'

'Sir William.' The commissioner inclines his head. 'Now, Birkett, what's going on?'

'Nothing, Commissioner Baxter.' Mr Birkett ties Agnes's hands behind the pole, 'Just a bit of dirt on her face, I believe.'

'Women! Are we ready now?'

'Aye, sir.' Birkett moves away from the staff.

The commissioner unfurls a scroll of parchment. 'We are assembled to carry out the sentence of the royal court. All present on this day are here to witness the execution of the witch Agnes Sampson. Mr Birkett, proceed.'

The other guard hands Mr Birkett a rope and a thick stick about twelve inches long and two inches in diameter. He wraps the rope around Agnes's neck and the pole. In her nightmares, the twine was coarse, thick and scratchy and was tugged and tugged until her head popped off. Now, it is like a glove. *Aye, that's it, a soft glove. How strange.*

Birkett ties two loose knots in the rope and threads the stick through them to give him a good grip when he rotates it to tighten the noose around Agnes's neck.

All eyes turn to Commissioner Baxter. The only sound is the cack, cack, cack of seagulls gliding on an invisible wire stretching from the hill out over the sea, and the song of a lark ascending far above the seabirds.

Agnes homes on its song. *It's a sign! I know it! It's a sign!* She looks up, imagining she is in the wispy clouds with the bird.

The commissioner raises his hand then drops it. Birkett starts turning the rod, and the glove caresses and squeezes. Agnes pops out of her body and hovers next to it. It splutters and chokes. *Poor, poor thing.*

The commissioner raises his hand. 'Stop!' Birkett halts in mid rotation, holding the grip firm. As he releases the tension, Agnes's body convulses in a fit of coughing and retching. Back inside her frame, she pans the crowd but the people won't stay still; they undulate and sway like little fishing boats loose from their moorings.

Reverend McLaren comes into view beside the commissioner, and the witchfinder next to him, and then two boys. *Duncan and Matthew! John Fian's pupils. What are they doing here? John would be very angry. Go home, lads, go home! This is no place for you!*

A haze seeps through the group, dissolving the figures into a swirling blob … and blackness. It cocoons her in a warm, tender embrace, the deepest black she'd ever seen, yet, alive and loving, and … such peace.

Agnes is ten feet above her body looking down on it. *Hmm, that's funny.* She is curious, but nothing more. Her form is like a big rag doll slumped at the stake. 'Is that my body?' She no longer feels connected to it, only that it has served its purpose. And yet she can still see and hear up here.

The voices of the commissioner and Mr Birkett drift upwards. They seem far away, distant and echoing.

'Is she dead?' the commissioner enquires.

'Not yet … but…'

'To the fire!'

Bang! Agnes is back in her body. Her eyes snap open; every sinew of her is stretched taut like the gut on a fiddle. Her throat is on fire. The crowd whirls in front of her, going round and round. Her chin flops to her chest as the rope is released. She stares at her feet, small and white, streaked with dirt and little streams of blood. Her knees buckle as the cords around her waist and chest are loosened. Before she hits the ground, she is caught by Mr Birkett and his assistant, each gripping her under the arms and pulling her up. She notices her dainty white feet being dragged through the grass.

They stop before the pyre and Mr Birkett tilts Agnes back, sweeping her off her feet.

It's been a long time since anyone has carried her like this. A garden and a lake flash before her eyes, and a warm feeling of peace descends through her body from her scalp, forehead, jaw, throat, shoulders, downwards past her hips, legs and feet. *Everything will be all right.*

Mr Birkett stumbles and staggers with his burden over the planks and logs to the central column. As he places her feet first, she feels a hard flat surface – a plank of wood or a box, perhaps. He ties her hands, then lashes her back and hips against the thick post. Fleetingly his eyes meet hers. Gingerly, he steps back off the pyre.

Piles of roughly cut wood lie criss-crossed around the central stake. The crowd is stretched in a semicircle looking inland at Agnes as she gazes past them out to sea. A flicker at the edge of her vision draws her eye.

Mr Birkett has raised a flaming torch above his head. He sets it under the logs. Other guards step forward around the bonfire, placing their torches inside the woodpile. It begins to crackle as it catches, slowly burning, the flames licking upwards and inwards.

'Time to go, Agnes,' a voice whispers.

# Chapter Sixty

Trapped
Beaune

No one moves. Six men stand in the church entrance: four behind with their hands poised on the hilt of their swords, and two in front carrying no weapons.

One of the unarmed men steps forward and holds up his hand. 'Good brothers and sisters, do not fret. My name is Mr Noiret. We are on official business. We shall conduct that business and be gone.'

Still no one moves or speaks, but the soft tread of footsteps shuffling in the corridor beyond the small door at the back of the hall grows louder in the stillness. Mr Noiret creases his brow. The footfall stops on the other side of the door. The handle jangles and, with a cough and a grunt, the person behind it pulls it open. The abbot appears, then closes the door after him, making sure the latch is in place before unhurriedly walking towards Mr Noiret.

'Good day, gentlemen,' he says, looking from their faces to their weapons. 'I am Abbot Antoine. You are most welcome, as any soul is, but, alas, I'm afraid your weapons are not. Please give them to Brother Simon.' He swings his arm, beckoning the monk nearest to him. 'You may collect them when you leave.'

Mr Noiret pulls his tiny thin beard to a point. 'I'm afraid we can't do that. We are hunting a dangerous fugitive, a murderer, no less! A former physician who killed his patients!'

A metal basin clatters on the flagstaff floor and the racket echoes around the hall.

'There is no one like that here.' The abbot waves his hand as if swatting a fly.

Taking three paces into the hall, Mr Noiret pans around. 'Oh, but I think there is. He is dark and distinctive ... very distinctive. A Moor ... half-Moor, actually.'

His gaze settles on Assen and everyone follows his stare. Assen is hardly breathing, every muscle tight, poised and ready. He knows what he must do.

'Guards!' Mr Noiret bellows. The four armed men march the length of the hall to the bed booth where Assen stands. Two grab his arms and he shakes them off. They fall back and reach for their swords. Their blades are halfway out when he holds up his hands. 'Wait! I'll come. This is a house of God. I'll come peacefully – but do not touch me.'

He has been thinking about this day for some time and has resolved that if they ever caught up with him, he would return to Paris and clear his name. He has even considered returning himself. In his heart, he knows he could never allow the Verey name – his birthright – to be tainted with such malice. And yet, he also knows his work here is far from finished.

The guards step back, and Assen walks forward, head up, positioning himself between them. They march down the aisle to the entrance arch then stop beside the abbot and Mr Noiret.

'Wait!' The abbot looks up at Assen. 'This is a house of God, my son. Is your conscience clear?'

Water pools in Assen's eyes as he meets the compassionate stare of the abbot. 'I am no murderer. I was a doctor, I tried to be … to help… The plague – I only ever wanted to help. It took a lot of patients. God knows, we tried to save them.'

The abbot steps back, his gaze fixed. 'Then claim your right. Claim your right in the sanctity of this holy place.'

'What? Abbot—'

'Claim your right, the right of all human beings to—'

'Sanctuary! I claim sanctuary!' Assen falls to his knees, bowing his head.

The abbot rests his hand on Assen's crown, making the sign of the cross. 'This soul is granted sanctuary.'

The guards look at Mr Noiret.

# Chapter Sixty-One

A New Beginning
A Hill Overlooking North Berwick

The flames take hold; this is no time to linger in a human body. *Agnes floats high above, looking down at the limp figure as the fire edges closer. The puppet below no longer belongs to her. It was a vessel, a container, and now her need for it has vanished. She is peaceful and calm, hanging in mid-air, observing the crowd.*

*The minister's face is set hard. What happened to make him like this? A picture appears in her mind of a little boy in a room with a woman in a bed screaming and another woman holding bloody sheets. The child is petrified, tears streaming down his face. Agnes inhabits his terror, grief and confusion.*

*'You understand now?' a voice beside her whispers.*

*'Yes.'*

*Two tall beings have materialised on either side of her. They bob up and down with the breeze. They're like the ones that came with Gelly. Are these mine?*

*'That's right, Agnes. We're here for you now, just like we promised.' She looks at the male figure but his lips haven't moved. 'It is time to go.'*

*She looks down at the bound body, the flames almost upon it, and wonders how she can float here in the sky, alive – more alive than she's ever felt. She extends her hands and arms: they are long, smooth, pale and unblemished. A beautiful, silk-like skirt adorns her lower half, shimmering with orange and purple hues. There is a hint of white at her chest and elbow; she thinks she might be wearing a white blouse with matching trim. 'Wish I had a mirror.'*

*A shimmering form about Agnes's height appears before her. The glistening particles undulate, shift and coalesce into a mirror and Agnes laughs. She sees a striking young version of herself* with luminous blue eyes staring back in wonder. With long, luscious, caramel-brown curly hair reaching her chest, she looks in her late twenties or early thirties, full of life and joy. Her clothes, although immaculate, are a modest, peasant-type of dress. 'Just perfect.'

There is a tingly warm, expansive sensation in the centre of her chest, swelling from her body in a circle, growing and growing. 'My goodness. It doesn't have any limits.'

The iridescent mirror flickers and dissolves into the mist gathering around them.

'Are you ready?' asks the female angel.

'Yes.'

As the execution scene far below vanishes in the churning haze, there is a rumbling and roaring in Agnes's chest. Something is tugging at her heart, pulling her forward. She jolts, whoosh, as she is propelled at lightning speed upwards – or is it sideways?

She finds herself in a transparent tube, or maybe it is a corridor, with colours and shapes rotating and whirling past, faster and faster; a kaleidoscope of magenta, violet, lavender, indigo, thistle, cerulean, sapphire and colours she's never seen before. All at once, it ends and she is at the mouth of the tunnel surrounded by billowing white clouds. Shadowy figures appear one by one out of the vapour, some facing Agnes and others facing different directions.

As Agnes glides out of the channel, the figures become more defined and form a giant circle. They are dressed very similarly to Agnes, the women in peasants' skirts of kaleidoscopic colours and men in loose breeches, puffed shirts and vibrant waistcoats.

'Who are these people? Do I know them? Why are they here?' Everyone is chatting, laughing and nodding enthusiastically at Agnes.

'They are here to welcome you,' her female guide answers. 'Look closely.'

Agnes looks from face to face around the circle. She makes out Gelly, dazzling; John Fian, his smile as bright as the sun; John the smith; Maggie ... everyone she knows, except they are younger, brighter, more vibrant versions of themselves.

'They are souls. They are what souls look and feel like.'

*'Of course.'*

*A space opens up for her in the circle. On one side Gelly offers her hand and Agnes grasps it. A surge of electricity shoots up her arm and into her chest, bursting into gratitude ten times stronger than anything she ever felt on Earth. On the other side, another holds out their hand, and she steps forward, allowing her hand to slip into theirs.*

*She sees his face. Every emotion she has ever buried deep within her bursts out: grief, longing, fear, passion, all releasing and transforming into one love – a love she has only felt for one person. It overflows and pours out of her chest into her companion and all around the circle. They grasp each other's hands. The circle is complete.*

*Agnes's male guide places his hand on her shoulder.* 'A time for healing.'

*A bluish-silver mist swirls around the gathering, growing brighter and brighter, with shades of gold, sunflower-yellow and citrine streaking through the clouds, dissolving the ethereal beings into brilliant sunlight.*

# Chapter Sixty-Two

The Rose Stone
Beaune

'It is almost too bright.' Assen screws up his eyes and makes his way back into the interior of the Hall of the Poor.

He savours the cool, calm air. The sisters and brothers are going about their work. 'Bedpans and broth,' the old abbot used to say. Little has changed in twenty years, except the apothecary and physick garden have got much larger and better organised. Progress. Assen sighs contentedly as he treads slowly down the main hall towards the door tucked in the corner of the wall facing the entrance.

'Morning, Dr Verey!' Brother Sebastien smiles, little dimples forming in his cheeks. He is holding an unused bedpan.

'Good morning, Brother Sebastien. I trust you slept well in your new lodgings?'

'Oh yes, Dr Verey. It is a blessing to be inside these walls, close to our patients, where I can do most good.'

'That is commendable, Brother. We are glad to have you.'

The young monk beams and heads off in the direction of the kitchen.

Assen looks around. Not all the beds are filled. 'That's good.' He counts one, two, three, four, five unoccupied. 'Excellent.'

The drapes are pulled back and the sheets are clean and crisp. The chamber pots are hidden discreetly at the end of the bed. If possible, they try to give each patient their own pot; it was something Assen insisted on when he became head physician.

'That is good,' he says to no one in particular. 'We won't have to turn anyone away today.' Not that they ever did, not in all the time he has been here. People just share the beds, and they make up extra cots in the other buildings in the ecclesiastical infirmary. He is gratified to have carried on the old abbot's legacy as well as introducing some improvements, he hopes. 'Yes, I'm sure he would have approved.' Assen smiles.

Sometimes, when he's walking down the far corridor, Assen is sure he hears the abbot's familiar shuffling tread at his side. Other times, when he has been sitting at his desk – the old abbot's desk – staring into space, he has heard muttering in his ear. He wouldn't put it past the old churchman to be guiding him.

'You have got very fanciful, Dr Verey,' he whispers to himself. 'I know what you're doing. You're just trying to delay getting down to this month's accounts.'

He exhales heavily as he approaches the door onto the corridor to his office. It is dwarfed by the west wall and the enormous stained-glass window rising a third of the way up. His stomach sinks a little more.

He twists the iron knob, pushes the door open with some force and enters the dimly lit hallway. It is so dark he has to wait a moment for his eyes to adjust. Two sconces about head height are supposed to light the length of the passage. He makes a mental note to order more candles and holders; he'll get Brother Francis on to it. But, then again, money could be spent on a new store in the apothecary to preserve the berries.

'Preserved berries won't do you any good if you break your neck, Dr Verey,' he hears the old abbot say.

Assen laughs and says to the empty corridor, 'Why didn't you do it, then?'

The door to his office is ajar and the window wide open. 'Hmm, Brother Peter.' But the soft cool breeze does feel pleasant on his cheek. There will be no afternoon naps today; he's here to see to the accounts.

He inhales the soft summer scent of lavender, wafting from the pot outside the window. A pile of parchment sits in the centre of the desk; the chair is pushed back, waiting for him. The weight in his stomach gets heavier as he trudges over; to say administration was not his forte would be an understatement.

He sits down with a 'Right!' and takes up the quill lying in front of the pile. Two gigantic lit candles at opposite corners of the table illuminate the neat hand of Brother John and the not-so-neat hands of the town butcher, baker and granary master. Everything is ready for him to balance the books.

He takes up the first sheet, exhales and reads the first line. *For eight sacks of grain at—*

There is a knock at the door and a wave of relief passes through him. He reddens at his reaction and looks up, rubbing the side of his neck. Brother Francis's head appears around the door. 'Dr Verey, there are some people to see you.'

Assen lays down his quill and smooths the long, tapered feather, both relieved and irritated. He tries to persuade to himself that he could have finished the orders today; perhaps he should ask his visitors to come back. No. Brother Francis would only interrupt him if it was important. What could it be? Pray God not a disaster. A band as thick as a man's hand tightens across his upper abdomen.

'Very well. Show them in, please, Brother Francis.'

The monk steps aside, and Assen's elderly father walks in, followed by a young fair-haired woman.

'Father!' Assen jumps up, scattering the papers and almost upturning the ink pot. 'I–I did not know you were coming. The journey … your health. Please sit, sit. It is so far… I would have come to Paris – I was planning to. It's just that there was so much to—'

'Hush, hush, dear boy! I'm fine, can't you see? The journey was invigorating. What could be better than the French countryside rolling before your eyes?'

Assen squints, recalling his journey on Burgundy's back roads. 'Quite a lot, actually.' But his father is clean and groomed, with a tapered beard and apple-red cheeks, and his lips and eyes are creased in a smile.

'And,' the older man says, 'I had the loveliest company. Please come forward, my dear.' The young woman steps closer to the desk. She has a foolscap leather satchel draped over her shoulder.

Assen hurries around the desk, guides his father to a chair and pulls another from the corner for the girl. 'Please, both of you, sit, please sit. Are you hungry? Are you weary? Brother John can—'

'That can wait, son. There is something important I've come to discuss with you.'

Assen sits back down and places his hands in front of him on the desk. 'Very well, Father.'

'This is Hope. She is from Scotland,' Mr Verey explains. 'She came to France twenty years ago as a baby to flee the burning times. You've heard about those, yes?'

Hope leans forward and lifts the satchel over her head.

'I've heard something of it, yes. Sad times, very sad indeed.'

'Well, Hope's parents were caught up in it. They were one of the many victims of the madness.'

Assen turns to Hope. 'I'm sorry to hear that, I truly am. But, Father, what has this to do with me?'

'Hope has something for you. But first, she has to tell you about someone.'

'For me?' Something akin to thick black treacle lurks in the pit of Assen's stomach. 'I–I don't understand what any of it has to do with me!'

'Just listen. Go ahead, Hope.'

'I was born in North Berwick, in Scotland. Agnes Sampson, the town midwife and healer, brought me into the world.' A vision of another midwife and healer flashes in front of Assen's eyes. He blinks and focuses intently as Hope recounts the story of the infamous North Berwick witch trials. 'No one knows how many souls were sacrificed, maybe a hundred, maybe two hundred.'

'I am so sorry. It is unbelievably barbaric,' Assen says shaking his head. 'All those people… And the king! It's beyond reason. This woman, Ag…'

'Agnes,' his father says.

'Agnes, yes. She sounds courageous. I am sorry for her fate.'

'She *was* courageous and she was kind, too,' Mr Verey adds.

'You knew her, Father?' Little frown lines appear on Assen's forehead.

'I did. She was spirited, beautiful, clever and a natural healer.'

'When did you know her?'

'All in good time. First, Hope has something for you.'

Hope fishes into the bag lying across her lap and takes out a large package tied with twine and finished in a neat bow. She places it carefully on the table and pushes it towards Assen. 'She wanted you to have this.'

'Me?' Assen slaps his hand on the desk and the shock waves reverberate to his elbow and shoulder. 'I don't understand.' He rubs his upper arm. 'I'm sorry to hear what happened, but I ... I don't know this woman.' He looks from his father to Hope.

'They are letters,' continues Mr Verey.

'Letters?'

'Between your mother and Agnes.'

'They knew each other?' Assen stands, his chair screeching backwards. He walks to the window and looks out. Brother John is filling a pail from the spout across the courtyard. The monk always fills it too much, and then it splashes all the way through the kitchen and into the hall. He'll need to have a gentle word with him about it.

Assen half closes the window. 'Mother never said anything about knowing someone in Scotland. I've never seen her writing...'

'Are you sure?'

Pictures spring into Assen's mind as if someone has released the catch on a jack-in-the-box. *Mother in the chateau, quill in hand, with a pile of papers – letters – staring out of the window towards the lake.* His childish voice echoes, *'What are you doing? Are you coming out to shake the apples from the trees? We're going now.'*

*She smiles and pats him on the head. 'Not just now, darling. I have to finish writing to a friend. You go with Robert; I'll join you soon, I promise.'* He can still feel the soft pressure of her hand and the little knot of frustration in his gut from her refusal to come out and play. A lump plummets from his throat to his chest like a log wedged in the rocks of a river.

He walks back to the desk. 'I cannot read Mother's letters. They're private.'

'She would want you to,' his father says. 'She always wanted you to ... when Agnes agreed.'

'What has this Agnes got to do with what Mother can and cannot do?' he explodes. There is a fire in his chest. Who is this woman? And why is she, this stranger, dictating what happens between him and his mother?

Hope reaches into her satchel and pulls out another bundle of letters. These are tied up with a red silk ribbon. She pushes them across the table so they are level with the first package.

'These are Agnes's letters to your mother. Read the letters, son.' Mr Verey slowly rises. 'Hope and I will get some sustenance from the kitchen, and we'll sit ... under the yew, I think.'

'I'll get Brother Francis to arrange—' Assen heads for the door.

'Stop. Please. Sit down. I can see to it. Sit and read – for me.'

'Very well.' Assen pulls in his chair and rests his elbows on the table. He runs his fingers over the first bundle held together with twine. Releasing the knot, he lets the string loosen and it falls open. He carefully lifts the folded piece of paper.

Mr Verey and Hope rise and head to the door, then close it softly behind them.

With his heart beating irregularly, Assen opens the first letter and pulls one of the huge candles closer to cast more light. He recognises his mother's handwriting and immediately hears her voice.

*My dearest Agnes,*
*Our darling boy grows bigger as each day passes. I see you in his eyes sometimes. You both have that intense, uncompromisingly wonderful stare. Oh, he makes me laugh – so inquisitive. He has a real fascination for ducks at the moment! It was all we could do to stop him diving into the duck pond at the chateau. Truthfully, poor Robert came back with him soaked up to his thighs, and little Assen looking so happy with a lily in his hand. He reminded me so much of Galib when he was a boy.*

Assen rubs his eyes and picks up another letter.

*...You do not have to thank me, Agnes. It is I who am on my knees every day thanking you for what you have given us – a gift from God. We spent such a wonderful summer at the chateau, I wish you could be here. Assen is doing marvellously well in his education – his tutor has high hopes for him. He shows an aptitude in philosophy, the classics, astronomy. He is also interested in nature, plants, and my recipes and remedies. I have a secret hope he might become a healer one day. But he'll be better than us, Agnes, better than we ever were, or ever could be.*

*He'll have the finest education, from the Faculty in Paris and the best teachers. I know I'm getting ahead of myself. And only if he wishes. If it is truly his vocation.*

*My dearest Agnes*
*Our boy has started his medical training. He is passionate. He wants to change the world; it is a wonder. I am so proud of him, and I know you are too. Though I fear he is perhaps too enthralled with this new medicine. His teachers are exuberant. I don't want him to be disappointed or to disregard the old ways, traditions – there is so much we would lose. But he is a good boy, with such a good heart like you and his father – a gentle, kind but honourable heart. He will find his way.*

*My cough still troubles me, thank you for asking. But I'm sure it's just a pesky summer cold. Theo wants me to see Dr Brisbois. It's nonsense, really. In my next letter, I'm sure I will tell you I'm quite recovered and in the best of health.*

Assen sighs heavily, laying down the letters and smoothing out the folds. Placing them to the side, he looks at the other pile tied with a red silk ribbon. He is not sure he wants to read them. He glides his fingertips over the material, pulls the end and watches it unravel. The ribbon is soft and velvety beneath his touch. The sheets it encases are made of rough parchment and pieces of linen.

He doesn't know this woman; he doesn't care about *her*, he tells himself, but he knows it's a lie. He could burn the letters in the kitchen oven. No one need know anything about the woman who has just turned his life upside down and tossed all his cherished memories in the air, scattering them to the four winds.

*But it's not what Mother wanted, is it?*

He picks up the first sheet, and his fingers tremble as he unfolds the first letter. The paper is coarse and the ink faded. The large, confident lettering is in direct contrast to his mother Bahdeer's neat, measured script. He slides the pads of his fingers along the rows of whorls of writing as if reading through his fingers.

*My dearest Bahdeer*, it begins. He tries to imagine a strong, confident Scottish voice to match the script.

*I so look forward to your letters, I can't tell you how much. I pray God they always reach me. I read your last letter so many times, the writing has faded. My boy is happy. He is safe. He is loved and he thrives. That is all that matters. Nothing else in this world matters as much. You asked me about my life here. It is a good life. I've tried to make the best of things, I have a cottage with a clean stream, or burn as we say, nearby. I have a herb and vegetable garden, and they need me here. I've already brought five souls into the world. It's the best feeling in the world and the worst. It'll always forever remind me of him, my beautiful son. But I know he is safe with you and Theo and you love him. That's all I could want and it is what I've prayed for. Please, please, keep sending me news of how he grows. The way you describe him with his coal black eyes, dark curly hair and kind smile, I can see him before me. Stay well, Bahdeer, give my love and greetings to Theo, and once again, thank you, with all my heart, thank you.*

Assen brings his hand to his throat and caresses it. A lump like a skimming stone he once found on the beach has taken up residence. Determinedly, he picks up the next letter.

*Tell me more of his interest in the garden. Does he still follow you around? Perhaps he will be a healer, maybe a physician? Do you think? Please kiss my boy for me. I feel him in my heart; it breaks into a thousand pieces sometimes. You have saved me and my beautiful boy. God bless you.*

Assen lays the last letter down and stares into space. He clasps his hands to stop them from shaking. His mind is devoid of thoughts, sounds and pictures; it is an empty, expanding, comforting space. He doesn't know how long he's been like this, but the candle has burned down a few inches and the sun is much lower in the sky. He must talk with his father.

Getting up, he finds his lower back has stiffened and his thighs are taut. His whole body feels tight, like he has tensed everything ready for a fight or an escape. He jiggles his legs and straightens them. Then he sees something else, something protruding from under the pile of Agnes's letters. It looks like an old rag. He'll leave it for now. He takes a deep breath and walks towards the door.

As he grasps the cold iron handle he stops. Something is pulling him back. *Finish this. Find out what it is.* He sighs and turns around.

Dropping back into the chair, he runs his fingers along the edge of the rag, sensing the coarseness. It is a linen bag with a drawstring. Dragging it along the surface, he picks it up. Something is inside; it is the weight and shape of a large pebble and sits comfortably in his palm. He opens the bag and carefully allows the contents to glide onto the desk.

'No! It's not true! I won't have it!' He jumps up and sweeps the letters and contents of the bag across the table and onto the floor. 'This is not yours! It can't be yours!'

He clutches the locket hanging in the centre of his chest; the other half of the crudely fashioned rose heart stone lies in the centre of the desk. Squeezing his locket, he wants to rip it off and toss it across the room, but something stops him.

He sees Bahdeer standing in front of the fountain with her thick dark hair draped around her shoulders and her hand on her heart. Her eyes are brimming with love and compassion as her words swirl around him. *'And your mother always keeps it close to her heart. You are always there in her heart, every day. You know that, dear boy, don't you?'*

Another memory surfaces, this time of her sitting at her dressing table as her maid brushes her hair.

'*Mama?*' He picks up a silver comb on the vanity dresser. '*May I please go to the forester's cottage with Robert. He is taking the gamekeeper's son and William.*'

She half turns and reaches out to him. '*Come here… Thank you, Marie. Please leave us.*' Picking up pins and combs, Marie leaves with an armful of cloth. '*Now, Assen, come closer. What's all this about a trip to the forest?*'

'*Please, Mama, Robert is taking us. He'll make sure I get back before sundown.*'

'*In that case, how can I refuse?*'

'*Thank you!*' He can't wait to tell Robert and bolts for the door.

But she calls after him. *'Assen, haven't you forgot something?'*

*'Huh?'*

She points to her cheek, turns her head and screws up her eyes. Running back over, he pecks her on the cheek. *'That's better. Now—'* she touches his chest *'—your locket is safe? Remember. You have to take care of it.'*

Tugging his collar to the side, he shows her the gold chain and retrieves the locket from deep inside his shirt. *'I never take it off, Mama.'*

*'Good boy. I never take off mine, either.'*

Pulling it out further, he looks down at the smooth, delicately carved surface of lilies and ... thistles. Thistles! He opens it, lightly fingering his half of the rose heart. *'It's special, isn't it? Like magic.'*

*'Yes, it is like magic, and it is very, very special.'*

*'Can I see yours, Mama?'*

*'Yes, of course. Here it is.'* She lifts her chain and lets the locket dangle.

*'Will you open it?'*

*'Oh, darling, I never open mine. No one ever sees it. I don't need to see it to know how much you mean to me. It is enough that you are close to my heart.'* She crosses both palms over her breast, covering the locket. *'Don't ever ask me to open it. Is that all right?'*

*'Yes, Mama. I won't ever open mine either.'*

*'No, son,'* she laughs. *'You may open yours whenever you wish. Whenever you think of your mother and want to be close to her.'*

*'All right! Thank you, Mama!'*

The memory vanishes and a melody takes its place. A song. A woman softly singing a hauntingly beautiful song. The tears now press hard against the back of his eyes. The woman has long auburn hair. She is holding up a… a… a heart shaped rose stone dangling from a black ribbon. He can't understand the words, yet he knows what she is saying. *How can that be?* *'It's precious, little one,'* she whispers, *'the most precious thing in the whole world … our love.'* He falls back into his chair and cradles his face in his hands. *Mother?*

The hottest part of the day has passed. The sun is lower in the sky and downy clouds float across the bright disc, bringing with them a cooling breeze. Assen's father and Hope are sitting on the ground in the shade of the ancient yew, a spot Assen favours in the late afternoon.

Hope gets up as he approaches. 'Dr Verey, may I take a stroll in the garden?' she asks.

'Please do.'

She gathers her satchel, heads back to the church and takes the path veering around the corner to the physick garden.

'Come, sit.' His father pats the ground next to him. Assen sits down heavily. 'You have read the letters?'

'Yes.'

'Then you know.'

'Yes... But I don't understand! How can I possibly be a Scottish woman's child? Look at me!' He holds his hands out and turns them over. 'And look at you! How could you? How could you betray Mother? I thought you loved her. You always seemed to... You were happy, weren't you? You both seemed so happy.'

'Wait, wait! Hold on. You're not thinking properly. That's not how it was! I did not betray Bahdeer. How could I? She was everything to me. You know that. But ... just as Bahdeer was not your birth mother...' He inhales through his nose, cradling his hands in his lap. 'I was not your birth father. But we *were* your mother and father in so far as we loved you as our own child, maybe more. God in his wisdom chose not to bless us with our own children but blessed us in another way and we thanked Him every single day.'

'Then who...?'

'Was your father? One day back in 1561, a young, beautiful, intelligent serving girl came to Paris with her young mistress and master. The girl was in a new land, a strange place she didn't understand. But Bahdeer saw something in her; there was more to Agnes Sampson, you know. Your mother was like that – she could read people's souls, see into their hearts and she saw something in Agnes. She often said Agnes had the makings of a great healer, greater even than her, and she helped her, taught her about the flowers and herbs in the garden. How to grow them, their properties, various remedies. She did the same with you. Bahdeer also had a brother…'

'Uncle Galib?'

'You remember him?'

'I remember her talking about him a lot, telling me stories about his adventures in strange lands. He died in the China Sea, didn't he?'

'She wanted you to remember him, to know something about him. But yes, he died in the China Sea. You weren't born when he died. He was a great explorer. It was in the blood.'

The two men sit in silence, staring into the past.

'One day, Mother came in from the garden, laughing,' Mr Verey continues. She'd seen Agnes and Galib sitting together on the stone bench by the fountain.'

'By the fountain?' A memory stirs: Mother and Uncle Manny next to the fountain in the ethereal garden with the sweetest melody he's ever heard rising from its eternal flowing water. 'You have to go back…' The words float around his head.

'There was no impropriety,' his father continues. 'But your mother felt … well … she just knew things, did she not?'

'She did,' says Assen, nodding, still seeing the magic garden.

'But I don't think she took it too seriously at first, she just said Galib was smitten by the beautiful Scottish girl with the unruly hair and musical accent. I think she thought, even though her brother liked Agnes, was captivated even, he wouldn't pursue it. The social distance between them was too great. She had nothing – no dowry, no name, no family of any note, and Galib was too upstanding to have a mere dalliance. Your mother thought it would just fizzle out.'

'But it didn't?'

His father shook his head. 'We didn't know it, but it got serious – very serious. They were in love. Galib was desperate to marry her … even before the baby.'

'The baby? Me?'

'Yes, you. He told his parents everything, said he was going to marry Agnes even if it meant being disinherited. They said he would get nothing, they would settle it all on his younger brother. Your mother and I agreed – it was her idea – and we offered him half her dowry. He refused, said he would make his fortune in the China Sea.'

'And he died.'

'Yes. But he married Agnes before he left. They wed in secret, with just me and your mother there as witnesses. Agnes stayed with us until she delivered. You were such a joy, such a blessing to all of us. Then news came of Galib's death. It was a very hard time for Agnes. We said she could stay with us, we asked her to stay ... we were family ... and I think she would have, but the expulsions came soon after. There were killings, a lot of them; it wasn't safe for her.'

'Why not?'

'She'd been attending the Huguenot home meetings. She was curious and headstrong, that Agnes Sampson! She was interested in what they had to say, especially about healing and medicine and the church.'

'I see.'

'Agnes never trod an easy path; it wasn't in her stars. Your mother had them read them for her. Anyway, it was the 1560s. We offered to hide her, but she wouldn't have it ... said she wouldn't put us all in danger ... you.'

'She left me.' A rush of heat rises from Assen's chest to his throat and resentment tightens his windpipe.

'No! Not in the way you think. She sacrificed herself. She didn't want to put us all in danger. She knew we loved you ... and ... what could she take you back to? An unwed woman with the story of being married in Paris, and a brown baby in tow. You would have been outcasts. Think what your life would have been. I've no doubt you would have been a healer too, but do you think you would have escaped the flames? Son of a witch, and looking like you? She loved you, and she did the best she could for you.'

'What about Grandpapa and Grandmama?'

'They would have accepted Agnes in time, I'm sure of that, but there *was* no time. They went back to the Saadian Sultanate in Africa. Galib's body was on its way home, and they went to grieve and bury him. When they came back, Agnes was gone ... and you were here, and – well, you know how they were with you.'

Assen nods, smiling at the memory of sitting on Grandpapa's knee, the smell of tobacco wafting from his pipe, snuggling into his neck as he told Assen about the adventures of Prince Rupert. 'Yes.'

Mr Verey gets up, groaning and stretching his back. 'I must see your apothecary while I'm here and get some liniment for my lower back. Right here.' He places his hand on his lumbar spine and arches his back. 'I hear you have an excellent apothecary.'

Assen laughs. 'The best.'

'I know you'll need time to let this sink in. But in a way, you are very lucky. You have had four parents who loved you, who treasured you. Not to mention how you were doted on by your grandparents.'

'You're right,' Assen answers, because he thinks it's what his father wants to hear, but in truth he is numb.

As they begin walking back towards the church, Assen's sees Hope hovering around the corner of the building.

'Hope, join us,' Assen calls. 'There are some people I'd like you to meet.' As she approaches, he frowns. 'There's one thing I don't understand. How did you come to have all these things – the letters, the packet? You must have been only a baby at the time?'

'It wasn't me, it was my papa. He used to be the sheriff for the town where it all happened. He told me he didn't like the way things were going, they were getting out of hand. Neighbour was accusing neighbour and no one was safe. One night he and Mama decided to leave with me and my sister, Jennie. They weren't my real parents – I know what happened to my real parents because he told me. He went to see Agnes Sampson the day they were leaving to try and do something, to help, I suppose. She asked him to get something from her cottage – an old box – but not to open it. He was to take it to France with him and give it to a Mr Verey in Paris …and … this Mr Verey would know what to do. But…'

'Yes?' Assen looks up.

'Mama said that when we got to France, the plague had struck.'

'The plague, yes.'

'And so, they decided to go to the Low Countries 'til ... well, things had settled. We moved about a lot, and I think the box must have got lost or forgotten. But when Papa became ill, when he was dying last year, he got really agitated. He kept talking about this box wrapped in linen. He had to get it to someone in Paris. He couldn't die without handing it over. He told me about seeing Agnes and everything ... just before...'

'She was executed?' Mr Verey shakes his head.

'Aye, I think so. She told him she had a hiding place in her cottage. One of the stones by the fireside was loose, and there was a box wrapped in an old cloth in the hole. It contained important papers and something very precious. If he made it to France, he was to take it to Mr Verey. The Vereys had a residence in Paris that had been in the family for generations; he would find them easily. Or, if Mr Theo Verey was no longer with us, he was to look for a Dr Bris ... Bris ... Brisbois ... yes, Dr Brisbois at the Faculty of Medicine.' Hope stops, squeezing her knuckles and biting her bottom lip as if trying to decide something.

'There is something else?' Assen holds his breath.

'Aye ... yes ... yes... She asked him to burn down her cottage so nothing remained, and no one could pick over her life. All that mattered was in the box, and Papa was to get it into the hands of a very dear friend. The casket was ancient and the lock had been broken for many years, but he swore he wouldn't look inside and he never did. He made me swear, too. I think he admired her. He always seemed to when he talked about her ... said she was a remarkable woman. After he told me the story, I promised I'd get it to Mr Verey or the doctor, and my papa died peacefully.'

She releases a juddering breath and swallows. A fat tear overflows from the corner of her eye and slides down her cheek. Sniffing, she wipes it with her fingertips.

Assen takes out a clean piece of white linen and hands it to her. 'I'm sorry.'

'Thank you.'

An older woman and young man are ambling down the path from the kitchen towards the yew. The woman is handsome, in her mid-fifties, with striking silver-grey hair peppered with black piled on top of her head. She is wearing an off-white apron and a deep turquoise dress, with a tiny cream ruff at the collar.

'My apologies,' she says when she reaches the group, touching her hair. 'I don't know where my cap has got to. I must look very uncouth.'

'Ah, there you are.' Assen tries to lift his voice but it cracks and he coughs. 'Forgive me. The dust ... it sticks to the back of the throat.' The woman studies him. 'Hope,' he continues. 'This is my wife, Mrs Thérèse Verey.'

'I am very pleased to meet you, Hope,' Thérèse says, bowing her head.

Hope bobs a curtsey. 'Pleased to meet you, Madame Verey.'

'Thérèse, please.'

'Thank you, ma'am.' Dimples appear in Hope's cheeks.

'And this is our son, Lucas.' Assen gently guides his son forward by the elbow. 'And this is Hope from Scotland.'

A young man in his early twenties with thick, wavy, raven hair steps closer and bows to the girl. 'Hello, Hope from Scotland,' he says with an impish grin, raising his eyebrows.

Assen and Thérèse exchange a look, and Thérèse rolls her eyes.

'Hello, Lucas from France,' Hope says, imitating the young man's intonation.

Lucas bursts out laughing. 'It's good to meet you.'

They stand in silence then Thérèse breaks the spell, looking at Assen, 'I was on my way to find you. Supper is ready—' she smiles at Hope and Mr Verey '—and we would be pleased if you could join us. Please, this way.'

She steps back. Mr Verey, Lucas and Hope walk ahead, Lucas stealing another look at Hope.

'And what are your interests, Lucas? Are you going to follow in the footsteps of your father?' Mr Verey enquires.

'Yes, sir. I have trained in Paris and Padua, and I am now serving here in the Hall of the Poor.'

'Really? Most commendable.'

Thérèse slips her arm through the crook of her husband's elbow, holding him a little way back, out of earshot. She stops and turns to face him. 'Husband? You have something to tell me?'

So many sensations are competing in his torso for space—heaviness, tightness, tingling. He bites his lower lip. 'I—I… ' his voice quivers.

'But it can wait, I think,' she says lightly, 'til after supper and you're seated by the stove.'

'Yes,' he says gratefully, his chest and shoulders loosening. 'Thérèse?'

'Mm-hmm?'

'I love you.'

Thérèse laughs. 'I'm glad. I love you too … always have…'

Assen puts his arm around her waist and she does the same to him, leaning her head on his shoulder. In his mind, he is outside Mrs Lambert's door with little André, his fist poised to bang on the door that would change his life. 'We're very lucky.'

She breathes in deeply and glances around. 'It's amazing where our dreams will take us. I'm glad your mother told you to come here, to seek out healers on your way.'

'I am, too. It … you … saved me.'

'It was Abbot Antoine.'

'Yes, but you got my father, Dr Brisbois, Gérard and the Royal Court of Physicians. You and the good Abbot Antoine.'

'Everyone knew you were innocent.'

'Hmm. I made a lot of mistakes.'

'Everyone does.' Looking back at the yew, she sighs. 'Your mother must have been a very special person.'

A lump in his throat catches him unawares. 'My … my … mother?' he stumbles, his eyes stinging. 'Yes… I think she was.'

## Author's Note

This story was imagined from real events that took place in East Lothian in 1590–91, namely the infamous North Berwick witch trials. No one knows for sure how many people were executed for witchcraft, but it is estimated that from seventy to as many as two hundred lost their lives.

Among them were Agnes Sampson, Gellis Duncan, John Fian, Jannet Blandilands, Babara Napier, Euphamie MacCalzean, the smith of Bridge Hallis, and Robert Grierson, skipper.

Agnes was an older, highly respected midwife; John, the local schoolmaster; and Gellis Duncan, a serving girl in the Seton household at Tranent.

Gelly was the first to be accused by her employer, David Seton, a magistrate, for suddenly having miraculous healing powers and sneaking out in the middle of the night. When she couldn't explain her actions, she was arrested and tortured. Agnes, John and Gelly all withstood horrific torture before eventually confessing to meeting in a coven, conspiring to sink the king's ship and poisoning him.

For the purposes of this story, I've situated these people as living in or close to the village of North Berwick, but in reality they were dispersed in villages across the Lothians. For example, Agnes was from Humbie and lived in Haddington, John Fian dwelled in Prestonpans and Gelly in Tranent.

The other characters in sixteenth-century Scotland, such as the Reverend McLaren, Commissioner Baxter and Sheriff MacKay, were my own creation, as were all the characters and events in France and some of the places such as the plague hospital, St Marcel's, on the outskirts of Paris. However, the Hôtel-Dieu (House of God) in Beaune is very real and has been serving its community for hundreds of years. It is now a museum. Vézelay is also a beautiful village in the region of Bourgogne-Franche-Comté. Although, how I've imagined it in the sixteenth century is a little different from how it is now.

The descriptions of near-death experiences (NDEs) in this book are faithful to the accounts of those who've had them. The portrayals here don't represent any single account but rather are an amalgam of common elements that make up NDEs. I have based this on my research of over 400 NDE cases and the interviews I've conducted with many people who have experienced life after death. My findings appear in my two non-fiction books. *Showing Us the Way Home (2019)* and *The Joy of Moving On (2021)*.

Acknowledgements

My thanks go to Debbie Emmitt for her light-touch edit and helpful suggestions.
And finally…

Dear Reader, thank you so much for reading this book. Your time and effort is greatly appreciated. You would be helping me out enormously if you would leave a review on whichever platform you purchased it from. Without your reviews, this book will fall down the listings and out of sight on the various websites through their algorithms. I have tried to bring a certain dignity and humanity to people like Agnes Sampson, Gellis Duncan and John Fian, who suffered so much but are only known for the brutal nature of their torture and deaths. I wanted to bring forward their lives and spirituality even though it is largely imagined on my part. Thank you again for reading this and considering writing a review.

www.ingramcontent.com/pod-product-compliance
Ingram Content Group UK Ltd.
Pitfield, Milton Keynes, MK11 3LW, UK
UKHW020209190325
456407UK00011B/182